Is It a Crime:

20 Year Anniversary Edition

Is It a Crime:

20 Year Anniversary Edition

Roy Glenn

www.urbanbooks.net

Urban Books, LLC
300 Farmingdale Road, N.Y.-Route 109
Farmingdale, NY 11735

Is It a Crime: 20 Year Anniversary Edition

ISBN 13: 978-1-64556-500-0

First Trade Paperback Printing November 2023
Printed in the United States of America

10 9 8 7 6 5 4 3 2 1

This is a work of fiction. Any references or similarities to actual events, real people, living or dead, or to real locales are intended to give the novel a sense of reality. Any similarity in other names, characters, places, and incidents is entirely coincidental.

Distributed by Kensington Publishing Corp.
Submit Orders to:
Customer Service
400 Hahn Road
Westminster, MD 21157-4627
Phone: 1-800-733-3000
Fax: 1-800-659-2436

Is It a Crime:

20 Year Anniversary Edition

Roy Glenn

Is It a Crime was the inaugural novel of fan-favorite author Roy Glenn. With this debut, we were introduced to the fast-paced life of Mike Black, a vicious New Yorker running the streets. For two decades, Glenn has shaped the Mike Black saga with stories of assassinations, sex, and money, leaving readers at the edge of their seats. Dive back into the classic series with this re-edition of a certified hood classic.

This special rerelease is a celebration of Urban Books Publishing's twentieth anniversary. In the two decades that have passed since the origin of Urban Books, we have played a hand in launching the careers of *Essence Magazine* and *New York Times* bestsellers and continue to bring the hottest up-and-comers into the fold.

A lot has changed in those twenty years in the publishing landscape, for better or worse. From the bottom of my heart, I want to thank all our loyal readers, old and new. Whether you have been rocking with Urban since 2003, or you picked this book up by chance at your local bookstore, we couldn't do this without you.

As we celebrate our twenty-year anniversary, you can expect to find new editions of your favorite Urban Books originals by beloved authors like Ashley & JaQuavis, La Jill Hunt, Chunichi, and more. Be on the lookout for these hot new covers to add to your collection.

Sincerely,

Carl Weber
Founder and Publisher, Urban Books LLC

Other titles by Roy Glenn

MOB

Drug Related

Payback

Anthologies:

Girls From Da Hood

Gigolos Get Lonely Too

Dedicated to my father, Charles Glenn: it's about living your dreams.

CHAPTER ONE

Mike Black was 34 years old and controlled a profitable and growing business in New York City. For lack of a better term, Mike was a gangster. His business was gambling, prostitution, and number running. When he was 15, he and Bobby started out selling reefer and doing a little number running for André Harmon, who ran most of the illegal activity in the area. André was a drug dealer. As far as he was concerned, gambling and prostitution was just a sideline. As the years passed, André put them to work collecting. Enforcing André's law earned Mike the nickname Vicious Black, but everybody called him Black.

Mike and Bobby hung with their crew, which also included Wanda Moore, Nick Simmons, Perry Dukes, Vickie Payne, and Clyde Walker, who was from Jamaica, so everybody called him Jamaica. Soon Mike and Bobby went freelance and did a few jobs on their own. Wanda, who always had a head for business, insisted that the first thing they should do was to start a business to run their money through. The name of their company was Invulnerable Security, specializing in private security and personal bodyguards. Mike chose a security company because it would afford them a license to carry guns. They began hijacking trucks in New Jersey, northern Pennsylvania, and Connecticut. Sometimes they would park the truck on the block and give the stuff away. They robbed a few warehouses early on. However, Mike decided that all that time waiting to load the truck was time waiting to get caught. Hijacking trucks, on the other hand, was quick, clean, and extremely profitable.

Drug money was flowing, and they lived large, doing everything they ever imagined. But Mike soon faced the reality of his world. When Vickie died smoking cocaine, it caused his attitude on many things to change. He began to see cocaine as death and heroin as slow death. He became totally opposed to selling death to his own people. So when André met his untimely demise nine years ago, Mike took over and moved quickly to get out of the drug business.

The violent days were behind them now. Mike opened a supper club called Cuisine. Meanwhile, Bobby opened a nightclub named Impressions. Mike spent the majority of his time ensuring that every aspect of the operation met very high standards of quality. It took some time and a great deal of energy, but for the last three months things had been running smoothly and did not require as much attention. Now Mike found himself bored, looking for something to do with himself.

"Yo, Black!" Freeze yelled. "Are ya with me?"

"Leave him alone, Freeze. Can't you see he's in the zone?" Bobby said, looking back at Mike.

He sat in the back seat of Freeze's new Rodeo, looking out the window at the Hudson River. He had spent a month island-hopping in the Caribbean, hoping the change would bring him out of the funk he had been in lately. It didn't, so for the last couple of weeks Mike had been hanging out with Bobby and Freeze, trying to recapture a bit of the old days. Mike stared out at the water, and a blank expression covered his face. It felt good being back, feeling his power. However, he still felt empty.

"Like, you a zillion miles away. Something buggin' ya, man?" Freeze asked as he drove downtown along the

West Side Highway. Mike wanted to see a show at a club in Manhattan, so he had Freeze drive him. Although Mike could drive, he didn't like to.

"Just thinkin'."

"You ain't sick or nothin', are you?" Freeze asked, but Mike didn't answer. "We just need to get him inside," Freeze said, laughing as he pulled in front of the club. "Yo, Black, you just need to relax. You know what I'm sayin'? You're too uptight. Where's that fine-ass Melinda at?"

They entered the club and were escorted to a table next to the stage. As the show began, Mike noticed a lady walking by. She was the most beautiful woman he had ever seen. She had the type of smile that won you over almost immediately. As he watched her walk past him, he couldn't help feeling that there was something about her, a kind of familiarity. Nothing he could put a finger on, but definitely something. Mike turned to Freeze, who always seemed to know everybody. "Who is that?"

"Who's who?"

"The one in the black," Mike fired back.

"Oh, her name is Shy," Freeze answered.

"Who?" Mike said while he looked her up and down.

"They call her Shy. You know, like she's so shy. But she definitely ain't shy. Them guys with her are—"

Mike cut Freeze off. "I'm not interested in them. I'm only interested in her."

Freeze cut his eyes at Mike and looked away. "She runs that crew. They slingin' sacks."

"She's rollin'!" Mike stood up to see where she went. "There she goes. Let's go. I wanna get a closer look."

Shy, whose name was Cassandra Sims, stood five feet eight inches tall and weighed 150 pounds with a small waistline. She had deep brown skin, dark brown bedroom eyes, and shoulder-length black hair, which appeared to be her own. She was dressed head to toe in black, which always caught Mike's attention since he usually wore black himself. She wore a black cardigan trimmed with mink, a black wool and jersey tube skirt, and black leather boots also trimmed with mink.

Shy wasn't your average drug dealer. She had dual degrees in management and marketing and ran things like a business. In her view, cocaine was nothing more than a product to be marketed and distributed. She was with her associates: Jack, Tony, and Eddie, or E, as he preferred to be called. They had known each other since high school when they sold reefer for Shy. When Shy went away to college, each of them went their separate ways. When Shy returned to the city after graduation, unable to find a job in her field, she rounded up her old partners, changed the product, and went to work. Business was booming. However, lately, someone had been trying to move in on what they considered their "piece of the rock." Over the last month, several of her associates had been robbed. Shy had been unable to find out who was responsible.

They stepped to the bar to order drinks. Jack ordered his usual Red Stripe. Jack was a big guy, six five, and weighed over 300 pounds. Despite his size, he was always well-dressed and had a way with the ladies. He stayed in New York and attended City College, going on to earn his degree in public administration. Tony ordered juice and gin. Tony enrolled at City College also but dropped out during his freshman year. After that he got married and promptly divorced. Going from a bad job to a worse job, he finally ended up with no job, no money, and no plan. He was good-looking, always a smooth talker, and a sharp dresser. So when things got too thick, he began scamming rich white women. E had attended a college of sorts as well. He was caught in a failed armed robbery attempt and did three years at Rikers Island. He ordered for himself and Shy. E didn't drink much, so he had a Pepsi.

"What you want, Shy?" E asked.

"Gimme a sex on the beach." Shy looked up at him and smiled. "I might get chosen tonight."

Knowing that she wasn't serious, E laughed at her. "Fine as you are, you can get chosen anytime you want." But he wanted her. "Matter of fact, I might."

Shy threw her hand up in his face. "Don't even go there. You know we strictly business."

"All right, all right." He turned to the bartender. "Give the lady a sex on the beach."

"Hey, y'all, check them out," Jack said.

"That's Freeze. And ain't that Black and Bobby with him?" Tony said. He had known Freeze since junior high school.

"Where?" Shy stepped to the front.

"Right there." Jack pointed them out.

"Why they sweatin' us? Maybe it's Freeze who's been bitin' on us," E said.

"Hell no. If you knew anything about Black and them, you'd know that ain't his style," Tony said. "Black would just kill you."

Shy looked Mike up and down. She smiled and took another sip of her drink. "So that's Vicious Black. He's kinda cute for a killer."

Jack and Tony turned to each other and then looked at Shy in shock. This was a revelation. Shy noticed a man. It had been a little more than a year since Shy had broken up with Ricardo, whom she had been dating for three years. The breakup wasn't pretty. Since then, she hadn't shown any interest in men, preferring instead to concentrate on making money. This became her defense mechanism. When men would try to talk to her, she would play them off with, "I'm strictly business."

Shy's thinking that Vicious Black was kind of cute did not amuse E. "Fuck all that. That's just the kinda shit that dirty muthafuckin' Freeze would do," E said as he walked away and headed straight for them.

"Damn! Y'all go with him."

Freeze saw E coming, followed closely by Tony and Jack. "Here they come, Black."

Mike reached behind his back and cocked his .45, turning slightly to his right so the oncoming attackers wouldn't see his weapon.

"What's up, Tony?" Freeze shouted with his hand up to stop them.

"What up my ass!" E shouted. "Why y'all sweatin' us!"

"Bad taste, poor eyesight—you choose," Bobby said.

"I asked you a question!" E fired back, stepping closer to Bobby.

"Chill out, brothers," Mike said without taking his eyes off Shy. "I was just admiring the lady." Mike turned and put the gun away to be sure that they could see it. "Let's go."

"I thought you wanted to see the show," Bobby said, laughing as he followed Mike away from them. Freeze laughed at them and took a few steps backward before turning around and walking away.

"What was up with that?" Shy asked as her associates returned to the bar.

"Says he was just admiring the lady," Tony answered.

"Who, Freeze?" she asked, her eyes focused squarely on Vicious Black as he made his way through the crowd. She knew who was watching her.

"No, Black." Jack took a seat at the bar. "When we stepped up, kid had his gun cocked and ready."

"I tried to tell you, he ain't no joke," Tony reminded them. "If we had come wrong, he woulda shot somebody. And Freeze ain't no better."

"Who are you, their fuckin' press agent?" E shouted. "You bust a cap in they ass, they die like anybody else."

"Shut up, E." Shy watched as they left the club. "All right, Tony, you check it out. See if you can find out what, if anything, they're up to. Jack, you ask around. I wanna know everything there is to know about Vicious Black. If we gotta go up against him, I gotta know how he's coming. E, you just need to chill out."

On the way back uptown, Mike was very quiet, once again staring aimlessly out the window. As the events of the evening slowly faded away, he slipped back into his funk. No matter how he tried, he couldn't escape it. He would have to face it sooner or later. Meanwhile, Freeze and Bobby, who usually went back and forth about most things, were going back and forth about who was, pound for pound, the best fighter in the world. Bobby thought Roy Jones Jr. was the best. Freeze liked Bernard "The Executioner" Hopkins.

"You like Roy Jones Jr. 'cause both of y'all are old and played out. Next you'll be tellin' me that Oscar De La Hoya is the best fighter."

"Oscar ain't the one. And Bernard Hopkins? Shit, I could beat him."

"You should be more concerned about taking on Pam 'The Interrogator' when you get home," Freeze said.

Pam was Bobby's wife. Mike and his longtime girl-friend, Regina, introduced them eight years ago. Back then, Pam and Regina were best friends, so it seemed only natural to hook Bobby up with Pam. They were married two years later, an occasion that marked the end of Mike's longtime relationship with Regina. Mike and Regina got into an argument over, of all things, listening to Prince on the way to the wedding. That minor dispute escalated from there to open warfare throughout the day. It got to the point that when the bridal party was going to dance, Pam had to force them to dance with each other. There they were, dancing cheek to cheek, not saying a word. They stood quietly and smiled politely through the pictures. Once the last picture was taken, Regina turned to Mike and said, "I hate you." She left the reception, and they hadn't spoken since.

"You goin' in with him, Black?"

"Hell no. He gotta face the kraken alone."

"I'm gonna need the head of Medusa," Bobby said. "When I called Pam, she was mad as hell."

"Okay, I'll go with you. But I gotta leave sometime, Bob. Might as well face her now."

As they pulled up in front of his house, Bobby noticed that the lights were still on. "I knew she'd still be up. She loves David Letterman."

"Man, stop being such a punk and face that woman."

"Freeze, until you have a relationship that lasts longer than a day, shut up."

Mike got out of the car, shaking his head. Although he and Freeze would slay Bobby about it, he was envious of the flow that Bobby and Pam shared. Pam was good for Bobby. Sure, Pam talked a little shit sometimes, but so did Bobby. Actually, Bobby talked a lotta shit. Besides, most of the time she was justified. They loved and respected each other. She was truly his better half.

"Freeze, I'll get with you tomorrow," Mike said.

"You gonna babysit him, Black?" Freeze asked.

Bobby got out of the car as Freeze continued to laugh at him. "Get out of here!" Bobby shouted, but Freeze got out of the car.

"Why you yelling at me? It ain't my fault you got married. I tried to warn you before you did it."

"You don't know nothing about this," Bobby said as he sat down on the steps. "Being married ain't the death sentence you think it is. Most of the time it's pretty cool."

"That's 'cause Pam is cool, but suppose you get one of them nightmare bitches. You know what I'm talkin' about. The ones who are real sweet for a while, but then they become your worst nightmare. Followin' you around, goin' through your shit, fuckin' everybody," Freeze said.

"You just got to be smart enough to see it coming."

"How you supposed to see that shit coming?"

"When you're just messin' around with them, instead of being so preoccupied with gettin' tossed, watch them. Listen to what she says, tell her no a couple times, and see how she takes it. The ones who get mad got trip potential. A real player like you should know that, Freeze."

"No, a real player gets tossed and moves on. He doesn't wait for them to start trippin'."

"It ain't easy finding a good one. I ran plenty of women before me and Pam hooked up. Back in the day, me and old Vicious Black here used to be rough on the honeys. Right, Mike?"

"Right," Mike said, watching the cars roll by.

"You mean you used to be rough. Black's still rough on them. And if he weren't in the zone, he'd tell you that all them bitches want is money."

"Don't get me wrong. Some of them are like that. All I'm sayin' is that there are one or two cool ones out there, but it takes time and energy to make it work. And that's why you will never have a good woman. You ain't that patient!"

Freeze started to walk away. "Yo, Bobby, the only good ho is a fucked ho. No disrespect to Pam, but all them hoes are alike. I'm out. Yo, Black, I'll get up with you tomorrow." Freeze got back in his Rodeo and drove away.

"You don't have to come in with me, Mike. Pam ain't that bad this time of the month. She'll talk some shit, I'll ignore her, and she'll go to bed."

"You sure?"

"Yeah, it's cool, but come on in anyway. Have a drink."

As they entered the house, Pam was sitting in the living room watching Letterman. "Are you alone?"

"No, Mike's with me."

"Oh, come on in, Mike. He got you to come in with him to try to wait me out?" Mike and Bobby went into the living room. Bobby poured a couple of drinks as Pam continued, "Well, it won't work. Freeze, maybe, but I don't care if Mike hears what I got to say. But you know what? I'm not even mad at you, baby, but what I am is tired, so I'll say good night." Pam got up from her chair and went into the kitchen for a second before starting upstairs.

"Hey, Pam, how's Regina?"

"What!" Pam said in shock. Mike started to repeat himself. "No, no, I heard you. She's fine. I talked to her tonight as a matter of fact. Do you want me to tell her that you asked about her?"

"No. I'm just asking, that's all."

Pam shook her head and giggled. After a few steps she stopped. "You know, whatever happened between the two of you that day didn't make any sense at all. At least not enough to stop speaking for six years. Maybe the two of you should talk."

Mike finished his drink and poured another one. "Good night, Pam."

"Good night, Mike." Pam went upstairs and shut the door.

Bobby sat down and picked up the remote. He was a chronic channel surfer. "So what is this, comeback night or something? First you wanna go run with Freeze, which I can see. It was kinda fun. Then you wanna know about Regina. I never told you this because I didn't think you'd care, but for more than a year after that, Regina would call me every day, asking me if you asked about her. So what's next?" Bobby asked, flipping channels before stopping back at Letterman.

"I don't know, Bobby. I guess I'm just bored."

Bobby smiled at his partner. "You just miss the old days, man—you and me runnin' the streets. We were pretty rough back in the day. I miss them days sometimes too, but I get to spend a lot more time with Pam and the kids." Bobby and Pam had four kids: Bobby Jr., Barbara, and the twins, Bonita and Brenda.

"Do you remember when me, you, Nick, and Jamaica were on City Island?" Mike asked. "Waiting on André to come out of his meeting with Frankie and them, and everybody came running out shootin' at us?"

"Yeah, yeah, what was it, six, seven of them? I shot the first two, and then you, Nick, and Jamaica started poppin' them as they came out the door. You didn't think I'd remember that, did you?"

"No, Bobby, you don't remember much. That's another reason why I miss Jamaica. He never forgot anything." After Vickie's death, Jamaica started shooting heroin on a regular basis. He disappeared after a job nine years ago. No one had seen or heard from him since. "When we're old, sitting in rockin' chairs reminiscing about the good old days, you won't remember any of it. Anyway, then we went inside, and André was on his knees beggin' Frankie not to kill him. I knew then that he was weak."

"What's your point, Mike?" Bobby asked after a long silence.

"André was livin' it up, lettin' us do all the work, you know."

"Stop right there. You just getting a little off the chain. You ain't weak like he was. What's really bothering you, Mike?"

"To be honest, I don't know." Mike looked at Bobby and shook his head. "I really don't know. I really just feel kinda, you know, like watching something else."

Bobby laughed a little. "Guess that means you don't feel like talking about it?"

"No, it means that I don't know what to talk about, so I guess I'll go home."

"Okay. Well, if you feel like talking, you know where to find me. You want me to drive you home?"

"No. I'll walk." Mike finished his drink and left.

Bobby finished his drink and straightened up the living room before going upstairs to bed, or at least that was his intention. As he entered the bedroom, he found Pam lying on the bed, watching Letterman again. Waiting.

"Mike gone?"

Bobby nodded his head in response as he got ready to join Pam in bed.

"What's wrong with him? Does he ever ask about Regina?"

"No."

"I almost fainted when he said that. Wait until I tell Regina."

"You're not going to tell her anything. If he wanted you to tell her, he woulda said so."

Pam rolled over and folded her arms. "Why not? You know she asked about him tonight. She hasn't asked about him in a long time."

"Pam, that's between them."

"They are both my friends. Anyway, I'm gonna call Regina, tell her what's up. I think she has a right to know that Mike asked about her. Regina hasn't been happy since they broke up, and it seems to me that he's pretty fucked up too. We should do something. And the answer is not being out there runnin' the streets with Freeze's wild ass. You been runnin' pretty hard with him and Mike the last few weeks, hangin' around with those wild-ass bitches."

Bobby rolled his eyes and shook his head. He knew where Pam was going with this, and he really didn't want to go there with her. But before he could say anything, Pam continued. "Now, baby, it's not you I'm worried about, but I used to be out there. I know how they are, half-naked, shakin' their ass all up in your face. Yeah, I know how they are," Pam said as she sat up in bed.

Bobby looked at Pam and laughed. "So that's what this is about. Why does it have to be about other women? There ain't nothing out there that I'm interested in. They want money, and you know I'm not the one. You know it's you I want. They can kiss my hungry black ass."

"You wouldn't be hungry if you had brought your hungry black ass home for dinner," Pam said jokingly.

"You think you're slick, don't you? You think if you can get Mike and Regina back together, he'll stop wantin' to hang out and I'll be here with you. That's your plan, ain't it?" Bobby lay down, thinking that he got her off him.

"What's so bad about that?" she came back with attitude. "You make it sound like being with me is the worst thing that ever happened to you."

"That's not what I'm sayin', Pam."

Pam stood up and put her hands on her hips. "Just what are you sayin' then? Come on now. This is not a real tough question."

Bobby got out of bed. He didn't like anyone standing over him. "If you'd chill for a second, you'd know I love you and I love what we got goin' here. You'd know that. But you don't understand."

"Well, make me understand!" Pam said, head and shoulders rockin' from side to side.

"Look! Mike is my friend and I thought he was your friend too. All that 'you're like a brother' shit you talk. Now there is something buggin' him. You can see that, can't you? I don't care if he wants to run the streets or if he wants to start making the rounds for Freeze. I don't care. I'm down with him. It doesn't matter to me what you say. I got his back! Just like I always have and just like he's had mine hundreds of times." Bobby opened the bedroom door and started down the stairs, slamming the door behind him.

Pam fell in behind him. "Wait, Bobby. Come on! Wait a minute. Don't walk out on me like this."

"What!" Bobby headed for the bar in the living room.

Pam sat down on the couch. "Come here, Bobby, please. Come here and sit down. Please, baby. Come sit down with me." Bobby didn't answer her, but Pam continued anyway. "I just wanna say I like what we got going on here too. I always have. But the last couple of years with you being home more have been great. I'm sorry, but I'm not ready to give all that up. Not for Mike. Not for anybody. Now I'm not askin' you to choose, but try to see my point here."

"You still don't get it, do you?"

"No, Bobby, you don't get it. What happened tonight?"

"Some toy gangsters stepped to us, that's all. No big deal. Why?" Bobby asked, wondering where she was going with this.

"See, that's my point. It was no big deal tonight, but what about the next time? How many was it?"

"Four. If you count the girl."

"You could have been killed, baby. Maybe I'm gettin' to be a punk or something, but it worries me more now than it used to. I just keep thinking about being broke with four kids and no man. All I'm sayin' is to think about that when you're out there runnin' the streets."

Quiet set in as each simply looked at the other. Finally Bobby sat down next to Pam. He grabbed her hand, kissing it gently. "All you say is true, but you don't have to worry about money. Wanda got that handled. But this is something that I have to do. I gotta be all over this for him. I'm not gonna let him go too far, and I'm not gonna let him get us killed."

Pam leaned over, kissed Bobby on the cheek, patted his hand, and said, "Problem is, you can't promise me that, now can you?"

Mike walked over to the window in his bedroom, his mind racing. His mind began to drift to the events of the evening. Not that people stepping to him was any big deal. Back in the day, that type of thing would happen all the time. The question was why they stepped. As far as he was concerned, he was just admiring the lady. She was quite a lady, all dressed in black. He couldn't help feeling that there was something about her. It wasn't just because she was pretty. Like Smokey Robinson said, "Pretty girls come a dime a dozen." Maybe it was that she was a player? Doubtful. He'd been with female players before and always found them to be a little too much like the brothers for his taste, so that couldn't be it. There was something about her eyes. They were very expressive eyes, like an open window to her mind. Although he was happy for the little excitement tonight, he still felt empty.

"Black, is everything all right?" said a soft voice from the bed. The voice belonged to Melinda Brown. When he got there, she was waiting in bed. He noticed that she was asleep, so he didn't say anything to her. Melinda was 25 years old, the youngest of four beautiful girls, each of whom had their first child before turning 16. Melinda knew that wasn't what she wanted. She parlayed her looks into getting what she wanted.

"Yeah," he said.

"You've been real distant the last few days. You mad at me? Did I do something wrong? What's up?"

"I just have a few things that I need to sort out, that's all. It's not you." *But maybe it is you.*

Melinda was tall and fine. Her hair was cut short, which highlighted her features. Melinda's eyes were oval, she had high cheekbones and full lips, and her skin was light brown. Mike had been introduced to Melinda by Freeze, who else, at a strip club. Melinda was trying to get a job as a dancer, but she just didn't have the patience for dealing with the clientele. It definitely wasn't because she couldn't dance. What Mike liked most about Melinda was that she was no trouble at all. Like the man said in *Total Recall,* Melinda was "respectful, compliant, and appreciative . . . the way a woman should be." His problem with her was that she didn't have any fire.

"Baby, why don't you come to bed? I'll make all your problems go away."

Except in bed. There the girl definitely had skills.

Mike sat down on the bed, and she began to dance for him. Slowly, she moved her hips in a circle, arching her back, and then she dropped slowly down to the floor. Melinda crawled to Mike and kissed her way first up one leg and then down the other before joining him in bed.

CHAPTER TWO

The one good thing about being stuck in traffic is that it gives you a chance to think. Mike sat in the back seat of a cab on the Cross Bronx Expressway on his way to Impressions from Wanda's Manhattan office. Mike owned a black '78 Seville, which he drove when he had to, and a black '89 Corvette convertible, which he drove on rare occasions. Mike had gone to see Wanda about some legal matters. She had played around in the game for a while, but Wanda always wanted to be a lawyer. So Mike paid for her to go to law school. He used his influence to get her an internship in the district attorney's office.

When Wanda passed the bar, she went to work as a prosecutor for the DA. The association didn't last. It wasn't long before she went into private practice with one major client. Wanda had gotten them out of more cases than he could remember. She was smart, careful, and just a bit ruthless. Over the years, Wanda managed the money, making a small fortune for her partners in addition to developing a reputation as an excellent entertainment lawyer.

Mike relaxed on his way back uptown. His mind began to drift once again, thinking about the things that had been bothering him the last couple of weeks. Mike continued to focus on one of the symptoms—boredom— instead of focusing on the real issue. And what about her—the woman who had dominated his thoughts since he saw her the week before?

Traffic finally broke loose. "A cop had someone pulled over. I hate rubberneckers," the lady cab driver said.

"I hate cops."

The driver laughed, but she had to agree. "I hate them too." As they passed the cop, both Mike and the cab driver gave him the finger.

Upon arriving at Impressions, he made his way through the crowd on his way to Bobby's office on the second floor. The office overlooked the dance floor with a two-way mirror so you could see the stage from the office. It was also equipped with video monitors. Cameras were located throughout the club for security reasons, not to mention watching women. The office was well furnished with a small but well-stocked bar and a small kitchen. Mike entered the office to find Bobby sitting at his desk looking over some paperwork.

"What up, Vicious?" Bobby always thought the whole Vicious Black thing was funny and would tease him about it from time to time.

Mike didn't answer. He went behind the bar and poured himself a glass of Rémy Martin VSOP, drank it down like water, poured another, and sat down. "Looks like you've got a real crowd. What's the count?"

Bobby looked through the papers on his desk. "Nine hundred sixty-four."

"Pam coming out?"

"No, she couldn't get anyone to watch the kids, so I can hang tonight," Bobby said with a smile.

"She still sweatin' you about hangin' out with me?"

"Mike." Bobby looked down and shook his head. His smile had turned into a frown. "You just don't know. She's been on it hard. Every time you call, she starts trippin'. She just don't get it. I'ma do what I'ma do. You're my partner. She can't come between us. Besides, she thinks we should hook you and Regina back up."

"You know, as soon as I said it, I knew it was a mistake," Mike said. "As far as I'm concerned, what's in the past should stay there."

Bobby laughed and pointed at Mike. "Still kinda touchy about this Regina thing, ain't you. What really happened that day?"

Mike looked at the monitors. "You still don't get it, do you? You're just as bad as Pam. It's over! And not worth talkin' about!"

"What ain't worth talkin' about?" Freeze asked as he entered the office.

"What's up, Freeze? Bobby and Pam on this Regina kick, that's all."

"Regina, now there's a blast from the past."

"And that's where she should stay!" Mike walked over to the bar. "Anybody want a drink?"

"Who are you?" Bobby asked. "You don't even got to ask."

"Freeze, I want you to do something for me."

"How long I been workin' for you, Black? I know what you want me to do, had Jap check it out this morning. Them boys stepped to us last night 'cause they think we tryin' to roll on them. Two of them been askin' questions about you and about the operation all day," Freeze said as he sat down at the monitors. "Yo, Bobby, there sure are some fine-ass honeys up in here tonight. Talkin' about fine-ass honeys, yo, Black, there goes your girl."

Mike walked toward the monitors. "Who, Melinda?"

"No, Shy." Freeze pointed to the front door monitor. "Right there at the door, with the red dress and black coat."

Mike walked to the house phone and called the front door's security station.

"Security."

"Yeah, this is Black. Who's this?"

"Yes, sir. This is Greg."

"Greg, right in front of you there's a lady in a black coat with a red dress and hat. I want you to keep her and her party there until somebody from hospitality comes for them. Got that?"

"Yes, sir."

Mike hung up the phone and dialed another number while Bobby and Freeze looked on in disbelief.

"Hospitality. This is Tara. Can I help you?"

"Tara, this is Black."

"Hey, Black," Tara responded with a smile and nasty thoughts on her mind, hoping that he was calling with an invitation to go fool around above the stage again. "What do you need, baby?"

Mike checked the monitor again. "I have some guests who don't know they're gonna be my guests at the front door with Greg. Go get them, take them to my table, and have a waiter bring them a bottle of Dom '87."

Tara wrote down the order and handed it to a waiter. "Anything else, baby?"

"No, Tara, that's it for now, but come see me later." He hung up the phone and dialed again.

"Coat check."

"This is Black. If the flower guy's near you, have him take one red rose to the lady at my table." He hung up. Mike sat down at the monitor to watch the drama he had set into motion unfold.

Meanwhile, at the front door, Greg proceeded to carry out Mike's instructions. As Shy moved toward him, Greg moved to block her path. "Excuse me, miss, would you and your party mind waiting here for a minute please?"

Shy stopped, and her associates gathered around her. "Why? Is there a problem here?" she asked.

Before Greg could answer, Tara arrived. "That's okay, Greg. I'll take it from here." Greg returned to his station as Tara posted her best smile and continued. "Welcome to Impressions. My name is Tara. I have a table waiting for you. Would you follow me please?" Tara started to walk away, but Shy stopped her.

"Hold up, we didn't make any reservations."

"You are personal guests of the house. Would you please follow me?"

"No, I wanna know who . . ." E said, but Tara didn't answer.

Shy held E back. "Never mind, honey, I know you're just doin' your job. You lead and we'll follow."

Tara thanked Shy for understanding and led them to a table down front just to the right of the stage. Two members of the hospitality staff awaited their arrival. The waiter took Shy's coat and pulled out her chair as the waitress announced that she would be serving Dom Pérignon 1987. She opened the champagne and poured each of them a glass, took their drink orders, and departed as the flower man arrived with one red rose for Shy.

As Mike moved to the mirror, Bobby sat down at the monitors and used the zoom to get a look at Shy. "I see what you like. She's a nice piece of business," Bobby said as Freeze joined Mike at the mirror.

"Yo, Black, I'll handle Melinda when she gets here."

"Freeze, that's why you're my nigga. But let Jap handle that. What do you know about who's been robbin' her?"

"Nothing really. Seems like something's happening, but nobody knows nothin'. Four of her dealers got robbed. Couple of them got hurt pretty bad. But it's like ghosts or something robbed them. Jap's still on it."

"I want you to arrange a meeting with our guests. Since she thinks we have a problem, we should meet to discuss it," Mike said with a devilish look in his eye.

"I'll set it up. I'll have the front door page Jap if Melinda shows up. What time you wanna meet?"

"Any time after the show," Mike replied, and Freeze left the office to make arrangements for the meeting. He knew he could depend on Freeze. He ran the day-to-day operation with Mike and Bobby being semiretired.

Freeze had worked for Black for twelve years. The day Freeze got out of jail, he saw Mike on the street. Freeze was 16 years old.

"Yo, Black, wait up!" Freeze yelled.

"Yo, Freeze, what's up? I thought you were on lock-down for murder."

"I got the murder charge dropped on a tech. Cops fucked up the arrest. So I got a year for aggravated and walked. Yo, Black, so like, where you headin'?"

Mike just looked at him.

"What I really mean is, like, you know, a nigga like me could learn a lot from a nigga like you," Freeze said without making eye contact with him.

Mike laughed, "Yeah, like how to stay out of jail."

"You never been to jail, Black?"

"Never even been cuffed," Mike said confidently.

"That's what I'm talkin' about. After bein' on lockdown for damn near sixteen months, I know that I never want to go back. Lockdown ain't no place for me."

Mike looked at Freeze for a minute, contemplating his proposition. He thought about the night that he met him.

Freeze had come to Black's after-hours spot and pushed up on the girlfriend of a drug dealer named Darren. When Darren noticed Freeze was at his girl, he and two of his boys grabbed Freeze and attempted to teach him a lesson. A lesson was learned, but not by Freeze. Each time they put Freeze down, he got right back up and went right back at them. Mike was impressed as he watched Freeze continue to fight back. Darren hit Freeze again,

and he fell over a table next to Mike. He motioned for
Freeze to stay down. As they approached, Mike stood up
and drew his weapon, pointing it at Darren's head.

"Yo, Darren, I think he's had enough. Don't you?"

Not wanting any part of Black, Darren stopped. "Yeah,
Black, he's had enough," Darren said, backing away.
Three days later, Darren and his boys were dead, and
Freeze was in jail for murder.

*"Okay, you come with me. You do exactly what I say.
And I never, and I mean never, want to hear you say shit
unless I ask you. Got that?"*

Freeze nodded his head without saying a word.

"Good. Now let's go."

Since that day, Freeze had worked for Mike.

Mike went to the bar to fix the drinks he had offered
earlier. He handed Bobby his drink and took a seat on
the couch. "Thanks. It sure took you long enough. Now
I don't mean to pry into your personal affairs, Vicious,
but is this what you been trippin' about lately?" Bobby
inquired. "'Cause if it is, I coulda had her in here hoppin'
on one foot and barkin' like a dog."

"Bobby, I don't think so. I was feeling like this before
I saw her. But maybe she's the answer. She is beautiful.
And her eyes. You know Melinda is cool and she's fine
and all that, but unless she's naked, she just doesn't
really interest me. Up 'til now that's been cool, but lately
I was thinkin' that I want more from a woman. Somebody
to talk to, you know what I'm sayin'? Like you, Bob. You
and Pam got it goin' on together."

"Yeah, but you're tryin' to fuck that up."

"Sorry, man, I don't mean to. Who else can I hang with?"

"Regina hurt you didn't she, Mike? You know you
haven't really taken any women seriously since then.
What happened that day?"

Mike had never told anybody what actually went on that day, not even Bobby. Apparently Regina never did either, or Pam would have known, and she certainly would have told Bobby.

"Yeah, Bobby, she hurt me, but I couldn't let any of you know that. I mean, what good would I have been to myself or any of you walkin' around, lookin' stupid?"

"Like you're doin' now?" Bobby teased. Mike gave him the finger. "Sorry, I couldn't resist that one. I think old Dean Martin had it wrong. It should be everybody gets hurt by somebody sometime. It happens. It happened to me. Do you remember Camille?"

"How could I forget her? I almost had to shoot you about her and Nick, remember? Did you know that Nick was out of the army and back in the city?"

"Yeah, I heard," Bobby said, nodding his head. He stared at Mike. He didn't like being reminded about the little incident between him, Nick, and Camille. But since he brought it up, he knew he had it coming.

"Callin' himself a private investigator. But knowing Nick, he's probably still doin' that black bag stuff." Bobby didn't say anything. "I'm sorry, Bobby. What were you sayin' about Camille?"

"Just that she had me goin' in circles for months. You're no different. I know you got feelings. You just don't show them."

"Are you my shrink now?"

"I'm your friend, one of the only real friends you got left. I don't want to see you out there like I was. I mean, she had me goin'."

Mike got up and started walking toward the mirror, then stopped suddenly. "I was out there like that too, I guess. But I had to go through those changes by myself. You were gone for damn near two months on your honeymoon. I went through it in phases. First, I just felt like shit, you know. Then I was in denial, like 'this ain't happening, not to me.' Next I started trying to blame someone, and that's when I really started trippin'. First I blamed myself, then I blamed Regina, and that circle continued day after fuckin' day. Me, her, me, her. That was the dangerous part, because the next phase was hate. You hate the one you blame. So if you blame yourself, you end up hating yourself. Bobby, I hated her. For a while it was all I had. And I took out my anger on all women. Not trustin' them, never lettin' them get close enough to hurt me," Mike said, pacing back and forth.

"I know what you mean, man, but you just gotta find the right one, you know. I was one of those guys who'd say anything to get some. My favorite line would be, 'I'm not like that.' Tell them what they wanna hear and they will do anything you say. Dog them out, treat them like shit, and they'll love you. Most important, you gotta lie to them. Them knuckleheads love it when you lie to them," Bobby said, taking another sip of his drink. "Where you went wrong is you treated her right, and that's why you got hurt. You treated her like a lady instead of like the bitch she was."

"Yeah, man, she hurt me back then. But now, thinkin' back, I can see that it was me," Mike said, beating his chest.

"What are you talkin' about?" Bobby asked with a surprised and puzzled look on his face. "You just said you blamed her. It don't go both ways."

Mike walked over to the mirror. "Show's gettin' ready to start."

"You know I hate it when you do that," Bobby said angrily.

Mike laughed. "Lighten up, man. You're too intense. You should drink more water. Leave that fried food alone. All I'm sayin' is that I let it happen. So the only one I can blame is myself. Regina only did what any bitch would do—dog a brother out, take his money, and play him, 'cause he's weak for her. And I was so weak for her."

"You're the one who needs to lighten up. Maybe you'll get lucky and find somebody cool." Bobby paused, then continued jokingly, "Like Pam's shit-talkin' ass. But she's a good girl, and I know she's down for me. But it's like she said, I let her get comfortable with me being around the house. That's why she's been trippin' lately."

While Mike and Bobby looked on from the office, Freeze prepared to set up a meeting with Shy and her associates. First, he had to handle Melinda. When he arrived at the front door, Greg informed him that he just missed her. Melinda was already in the club. Freeze told Greg to page Jap and Kenny and have them meet him at bar number one, and then he made his way to the bar to meet them.

"Y'all spread out. Find Melinda's fine ass and bring her to my table. If she asks you why, tell her y'all don't know shit but what I tell you. She shouldn't be hard to find. Now go," Freeze said before starting out in search of Melinda himself.

It was her night off, so she had simply been wandering around the club. She went to bar number three to get a drink and talk to Marcus, whom she considered her personal bartender. Then she hollered at a couple of waitresses and then headed to the ladies' room to check her 'do. With everything in order, she started for her table, which to her surprise was occupied. Melinda started for the table to tell them that they were sitting at her table, but she decided to have security do it. She turned around and walked up to Thomas, a member of the security staff.

Thomas smiled when he saw her coming, as men usually did when they saw Melinda walking toward them. "Melinda, you look fantastic tonight."

"Thank you, but who are those people at my table?"

"I don't know who they are, but I saw Tara bring them there."

"Well, just where is Tara?" she asked with much attitude. "That bitch probably put them there just to piss me off." Melinda stormed off to find Tara and walked right into Freeze.

"Yo, Melinda, what's up? Damn, you look good tonight. Sometimes I wish I had never introduced you to Black."

"You know you're too little for me, Freeze. I would hurt you. But fuck all that. Who are those people at my table?"

Freeze explained to her that they were just some people who had business with Mike and Bobby and that he would be more than happy to have her sit at his table. Which, by the way, was located on the other side of the club. He assured her that Jap or Kenny would be nearby if she needed anything. Melinda accepted his explanation for the time being and followed him to his table. Freeze moved through the crowd and passed the table where Shy and her associates were enjoying the perks of the house. As she passed, Melinda couldn't resist rolling her eyes at Shy.

"What's her problem?" Tony asked.

"She fuckin' somebody in here," Shy replied. She had a good idea who.

As the euphoria of free food and drinks started to wear off, Shy began to question what was going on. Why the royal treatment? Were they being lulled into a false sense of comfort? By this time, somebody other than the waitstaff should have come and said something.

"You can stop wondering, Shy. There goes Freeze," Jack advised.

"Where?"

"Over there at the bar with the honey who rolled her eyes at you."

"Everybody stay sharp and be ready for anything. Ain't no tellin' what they're up to. I'm sure it's them who's at us," E said, checking his weapon.

"Now just how do you know all this? You call Miss Cleo or something? You don't know what's goin' on. Just be cool. Let's see what he wants, but like E said, everybody stay sharp. Can't be too much because they didn't make us go through the metal detector, and they let us keep our guns. If they were gonna try something, they would have disarmed us. At least, I would have. Anybody seen Black?" Shy asked, looking around the club.

"No, but he's probably up there behind that mirror," Tony replied.

Mike smiled to himself as Tony pointed him out to Shy like she could see him through the mirror.

"Here he comes."

"Showtime. E, you don't say a thing, okay? Let me do all the talking, understand?" Shy ordered. E frowned and turned away.

"What's up, Shy, fellas? Mind if I sit down?"

"No, sit down. After all, it is your party," Shy replied.

"Thank you." Freeze sat down and motioned for Angela, the waitress.

"What can I get for you, Freeze?"

"Yeah, Angela, bring our guests another bottle of DP and bring me a shot of VSOP straight up."

"What can I do for you, Freeze?" Shy asked. "And more important, what did we do to deserve this hospitality?"

Freeze smiled at her and said, "Look, let's get right to it. You seem to think that we got a problem. You had your boys rollin' around askin' about us."

"What about it?" E fired.

"Shut up, E!" Shy demanded and calmly turned back to Freeze. "Go on, Freeze."

"Well, we'd like to have a little meeting to discuss it."

"Where and when?"

"Do you see that door over there that says *authorized personnel only*? Any time after the show, just tell security that I'm expecting you and he will show you where to go."

"That's cool. We'll be there." Freeze left the table and headed for the office.

Shy looked around the table, shaking her head. "I don't think that's all there is to it. And you two . . ." She looked at Jack and Tony. "What did you do, announce what you were doin'? I'm tellin' you, he just knows all our business now, don't he?"

"See that's what you get. Shoulda let me handle it," E said.

Jack and Tony both tried to explain. "But, Shy—"

She cut them off. "'But, Shy' my ass. That's okay. This may work out better anyway. Better it all be out in the open so there's no misunderstanding. Now whatever happens up there—and, E, I am talking to you—let me do the talking. Got that, E?"

E didn't answer. He simply turned away.

As the show drew to a close, Shy got up and started heading for the door as instructed with her crew not far behind. Shy told the man at the door that Freeze was expecting her. He pushed a button on the wall, and before too long, Kenny opened the door. Kenny led them up the stairs to Bobby's office. As they arrived at the door, two gentlemen stopped them and asked them to turn over their weapons. Kenny told them not to worry about their weapons and that he would take responsibility for them.

Kenny knocked on the door and announced himself. Jap opened the door and invited them into the office. They entered the office only to find that Jap was the only one in there. He asked them to have a seat and told them that Freeze would be with them soon. When they were seated, Jap knocked once on the other door in the office, and Freeze came out.

"Black will be with you in a minute," Freeze said as he entered the office followed by Bobby.

"My name is Bobby Ray. I hope that you enjoyed the hospitality of my club," Bobby said as he sat down at his desk.

Mike entered the office and stood in the middle of the room, making eye contact with everybody. Then he walked over to Shy, sat down next to her, and extended his hand. "My name is Mike Black, and you are?"

"Shy, but you knew that." She smiled. "Anyway, it's good to finally meet you. I've heard a lot about you," Shy said, accepting his hand. She felt goose bumps as Mike kissed her hand.

He looked around and asked if anybody would like something else to drink. Mike smiled at Shy, finally releasing her hand. "Let's get to it." He got up and returned to the middle of the floor. "I understand that you think we have a problem. Freeze tells me that you've been hit a few times," Mike said, looking directly at Shy as if nobody else were in the room. Her eyes fascinated him. It was as if she were looking inside his mind. Entering his heart.

"That's right. A couple of my people got hurt pretty bad, too. Now I've been checking around, and I really don't think it's you personally, but E here thinks it's maybe some of your people," Shy said, looking at Freeze.

E started to speak, but Shy cut him off before he could say anything. She turned to Mike and continued with a smile.

Shy had the type of smile that put you at ease. He looked at her lips as if they were saying, "Love me," but only he could hear her.

"Now I don't really care who it is, but I can guarantee you this: whoever it is, well, let's just say there's a price to be paid."

Mike grinned at Shy before responding. "Let me assure you that we do not have a problem. I have no interest whatsoever in your business as long as it doesn't conflict with mine. However, you do have a problem. I've done some checkin' too, and nobody knows anything about it. If you like, I can push a little harder."

E could no longer contain himself. He got up and started moving toward Mike. "What makes you think we need you to handle our business?" he shouted.

Mike turned his back as E moved toward him and walked to the bar. As he turned away, Jap and Kenny moved to either side of E. Not too close, but close enough that E stopped. Mike poured a drink for himself. He asked Bobby if he wanted one too. Jack and Tony leaned forward in their seats.

Sensing that things were about to escalate, Shy motioned for them to chill. She stood up and joined Mike at the bar. "Look, Black, I think things are about to get out of control. I really don't want to go there, so we'll go now. But if you hear anything, please call me." Shy handed Mike a business card with only a number on it.

"Kenny, why don't you see our guests out? Jap, don't you have somewhere to go?" Freeze said, reminding Jap that his job was to take care of Melinda. Jap left the office.

"I'll get the car, Shy," E said, and he followed Jap out of the office.

"Thank you, Mr. Ray, for your hospitality. I enjoyed the show," Shy said as she walked over to the desk where Bobby was seated. She extended her hand, and Bobby shook it.

"Please, call me Bobby. Anytime you or your associates want to come again, just call me. I'll make sure you have a good table."

"Do you mind if I walk out with you, Shy?" Mike asked.

Shy stopped and thought about it for a second before saying, "No, not at all." She continued out the door and down the steps.

"It was a pleasure meeting you, Shy. Sorry it had to be under these circumstances," Mike said as they walked across the club. He looked around the floor. Melinda wasn't anywhere in sight. When he looked back, Shy had walked a little ahead of him. He watched her walk. She moved gracefully, seeming to glide across the floor. He could feel her strength, her power. Watching the way she handled her crew was almost sexual to him.

"Don't worry about it. It's just business, and this is the nature of ours." Shy could feel his eyes all over her body as she walked. Thoughts of his hands caressing her body intrigued her. Reminding herself that she was strictly business, Shy got her coat and continued out of the club.

"I saw you last night. I tried to talk to you, but your boys are kind of overprotective of you. They wouldn't let me get near you."

"Yeah, they're protective, but you gotta admit you have quite a reputation, don't you, Vicious Black? Do you blame them?" Shy asked, smiling.

"Touché. But I'm really not like that, at least not any-more. Those Vicious Black days are long gone. I was a younger guy then. Tell you what. Why don't you have dinner with me tomorrow and you'll see that I'm not that guy anymore?" Black said as he and Shy got outside of the club.

"I don't think so, Black." Shy looked around for E with the car. Jack and Tony had walked a little ahead. "Why don't we keep our association on a strictly business level for now, okay? At least 'til I work these problems out."

"Nothing I can do to change your mind?"

"No. Not tonight anyway, but call me if you get some-thing I can use," Shy said as she walked away to catch up with Jack and Tony.

Mike watched Shy walk down the street, smiling as her coat moved from side to side in unison with her hips. As Tony and Jack continued up the street, they passed a blue Taurus double-parked with two occupants: one man at the wheel, the other in the back seat. As they passed, the one in the back seat got out, looked back at Tony and Jack, and then started walking toward Shy. The driver started up and rolled slowly down the street. Mike saw the car coming with no lights. He looked in Shy's direction, and he could see that the man walking toward her had a gun in his right hand. Mike started running after her, watching as she got closer to the man. Mike caught up with Shy as the man pointed his gun at her.

"Get down!"

Mike pushed Shy out of the way, pulled out his gun, and fired one shot to the head of her attacker as Shy fell to the ground. When Tony and Jack heard the shot, they turned and ran back to the area as E pulled up in the car. Mike watched the Taurus speed away. All arrived at the scene in time to find one man lying on the ground with a fatal gunshot to the head. Mike looked over at the dead man. It had been seven years since he had fired a gun, much less killed somebody. His mind drifted back.

Freeze had been dabbling in counterfeit money and had put a deal together to sell some to a couple of guys from North Carolina. Mike and Bobby went along for the ride. They arrived at an empty office building. There were two cars in the parking lot, neither with North Carolina plates. One was from Connecticut, and the other was from Vermont. Mike and Freeze walked up ahead while Bobby looked at the two cars.

"Freeze!" Bobby yelled.

"Yeah, Bobby?" Freeze said, turning around to see what Bobby wanted.

"I thought you said these hillbillies were from North Carolina."

"Yeah, why?" Freeze and Mike walked back to the cars to take a look.

"Yo, Black, last time we did business, these boys were in a red Dodge pickup beat to shit with Carolina plates."

"Okay," Mike said, reaching into his coat pocket. He cocked his gun and returned it to his pocket. "Maybe they're just in different cars." He reached into the other pocket and cocked his other gun. "Or we're walkin' into a setup."

Bobby and Freeze both checked their weapons, and then Freeze led them inside the building to suite 107. As they entered the room, the two men Freeze was to meet with, Zek and Emmet, were seated at a table with two briefcases on it. Another man Freeze had never before seen was standing in the corner next to the door. The back door to the office was glass and opened outward so you could see reflections from the outside of the building.

"Hey, Freeze, who are your buddies?" Zek asked.

Freeze stepped straight up to the table. "That don't matter, Zek. Let's just get to it."

Mike and Bobby moved to either side of the table and began to look around. Bobby went to the left to cover the back door while Mike went to the right to watch Bobby's back.

"What you so uptight about there, Freeze? We done this before, smooth as a baby's ass. Let's see what grade of paper you got," Emmet said.

Mike looked at the glass door and could see that one man was moving slowly along the side of the building toward the door. Then he stopped. Mike motioned to Bobby, who nodded in response.

"No, let's see your money first, hillbilly!" Freeze said, pointing in his face.

"*Fuck this!*" *Mike walked up to the table, pulling both guns from his pockets. He turned to the man standing by the door and fired two shots. Both hit him in the head. Mike turned to Emmet and hit him with one shot in the head. Freeze moved to cover Zek. Bobby pulled his shotgun from under his coat. At that moment, a man came running through the door. He received both barrels in the chest. As the shooting stopped, one man remained, still sitting at the table with his hand two inches from his weapon. However, there were two guns pointed at him, one at each temple. Zek drew his hand back slowly. Freeze put his gun in Zek's mouth. "Now, hillbilly, I want to see you open up them cases."*

Bobby walked up to the table and patted Freeze on the shoulder. "Freeze, you just calm down. Give this hillbilly a chance." Bobby looked at Zek and smiled. "You ever watch them game shows on TV? I know you can't talk, so you just wiggle your ears or something."

Zek nodded.

"If there's money in those cases, you can go with what you came for and never come any farther north than the state line ever again in life. But if there's no money, well," Bobby laughed, "Freeze is gonna blow a hole out the back of your head. At the same time, Mr. Happy here is gonna blow your brains out the right side of your head."

Mike grew impatient. "Freeze." Both men fired.

"Damn, you two ain't no fuckin' fun at all," Bobby said.

"Bobby, check outside. Make sure there's no one else out there," Mike said as he looked in the cases. "Shit! Freeze, check the other offices. See if there is any money anywhere."

"Yo, Black, I'm sorry."

"Don't sweat it, Freeze. Shit happens. Now go."

Mike had just killed another man. The feeling wasn't the same. Mike looked down. Shy was still on the ground. He stood over her with his hand extended to help her up. "Are you all right?"

"Yeah, I'm all right, except for my pride," Shy said, as she got up and dusted herself off. "Thank you."

"Now will you have dinner with me? Please."

Shy looked in his eyes. She could feel the warmth of his touch. She stood speechless as part of her demanded she be strong and refuse. "I guess saving my life is at least worth dinner. You just tell me where and when, and I'll be there," Shy answered before turning to her associates. "Where were y'all? He coulda killed me." They tried to explain. "I don't wanna hear that shit. Let's just get out of here." As they walked toward the car, Shy walked over to Mike, who had been joined by Freeze and Kenny.

"Thanks again, Black. Where do you want to eat?"

"Do you know where Cuisine is?" Mike answered as he escorted Shy to the car.

"Yeah, I've eaten there before. Good food, but aren't they closed on Sundays?"

"They are, but I know they'll open for me." Mike smiled. "I own the place. Is six o'clock good for you? Should I send a car for you?"

"That's cool. Yeah, six is fine. I guess I can count on them to drive, so I don't think I'll need you to send a car for me. But thank you for offering." She closed the car door, and E drove away.

Kenny and Freeze looked at the body. Freeze told security to get rid of it. Mike joined Freeze and Kenny as the body was carried off by security. Mike asked Kenny if he'd ever seen the guy before. He hadn't. Mike explained what happened and that as the car drove away, he thought it had Michigan plates. His hope was that since Kenny was from Detroit, he might know him. Mike gave Kenny his gun and told him to get rid of it.

"Then I want you to go to Detroit. By the time you get there we'll know who this guy is. See if you can find out anything." Kenny went with security to oversee the disposal of the gun and the body.

"Yo, Black," Freeze said. "When you try to impress a bitch, you go all out. If I were a bitch and you saved my life, I'd hop up on a car and fuck you on the spot."

"Glad you ain't no bitch."

CHAPTER THREE

The next afternoon, Jack and Tony arrived at Shy's apartment for a quick meeting before escorting her to dinner at Cuisine. They arrived a little early. Shy answered the door in her robe.

"What's up, y'all? Where's E?"

Both men told her that they hadn't seen him all day. They discussed the events of last evening. The overriding question was, who would want to kill Shy? Was the assassination attempt connected to their associates being robbed? How, if at all, was Vicious Black involved? Neither Tony nor Shy believed that Black was involved. However, it may be somebody who worked for him. Jack told Shy that he didn't think so. Based on the checking that he did, no one in Black's organization was interested in their line of work.

"The feeling is that Black would kill them if they did," he said.

"Then who?" Shy asked. "Freeze maybe?"

Tony commented about the way that Black dissed them the night before, especially E. Shy explained that she thought that it was all a mind game that he was playing with them, first and foremost to show that he was in control of the situation. For them, he wanted to show that they were not important enough to talk to. It was a test for her. Black wanted to see if she was really running things, which E went a long way toward blowing.

Shy returned to her room to finish dressing. She re-emerged forty-five minutes later wearing a rust-colored satin fitted minidress, which highlighted every contour of her body, accented by a diamond necklace with matching bracelet. Tony looked at Shy and told her that she was dressed to kill, which was cool since she was having dinner with a killer.

Shy looked at him and smiled. "Let's just hope I'm not dressed to get killed, but I'll be all right. I'm sure all he wants is some pussy. Not! You know I'm strictly business. After dinner we need to go to Brooklyn to check out somebody E put me on to. Says this guy got some info we can use. I don't know the whole story. That's why I was hoping he would show."

A short time later, E rolled up in front of a building on Barnes Avenue. He sat for a while looking at the building and the boys playing outside. E got out of his Lexus and turned on the alarm. As he walked toward the building, E gave two of the boys $20 each to watch the car. He promised to give them $20 more each when he returned.

He went inside and rang the bell to the downstairs apartment. The door opened only a crack.

"You're getting kinda bold, ain't you, E?" came a woman's voice.

"Don't worry, he'll be gone for hours."

"As usual. He's never here."

"I know. That's why I'm here. I know you get lonely being here by yourself all the time. I wouldn't do my lady like that. I just wanna take care of you. Make you feel good. You don't need no weak man like that."

"Oh, really? Just what type a man do I need?"

"I got whatever you need right here waitin' for you to take it."

"You think so?"

"I know."

"I'd be interested to see," she said, opening the door to let E inside and closing it behind him.

Shy and her associates arrived at Cuisine at about a quarter to six. Cuisine was a small supper club that offered fine dining, an intimate atmosphere, a jazz combo called Que with a female vocalist, and a small dance floor. They entered the building and found it in darkness except for the bar.

"Hello! Is anyone in here?" Shy yelled.

Freeze, Jap, and Freddie the bartender were seated at the bar. Freeze got up and came to greet her. "What up, Shy? Are you all right?"

"It's not every day that someone tries to kill me, but I'm fine."

"You're a little early. We're not really ready for you."

"Is Black here yet?"

"Yeah, he's in the kitchen. I guess it's cool if you go on back. Go through that door there, to the right and down the hall, through the double doors at the end of the hall."

"Thanks, Freeze." Shy took off her coat and then turned to Tony and Jack. "Stay here. I'll be right back. And try not to get in any trouble," she said as she walked through the door.

"Don't worry, Shy. I'll take good care of your boys," Freeze said cordially, and then he turned his attention to Jack and Tony. "Y'all gotta give up that hardware," he said, no longer cordial. "Either of you seen that movie with Nick Nolte, *Q&A?*"

Both Jack and Tony nodded.

"You know what to do then. You wanna look around first?" Tony had a look around, then patted down Freddie. After Tony looked behind the bar, all four men gathered around a table.

"Okay, we go on three," Freeze said. "One, two, three."

Each man removed his gun and placed it on the table.

"Bar's open. Freddie, come here and see what they want."

Shy walked down the hall, hoping she could get through this as quickly and as painlessly as possible. She found Vicious Black very attractive, and if circumstances were different, maybe . . . *But not today.* She was anxious to get to Brooklyn to check out E's tip. *A little polite conversation, maybe a quick drink, and I'm out.*

She pushed open the kitchen doors to find Mike with an apron on, black of course. There he was, standing in front of the stove, pot in one hand, spoon in the other stirring the contents. Shy couldn't believe her eyes.

"Hello," she said as she walked toward him.

Mike looked at the clock on the wall. "Hello, Shy. You look incredible tonight."

"Thank you, Black. So tell me, just what are you doing?"

"Cooking, why?" Mike answered, continuing to stir.

"You're cooking dinner for us?" Shy asked with a look of disbelief in her eye. *Picture that. Vicious Black in an apron.*

"Yeah, but trust me, I'm really good at this."

"Well, what are we having?" she asked, leaning over the prep table.

"This is lobster Newburg, or at least it will be once I smooth out this sauce. You have to stir it just right. Come here."

Shy made her way around the counter while Mike continued to stir. Just as she got to him, he removed the spoon.

"Taste this. Tell me what you think."

Mike raised the spoon to her mouth, and his hand shook a little as he placed the spoon on her lips. Shy tasted the sauce. She smiled.

"That's very good. What's that I taste?"

"It's dry sherry and just a touch of Rémy Martin," Mike answered while he placed the cut-up lobster tails in the sauce. "I didn't know what kind of food you liked."

"Let's just say I like food. What kind doesn't matter. As long as it's food, I'll eat it. I should be as big as a house the way I eat," she said, motioning with her hands. "So what else we havin'?"

"I got a couple of steaks and some chicken in the broiler. I'll smother them with sautéed mushrooms and onions that I cooked in a wine sauce. Steamed broccoli with a cheese sauce. And a little rice and veal thing I threw together," Mike said, pointing to each item without taking his eyes off her.

"That you threw together?"

"Yeah." He had lost himself in her eyes. "I'm not much of a baker, so there's no dessert."

"I'm glad that I'm hungry. I don't think that I'll want to see dessert after all that. Maybe an apple to stuff in my mouth like a pig."

Mike finished with the lobster while Shy looked on. Michelle, who did food prep at the restaurant, and Diane, a server, entered the kitchen.

"Hi, Black. Sorry I'm late. Is everything ready for me?" Michelle asked while going to get started prepping the food to be served.

"What's up, ladies? Shy, this is Diane. She'll be our server tonight. And that's Michelle. She is going to prep the food. Yeah, Michelle, everything's ready for you here. Diane, everything all set outside?"

Diane simply nodded her response.

"Cool. Go tell them to get started."

As Diane left the kitchen, Mike looked up at the clock. "Six o'clock. Now this is when you were supposed to get here," Mike said, taking off his apron as he walked toward Shy. He couldn't stop himself from looking in her eyes.

She looked back at him. He frightened her and excited her all at once. "If I hadn't been early, I wouldn't believe you cooked all this."

As they walked through the kitchen doors and started down the hall, Shy heard music begin to play. *Maybe he's not so terrible after all. He didn't have to go to all this trouble for dinner. He could have just as easily told the chef to come in and throw something together. And with all that's going on, Vicious Black is a good person to know. Besides, he is kinda sexy, for a killer.* Her defenses began to melt away with the sound of the music.

Mike opened the door for Shy, and she thanked him. As Shy walked through the door, she could see that a candlelit table was now in the middle of the dance floor. The music that she heard coming down the hall was live. Que was on stage playing "The Girl from Ipanema," one of Mike's favorites. They usually played it for him anytime he came in the club.

Mike and Shy walked to the table. Diane pulled out the chair for Shy and poured the champagne: Dom Pérignon 1982, from Mike's private stock. Diane served the salad and asked Shy if she would like fresh pepper on her salad. Freddie placed a glass of Rémy Martin VSOP to the right of Mike's champagne glass, then came around to Shy's side of the table and asked if she would like a cocktail with her meal. Shy declined but asked him to come back after dinner and check on her.

The evening went on. Diane served the meal. The music was excellent, and the conversation twisted and turned in many different directions. They laughed and talked like two old friends who hadn't seen each other in years.

"Black, everything tastes delicious. You really are a good cook," Shy said, trying not to talk with her mouth full but not succeeding. "This is really nice. You arranged all this for me. You cooked all this food. I'm really impressed."

"Thank you. I'm glad you like it. Freeze thought that saving your life was impressive. Said I went all out. But I really didn't think that it fazed you."

"You know, I thought about that when I went to bed last night. That I really didn't seem like I appreciated you saving my life." She held out her hand and looked at Mike. "Thank you, Black."

He took her hand, stared into her eyes, then said to her without letting go of her hand, "Has anyone ever told you that you have very expressive eyes, beautiful eyes?" He let go of her hand. "So forgive me if I stare sometimes."

Although he had let go of her hand, Shy left it out there. "Thank you, Black." Finally realizing he'd let go of her hand, she jerked it back quickly.

"Do you have any ideas about who would want to kill you?"

"Not a clue. I was having a hard enough time trying to figure out who was robbin' us. Why would anybody want to kill me?"

"It's probably not you personally. It's just business, remember. And that's just the nature of our business."

"Touché."

"But your attacker was from Detroit. I sent Kenny there to check it out. His name was Leon Thomas. That sound familiar to you?"

"No, I've never heard of him. It still doesn't seem possible that someone wants to kill me," Shy said, sipping her champagne. "But I don't really want to talk about it now."

"So how'd you get the name?" Mike inquired, motioning for Freddie to freshen his drink. "Are you just shy, or were your parents just in one of those moods when you were born?"

"No, it's just a nickname," Shy laughed. "It's short for Chicago. That's where my father's from. My name is Cassandra, Cassandra Sims."

"Well, it's a pleasure to meet you, Cassandra Sims," Mike said, extending his hand.

Shy accepted his hand and replied, "Well, thank you very much. The pleasure is all yours."

Mike laughed. "I like that. I like a woman with confidence."

"I thought it was my eyes," Shy said very sexually.

"Why'd you have to go there? Now I have to stare at your eyes and hold your hand for a while," Mike said in his sexiest voice. "But it's really hard to eat like that."

"We could go on like this for hours, but I'm hungry too. So I promise not to say anything about my eyes . . . if you promise not to look at me like that," Shy said very slowly.

"How am I looking at you, Cassandra?" Mike asked, still holding her hand.

"Well, it's like you're looking through me. I don't know," Shy said with an innocent giggle.

He continued to stare at her. Shy felt her last layer of defense slip away. She struggled to maintain it. She closed her eyes and pulled her hand back slowly.

"Okay, I promise," Mike said, letting go of her hand. "But how did you get to be nicknamed after your father? Usually, it's boys who get named after their fathers."

"Well, I'm the youngest of five children. My oldest brother Harold is ten years older than I am. George is eight years. Gary is five years, and Randy is a year older than me. Me and him are real close. When I was a little girl, my brothers would pick on me. So my father would take me around with him wherever he went. At first people started calling me little Chicago, then little Chi-town, then little Chi, and finally just Shy. So what's your story, Black? How did you get the name Vicious Black?" she asked. "'Cause you're not vicious at all. Actually, you're kind of nice."

"Do you really wanna know?"

"Yeah. I really wanna know. I know it's probably real violent, and it's probably not good dinner conversation. But I really wanna know."

"I was fifteen when I got started working for André. Me, Bobby, Nick, and Jamaica. First, we were runners. Then we started collecting for him, but he liked me and Bobby. So he started taking us around with him. Sometimes we felt like pets, you know, two pit bulls. So one day André takes us to collect from some guy who owed him twenty-five grand. I was like seventeen, eighteen by then. So we tie the guy up, and André starts goin' through the 'where's my money' shit. Bobby's torturing the guy when his wife comes home. André takes the bit—I mean, woman—in the back and rapes her."

"What were you doing while all this was going on?"

"Watching some movie, *The Soldier,* on TV."

Shy laughed as she pictured him calmly watching TV surrounded by the screams of rape and torture.

"Now Bobby's idea of torture is while he slaps the guy around, he tells him jokes. Some of them are funny, some aren't. If you laugh, you get slapped. If you don't, you get hit. Hard. Anyway, André gets through doing his thing with the wife and comes out of the back. André slaps the guy a couple of times and asks him where the money is. But by now the guy is too out of it to talk. André says, 'Yo, Black, come here.' I don't even answer him."

Shy listened quietly. She called Freddie over to the table. Shy asked him to get her a drink. "Doesn't matter what."

"So then he says, 'Yo, Black, I think this guy's dead.' I looked at them, got up, and walked over to the guy. I told the guy to look at me, but he didn't move. So I said it

again, but this time he looks up. I took out my gun, held
it to his forehead, and shot him. One shot in the head.
Then I looked at André and said, 'Now he is.' André
freaks. Says, 'Damn! You just a vicious muthafucka, a
vicious black-wearin' muthafucka, ain't you?' I said,
'Whatever, can we go now?' And the name stuck." Mike
sat back in his chair and waited for Shy to say something.
Freddie returned with a rust-looking drink to match her
dress.

"Yeah, I was right. Rape, torture, murder—not exactly
dinner conversation. But I did ask." Shy sat back in her
chair and pointed at Mike. "You know what? You are
not at all what I was expecting. I'm not sure what I was
expecting. Yes, I do. I was expecting the guy in that story.
But you . . . no, I wasn't expecting you. I didn't even like
you yesterday." But she knew she was lying. "But tonight
I've really enjoyed myself. You're quite intelligent for
a killer. I mean, last night you push me down and shot
somebody. Then today you cook me the best meal I ever
had. Arrange all this. And I have had so much fun talking
to you. No, Mike Black, I wasn't expecting you."

"You think that's something. 'I got a Balinese dancing
girl tattooed on my chest.'"

"Humphrey Bogart in *The Big Sleep*," Shy said quickly.

"What?"

"That was a line from *The Big Sleep* with Humphrey
Bogart, right?"

"Yeah, how did you know that?" Mike said, looking
kind of puzzled.

Shy smiled at Mike. She leaned forward and said, "I
told you I have four older brothers. I had to watch a lot of
gangster movies growing up. Now I just love them, being
kind of a gangster myself."

"Where are your brothers, Cassandra?"

"Baltimore-Washington area. My oldest brother teaches college English, one is a supervisor for the IRS, one writes programs for a computer company, and the last is a doctor."

"So with a family résumé like that, how'd you become kind of a gangster?"

"I've been selling drugs since high school. Reefer back then. When I went to Syracuse, that was my work-study program. I graduated with a dual degree in management and marketing. When I came home, my brother Randy was waitin' tables in Brooklyn, trying to get into medical school. The money that my father had left us to go to college with was gone. Everybody in the family was struggling. He would have never gotten the money for med school waiting tables. So I told him when I got a job I would help him and when he graduated from med school, you know, I would go back and get my masters in marketing. See, I wasn't even thinking about rollin' then, college girl, you know. But reality set in quick. After four months of looking for a job—any job—we were both broke, both of us waitin' tables in some dive in Brooklyn. I said, 'Hold up, I got a marketable skill.' So I went to see one of my father's old business associates, who turned me on to someone to do business with. After he gave me a lecture about what I was getting myself into, he fronted me a couple of ounces. I rounded up my old partners, and we went to work."

"I'm impressed. What's the secret to your success?"

"No secret. I run a business. It's just that simple."

"No, Ms. Sims. The way I hear it, you run a high-volume and extremely profitable business that you grew from a couple of ounces. There's an art to that. So I say again, what's your secret?" he said, leaning toward her.

Shy leaned right back at him. "And I say again, it's no secret. It's just business." Shy sat back in her chair and smiled playfully. "It's just not business the way you know it." The smile was now a superior one. "I do business just the way they taught me. I market a product. I manage people and money."

Mike sat and listened intently as Shy defined in a fair amount of detail how she structured her business, how she applied what she had learned and, in seven years, turned a couple of ounces into a company with annual sales projected to top $4 million. The concept intrigued him. His eyes began to open to new possibilities as Shy talked optimistically about her plans for future growth.

Her mood changed as she began to reflect on the past and the choices that led her to this point. "I told myself I was just gonna do it 'til he got through med school. Not."

"Have you ever thought about goin' back, getting your masters?"

"Yeah. I think about it," she said, her eyes displaying the regret she felt. "I even took a few classes early on. But that was just to get a higher-price clientele, that's all. I still think about it, but I'm definitely not motivated," Shy said, looking kind of sad when the vocalist began to sing "You're All I Need to Get By," a cappella at first. Her face came alive, her head drifting back slowly. "I love this song."

"So do I." Mike stood up and held out his hand. "Come dance with me."

Shy looked up at him and accepted his hand. "I'd love to."

As Mike and Shy got up to dance, Jap leaned toward Freeze and said, "Touchdown."

"I was wondering what was taking him so long," Freeze replied as he stood up. "Yo, I gotta get out of here. This shit is making me sick. I'll make the rounds tonight. You stay here and watch them. Call me on the cell if anything goes down."

"You want me to tell Black where you goin'?"

"Nah. I'll tell him as soon as he gets through doin' his thing."

As the music played, Mike and Shy danced very slow and very close. Shy rested her head on his shoulder. *I guess this is the part when I'm supposed to exhale,* she said to herself. Maybe it wasn't all that, but he definitely felt better than her pillow. Shy closed her eyes and allowed herself to drift, wishing he'd hold her tighter.

He drew her closer as if he had heard her wish. He looked at Shy. Her eyes closed, and she mouthed the words to the song. Like a rush of adrenaline, all at once everything became very clear to him. All his questions seemed answered. All of his doubts seemed illogical. "I could really get used to this. It's been a long time since I danced with a woman."

"Why? I know it's not because you don't like women."

"It's a long story."

"Oh, really? Long story? What was her name?"

"What makes you think . . . never mind. Her name was Regina."

"Did she break my . . ." Shy caught herself. "I mean, that baby's heart?"

"Baby, huh? Yeah, she busted me out."

As the song ended, they stood staring at one another, each searching awkwardly for something to say. They walked hand in hand back to the table without saying a word. Mike held out the chair for Shy as Freeze approached to break the spell.

"Yo, Black, I gotta break, go do my thing. Jap's gonna stay, make sure her boys behave themselves. If you need me, you know the routine. I'm out. Peace, y'all." Freeze grabbed his coat and pointed at Tony and Jack on his way out the door.

"So do you have any plans for the rest of the night, Cassandra?"

"I do, but that's not a problem. I'm enjoying myself too much to deal with what I got to deal with. Besides, that's what they're for, right? Yo, Tony, come here."

Tony stood up and came to see what Shy wanted. "What's up, Shy?"

"You remember that business we discussed on the way here?"

Tony nodded.

"I need you to go out to Brooklyn and check it out, see what's up. Jack will stay here with me. I'll be okay."

Tony accepted his assignment and departed the table. He went over to Jack to let him know what was going on, finished his drink, tipped Freddie handsomely, and left the club.

"Now that that's settled, what did you have in mind for the rest of the evening, Mr. Black?"

"Well, Ms. Sims, I was hopin' that you would come . . . and take a walk with me."

Picking up on the play on words, Shy responded, "Where do you want me to come and walk to?"

"Just around. I promise to behave myself, Cassandra."

"Since you put it that way, how can a girl refuse?" Shy stood up and started walking toward the bar. "Jack, get my coat please."

Mike thanked the band for coming out and especially for playing "You're All I Need to Get By." He handed them an envelope. He went into the kitchen to pay Diane and Michelle. He thanked them for helping him out on their day off and told them that they could go when the place was clean. Jap took the opportunity to call Freeze and make him aware of the change in the evening's agenda and of Tony's sudden departure, which seemed to be of particular interest to Freeze.

Mike and Shy left the supper club and walked down the street with Jack and Jap not too far behind. As they walked down the street, most of the people they passed said, "What's up, Black?" Some of the older folks still called him Mike, but they spoke too. They walked and talked for over an hour. Mike would stop from time to time to talk to somebody.

Watching him, Shy got a sense of the respect he commanded. "So who are you anyway, Don Black?"

"Well, I do suffer from a godfather complex, but no. I grew up around here. Everybody knows me. I wanted to show you off. And by the way, you've gotten a few compliments." Mike stopped and smiled seductively at Shy. She returned the smile as she walked toward him. Their eyes locked, the energy between them building to a crescendo, but before she could say anything, a young brother came running up to them.

"Yo, Black! Yo, Black, man, it's a goddamn shame! You know there just ain't no reason for this to be happening! You gotta do something about this 'cause yo, I'm tired of this!"

"What was the damage today, Larry?"

"Forty-four to ten," Larry said. "Yo, Black, it was embarrassing just to sit there and watch. Why don't you buy the Jets and clean house, man?"

"I ain't phat like all that," Mike said as he and Shy walked away. "I was gonna ask you for some spare change so a brother could have something."

"Yo, Black, you could have introduced me to the honey. She sure is fine!"

"Does he always get that excited about football? I mean, I thought something was wrong the way he came runnin' up on you. I was getting ready to cap his ass," Shy said, removing her gun from her left coat pocket and then putting it back.

"Maybe he was excited about your eyes, Cassandra. Anyway, if it were like that, I would've shot him myself," Mike said, removing his gun from his right coat pocket and then putting it back with a smile.

They continued up one street and down the next. They stopped in front of a three-story house. It was the home of Emily Black, Mike's mother. "This is where I used to live," Mike said, pointing to the house before walking on.

"Must be some bad memories there."

"No, life was good here. When I see that house, I still think of home."

Mike and his mother came to New York from Saint Vincent in the West Indies when he was 4 years old. Arriving in New York with no family or friends or much money to speak of, they moved into a small one-room flat in the South Bronx. After she completed nursing school, Emily got a job at Lebanon Hospital working the evening shift when Mike was 6. With a new job, Emily was able to move out of the South Bronx into the basement of a two-family house in a section of the Bronx with a large West Indian population. After a few years, they were able to move upstairs. Emily still lived there, but now she owned the house. With Emily working evenings, Mike would stay upstairs with her friends, George and Daphene Smith, and remain until his mother came for him. This lasted a couple of years until he decided he no longer needed a babysitter. From that point, the streets and television raised him.

As a result of this independence, Mike's attitude began to change. He became very aggressive, cold, and hard, showing little emotion if any at all. Vicious Black's reputation grew. Everybody knew who he was and what he did. Knowing that her son was a criminal caused Emily tremendous grief and brought on ten years of silence between them.

"I've done a lotta things in my life that I'm not proud of. I've done my best to do some good around here. Make up for some of the destruction I caused," Mike said, coming around the corner down the block from Cuisine. "Like everyone, I've got some regrets. Things I shoulda done smarter."

"Like what?"

"That's a long story too, Ms. Sims," Mike replied.

"Regina, right?" joked Shy.

But Mike didn't answer. He stopped in front of Shy's car and waited quietly until Jap and Jack caught up.

"I really enjoyed the evening. I think that was the best meal I ever had, Black. You really are an excellent cook."

Mike opened the car door. "Good night, Cassandra. I enjoyed your company." Mike turned and walked into Cuisine with Jap following close behind.

Shy watched as the door slammed shut. She turned to Jack and let out a little giggle. "Was it something I said?"

CHAPTER FOUR

Shy woke up to the sound of her phone ringing. "Hello."

"Good morning, baby. Did I wake you?" It was her mother, Joann Sims, calling.

"No, Mommy, I needed to get up anyway. How are you?"

"I'm fine. I was just calling to make sure you were coming next Friday and see whether you were going to bring somebody with you. If you are, I hope it's not that lowlife you brought with you last year. I mean, he reminded me too much of your father. Old slick, shit-talkin' nigga. What was his name anyway, Cassandra?"

"His name is Eddie, and no, I'm not going to bring him. And don't be so hard on him, Mommy. He's been a good friend. When we came down there last year, it was just after I went through that thing with Ricardo. I was feeling pretty low. E was there for me when I needed somebody. He helped me get through it. That's all."

"I still don't like him."

"There is someone I might like to bring with me, but I think I hurt his feelings last night. I don't know if I'll even hear from him again, much less invite him to our family reunion."

"Is this somebody new? What's his name? What's he like? Is he good-lookin'? Come on now, I want to hear everything," Joann said, obviously excited that her daughter had finally shown some interest in something other than money.

"Calm down, Mommy. One question at a time. Yes, he is someone new. His name is Mike Black. And yes, he is very good-looking. He's not like most guys I've met. He's intelligent, so he can hold a conversation. Mommy, guess what?"

"What, baby?"

"He can cook!" Shy shouted. "Mommy, last night he cooked me the best dinner I ever had. That is, other than your cooking, of course."

"Well, thank you for showing me some respect."

"He owns a nice little supper club, and they're closed on Sundays. So he had the house band playing just for us. He had people come in to serve, and he cooked."

"He probably had the chef cook and he took the credit for it," Joann said suspiciously. Her personal experience with men in general, and with Shy's father in particular, led her to be leery of all men.

"No. I got there early and found him in the kitchen throwin' down."

"Really? I'm impressed. And I'm glad that you finally met someone respectable. Maybe he can square you up, make a respectable citizen out of you."

"Well, Mommy, he's not exactly—" Shy was interrupted by a loud knock at the door. "Hold on, Mommy, there's someone at the door."

Shy got out of bed and put on her robe. She took her gun from under her pillow, took the safety off, and cocked it before moving to answer the door. She stood to the right of the door. "Who is it?"

"Flower delivery, ma'am. I have flowers for Cassandra Sims!" yelled the voice on the other side of the door.

"Hold on a second. I gotta put something on." She walked to the window to see if there was a delivery truck parked outside. Sure enough, she could see a small van double-parked across the street, but she couldn't make out the writing from fifteen floors up. *What if it's a setup? Anybody can steal a truck.* Maybe she was just overreacting. But who would be sending her flowers? Then all of a sudden it hit her like a shot.

"Black!" she shouted, walking quickly back to the door. In her excitement, she didn't forget that this still might be a setup. So she unlocked the door, then moved back to the right before yelling, "Come in, it's open."

The door opened slowly, and in walked a man with his arms full. The delivery driver carried in three vases of three dozen long-stemmed red roses.

"Somebody must really think a lot of you, which I can understand," he said, looking Shy up and down, nodding his head in approval. "Or he messed up really bad, which he should die for. Where do you want these, lady?"

"Just put them on the table here," Shy replied, clearing a spot on the dining room table. She thanked the man for bringing up so many roses and gave him a $10 tip before letting him out. Shy returned to the dining room. She smelled the roses and looked at the card, which read:

> *Cassandra,*
> *I really did enjoy your company last night. I hope that we can get together again soon.*

The card was unsigned, but she knew they were from Black. She picked up a vase and returned to her bedroom to tell her mother about the flowers. Shy lay down on the bed, closed her eyes, and took a deep breath. She smiled and picked up the phone. "Mommy."

"Well, it's about time. I thought that you forgot about your poor old mother on hold long distance. So who was at the door?"

"Mommy, you'll never guess what I just got." But before Joann could answer, Shy yelled out, "Three dozen roses!" Removing the roses from the vase, she threw them in the air and watched them fall down all around her on the bed. "I always wanted to do that." She smiled.

"Child, what you doing?"

"Just being silly. Anyway, the guy I was just telling you about sent me three dozen roses. Nobody ever sent me roses before. Mommy, what do you do when somebody sends you roses? I know, I should send him some . . . no, I'll send him one black rose."

"Black! What you want to send him a black rose for? He an undertaker or something?"

"It's a long story, Mommy, but I gotta go. So I'll see you either Friday night or Saturday morning. Bye-bye, Mommy. I love you."

"Hold on, girl. Slow down. I got something else to ask you before you run off. Do you need me to send someone to the airport to pick you up?"

"No, I'll rent a car and drive out, okay? Gotta go, Mommy."

"See you when you get here. I love you too, baby." And with that, Joann hung up the phone.

Shy flipped through the yellow pages, looking for a florist. She found one and dialed the number. Shy asked if they could dye one rose black. Once the attendant got through laughing at her request, he explained how the process worked and explained the significance of her choice of color. Shy promptly told him to mind his business and gave him her credit card number. He asked where she wanted the flower delivered. It was then she realized that she had no idea where Black lived. Shy asked the man to hold on while she thought about where to send the rose. She could send it to Cuisine. But how would it look, Vicious Black getting a rose? *Well, at least it's a black rose.* Shy told the attendant where to send it and gave very specific delivery instructions. She wanted to make sure that he was there and alone before they attempted delivery.

Shy called Tony and told him to meet her on Gun Hill Road about noon so they could talk about what he found out the night before. Shy asked if he had heard anything from E yet. They were accustomed to E disappearing for days at a time. With all that'd been going on lately, Shy thought it was best if all of them at the very least checked in with one another every day.

Shy returned to her room to get dressed. As she stood in front of her closet, she began thinking about the night before and how it was kinda cruel to bring up Regina. Black had already told her that this woman broke his heart. Somehow she never expected Vicious Black to be sensitive about anything. He appeared to be so strong and in control of everything around him. One thing Shy was sure of was that she liked him, sensitive or not. Mike Black was the most interesting man she had met in a long time. On top of that, he was fine, but this was no time to get all involved with Black or anybody else for that matter. Somebody was trying to ruin her business, not to mention kill her. For the time being she would have to kick her feelings to the curb. They usually got her in trouble anyway. That was a lesson Ricardo had taught her. Ricardo devastated Shy, but all that seemed so far away now.

While she got dressed, as hard as she tried to focus on more important issues, her mind kept drifting back to Black. She picked out something to wear: a burgundy wool jacket, trimmed in lambswool, with a matching skirt. She wondered whether he would like her in it. Finally, by twelve thirty, Shy was dressed and ready to go, but she would be late meeting Tony. Shy rushed to get herself together and out of the house. She opened the door, and to her surprise, E was standing in the doorway.

"What are you doing out there? You scared the shit out of me."

"Ain't you gonna say hello? Invite me in or something?"

"No. We gotta meet Tony and we're late. So come on, you can drive. Where you been anyway? With all that's goin' on, the least you could do was call and let me know what's up. Did you get a chance to check out them leads?"

As they got into the elevator, E explained that he was following up on some business that would benefit everybody involved. He didn't want to tell her about it until he had all the details worked out. E told Shy that if everything worked as planned, they would all have enough money to retire.

"What you talkin' about, E? It's gonna take a lot of money for me to retire."

"Don't worry about that, girl. I got this. You just worry about stayin' your fine ass alive." E opened Shy's car door.

"Okay, E, but I wanna know what's up with this before you get too far out there. Money's gettin' tight, so we can't mess around and lose any," Shy cautioned. She trusted E, but she knew to keep a tight rein on him.

"Trust me, Shy," E said as he closed her door.

They drove to Gun Hill Road where Shy was to meet Tony. Although they were late, there was Tony, standing on the corner, waiting. He got into the back seat, and E drove off.

"Where you been, E?"

"Handlin' my business. Not mindin' yours."

"Y'all kill that noise!" she demanded, noticing that there was a lot of tension between Tony and E. More than usual. It was becoming more apparent to Shy that something was going on between the two of them. She would have to handle that too, but this was really not the time. Everything seemed to be crashing down around her. "We got important matters to deal with. We can't afford to get into this now. What happened last night in Brooklyn?" While Tony described what happened in Brooklyn, Shy slowly drifted into another world, thinking about Black and wondering if he was thinking about her.

"Shy! Yo, Shy, are you listenin'?"

"I'm sorry, Tony. You know I got a lot on my mind. That's all. What did you say?"

"I said that I went to see that guy Tim last night. He fed me some bullshit for a while, and then something funny happened. The phone rang, and I heard him say, 'Yeah, he's here.' I guess who ever called was talkin' for a while, and then he said, 'No, she ain't with him,' like he was expecting you. How would he know that?"

"Makes sense. Ain't too many people who don't know what's goin' on," E said. "It might have been a setup for Shy. It's a good thing you sent Tony alone, Shy."

But Shy was back in her zone and said nothing about the setup. "E, swing by Jack's," Shy said.

"How was the date last night, Shy?" E asked.

"That's why she ain't listening," Tony said, smiling at her. "She got them 'I'm in love with a killer' blues."

Shy looked back at Tony. "You just want me to have something to say, don't you? I mean, I try to be nice, but you're not happy unless I'm goin' off on you. Is that what it is? I heard what you said. Nobody is more aware than

I am of the fact that somebody tried to kill me. Anyway, as far as Black is concerned, I can't be so bothered right now," she said in denial. "So can we get back to business now?" She knew Tony was right. She was finding it hard to concentrate. It was like being at the crossroads, and all the roads led her back to the same spot.

E turned onto Jack's block and found him standing by his car, talking on his cell phone to Trevor, one of the associates who worked for Jack. E parked the car and called to Jack to come over to the car.

"Hold up! You rude muthafucka," Jack shouted as he walked across the street. "Okay, I'll tell her. What's up, y'all? Shy, that was Trevor. He just got home and found his girl Janet dead and the dope gone."

"Damn, they killed his girl. Take me over there, E."

"No. Trev said the cops are there," Jack said.

"You just meet us there, Jack," Shy commanded.

"How did it happen?" Tony asked.

"Trev said that Janet usually gets home about seven in the morning. Said when he got there, he found her by the door. They shot her in the back."

"Sounds like she walked in on something," E said.

When they arrived at Trevor's apartment, the police were all over the place. Shy wanted to go in and tell Trevor how sorry she was about Janet. She felt like it was her fault that Janet got killed. The cops wouldn't let Shy in the apartment, so she sat quietly in the hallway until the cops left.

"Trevor, I am so sorry this had to happen," Shy said with tears in her eyes. "I never wanted anything like this to happen. It's all my fault. Trevor, I'm sorry."

Trevor and everyone else told Shy that this wasn't her fault, that it was just one of those things that happened in this game. Shy would not accept that as an answer. It would strengthen her resolve to find the people responsible. Jack stayed with Trevor while Tony, E, and Shy started to leave.

Before they left, Trevor stopped Shy in the hall. "Shy, I don't want you to carry this around with you. I mean it. This wasn't your fault. Shit happens sometimes. We got no control over it," pleaded Trevor.

Shy wasn't hearing any of that. "No. If you had died, yeah, okay, that's just business. But Janet didn't have no part in this. She didn't have to die. She died for me." Shy turned and got in the elevator.

CHAPTER FIVE

The delivery driver arrived at Cuisine at about three o'clock that afternoon. The restaurant was in transition from lunch to dinner. The staff had finished cleaning their stations. Those who remained were sitting around talking. Mike was there working in his office with Bobby. Michelle came into his office to tell him that there was someone to see him. She did leave out the part about the rose. Michelle wanted to see the look on his face when he got it. Luckily, Mike told her to send whoever it was in without asking who it was. When the delivery driver came in, half the waitstaff came in with him. That was exactly what Shy wished to avoid. Mike read the card:

> *Thank you for the roses.*
> *I enjoyed my evening with you too.*
> *See you very soon.*
> *C*

The waitstaff clapped while he read the card. Then Mike kicked them out of his office. Mike tried to call Shy to thank her for the rose and to see if she wanted to have dinner or do something later that evening, but there was no answer.

Bobby, who had been sitting quietly through it all, said, "Well, isn't that just the sweetest thing you ever did see? Old Vicious Black getting flowers. Times, they sure are a-changin'."

"You're working me, Bobby," Mike said, still staring at the card.

"I guess I don't have to ask you how the little meal went last night. She must have been impressed. She sent you a rose," Bobby said sarcastically.

Mike thought for a second or two. "Dinner went all right. She's fine. That's what she is. Goddamn, Bobby, I caught myself a couple of times sitting there staring at her. Looking at her eyes, you know. On top of that, she has a brain. She's got a dual degree in management and marketing."

"Impressive, but can she fuck?" Bobby asked, waiting for more details.

Mike leaned back in his chair. "Didn't even crack."

Bobby picked up the phone and started dialing.

"Who you calling?"

"I'm callin' Perry, man. You need a doctor," Bobby said, laughing while he hung up the phone. "You didn't talk up on it, something ain't right. You ain't in love?" Bobby asked. Then he stopped laughing. "Are you?"

"I don't know, Bobby. The way she runs her business fascinates me. There are some things we can draw from her. But other than that, I do know that she's all that. And a bottle of Remy."

"I'll drink to that, but I'll drink to anything. But just a short one. I'm going to take Pam to dinner," Bobby said while pouring the drinks. "Kinda make up for the last couple of weeks hanging out with you and Freeze."

The phone rang. It was Freeze. He had just heard what happened with Shy. Bobby answered the phone.

"What's up, Bobby? Where's Black?"

"Hold on, Freeze. I'll see if lover boy can come to the phone."

Mike grabbed the phone out of Bobby's hand. "Asshole." He turned his attention to Freeze. "What's up, Freeze? Did everything go all right last night?"

"Yeah, yeah, all that's cool. But your girl Shy got robbed again this morning. This time some girl died."

"Shy all right?"

"I guess so. I haven't got the details yet. But before you say it, Jap is on his way over there now. He'll call me when he finds out what's up."

"Once he finds out all the details, you have him stay with her, but stay out of sight. Just make sure she's safe."

"You got it. I'll find out if she's all right and call you back."

"No. Where are you?"

"Rollin' down Webster."

"Come down here. I want to see Angelo today. Call him and set it up."

Mike explained to Bobby what happened. Bobby didn't say much. Once Mike had finished talking, Bobby said, "Mike, are you sure you want to get involved in this? Whatever's going on with her and her business is her business. I know you like her, but we don't need to get into no covert drug war. I gotta get out of here, but you think about this. Whatever you decide, I'm down with you. But make sure it's a war worth fighting and one we can win."

"That's why I'm going to talk to Angelo."

"You want me to go?" Bobby asked, hoping he'd say yes.

"No. You take care of Pam."

Bobby left the office, and Mike waited for Freeze to get there to drive him to Yonkers to see Angelo Collette. Mike and Angelo were in the same homeroom in high school. Back in the day when they both were freelancing, they did a few jobs together.

Freeze arrived at Cuisine, and he and Mike drove out to Yonkers. They pulled up in front of a small private club and were met at the curb by two large gentlemen.

"Here comes that fuckin' Jimmy. I hate that fat bastard, Black. I'd like to cut that fat muthafucka's throat," Freeze said as Jimmy and his associate approached the car. In the old days, Jimmy would talk big shit to Freeze. Jimmy used to call him "Black's little errand boy."

"Don't let him get to you, Freeze. Jimmy still fucks with you 'cause he knows it gets to you. Go ahead. You get out first. Make him show you respect. And remember who runs shit and who's always gonna be the errand boy."

"What's up, Jimmy? Black is here to see Mr. Collette." Freeze would have rather shot him than talked to him.

Jimmy looked at Freeze but didn't say anything.

Mike got out of the car. "Jimmy, how are you?" he said as he and Freeze followed Jimmy inside the club.

"I'm okay, Black. Where's Bobby? He always cracks me up."

"He's having dinner with the wife," Mike said, handing Jimmy his guns. He patted down Mike. Freeze sat down at the bar without offering his weapon.

"Angelo's in the back. He's waiting for you."

"Thanks, Jimmy. Good seeing you again. How's the wife and kids?"

"Helen's good, and we just had our sixth," Jimmy shouted as Mike went in the back.

Mike knocked on the door to Angelo's office.

"Come on in, Mike. Sit down. Hey, Joey, get Mr. Black a drink. Rémy Martin VSOP straight up, right? Then get out."

"Greetings and much respect, Don Collette," Mike said as Joey left.

"I ain't no fuckin' don, Mike. And if you try to kiss my fuckin' hand, I'll shoot you. We go too far back for all that don stuff. But I appreciate the respect." Angelo stood and shook Mike's hand.

"How's it going, Angee?"

"A little older, but I'm good."

"How's Carmine? How's his health?"

"Not good, Mikey. You should go see him. He always liked you. So tell me, Mike, it's been over a year since you came to see me. You could come by and take me to a ball game or something."

"Come on, Angee, you should be taking me to the game. You guys got the skybox at the Meadowlands. Remember?"

"Maybe I'll come get you one Sunday, Mike, take you with me."

"Bullshit, Angee. I can see it now, me walking in the skybox. I'd get shot on sight."

"Mike, you just don't realize how much respect you have in some circles. Vincenzo, God rest his soul, had respect for you and what you did. Getting your people out of the drug business, cleanin' up your hood and all that. Enough bullshit, Mike. You didn't come here to tell me how pretty I am. So what gives?"

"You know a woman named Cassandra Sims, calls herself Shy?"

"Yeah, she does business. Why, Mike, what's your interest?"

"Personal, for the time being."

"I understand. She's a beautiful woman."

"Are you aware of the problems she's been having lately?"

"Been robbed a couple times. Why you askin' me this, Mike?"

"'Cause Freeze can't get a line on it."

"Get the fuck outta here. Fuckin' Freeze is better than the fuckin' *Times*."

"That's my point, Angee. If Freeze can't run it down, either it ain't happenin' or whoever's doin' it has excellent security. That's why I came to see you."

"I get your point, Mike. I don't know anything about it. You have my word on it."

"I was hopin' you'd say that, Angee. If I decide to involve myself in this, I don't feel like messin' with you. I didn't want to bury you. No disrespect."

"None taken," Angelo laughed. "Where's Bobby at, Mike? He still married?"

"That's where he is, out with the wife."

"You tell him that he cost me a couple a grand. I bet that it wouldn't last two years. How long has it been, Mikey?"

"Six years, Angee."

"Six years. Go figure. Guy like that married for six years. Who'da thought? But anyway, Mikey, Shy's a good girl. She runs a good operation. Nothing like her father, that scumbag."

Mike looked puzzled. "Her father? Who's her father?"

"What, are you kiddin' me? You of all people should know. Chicago's her father."

Mike looked at him in shock, and his mind began racing.

"Oh, shit, Mike, you didn't know? Shy, Chi-town, Chicago . . . This ain't rocket science."

"Angee, I must be slippin'," Mike said, obviously shaken by the information. His mind flashed back, and he could see those eyes that haunted him for years. "She told me last night over dinner that she got the name from her father, and I just didn't put it together."

"So she doesn't know. You gonna tell her?"

"I need a drink, Angee," Mike said, helping himself to another shot of Remy. "I oughta kill Freeze."

"Why? The only ones who know about that is me, you, and André. And that bastard ain't tellin' nobody. I never said anything about it, and unless you told somebody, who would know? How would Freeze know that it was important enough to mention?"

"You're right, Angee. I mean, she laid it all out. Said she went to see some of her father's old partners. Carmine, most likely, who probably sent her to you."

"Guilty."

"Said you gave her a lecture. I should have known it was you she was talkin' about when she said 'lecture.'"

"You were probably too busy looking at them titties. No disrespect to you, Mikey, but she is a beautiful woman."

"You know me too well, Angee. But actually it was her eyes. And now I know why. I've taken up enough of your time. We both have work to do. Angee, thanks for everything."

"I'm serious about going to a game. But let me give you a little advice, Mike. This should be a warning to you. Think and see this thing with Shy with your brain and not your dick. You know I'm right about this, Mike. If you can let a point like that slip by, what else have you missed? You take care of yourself, and game or no game, you come see me," Angelo said as he hugged Mike.

"I will, Angee. You could come up to the Bronx every once in a while. Come by the club."

"Nah, Mikey. Your new spot's a little too highbrow for my taste. Not like the old days when you had the after-hours spot."

"See ya, Angee." Mike walked out of the office and leaned against the wall. He stood for a minute, his mind racing, flashing back to that day. Angelo was right. He let his feelings cloud his judgment. He gathered himself together and continued walking toward the bar.

He saw Freeze standing by the bar with his back turned. As he got closer, he could see that Freeze had his gun pointed at Jimmy's head. Everybody else in the room had their guns pointed at Freeze. Mike laughed and went back in the office to tell Angelo.

"Yo, Angee, it's finally happened. Freeze finally stood up to Jimmy."

"I don't believe it. This I gotta see." Angelo got up and followed Mike out of the office. "Well, what have we got here?" Angelo asked, grinning from ear to ear.

"Looks like a New York standoff to me," Mike said.

"Yo, Black, I told you I'm tired of him fuckin' with me," Freeze said.

"All right, everybody, just ease off. Nobody's going to die here today." At Angelo's command, everybody slowly lowered their guns except Freeze.

With almost all the weapons down, Mike crossed the room, passing Freeze. "Jimmy, you all right?" Mike asked.

Jimmy nodded his head, sweating like a pig.

"Freeze, I don't know about you, but I'm ready to go, and you have the keys to the car. So give me the keys."

Freeze handed Mike the keys. Mike thanked him and walked out. Freeze finally eased the gun away from Jimmy's head and started to back out the door. Jimmy didn't say a word. He just smiled.

Freeze walked out to the car and got in, started the car, and pulled away. Freeze looked over at Mike. He smiled at Freeze. "He'll respect you now."

Mike and Freeze arrived back at the supper club. Sylvia, Mike's secretary, told him that Kenny called while they were gone. She told them that Kenny said that he got some info on Leon Thomas but nothing on why he was in New York, much less who hired him. Hopefully he'd be back in a few days.

"Did he leave a number where he was?"

"Kenny said he was on the go and couldn't be reached. He said he would call tomorrow around five."

"Knowing Kenny, he's partyin' too hard and doesn't want you to give him more to do," Freeze said as he entered Mike's office.

"Have you heard anything from Jap?" Mike asked Sylvia.

"Not yet, but I can stay another hour or so if you need me."

"Another hour? Who's gonna pick up your son?" Mike asked on the way into his office.

"I'll call my sister," she said.

"No, you go home. Take care of that man-child. But thanks for asking," Mike said, closing the door behind him.

As he sat down on the couch, the phone rang and Freeze answered it. It was Jap. He explained the details of the robbery to Freeze, which he in turn relayed to Mike. He said that Shy was pretty shaken up about the girl who died because she felt responsible for it. Jap also let Freeze know that he was still on Shy.

"Yo, Black, Jap wanna know how long he should stay with Shy," Freeze said.

"Until I tell him otherwise," Mike fired back.

Freeze relayed Mike's instructions and told him to check in a little more often and he might arrange some food. Freeze hung up the phone, putting his feet up on Mike's desk. "What you gonna do now, Black?"

Mike looked at Freeze. He picked up a bottle and poured. "Nothing."

CHAPTER SIX

Mike paced aimlessly around his house. He couldn't seem to sit still, wandering around the house like a nervous cat. He tried to go to sleep, but he was restless. He tried reading, but he couldn't concentrate. He turned on the television and channel surfed for a while, but nothing was ever on cable anyway. He put on some music—Johnny Hartman on vocals backed by John Coltrane on sax—and started to work out, but he couldn't get motivated. Love songs weren't exactly music to work out with, but that was the way he was feeling. He thought he might take a ride, but he didn't want to leave the house. So he paced, always ending up back in the same spot: standing in front of the phone with the hope that he could make the phone ring. *Maybe you should use the Force.* Back and forth he walked around the house. When the phone did ring, the name on the display of his caller ID was always Melinda. Mike wanted to talk to one person and one person only: Shy. He had dialed her number a hundred times in his mind. He refused to call again. His pride and his ego would not allow it. That was the same reason that he wouldn't call Jap to find out where she was. He didn't want Jap to know the deal. He felt bad that he had Jap following her. He didn't want a spy, just a bodyguard. After Saturday night, he didn't think that her boys could protect her.

The phone rang, and once again, Mike ran to the phone. It was Melinda again. He had to give her credit for being so determined. By this time most women would have given up. Mike turned off the music and went back to bed. The phone rang again, and once again, it was Melinda. Mike answered the phone this time. Melinda asked if he was all right, because she hadn't heard from him in a few days. Mike said that he was fine but had a lot going on lately. Melinda said that she had something that she wanted to talk with him about. "So if you're not doing anything, is it cool if I come by for a while?"

Mike said that he wasn't doing anything and told Melinda she could come over. He hung up the phone with the thought that maybe fucking Melinda would take his mind off Shy. For what may have been the first time in his life, he was unsure of what he should do. This was not a feeling that he was accustomed to. One thing Mike was sure of was that he didn't like it. He had been making decisions, tougher ones than this, since he was 6. It was becoming clear to him that this whole situation had him far more shaken than was necessary. Things had gotten further complicated because there was now the matter of whether to tell Shy about what happened with him, André, and her father.

The doorbell rang. It hadn't even been five minutes since Melinda called. Mike put on his robe and looked out the window to see who it was. It was Melinda. Mike thought that she must have been around the corner to get here that quick. Since he had been at the window at least twenty times, he knew that she hadn't been parked there all along.

Mike opened the door. Melinda entered. As usual she was looking good, dressed in a leopard swing coat that hit about mid-thigh and tied at the waist, with bare legs and black fuck-me pumps. Melinda sat down on the couch and crossed her legs.

"Didn't take you long. You must have been in the area."

"To tell the truth, I've been riding around for hours waiting for you to answer the phone." After dispensing with the pleasantries, Melinda got right to it. "Who was that woman at your table Saturday night, Black?"

"Her name is Shy. The brothers with her—"

"I really don't care about them, Black. Who is she, and what is she to you? She's a dealer, so I know that you don't have any business with her. Unless you're plannin' on gettin' back in the game. Is that what this is about, Black?"

Mike shook his head.

"I didn't think so. So what's up with that? And don't ask me how I know she's a dealer." It was as if Melinda was anticipating each answer as she went along.

"What's your point?" Mike asked, not wanting to commit himself to anything until he knew where she was going with this. He didn't even know where, if anywhere, he was going with Shy. If he knew it was on with Shy, he wouldn't hesitate to tell Melinda that her ride was over.

"You know what I'm sayin', Black. Why you wanna play with me? Are you fuckin' her?"

"No," Mike said confidently.

"Are you going to?"

"I thought about it," Mike said, trying to hold back the excitement he felt just thinking about it. He had been thinking about what sex with Shy would be like since he first saw her. Would Shy be able to keep up the high standard that Melinda had set?

"You thought about it," she spit out angrily. "You thought about it. Well, ain't no law against thinking, I guess. So where does that leave me?"

"Honestly, it doesn't leave you anywhere. Especially since it ain't happened. If and when it does happen, you will be the first to know."

"So you're gonna cut the dick off. Aren't you?"

Mike smiled and shook his finger at her. "What do you mean, cut the dick off? I can guarantee you that I'm not gonna cut my dick off. So you planning somethin' you wanna tell me about?"

"Nothing like that, baby. I would never do that to you or my friend there. I just wanna know if you don't wanna fuck me anymore."

"Do you really think it's necessary to ask me that question?"

"No. So what's up? I ain't had none since Saturday morning. You know what a junkie I am. You know you are my fix." With that, Melinda stood up, untied her coat, and let it drop to the floor, revealing that she had nothing on under her coat.

Mike was right. At that point he could think of nothing but penetration. Mike leaned back in his chair. He took a deep breath and another swallow of his water.

"You can't tell me that you don't want any more of this pussy, can you, Black?" Melinda started walking toward him until she was close enough to touch. "You know how good this pussy is and how wet it gets for you, Black. Don't you want me, baby?" Melinda said, using her body like a weapon.

"You're not going to hurt me, are you?" Mike asked, running his hands up and down her thighs.

Melinda spread her legs a little wider. "I would never hurt you. I just want to feel your hands on my body."

As her legs opened, Mike ran one hand on the inside of her thighs. He ran his hand up one thigh and down the other, barely brushing her neatly trimmed hair. He grabbed her ass with the other hand and pulled her closer. Melinda kicked off her pumps.

"You make my legs shake when you touch me like that." She grabbed his head and slowly tried to move it closer to her.

Mike stopped her, removing her hands from his head. Melinda leaned forward and kissed him on the neck, working her way down to his chest, then stood straight up again. She moved a step back, but Mike did nothing to stop her. Mike sat back in the chair and looked at her body. Melinda really was a beautiful woman.

"Turn around," Mike said, and Melinda quickly complied.

"You like this ass, don't you? You want this ass, don't you?" Melinda said, looking back at him over her shoulder.

Without a word, Mike stood up, grabbed her by the throat, and kissed the back of her neck. Melinda's eyes closed, and her head went back as he rubbed her stomach with his other hand. Mike let go of Melinda's throat and began to move his hand slowly over her chest without touching her nipples. Melinda's back arched as his right hand glided between her legs. He lightly squeezed her nipple. He began to move her body, arching her back and then bending her over and back up again. Melinda moaned, "Baby."

"Bend over and grab your ankles."

Melinda spread her legs and bent over. Mike took off his robe and ran his hands over her ass and then up and down her back. Melinda's body shook a little when he ran one finger down from her clit, along her lips to her ass, squeezing it with the other.

Melinda moaned, "I want to feel you inside of me." He spread her lips. Melinda moaned louder.

"Oooh, yes, it feels so good. Fuck me!"

Mike rolled over and looked at the clock. It was 6:15 a.m. He still couldn't sleep. He looked at Melinda. Like a junkie who just had her fix, she was in a deep nod. He felt bad about having sex with her. *First you can't make up your mind, and then you feel bad about gettin' some pussy. Bobby was right. I do need a doctor.*

Mike got up and put his pants on, grabbed his robe, and went outside. He sat down on the porch and watched the sun come up. He'd seen the sun rise before, but he had never watched it. Mike was right about one thing. Melinda did take his mind off Cassandra Sims for a couple of hours. But that was then. Now she was the only thing on his mind. He wondered what she was doing. Was she asleep like he should have been? If she dreamed, did she dream about him? Had she even given him a second thought since she sent him the rose? Mike tried to rationalize the fact that someone was trying to kill her and that she blamed herself for someone dying.

"Fuck that! She coulda called and at least said, 'Hey, muthafucka! Sorry I didn't call, but I'm feelin' pretty shitty right now.'" At least he would know that she felt something too.

If only he knew that Shy spent the night in much the same manner that he did. Shy sat in her favorite spot by the window most of the night, gun at her side, thinking. Thinking about her business and how the price of doing business had just gotten a little higher. Everybody, including Trevor, tried to tell her that Janet getting shot like that was not her fault, and to a point she agreed. Trevor, like everybody else who worked for her, was responsible for their own security, but somehow she still felt responsible.

"She didn't have to die."

Then there was Mike Black inside her mind. Shy tried unsuccessfully to focus on her problems and a solution to them. No matter how she tried to push him away, Black stayed on her mind. So she'd sat, looking at the moon, thinking about Black. Naturally, there were a few differences in their night. Shy spent the entire night alone and tried not to think about him. But just like Black, she absolutely refused to pick up the phone and call him. She wanted to call him and tell him what was going on with her, explain why she thought that it was a bad time for her to be starting a relationship with someone.

Although it had been more than a year, Shy was still feeling the pain that Ricardo had caused her. At one point, she had even thought about changing her lifestyle and marrying Ricardo. Each time she brought the subject up, Ricardo would tell her that he wasn't ready and that their relationship was going too well to spoil it by getting married. But Ricardo had been living a double life. Shy had no desire to feel that pain again.

On the other hand, she wanted to tell him how much she had been thinking about him, how at times she felt overwhelmed by everything about him: the way he looked, the way he walked, the way he talked, the way he looked in her eyes, and how good it felt in his arms. "Take your lovesick ass to bed."

Shy went to sleep.

Mike sat outside until about 7:00 a.m. before going back inside. Melinda was still asleep, so he quietly got in bed with her and finally went to sleep. When he woke up, Melinda was gone.

It was almost 5:00 p.m. Mike looked at the phone. Melinda had turned the ringer off. He called to check his messages. Bobby called twice. Freeze called to tell him that Shy hadn't been out of her apartment since late last night. Sylvia called to say that Kenny had nothing new to report. But these were not the call he'd been waiting for. *No Shy.*

He called Freeze to get the details. Freeze told him that she just sat in the window for hours. The light finally went out at about 4:30 a.m., which, coincidentally, was about the time Melinda showed up. As far as he knew, Shy was still there. Mike told him to send Jap home to get some sleep but to be ready to go when he called.

"What about Shy?" Freeze asked.

"Don't worry about it."

Mike hung up the phone quickly.

Freeze held the phone in his hand and shook his head. "We in trouble. That nigga's in love."

Mike wasn't sure how to take the report from Jap. It only gave him more questions. Why was she up all night? Since she was up all night, why didn't she call him? Mike could no longer contain his pride. He dialed her number.

A still-sleeping Shy picked up the phone. "Hello."

Mike smiled when she answered. "Hello, Cassandra. Did I wake you up?"

"Yeah, but it's cool," Shy said, sitting straight up in bed when she realized who it was. She started to tell him how much she had been thinking of him, but she didn't. "What time is it?"

"It's a little after five."

"How you doin'?" she asked.

"I'm fine." Mike wanted to tell her that he had thought of little else but her since seeing her and how he had stayed up all night, wishing she would call. "I was hoping that if you didn't have any plans for tonight, we could have dinner together, maybe see a show or something. Do you like the theater?"

"I love the theater, and I would love to have dinner with you, Black, but I can't," Shy said, knowing she had nothing to do. "I got some business to take care of tonight. Maybe we can get together Saturday night." She couldn't tell him that she didn't want to see him because she was afraid that she was falling in love with him.

"I wanted to say thanks for the rose. It was my first. I got a standing ovation from my staff at the club when the guy brought it in."

"I'm sorry. I knew that was gonna happen. I gave the guy specific instructions to give it to you when you were alone. I didn't know where else to send it. Which reminds me, how did you know where I lived?"

"I have friends. They have friends who have cop computers. Probably because they're cops. I hope that it was okay. I don't want to invade your privacy. I wanted to say sorry for trippin' on you, that's all."

"That's okay, baby. But it's me who should be sayin' I'm sorry. I shouldn't have gone there about what's-her-name."

"I like it when you call me 'baby.'" Mike paused, awaiting a response. When none came, he continued, "No, it's just that her name's been coming up a lot lately. Which is my fault for asking Bobby's wife how she was. But since then, everybody's been throwin' it at me."

"Maybe one day you'll feel comfortable enough with me to talk about it. You seem like the type of guy who doesn't like to talk about stuff like that."

Mike smiled when she said that. "Does that mean you'll be staying around long enough to get comfortable with me?"

Shy laughed it off. "Who said that? Did I say that? But seriously, you probably have never talked to anyone about it. It might make you feel better if you talk about it."

"You're right. I never have talked about it. And just how did you know that expressing my feelings is not one of my strengths?"

"It takes one to know one. I kinda have a problem talkin' about mine too."

"We're gonna have a problem, aren't we, Cassandra?"

"For some reason, baby, I don't think so." Shy laughed to herself when she said it because she was having a problem with it right now. She didn't know about him, but she could write a book filled with all of the things she wanted to say to him. "Don't ask me why, but I feel very comfortable talking to you." Shy kept telling herself that this was not the time for this. *I got too much goin' on right now. It's just not a good time.* "It's like we've known each other for years." It was like she couldn't stop herself from talking.

The conversation continued in much the same manner for hours, each very careful not to say what they were actually thinking. Mike thought about telling her about him and her father, but he didn't. He wanted to see her face when he told her to be able to gauge her reaction. Besides, he didn't want to ruin the relationship before it ever started over something that happened nineteen years ago. Timing would be everything, so he decided to take it slow. The way Mike saw it, he was taking a huge risk here. He hadn't felt this way about a woman since Regina kicked his insides out. He would not allow that to happen again, especially since he really didn't know how she felt about him. And he was afraid to ask. *Fear. Another unfamiliar and unwelcome emotion.*

The longer they talked, each found more to like about the other. It had been a while since Shy had a conversation with a man that had nothing to do with business. "You know what I haven't done in years, Black?" Shy asked.

"What's that, Cassandra?"

"I used to love to go to Great Adventure and ride the roller coasters. My moms would take us at least twice every summer."

"You're not going to believe this, but I've never been to Great Adventure. We used to hop the train and go to Coney all the time. I dug the coasters, but my favorite was the bumper cars."

"Naturally. What else would Vicious Black like but delivering pain?" Shy joked. "Look at the time. It's almost eight o'clock. Have we been talking for three hours?"

"I guess we have. You're not going to be late, are you?"

"Hell no," Shy replied with a hint of arrogance. "I run things in this camp." *Especially since I have nothing to do and no place to go.* She had to laugh at herself. "I gotta get dressed and get out of here. But I still want to have dinner with you Saturday night." She was hungry, and she really wanted to go tonight, but she had already put her foot in that one, and she wasn't about to back off now.

"Why don't I pick you up around six?" he said. "And after dinner we'll catch a show."

"That's sounds wonderful. I'll see you Saturday. I'll wear something black. I believe that's your favorite color. By the way, I love talking to you. Bye-bye." Shy quickly hung up before Mike could say anything and before she could say anything else. "'I love talking to you'? I can't believe I said that."

Mike sat holding the phone and laughing. "So she loves talking to me." He rolled over in bed and began to dial Freeze on his cell phone. "Be careful, Ms. Sims. It's little comments like that that'll get your fine ass in trouble."

"Yo."

"This is Black. Get Jap back on her. And, Freeze, I really don't need to know where she goes or what she does. Just keep her alive."

"You still want him undercover?" Freeze asked.

"Hell yeah," Mike said quickly. "She don't need to know all that."

"She oughta appreciate a nigga tryin' to protect her. With them three low-stress toy gangsters she got," Freeze said, but Mike didn't comment.

"Where you at?" he asked.

"At the club. You comin' up here?"

"Bobby up there?"

"Yeah, he's here. Maybe you shouldn't come up here, man. Bobby's in the zone. He's been workin' you over for about an hour. He thinks you're in love."

"What are y'all doin' up there? I mean, other than workin' me?"

"Just listening to Bobby trip."

"Who's up there?"

"Me and Paulleen, Bobby, Pam, a couple of barbacks workin', but he's crackin' them up, too."

"I might come up there later. Tell Jap he's got about forty-five minutes to catch her."

CHAPTER SEVEN

On Saturday night, Mike began to prepare for his dinner engagement with Shy. He put on some music and headed for the shower. As the running hot water hit his body, he felt excited and yet at the same time he was very nervous about seeing her again. Bobby and Freeze kept telling him that he was in love with her. This was a concept that he was unwilling to accept. But how else could he explain his inability to concentrate on anything without thinking about Shy, the rush of conflicting and unwelcomed emotions, his newfound need to lie about what he was thinking or feeling, the sudden attack of morals he felt about Melinda? This last one in particular bothered him. Mike had always considered himself a ladies' man. He had never been tied up with any one female. So why did he feel so bad about having sex with Melinda? Especially since it was so good. *A man shouldn't feel guilty about anything that feels that good.* And besides, as much as he had thought about it, he hadn't even so much as kissed Shy, a situation that he planned to remedy this evening.

Mike got out of the shower, dried himself off, and opened the closet to pick out something to wear. He pulled out a black double-breasted suit and a charcoal gray silk shirt and tie. He proceeded to get dressed, imagining what Shy would wear.

Mike got in his Seville and set out for Shy's apartment. *You know, maybe if you stopped listening to all these love songs, you wouldn't be feeling this way.* He reached in the glove compartment and put in some vintage James Brown: "Cold Sweat." The horns jumped off, backed by a heavy bass line, and then Brown opened up.

> I don't care about your past
> I just want our love to last

"Damn, James, not you too," Mike said, shaking his head as he drove off.

He stopped at the florist to pick up some flowers for Shy and then headed for her apartment building. On the way there, Mike gave some thought to how he would tell Shy about her father. First, whether it was worth telling her at all. After all, it really wasn't all that. But he would rather it come from him than have it come out later. Mike had no idea who else was in on it, although he was pretty sure that this was not the type of thing that André wanted to get out. He didn't think Angee would tell her anything, but in any given circumstance, Mike had no delusions that Angee would if he had to. Yes, telling her now would be the best way. The question was how and when.

"You can't just bust out with, 'Oh, by the way.'" *Timing is everything. Which brings up another matter.* Something in the back of his mind told him, *fuck her a few times first, then tell her. No. For once be straight up with a woman, especially this woman. No lies, no secrets, since you plan on keepin' this one.* Then he thought about Melinda. Mike laughed, "Ain't no point being that honest, at least not yet. Besides, you're gettin' just a little ahead of yourself anyway."

Mike pulled up in front of the building expecting to see Jap on the case, but there was no sign of him. Either Jap wasn't on the case or Shy wasn't there. He checked the clock in the dashboard. It was a little before six. Mike went inside and rode the elevator up to the fifteenth floor. He knocked on the door, and as he expected, there was no answer. Standing there with an armful of roses and no one to give them to, he felt kind of foolish. *What now?* Should he leave or continue to stand there looking stupid? He chose the latter.

After fifteen minutes of that, Mike decided to leave, laying one rose at her door. The elevator door opened, and Mike got in. He had hoped that the door would open and Shy would be standing there, but the elevator was empty, which was exactly how he was feeling. Getting stood up was something new. He had never had anyone stand him up before. It was usually he who did the standing up. It didn't feel good at all. *I'm not sure if I'm built for this shit.*

The elevator door opened in the lobby, and there was Shy, out of breath, dressed in a black leather coat and pants and silk-charmeuse turtleneck, with a scarf tied on her head. Mike smiled, and everything that he was feeling was now a blur.

"Oh, hi, Black!" Shy said, grabbing the scarf off her head.

"Hello, Cassandra. It's too late. The damage is done."

"I guess so. I really didn't want you to see me like this, Black. I'm sorry I'm so late."

"It's okay. I'll forgive you, but only because you look good in black."

"Thank you. It's funny. For some reason it's all I've felt like wearing lately," Shy said, smiling as she looked at him. "Are those for me?" She pointed to the roses.

"Yes, they are. I almost forgot," Mike said, handing her the roses.

They got out of the elevator and walked down the hall to her apartment, each glancing at the other and looking away before being discovered. Shy stopped. "Wait a minute. There's only eleven roses here."

Mike stopped and pointed down the hall to her door.

"Were you up here already? I was sure when I ran up and heard the elevator door close that you had just gotten here." Shy unlocked the door and they went inside. "How long have you been here?" Shy asked, looking at the clock.

"Not long," Mike replied, looking around her apartment.

"I know it's late. Do we still have time?"

"Does it matter?"

"Does what matter?" Shy asked as she walked toward Mike, stopping right in front of him. Close enough to kiss.

"I mean, it doesn't matter whether we're late. I really don't care what we do as long as I'm with you." He wanted to be alone with her.

Shy didn't say anything, she just looked up at him.

"You know, you really are beautiful, Cassandra." Those were kissing lines. There she was, standing right before him. But he was scared to touch her.

"I guess you're right. I really just wanted to be with you too." She wanted to kiss him, but she didn't want him to think she was going to be easy. "But I am hungry. So where do you want to eat?" Shy asked, walking away before she changed her mind.

"How about that dive in Brooklyn?"

"No. I want to dress up for you. Someplace nice."

"You go ahead and get ready. I know just the place."

He thought he would take her to his house. The atmosphere would be more intimate. He could throw something together quickly, or better yet, he would call Cuisine and have the food prepared, delivered, and served in the comfort of his home.

"We aren't goin' to your place. If we are, tell me now so I won't spend an hour getting ready."

"You're lookin' through me, Cassandra. How did you know?" He was mystified and at the same time excited by the way she seemed to know him so well so soon.

"That slick West Indian smile gave you away."

"How you know me West Indian, girl?" he asked, turning on his accent.

"Me know everyt'ing about you, Black," Shy said in her best West Indian accent.

Mike laughed, "Next to Bobby, that was the worst accent I've ever heard."

"Ain't it bad? What's worse is I've been working on it," Shy laughed. "I'm gonna get ready. Now you promise not to peek?"

"No. I promise if you leave the door cracked, I'm gonna peek."

"In that case, I'll make sure I leave the door cracked," Shy said, walking into the bedroom. Then she closed the door.

Mike sat down by the window and stared at the setting sun. He asked himself why he didn't even attempt to kiss her when she was standing right in front of him. He had no logical answer. He looked down to the street. He could make out what appeared to be Jap's car parked across the street from the building and someone standing next to it. Mike asked Shy if he could use the phone. Naturally, she said yes. So Mike made a couple of calls to make arrangements for dinner, and then he called Freeze. He told him where he was and told him to call Jap. "Tell him to take some time off but be ready later on tonight."

"Later! Tonight! And you said you were where? Who are you, muthafucka? And what did you do with Black?" Freeze said jokingly.

"I don't know where he is, but tell him that I need his skills." He, too, had been wondering who he was lately. "In either case, get with me tomorrow. Peace."

Mike returned to the window and looked out at the cars. It must have been Jap, because shortly thereafter, he got in his car and drove away.

Although it had been less than half an hour, it seemed like he had been waiting a long time. Mike hated waiting for women. It reminded him of the old days, robbing warehouses, waiting for the truck to get loaded. He got up and began to wander around.

"Mind if I look around, Cassandra?" he yelled as he walked past her bedroom door.

Shy stuck her head out the door. "What did you say?"

Mike turned to repeat his question. He noticed she wasn't wearing anything.

Shy smiled and said, "I'm sorry. I didn't realize you were standing there."

"I said, do you mind if I look around?"

"Yes, I mind. And besides, I'm gonna need your help in a minute. So be patient with me. I'll be ready for you soon," Shy said flirtatiously.

She walked away, but this time she didn't close the door. So Mike, being true to his word, looked as she walked away. Her body was beautiful. Her skin seemed to glisten. Mike hoped that she would turn around, realizing that she had left the door open, so he could see the rest of her body, but she disappeared from sight.

"Have you decided where we're going?" Shy yelled.

"I was thinking about a hotel downtown, but I had a better idea."

"Well, what is it?"

"It's a surprise. Just be patient."

"I like surprises, but can you give me a hint?"

"It's bigger than a bread box."

"You're funny," Shy said, sticking her head out around the corner. "You're fine, too." After a brief silence, Shy said, "Why did I say that?"

"I guess it was a bribe to get me to tell you where we're going, but it won't work."

"Suppose I torture you?"

"Been tried."

"Yeah, but not by me." Shy emerged, walking slowly toward him, carrying a triple strand of pearls. She was dressed in black heels and black silk stockings. Her off-the-shoulder dress was also black with a plunging neckline, which revealed her cleavage.

"Now that's torture," Mike said, watching Shy walk toward him.

Shy stopped in front of him and turned around slowly. "Zip me up, please."

Mike's hands shook a bit, but he managed to zip up her dress. Without asking, he took the pearls from her hand and put them on for her. "Cassandra, you look fabulous."

"Thank you, Black." She turned around slowly and walked past Mike into the living room. Mike followed her. She went into the closet and pulled out a black full-length mink coat and handed it to him. Shy turned around. Each time she turned, each move she made was more seductive than the last. Mike helped her on with her coat.

"You're trying to seduce me, aren't you, Cassandra?" Mike said, opening the door to leave.

"Not yet. You won't have to ask when I do," Shy replied seductively, handing Mike her keys to lock the door as she walked past him.

They took the elevator down, neither saying a word. They stared at each other like two boxers before a championship fight. They walked out of the building to the street where Mike had a limousine waiting. The driver, seeing Mike approaching, opened the door.

"Your limo?"

"For a while," Mike replied as he watched Shy get into the limo. Mike got in, and the driver closed the door behind them. While Mike and Shy sipped champagne, the driver drove to an open field in Mount Vernon.

"Where are you taking me?" Shy asked. A few minutes later she could see a helicopter.

"I hope you're not afraid of flying, Cassandra."

"No, I'm not. But I still want to know where we're going, Black."

"I thought you wanted to be surprised. Don't you trust me?"

"See, there goes that slick West Indian smile again. And it's not that I don't trust you. But with everything that's been happening, I am a little more cautious," Shy said as the limo stopped.

The driver got out and came around to open the door. Mike got out and extended his hand to help Shy get out of the limo. Shy took his hand and got out smiling. She loved being treated like a lady. However, she still wanted to know where he was taking her in a helicopter.

"Come on now, baby, tell me where we are going. Please," she said as they walked toward the helicopter, hand in hand. Mike still wouldn't tell her where they were going. He helped Shy get into the helicopter, and after some brief do's and don'ts from the pilot, they were on their way.

The suspense and excitement were about to kill Shy. She continued to try to get Mike to tell her where they were going. He would simply avoid the question. "This your first time in a helicopter, Cassandra?"

"Yes, it is. The view of the city is magnificent from up here. Please tell me, baby."

"Okay, if you really have to know. We're going to Atlantic City. We're having dinner at the Trump Castle."

"This is really wonderful. First the limo and now this. You make me feel so special when I'm with you. You're going to spoil me rotten, Mr. Black. I hope you can keep it up."

"I don't think you have to worry about that. I'd give you the world, drop it in front of you, and ask what's next."

"You probably do this for all of your women," Shy said, trying to get a feel for the competition. "I know I'm not the only one who gets this type of treatment."

"No, I've never done this for a woman before. I mean, flying to Atlantic City like this. Usually, me, Bobby, and Freeze fly down here," Mike said, avoiding the real question. There would be plenty of time for that conversation later. He knew that Shy wouldn't let it go just like that. What woman would?

The helicopter landed at an airfield outside of the city limits. Another limo was waiting there to take them to the Castle. They arrived at the Castle for dinner. The maître d' seated them at their table. It was nothing extravagant, just a small table off in a corner. Shy said it was intimate and loved it. Mike thought it was the type of table they saved for black people. In spite of that, Mike didn't say anything. He was too happy to be with Shy to care where they sat. Mike ordered their meal and a bottle of Dom Pérignon 1982. He gave the waiter a $50 bill to make sure that he would get lost and not bother them. They had a casual conversation over dinner, nothing on the level of the hot and heavy flirtation that they had enjoyed to this point. After dinner, they both stopped talking until Shy broke the ice.

"Black."

"Yes, beautiful."

"I wanna ask you something."

He was sure that she was going to ask if he was seeing anybody. He wasn't sure what he would say. "The floor is yours."

"My family is having their reunion next weekend, and I want you to come with me."

Mike looked shocked. He didn't know what to say. He had never considered himself the type of guy a woman would bring home to meet the family. But after all, this was different. Now he was sure that he wasn't alone. He was sure that the woman sitting across from him felt the same way about him that he felt about her. He was in love with her. He still wasn't quite ready to say it out loud.

"I would love to go with you, Cassandra. Thank you for asking."

"Good. 'Cause I kinda already told my mother I was going to bring you," Shy said with a smile.

"You told your mother about me?" Mike said, pouring them each another glass of champagne.

"Monday morning. I was tellin' her about you when the roses came. I told her that I thought that I had hurt your feelings and you probably would never speak to me again. And that was the minute the roses came. So she is just dying to meet you."

"Dying to meet me, huh? Is your whole family going to be there?"

"Yes," she said, and then she qualified it. "Well, almost everybody. Only some of my father's people get invited. My sister usually comes."

"Your sister?"

"Half sister." Shy paused for a moment, and then she decided to offer an explanation. "I have two half brothers and two half sisters. The one who usually comes is a year younger than me. Her name is Porsche. You might even know her. She gets around. Anyway, all the rest are just teenagers. Papa was a rollin' stone."

"Well, while we're kinda on the subject, there's something that I have to tell you. Do you want the long version or the short version?"

"Let me see," she said, not really knowing what to expect, so she made light of it. "You tell a good story, so do the long version. I'll stop you if it bores me."

"When I was coming up, me, Bobby, Nick, and Jamaica ran the block. Our crew sort of protected everybody who lived there. It started when we were young. My mother would make us carry packages for the ladies on the block. When we got older, we would walk them places at night. We wouldn't let anybody who didn't live there hang out there. One day, when I was fifteen and some brothers tried to sell drugs to some kids on the block, we chased them off the block. You know André, don't you? Well, he saw the whole thing. He calls me over and tells me that it was good what we were doing, but it wouldn't last. He said, 'Those are small fish. If you want to put a stop to it, you gotta cut off the head.' So André tells me who they work for and says it will never stop until I killed him. I really looked up to André back then. Believed everything he said. I was a wannabe gangster, and I wanted to be down with him."

"I can see you now. Young Mike Black."

"You remember *The Petrified Forest*?"

"Yeah, Bogie, right?"

"I thought I was Duke Mantee, the killer. So André gives me a gun, and I went after him."

"Just like that? You went after him?"

"No. I followed him around for a couple of weeks so I could see the best time to hit him. He was a hustler, but he was a creature of habit. He would leave his house about the same time every day. That's where I'd hit him, right in front of his house, to send a message: you mess with me at my home, and I'll mess with you at yours. So I get Angelo to drive for me. You know Angelo, don't you?"

"Collette?"

"The same. He's the one who put me on to this 'cause I had no idea."

"No idea of what?"

"Let me finish. I get Angee to drive, and I go to whack the guy. He comes out of the house, heading for his car. Angee starts to roll. We get up on him. I pull my gun, ready to kill him. But I hear, 'Daddy, take me with you.' He stops. I look back, and I see a little girl standing on the steps looking dead at me. I couldn't do it. Those eyes went right through me. I just told Angee to drive. André didn't seem to care. He just laughed it off and gave me something else to do. But I never forgot those eyes," he said, looking in her eyes. "Your eyes, Cassandra."

"Wait a minute. What are you sayin'? That was me? You were going to kill Chicago?"

"And I would have if it weren't for you," Mike said quietly. "What makes the whole thing worse is it wasn't Chicago them guys worked for anyway."

"I know. Chicago was a lot of things, but he was too sorry to be a dealer. So why did André want to kill him?"

"I didn't find that out until that woman shot Chicago six years later. One of the old heads says to me, 'Well, I guess now Chicago will stop fuckin' André's wife.' André just tried to use me 'cause he was too weak to handle his own business."

Shy sat there looking at Mike without saying a word. Finally she took a deep breath and said, "Why are you tellin' me this now? Chances are I would have never known."

"Well, Cassandra, I like you. More than I have any woman in a long time. It's like you've become very important to me. I couldn't take the chance that anything would ever come between us. I had to take the risk and tell you now."

Shy got quiet again. "I'm gonna need a minute to take all this in," she said, drinking the rest of her champagne and then pouring another glass. "Can we just get out of here? Go for a walk or something?"

"We can do anything you want." Mike called the waiter over and paid the check. He felt relieved that it was behind him and that she appeared to take it well.

Mike and Shy left the Castle and began to walk. As they walked, neither said a word at first. They just walked.

"Say something, Cassandra. Tell me what you're thinking."

"Why? I know you're not nervous about what I'm thinking."

"Yeah. You could be planning your revenge."

"No. Just thinking." Then she reached for his hand. "Don't worry about it. That was a long time ago. You were a kid, a sucker that André used 'cause, like you said, he was weak. Everybody knew you and Bobby were his power.

"Now about my father. When I was a little girl, yeah, I was a daddy's girl. But then I got older, and I saw how he was doggin' my moms. Bitches callin' and comin' to the house at all hours of the day and night. He used to beat my moms. So you don't worry about that."

Suddenly Shy stopped dead in her tracks. She hesitated briefly. "You know, it's funny. If I hadn't come outside that day, I could have saved my mother six years of grief. Don't get me wrong. It's not that I'm glad you were trying to kill my father or that I'm glad he's dead. But me and my moms got real close when I was a teenager. You know girls gotta stick together. Anyway, I went through a lot of that pain with her. I know what it's like to have a man lie to you, disrespect you, cheat on you."

They walked in silence for a block or two. Mike worried that he had dropped it on her too soon. Although she seemed to understand, the revelation may run her away. He hoped his decision to tell her now wouldn't backfire on him. He watched her walk, observing the thoughtful look in her eyes, not anger as one might expect with what she had just heard. It was as if she were trying to reconcile her feelings about her father. He impatiently awaited the verdict.

"In so many ways I want to tell you that I don't want to get involved with you. I know you're no angel, Black. I'm not that big a fool to think that a man like you doesn't have a gang of women runnin' behind him," Shy said and looked at Mike. "I'm sorry. I didn't mean to go there. But I meant what I said about not being sure about getting involved with you. And it has nothing to do with you trying to kill Chicago. But in a way, I guess it does, and until tonight, I didn't realize how. But it all goes back to Chicago. Growing up, watchin' him dog my moms, laid the foundation for how I feel about men. Of course, my personal experience has proved me right every time. Y'all are dogs."

Mike didn't say anything. He had given up years ago defending the "all men are dogs" thing. It was a no-win scenario.

They continued to walk, and Shy continued, "I like you too, Black. I mean, I really like you. I just don't want to be hurt again."

"That's good to know. I mean, the part about really liking me."

When they got to the boardwalk, Shy sat down, and Mike leaned over the rail and looked out at the ocean. "So what's up, Black? I know you got a little fan club goin'. There were too many women rollin' their eyes at me that night at Impressions."

"Who was rollin' their eyes at you?" Mike asked, even though he could think of a few candidates off the top of his head.

"First, there was the honey who took us to your table. That was your table we were sitting at, wasn't it?"

"My table, and yes, I can see Tara rollin' her eyes at you," Mike said, wondering just how honest he was going to be with her.

"And then there was this other honey. I don't know where she came from, but if looks could kill . . . I mean, this woman looked like she wanted to kill me."

Mike knew that she was talking about Melinda. Now was his big chance to lay it all out for her, right here, right now. *Remember, no lies, no secrets.*

He decided to be a typical man.

"That might have been anybody. I do know a lot of women. I happen to like women. I don't necessarily trust them, but I like them. But I've never met anybody like you. I can't stop thinking about you," Mike said as he turned to face her. "I know all that sounds like a line from a bad movie, but it's true. Since the first time I saw you, I haven't been able to think about anything without thinking of you. Sounds pretty corny, right?"

Shy got up and stood in front of Mike. She put her arms around his waist, and he put his hands on her shoulders. She said, "No, it doesn't. Actually, it's kinda sweet. To be honest with you, I'm in the same shape. As hard as I try, I can't stop thinking about you either."

"We're both kinda pitiful. What are we going to do with each other?"

"Just don't dog me, Black. I don't think I can stand it. Let's take it slow."

"I'm in no hurry at all, Cassandra." Mike touched her face with both hands and kissed her passionately.

"I like that. I'd like more," Shy said in as close to a Lauren Bacall impression as she could muster. She put her arms on his shoulders and kissed Mike. He ran his hands down her back, then held Shy tight.

"Now that was a kiss," she said.

"You ain't so bad yourself."

They began to walk back to the Castle, holding each other's hand. When they arrived back at the Castle, they got into the limo and rode to the helicopter for the flight back to the city. When they reached the city, Mike and Shy got into the limo and headed back to Shy's apartment building. They hadn't talked very much on the way back. Shy laid her head on Mike's shoulder, and he refused to let go of her hand. Every once in a while, without provocation, one would lean over and kiss the other.

The limo pulled up in front of the building. They got out and walked hand in hand slowly toward the building. They got in the elevator and kissed their way up to the fifteenth floor. The door opened, then closed. They were still kissing. Finally, Shy pushed the button to open the door. They walked down the hall to her door. Mike unlocked the door and handed the keys back to Shy.

"Good night, Cassandra. I had a wonderful evening."

"I am great company. And so are you. Can I see you tomorrow?" Shy said with childlike enthusiasm in her voice. "Why don't I call you around one? Maybe we can have a late lunch or something."

"I'll look forward to your call."

After one last kiss, Shy said, "Good night, Black."

CHAPTER EIGHT

Mike paced around his house waiting for a call from Shy. The phone rang a few times, but it wasn't Shy, so he didn't answer. Mike let his pride get the best of him and called her house, but there was no answer. He began to second-guess himself. Maybe he should have waited to tell her that he tried to kill her father. Shy appeared to take it without too much grief. Maybe he was moving too fast or too slow for her. Perhaps he should have at least made an attempt to seduce her. It wasn't like he didn't want to. He felt he should take his time and cultivate a relationship that would last, one that was based on communication and trust. His success rate at building a relationship based on sex wasn't that great. Trust? He thought about the fact that he hadn't been completely honest with Shy. That couldn't be it. How would she know? Unless she had a spy. Why not? He had Jap following her. Suppose she had somebody following him. Mike got up and started to look out the window for suspicious cars, but he stopped himself.

"Lighten up, Black. You're startin' to trip."

This was one of the rare occasions that he regretted not having a beeper or a cellular phone. Mike really didn't like being that accessible, but now he felt chained to his house, waiting for a call. By the time six o'clock rolled around, Mike had just about given up on hearing from Shy. Although he still wanted to know why she didn't call, the confusion and self-doubt that he was feeling earlier had given way to clarity and anger. Anger made his disappointment easier to take. With that clarity, Mike focused in on two things. In his excitement last night, he didn't put Jap back on Shy. He had counted on picking her up earlier, so there was no need to call in Jap. It also dawned on him that he had not seen or heard from Melinda since Tuesday morning. Since she already knew of his interest in Shy, perhaps Melinda decided not to wait to be asked to step down. Not likely. Melinda enjoyed the perks too much to give them up voluntarily. He decided to do nothing about either one. He decided to leave the house before he went crazy. He got up and started out the door. When he opened the door, Bobby was coming up the stairs.

"What up, Bobby? Come on in."

"What's up, Mike? I saw the lights, and I didn't see your car," Bobby said, entering the house. "I thought something was wrong."

"I was getting ready to leave," Mike replied. "Were you at the club last night?"

"Most of the night. Why?"

"Was Melinda up there?"

"You know she was. For a couple of hours. Why?"

"Just haven't seen her in a couple of days. That's all," Mike fired.

"What you so touchy about? It's this whole thing with Shy, ain't it, Mike?" Bobby went to the bar and poured a couple of drinks. "You better have a drink."

"Make them to-go, Bobby. I gotta get outta here."

"Couple to-go it is."

"Come ride with me."

"Well, Pam was expecting me. Let me use your phone. I left mine in the car," Bobby said as he dialed the phone. "You eat anything today?"

"No."

"She got you all fucked up, don't she?"

"Why it gotta be all about that?"

The phone rang at Bobby's house. Pam answered, "Hello."

"What you doing, baby?"

"Feeding the kids. Why?"

"I'm on my way. Mike's comin' with me."

"That's cool. I got enough for him. How long y'all gonna be?" she asked.

"We're at Mike's house, so no more then ten, fifteen minutes."

Mike and Bobby left the house, taking the bottle with them. "Pam know about Shy?" Mike asked.

"Only her name," Bobby replied. "I'll drive, Mike. That way I have a reason to leave the house."

Mike got into Bobby's car. "Sometimes I wonder if you're the same guy I used to hang out with back in the day. You know, the one who used to tell jokes while he killed and tortured people."

"Same guy. Just smarter. Given a choice between a gun or Pam, I'll pick the gun every time."

"Get the fuck outta here."

"A man with a gun ain't got nothing on Pam. Check it out. I can outshoot most people, but I can't outtalk Pam. And besides, they ain't cookin' no food, cleanin' no house, washin' and ironin' for me, raising my kids, and they damn sure ain't fuckin' the shit outta me."

"Is that what I have to look forward to?"

Bobby slammed on the brakes. "Is there something you ain't tellin' me?"

"Shit! You made me spill my fuckin' drink."

"Fuck that shit. You plannin' on getting married? She's bad, but she ain't that bad to have your ass proposin'."

"You're right, she ain't. Hope you brought the bottle."

"Behind my seat. So what's this 'look forward to shit' all about?"

"All right. So I have given it some thought. What's so bad about that?"

"You? Thinkin' about getting married? You? And you asked me if I'm the same guy. I should be askin' you who you are."

"Freeze already did."

"Must be pretty obvious if Freeze sees it. So what's up with her?"

"I don't know, Bobby."

"You better think of a better answer than that before you run up on Pam."

"I thought you said Pam only knew her name." Mike thought about Pam's tendency for relentless questioning. "Never mind. That's all Pam needs."

"So you can talk to me now or the interrogator later. It's your choice."

"Okay. Let's just say I am very interested in her."

"Oh, bullshit. You're in love with her. Or you're just infatuated with her fine ass. You probably haven't even fucked her yet, have you?"

"No." Mike dropped his head as if he were ashamed to say it.

"See, that's infatuation. You just think it's love because your dick's hard. But fuck her for a while. Better yet, spend some quality time with her. If you feel this way next year or something like that, maybe then you can call it love." Bobby pulled up in front of his house, put the car in park, and then looked over at Mike. "So what's up with you? Why this woman got you so far out there?"

"I don't know, Bobby. She just got me," Mike said as he got out of the car and turned to walk inside the house, followed closely by Bobby.

Once inside the house, Bobby called to his wife, but there was no answer. Mike made himself at home, helping himself at the bar while Bobby looked for Pam. The table was set for three. The food appeared to be ready, but there was no sign of Pam. Bobby went upstairs to the bedroom. He found Pam on the phone. Pam motioned for him to be quiet as she continued her conversation. Bobby went back downstairs to join Mike at the bar. He explained to Mike that Pam was on the phone. "And I guess she'll be down soon."

Bobby poured himself a drink and freshened up Mike's. They sat down at the dining room table and waited for Pam to arrive. While he waited, Mike's mind turned once again to Shy. Why didn't she call? All of a sudden it dawned on him that maybe something was wrong. After all, someone was trying to kill her. He was too busy feeling sorry for himself to put Jap back on her. Mike asked Bobby for his car keys. Mike ran outside, got in the car, and frantically dialed the phone. Bobby followed him outside, laughing at him.

Freeze answered, "Yo."

"Freeze. Where's Jap?"

"I just sent him to make the rounds. Why? You want him back on your girl, don't you? I started to call you before I sent him out."

"You should always follow your first mind."

"Where she at?"

"That's the problem. I don't know where she is."

"Don't sweat it, Black. I'll find her. Her boys always leave a trail. They talk too fuckin' much. When I find her, I'll put Jap back on her. I'm out." Freeze hung up.

Mike got out of the car and turned right into Bobby.

"You feel better now, Vicious?"

"Shut up, Bobby," Mike replied. "Let's just go eat."

Where was Shy, and why hadn't she called? Shy was in the street, making the rounds, trying to collect as much money as she could. She hadn't called Mike because she lost the number. She called and left a message for him at Cuisine. Sylvia promised to call Mike and give him the message, which she did. There was no answer, so she left a message on his voicemail, which, by the way, she checked more than he did. Then Shy tried calling him at Impressions. She left her pager number for him to call. Shy had to remind herself, "I do have a business to run." She still waited for a couple of hours before hitting the streets.

Shy hooked up with Jack and E later in the afternoon to try to put a deal together so they could start to recoup some of their losses. Shy couldn't call Angelo because she owed him too much money. She thought about asking Black if he could put her on to somebody, but he hadn't paged her. Jack told her about a crew that said they could do business tonight around ten, and their price was right. Shy didn't like doing business with people she didn't know. However, time and money were both short, and she needed to make something happen now.

Bobby and Mike reentered the house. They found that Pam was off the phone and had served dinner.

Pam kissed her husband and then turned to Mike. "Mike. You know I love you, right? But I'm starting to get tired of the lonely hearts club you got. That was Melinda on the phone again. She's all hurt 'cause you haven't called her all week and because you had this other woman sittin' at her table at the club last Saturday."

Mike and Bobby looked at one another and started laughing.

Pam laughed with them and continued, "She wanna know what's up with this woman. But she seems to know all about her. She wants me to tell her what she should do. I told her I don't know what she should do, but she should talk to you about it." Pam sat down at the table. "So who is this woman? What's her name? And more important, when do I get to meet her?"

"Her name is Cassandra Sims. She is the most beautiful woman I have ever met."

Pam looked at Bobby nodding in agreement as Mike described Shy. Bobby reached for Pam's hand. "Next to you of course, baby."

"Everyone calls her Shy. She's funny, she's very intelligent, and she is very seductive."

"So when do I get to meet this woman, Mike? Check her out, make sure she's the right one for you? And what about Melinda? She does have the right to know."

"You're right. She does. The last time I saw her we talked about it. Then she . . . she . . ."

Pam helped Mike finish his sentence. "She fucked you."

"Yeah. Well," Mike said with a smile.

"See, that's where you went wrong, Mike. You should have stood your ground and made sure that she understood that it was over and why. But no, you fell right into her pussy trap. See, she knows as long as she can fuck you, she can stay. Have you told Shy about Melinda yet? Or maybe I should say, do you plan to?"

"No, I haven't told her. And yes, I intend to tell her. I just haven't had a chance yet."

"That's bullshit, Mike, and you know it. You should have told her right from the start. I know how y'all are. Bobby didn't tell me about Cynthia for a long time. But you gotta be careful 'cause Melinda knows all about Shy. First chance she gets, she is gonna step to Shy. So ask yourself, is this what you really want to happen?"

"No, she needs to hear it from me."

"So when you gonna tell her?"

"I don't know."

"That's 'cause he doesn't know where she is," Bobby threw in.

"What?"

"It's a long story, Pam."

Following Bobby's lead, Mike said, "Yeah, it really is. But thanks for dinner, Pam." He got up from the table. Bobby got up and started to help Pam clear the table.

"What are you doing, Bobby?"

"What does it look like? I'm helping you."

"Get out of here, Bobby. Don't be too late. I got something for you," Pam said, taking the dishes from him.

Bobby kissed his wife goodbye, and he and Mike left the house, got into Bobby's car, and drove away. Freeze would find Shy, and everything would be all right.

CHAPTER NINE

Shy prepared to do business Thursday night. She wasn't particularly happy about the choices she was faced with or her situation. Things had been quiet for a while. No one had tried to kill her, and none of her people had been robbed or killed. Shy thought it best not to make herself such an easy target, so she'd been keeping a low profile for the last couple of days. From time to time, Shy wondered why she hadn't heard from Black. Maybe he was busy. Or maybe he hadn't gotten any of the messages that she left for him.

Not wanting to appear to be a pest, she didn't call him again.

But tonight she was feeling kinda horny. *After all, it has been more than a year.* She definitely had sex on her mind. "Focus, Cassandra." She sat down next to Jack. "Things just may be getting better. All we need to do is make this deal tonight, and we'll be back on track," she said more to reassure herself than anything else. She got up, returning to her spot in the window.

"Everything should be cool tonight. Don't worry," Jack said, noticing the troubled look on her face.

E walked over and put his arm around Shy. "Jack's right. Don't worry about a thing, Shy. Nobody is going to kill you tonight. Not while I'm here."

"Where's Tony? We could use another gun tonight in case something goes wrong."

"He's been having problems with his girl Rita lately. So they're trying to work things out. I guess they went out," Jack replied. E smiled at Jack.

"That's real sweet, but we could still use him," Shy said.

"You shoulda got your new friend to back us up," Jack said.

"Fuck him. We can do this without any help from him. I keep telling you, Jack, we don't need him to handle our business. Believe me, Shy, he ain't even thinkin' about you. He's probably out somewhere with somebody else having the time of his life," E said with fury.

"Where do you want to go, Mike?"

"Let's go see Cynthia," Mike replied. Cynthia ran a gambling house for them.

"Cool. I haven't been up in there in a long time. I wonder if Sammy is still pourin' drinks there."

"That ain't what you're wondering about."

"What do you mean?"

"You were wondering if Cynt still gives head like she used to."

"That was a long time ago, Mike. I'm sure by now her skills have eroded. But . . ." Mike and Bobby both laughed.

This seemed to be just what Mike needed, to hang out for a while and have some fun. He'd had Freeze looking for Shy since Sunday. Freeze just missed her.

Bobby and Mike rolled up in front of Cynt's house, got out, and went inside. There were two doors: one led upstairs to the offices and was controlled by key card, and the other led to the bar area, which also featured erotic dancers on a small stage, but private shows were available. The gambling was run from the basement.

They were met at the door by security dressed neatly in blue double-breasted suits and white shirts. Ties were optional. There were new guys on the door who knew Mike and Bobby only by their reputations. After verifying their identity, Mike entered the house. Bobby stayed outside to talk with security before going in.

Once inside, Mike stopped to look around. Not much had changed in the last four years. Some of the old regulars were still regulars. Mike recognized most of the dancers from their appearances in the female revue at Impressions. He asked one of the dancers if Cynt was in the house, and then he saw Sammy behind the bar, still pouring.

"Sammy, how you doin'?" Mike said, approaching the bar.

"Goddamn, Black! I ain't seen you in years. Where's . . . Bobby! I knew you couldn't be far behind. Black drag you out the house?"

"What you talkin' about, Sammy?" Bobby said, sitting down at the bar.

"Freeze says your wife got you on lockdown, Bobby."

"She does. But I can always get him out," Mike said.

Bobby continued to talk with Sammy while Mike looked around the room. Like a magnet, he was drawn toward to the stage. Dancing on stage was a tall woman with beautiful dark skin whom he had never noticed before. He lost himself in the seductive manner in which she moved her hips. She reminded him of Shy. Mike stood for a while, watching, staring. He gave the dancer a $100 bill as a tip.

Mike decided to call Freeze to get an update on the search. He went to get the phone from Bobby, who was about to answer it.

"This is Bobby."

"Bobby, Black still with you?"

"Hold up. Here he comes now." He handed Mike the phone and told him it was Freeze.

"What's up, Freeze? You got her yet?"

"No, but I'm on her trail. I know where she'll be in an hour. She's tryin' to put a deal together. I'll pick her up there. Jap's going to meet me there, and I'll turn her over to him. Where y'all at?"

"At Cynt's."

"Yo, Black, tell Bobby to watch Cynt. She says the next time she sees him, she's gonna slap the shit out of him."

"I'll tell him. You call me when you got her," Mike said as he hung up the phone. Mike looked around for Bobby. He saw him going up the stairs to the offices. He returned to the bar. Sammy waved Mike on.

"Black, come here. Do you remember the last time you were here?"

"Sure. I gave you a bottle of Rémy Martin Napoleon."

"That's right. We had a few shots. And what did I tell you?"

"I think you said you were going to save it and only drink it when you see me. Don't tell me you still have that bottle."

"It's in the back. I'll be right back." Sammy went to the storeroom to get the bottle.

Just then, a guy walked up behind Mike and tapped him on the shoulder. "Hey, man, you're in my seat!"

Mike put his hand in his pocket and turned around slowly.

"And what happened to my drink? I left a drink sittin' right there."

Mike stood up with his right hand still in his pocket. "Sorry, brother. I didn't see you sitting there. As soon as Sammy gets back, he'll get you another drink." Mike turned to walk away, but the man walked up and grabbed Mike by the arm.

"No. You gonna buy me a drink."

Mike shook his head. He put his hand on the gun. "Look, brother. I am not having a good day. So take your hand off me. I'm not gonna ask you again."

"What you gonna do—"

Before he could finish, Mike grabbed the man by the throat. Mike pushed him against the bar and put his gun to the man's head. "I did ask nice, didn't I?"

"Yo, man, I'm sorry. Please don't kill me. Please, man, I'm sorry."

Sammy returned from the storeroom. The room was still as all eyes were on Mike. "It was a little dusty, but I'm sure it's still . . . Oh, my God. Tommy! Black, whatever he did, he didn't mean it. Please don't kill him," Sammy pleaded.

Mike looked at Sammy, then let Tommy go and put his gun away.

"This is Vicious Black?" Tommy said as he backed away, clutching his throat.

"Told you to be careful about who you fuck with. That man woulda killed you, Tommy."

"The night is still young," Mike said as he sat back down. Sammy poured Mike a glass of Napoleon, then poured himself one. "Brother says he had a drink sittin' here."

"That's just his hustle, Black. He gets people to buy him drinks that way. He just chose poorly tonight," Sammy said as he and Mike raised their glasses. "That sure reminded me of the old days. Things sure used to be wild up in here."

"I remember them days too, Sammy. I kinda miss them sometimes. I can't believe you saved this for four years. It sure is smooth. Pour me another and pour one for Bobby."

"Better just take the bottle just in case Cynt want one. I been keepin' it a secret from her, so don't tell her I had it."

Mike took the bottle and headed upstairs to Cynt's office. On the way up, he considered that he almost shot a man because he grabbed his arm. However, that wasn't the reason. The reason was Shy.

A little before ten o'clock, E pulled up and parked across the street from a building on the Lower East Side of Manhattan. The building looked empty, but there was one man standing outside. He approached the car and told them to follow him inside the building.

Freeze arrived on the viaduct down the block in time to see Shy and her associates enter the building. Freeze looked around for Jap. He was nowhere in sight. After they entered the building, Freeze saw movement across the street.

Meanwhile, Mike entered Cynt's office, finding her seated behind her desk. She smiled when she saw him. She got up and gave him a big hug and a kiss on the cheek.

"What's up, Mr. Black? I was wondering whether you were coming to say hello to me."

"How you been, Cynt? Can I offer you a drink?"

"You sure can. What's this?" Cynt looked at the bottle. "Remy Napoleon. I'm impressed. What's the occasion?"

"I knew I was going to see you," he replied as he sat down. "I thought Bobby was up here."

"He went to get something out of the car. He'll be right back," Cynt replied as the phone rang. "This is Cynthia."

"Yeah, it's Freeze. Is Black with you?"

"He's right here. Hold on." She handed the phone to Mike. "It's Freeze."

"What's up?"

"Yo, Black, I'm on her. She just went inside to handle her business."

"Good. Jap there?"

"Not yet. But there's something goin' on out here."

"What do you mean?"

"Looks like somebody setting up an ambush. See, the crew she's meetin' with is at war with some white boys over some stupid shit. Word is, they doin' the deal with Shy to get money to buy more weapons. Hold up. Here comes Jap." Freeze turned to Jap. "Yo, Jap, go over there so you can get a better angle on that crew across the street."

Bobby tried to reenter the building through the front door. Much to his surprise, the door was locked. Bobby banged on the door. The door opened, and Bobby started to walk in, but the man on the door stopped him.

"We're closed," he said and slammed the door.

"Closed at ten o'clock?" Bobby knew that something must be wrong. Bobby looked inside and saw that there were two different men standing in the doorway. Bobby knew that neither of them worked there because they weren't dressed right. There was no way of knowing how many of them there were, so he didn't want to bust in and start shooting.

Bobby went back to his car and opened the trunk. He returned to the door armed with a sawed-off shotgun and a hunting knife. Bobby kicked in the door, catching them off guard. He hit one in the face with the shotgun. Bobby grabbed the other before he could get through the door. Bobby took out the knife and stabbed him in the back, then used his card key to gain access to the offices.

"Yo, Black, it's cool. They're coming out now," Freeze said as Shy came out of the building.

"Cool. Why don't you meet us down here?"

"Oh, shit, Black! Boys across the street just opened up. Shy looks okay, but she's pinned down behind a car. It doesn't look like anybody's shootin' at them. They're just caught in the crossfire. It's pretty bad down there. What you want me to do?"

"Shit!" Mike thought for a second. "Do what you can to help her. But do not put yourself or the organization at risk in any way. You understand?"

"Understood. We can lay down some cover fire. That should give them time to make it to their car."

"All right. Do what you can." Just then, Mike heard the sound of women screaming coming from downstairs. "I gotta go, Freeze. There's something going on here. Remember, no risk." Mike hung up the phone as Bobby came into the office.

"Yo, Jap. Lay down some cover on that side. Aim high. We only want to draw their fire long enough for them to get clear." Freeze and Jap started to fire, and as expected, they drew fire from both sides of the street.

Still hiding behind a car, Jack noticed that there was no longer any shooting overhead. He looked around and saw that everyone was shooting in the other direction. "Shy! Now's our chance, while they're shooting over there."

"Okay, let's go!" shouted Shy. "Stay low!"

"Y'all go. I'll cover you!" E yelled. Shy ran out from behind the car. Jack moved out behind her.

Freeze saw them start to move out. "About time. Jap, let's go."

Jack made it to the car, got behind the wheel, and started the car. Shy jumped in the back seat. Jack turned the car around to pick up E.

Once Freeze and Jap stopped shooting, both sides began shooting at each other. Once again, they were in the line of fire. E rose, firing in all directions. Shy rolled down her window and fired to give E cover. Jack slowed down long enough for E to jump in the car. With everybody safely aboard, Jack floored it, rounded the corner, and sped away, right past Jap.

Jap smiled and said, "Like taking candy from a baby." He started up his car and fell in behind them.

"Bobby! What's goin' on downstairs?" Mike asked, drawing both of his guns.

"I'm not sure, but I think we're bein' robbed." Bobby told Mike what happened at the door. Bobby gave the shotgun to Cynt and cocked his Glock.

"Cynt, lock the door behind us," Mike said. Then he and Bobby left her office.

"I'll go back down to the front, Mike."

"I'll give you enough time to get set before I move."

"Don't you wanna synchronize watches or something?"

"I don't have a watch. But you'll know when to go."

"Yeah, right," Bobby said as he went back to the front door.

Mike moved slowly down the steps. The door to the gambling area was open, and there was no sign of security. He moved around to the archway, which led to the bar area. Mike peeked around the corner. He saw that two men were covering the area. One was by the door, and the one closest to him was standing by the stage. Mike slammed the door to the gambling area to prevent whoever was down there from hearing the shooting, not to mention leaving with his money.

It got the attention of both men in the bar area. They turned and started toward the archway. Bobby came through the door, firing. With their attention diverted, he had no problem picking one off.

Seeing his partner shot, the man who was by the stage fired on Bobby. As he turned, Bobby caught him with a shot in the chest. Bobby shot the man twice as he walked by. "In case you thought about livin'." Bobby came through the archway. Mike was watching the door to the gambling area.

"Thanks for your help, Mike," Bobby said sarcastically as he reloaded.

"Didn't want to give whoever's down there a chance to get away. Besides, there were only two of them. You didn't need any help."

"How many of them are down there?"

"How should I know?"

"You ready?" Bobby asked. Mike nodded. "Then let's go."

Mike and Bobby moved to opposite sides of the door leading downstairs. Mike opened the door slowly. There was nobody at the door. They started slowly down the steps. Once they reached the bottom of the steps, they found security tied up and all their patrons on their knees. There were three men, two of whom had their guns pointed at the heads of the female hostages. Mike fired one shot to the head of the one who didn't have a hostage.

"Hey, man! Don't come any closer or we'll kill them!"

"Go ahead. I don't know them hoes. Either way, you ain't leaving here alive," Mike said, moving closer to them.

"All right. We'll let them go if you let us walk."

Bobby laughed as he continued to move closer. "You ain't listening, asshole. You're not leaving here." Both Mike and Bobby were at point-blank range.

Both men slowly released their hostages. The women ran to safety.

"Thank you. Now drop your weapons and get down on your knees," Mike said. They followed his instructions. Once they were on their knees, Mike walked up to them and kicked their guns out of the way. Mike stood in between the two, raised his guns, and shot both of them.

Bobby untied security while Mike apologized to his customers. "Sorry for the trouble, everybody. It's been one of those days."

"That's right," Bobby said. "So the drinks are on him."

CHAPTER TEN

It was just before midnight on Friday, and it was pouring rain. Freeze dropped Mike off at his house, and he ran to get out of the rain. The rain had drenched him from head to toe. He took off his wet clothes, put on a black silk robe, poured himself a shot of Remy, and relaxed with the Miles Davis Quintet. He sat reflecting over the events of the last couple of days.

It had been a good day. Nothing like the night before. Mike spent the morning overseeing the repairs to Cynt's. The damage was minor, some broken tables and chairs. He spent the afternoon and evening with Bobby and Freeze. First, they met at Cuisine for lunch to talk about the robbery attempt. Freeze took personal responsibility for the breakdown in security. After lunch, they went to each of their operations and reviewed the security procedures. There were changes made to prevent it from happening again.

Being so busy all day gave him very little time to think about Shy. Mike did, however, break down and call her at home a few times. There was no answer, so he didn't leave a message. Mike still wondered why he hadn't heard from her. He knew that she too had a busy night and a business to run, so he tried not to let it bother him. If he had only checked his messages or talked with his secretary, he would have had his answer.

The phone rang and Mike answered it. "Hello."

"Black, this is Jap. I'm sorry to bother you, but are you expecting company?"

"Why?"

"'Cause it looks like Shy is on her way to your house. She camped outside your mom's house for a while, and then she saw Larry. She got out and ran him down. They talked for a while, and then she got back in her Beemer, and now she's headed straight for you."

"How long, Jap?"

"She should be on your door in five minutes."

"All right. Stay with her 'til she gets here. Then you go find Larry and step on his neck. Don't hurt him. Just let him know that ain't cool. Then you get some rest." Mike hung up the phone.

The mention of her name excited him. The fact that she was on her way was almost overwhelming. Mike walked around the house, straightening up. Although he told Jap to deal with Larry for telling Shy where he lived, he was very happy that he did. He would have to do something nice for Larry.

Now that everything appeared to be in order, Mike sat back down, picked up a book—*Player No More* by Thomas Green Jr.—and turned Miles up a little louder. What would he say to her? Would he play hard about her not calling?

The doorbell rang. Mike waited for a second before getting up to answer the door. He walked slowly to the door and opened it. There was Shy, dressed once again in black: a leather jacket with a leather skirt. She was soaking wet.

"Hi. Can I come in?" Shy said with a smile.

"I really don't like unannounced visitors, but in your case, I'll make an exception."

He stepped aside, and Shy came in. He closed the door and turned back to Shy. When he turned, she threw both arms around him and kissed him. Mike dropped the book to the floor and put his arms around Shy. He kissed her lips and then her neck. Shy stepped out of her shoes. They stopped to breathe, but only for a second.

"You should get out of those wet things."

"I plan to."

Mike took a step back and zipped down her jacket as they continued kissing. Shy wore only a black lace bra under her jacket. He slipped her jacket slowly off her shoulders, allowing it to fall to the floor. He paused to admire her beauty. Shy pulled open his robe and ran her hands across his bare chest and kissed his nipples.

"Why didn't you call me back?" Shy asked while she kissed his chest.

Mike ran his fingers through her wet hair. "Call you back? I've been calling you for two days. Why didn't you call me?" Mike asked, kissing his way down to her neck and then biting her gently on the shoulder.

"Ahh. I lost your number, so I called you at Cuisine."

As soon as she got the words out, Mike kissed her on her lips again. Shy began to untie Mike's robe. "I haven't checked messages in two days," Mike said, pulling her closer and kissing her on the lips, then on her neck.

"I thought you were avoiding me. I'm sorry," Shy mumbled while Mike kissed the exposed areas of her chest. Shy slid Mike's robe off his shoulders.

"I'm sorry too. I was sure you were avoiding me," Mike said, standing before her, naked and rock hard.

Shy stood back and looked him up and down. She tipped her head to the side and said with a straight face, "From where I'm standing, sorry isn't even a word I can associate with you."

He ran his tongue along the lace of her bra. Mike reached behind her back. He unhooked her bra with one hand, then slid it off her arms slowly. "I was mad at you for not calling me. Now I feel bad about it," Mike said, pausing for a moment to admire her body. Her breasts were firm, and her nipples grew harder as he ran his tongue across them. Now on his knees, Mike placed his hands around Shy's waist. Shy grabbed his head as he kissed her stomach and tongued her navel.

"Don't feel bad, baby. I was mad at you too. I came here to curse you out 'cause I thought you were trying to play me. You see how that turned out."

Mike pulled down the zipper on her skirt and eased it down as Shy wiggled her way out of it. She kicked out of the skirt. Her panties were black lace to match the bra. Mike again ran his tongue along the edges of the lace and down the inside of her thighs. Mike began to tease Shy, running his tongue up the seam of her panties. Shy moaned quietly as he slid them off.

Suddenly Mike stood up. He smiled at Shy, then picked her up in his arms and carried her off while he kissed her. He carried her up the stairs into the bedroom and laid her down on the side of the bed. Mike knelt down on the floor and started kissing her left leg until he got to her thighs. He sat down on the bed and massaged her thighs while he stared into her eyes.

"I haven't done this in a year," Shy said, then giggled, "so be gentle with me."

Mike didn't answer. He simply leaned forward and kissed her thigh and continued to massage the other. The closer he got, the more Shy would squirm. Mike started working his way up the other thigh while he brushed her hair with his hand. Mike sucked her lips gently. He glided his tongue slowly along her lips, first one side and then the other, while he made circles around her clit with his index finger.

"Oooh, that feels so good."

Mike very gently slid one finger inside of her, moving it in and out slowly, then in small circles, keeping pace with his other finger, still making slow circles around her clit. The circles became smaller and smaller. Mike massaged her clit lightly.

"I can feel you, Shy."

"You're going to make me cum."

"Shhh." Mike looked up at Shy and smiled. He slid his tongue around the edges of her pubic hair, and then he parted her hair and spread her lips. Her back arched as Mike stuck his tongue inside her, moving in and out slowly and gently as Shy had requested.

She moaned and rotated her hips. He spread her lips with two fingers and with the tip of his tongue made small circles around her clit. As the circles got tighter, her clit got harder. Her moans got louder.

"What are you doing to me?" Shy reached out, holding his head in place. Her stomach muscles tightened. Her thighs pressed together as she arched her back and screamed in ecstasy.

Mike lay beside Shy. She rested her head on his chest. Shy stroked his chest, fingering one nipple as she kissed the other. She got up on her knees and started kissing her way down Mike's stomach. Shy sat up in the bed, straddled Mike's body, placed her hands on his chest, and slid down gently on him. Mike grabbed her hips and began moving her slowly up and down until his entire length disappeared inside her.

"You are so hard."

They looked in each other's eyes as Mike held on tightly to her hips. Shy ground her hips in a slow, almost methodical motion. Now it was Mike whose back was arched. He reached for her face and pulled her toward his. Their tongues met, entangled in their passion. Shy opened her mouth wider and slowly began to suck his tongue. She leaned back slightly and swayed side to side, rubbing her nipples against his. Mike returned his hands to her hips and planted his feet on the bed. He arched his back and quickened his pace. Shy moaned as she placed her hands on his chest. She sat up straight and ran her fingers through her still-wet hair as each pulled harder, faster. Shy screamed. Mike followed. Their motion became fluid as they melted into each other. She collapsed on top of him, their movements slowing, but neither one stopped moving.

They made love in much the same manner well into the morning hours. Mike no longer had any doubts. Melinda was out. Shy left no room for any other choice. They were incredible together.

"If I smoked, I'd definitely want a cigarette now," Shy said. "I tell you what. A woman shouldn't take a year off and try to make a comeback with you."

"Did I do something wrong?" Black said sarcastically.

"No, it's not that."

"I know what's wrong," Mike said as he got out of the bed. "You were expecting Quick Draw McGraw."

"No. You are definitely more like El Kabong. 'Cause it damn sure feels like I been hit in the head with a guitar."

"I'm gonna get something to drink. Do you want something?"

"Just some water. What time is it anyway?"

"Quarter to three," Mike said, leaving the room to get the water.

"Yeah, just some water. We got a plane to catch in the morning. That is, if you're still coming with me," Shy said loud enough for Mike to hear her.

Mike returned, carrying a tray with two glasses and a pitcher of water.

"You are still going with me?"

"You didn't think you were just going to come over here, fuck the shit out of me, and leave? I'm not that kind of man," he said, trying to sound innocent. "You're stuck with me now."

"Stuck with you, huh?"

"For as long as you can stand it," Mike said, getting back into bed.

Shy curled up close to him. He leaned over and kissed her softly. They lay quietly and held one another for a while. Shy looked at Mike, smiling.

"What?"

"You're just fine, that's all. Most good-looking men are too busy being into themselves to satisfy a woman. It's kinda scary."

"What do you mean?"

"It seems like we've known each other for years. It just didn't seem like the first time we made love. It was like you could sense what I wanted you to do."

"Do you want to know why?"

"Why?"

"'Cause you were meant for me, and I was meant for you."

"I don't know about all that."

"You will. All you got to do is stick around."

"So you ready to tell me about what's-her-name?"

Mike looked at Shy, frowned, and rolled his eyes. He took a deep breath. "I'll make you a deal. I'll tell you my broken-heart story on two conditions."

"What are they?"

"I'll tell you mine if you tell me yours."

"That's cool. What's the second?"

"This." Mike placed his hands on her shoulders and drew her closer to him. "I'm glad you're here." He kissed her delicately. Here in his arms was everything he had always dreamed a woman would be, but never thought possible.

Shy touched his face gently with both hands. The way she looked at him made him want to spend every minute of the rest of his life with her. Share everything with her. Tell her everything. But he really didn't want to talk about Regina.

She inched closer to him, her hands sliding across his chest. Shy gave him what amounted to a peck on the cheek. "So. You wanna go first? Tell me how what's-her-name broke your heart."

Mike shook his head and smiled. "Her name is Regina. We broke up on the day that Bobby married Pam. Regina and I introduced Bobby and Pam to each other. I was Bobby's best man, and she was Pam's maid of honor."

"How long were you two together?"

"Five years."

"What happened?"

"Prince."

"Prince?" she asked curiously. "You're gonna have to break this one down for me."

"Well, first let me ask you a question. Do you like Prince?"

"Before I answer, is this a test question? Like does the future of our relationship depend on my answer? 'Cause if it does, I refuse to answer until I get more info," Shy said jokingly, but she was serious. She wanted this to work.

Mike laughed, "No, it doesn't." But in a strange kind of way, it did.

"In that case, I like him. Why?"

Mike smiled. "You do? What's your favorite?"

"'Automatic.'"

"Hmm, I'm going to have to torture you now," Mike said.

"What about you?"

"'Anotherloverholenyohead.'"

"It fits you."

"Anyway, Regina hated Prince. Since I knew she didn't like him, I wouldn't listen to Prince while she was around. If she was riding with me, I would take the CD out before she got in the car. For some reason that day, I left the CD in. She got in the car and went ballistic."

"You're tellin' me y'all broke up over Prince?" Shy asked, looking at Mike like he was crazy.

"No. That's just what started it. Regina was a bitch. No, that's not fair to say. She wasn't a bitch, at least not at first. She was very aggressive, you know. If she saw something she wanted, she went after it with a vengeance. I met her and Pam at a party out on the island. I was there to collect some money for André. Party was all right, so I stayed. It wasn't like anybody was going to throw me out. Anyway, I was standing outside talking to this lady I had just met. I saw her and Pam sweatin' me. Then Regina stepped up and started talking." Mike paused and took another sip of water.

"To tell you the truth, I really can't say what it was. Pride more than anything else. That was just a strange day. She said a lotta things, and I said a lot. We were both off the chain with it."

"Well, what happened?"

"Like I said, it started with her trippin' about Prince. That one lost me completely. Then she just kept throwin' little shit at me. Little smart remarks, you know, tryin' me. At first I was cool. But she just kept coming."

There was an uneasiness in his voice that Shy had never heard before. He turned away as he spoke, looking at the ceiling more than he faced Shy. She could tell it hurt him to talk about it. He almost seemed vulnerable, a crack in the invincible armor he displayed to the world.

"You really don't like talkin' about this, do you?" Shy asked.

"No. I really don't, but a deal's a deal. Anyway, she finally admitted to messin' around. I couldn't say nothin' about that 'cause I was out there too. She was givin' him my money. It wasn't the money. I got more money than I know what to do with. Like I said, it was my pride. But then she told me that she had a late-term abortion because she was mad about me and Bobby going to Saint Thomas with some hoes . . . I mean, women. That pissed me off. You know, it was just the accumulation of things."

"Time-out. She aborted a baby 'cause she was mad?"

"Yeah," Mike said.

"I bet you wanted to kick her ass."

"No. Pam made me dance with her instead."

"That's why you don't dance with anybody."

"See, that dual degree is useful. You're pretty . . . smart," Mike said, smiling at Shy. They both laughed. Mike got out of the bed and walked slowly toward the window. "I guess I should really be thanking her 'cause she taught me a lot about myself that day."

"Like what?"

"She told me that I was an arrogant, self-centered, egotistical asshole who didn't care about anything but myself and my boys. She said the only reason that I took the time to have sex with her was because I got off on making her cum."

"Was she right?"

"Yeah, she was, on all counts."

"I don't see all that when I look at you. Of course, I don't have as much experience as she did. But I see a self-confident black man who is not afraid of anything or anybody. I can see you being down for your boys and all that, but that's called loyalty. I bet y'all been through a lot together. I think she went off 'cause she was jealous. Because it wasn't her getting married."

"I guess. Can we talk about you for a while? I hate talkin' about this. That's why I never talked to anybody about it," he said, rejoining her in bed.

"That's why you went first. I figured it would pump me up hearing your story. I talked about mine before, but it doesn't get any easier, even after a year."

"Don't try to wriggle your way out now. What was his name?"

"Ricardo."

"What was he, Puerto Rican? Or did his people just love Lucy?"

"They probably loved Lucy. Anyway, we were together for almost three years. I loved Ricardo. I met him on Fordham Road. I was window shopping when he walked up behind me. I was looking at a dress, and he starts tellin' me that the dress was all wrong for me. We spent the rest of the day together. Everything was wonderful. We went everywhere together, did all kinds of things together. He's an investment banker. Wall Street type, very businesslike, very serious, but we had fun together. But he wasn't real. He made a fool out of me. One night we were at a club, and out of the blue Ricardo tells me that he could never see me again."

"Why?"

"He was getting married the next week," Shy replied sarcastically.

"Get the fuck outta here," Mike said, laughing.

Shy hit Mike on the arm. "It ain't funny."

"I'm sorry, Cassandra. It was just the way you said it. Go on."

"Thank you. Anyway, he got the nerve to tell me that the whole time I been callin' myself in love with him, and even before I met him, he had another woman. I started trippin' then." Mike could almost feel her anger building. "Then he tells me that she's not at all like me. She was an investment banker, very straitlaced. She worked at the same brokerage house he did, her parents live in New Rochelle, and they got money and whatever. And she's this and she's that. Like she's better than me. Then he flips, says, 'But we can still see each other after a while.'"

"No, he didn't go there," Mike said, holding back the laughter.

"Black, I got so mad. I got up, pulled out my gun, and I was about to kill him," Shy said as she sat up in the bed and started motioning with her hands. "But E saw me, and he ran up on me and grabbed the gun. By that time, Tony and Jack's big ass rolled up," Shy said with a smile. "I told them what was goin' on. I was cryin' and shit. I said, 'This bitch muthafucka gonna marry some other bitch and wants me to be his toy.' Jack snatched his ass up out of his chair. Then him and Tony dragged Ricardo outside. I never heard from him again. I never asked them what they did to him."

"Them overprotective niggas probably beat the shit out of him. Jack's a big boy," Mike said, trying not to laugh. "I know you must have been hurt."

"Yeah, I cried for weeks thinking I wasn't good enough for him. I trusted him, Black. That's why it's so hard for me to let you in, much less trust you."

"I know how you feel. I got a little problem with trust too, Cassandra."

"So what we gonna do?"

"I don't know what you're gonna do, but I intend to make you earn my trust, and if you're smart, you'll make me do the same. 'Cause I plan on seeing a lot of you and for a very long time, Ms. Sims."

"Oh, really? Well, if that's your plan, come on with it. I'll be right here. And by the way, you don't have to worry. You'll have to earn my trust too."

Mike thought that this probably would have been a good time to tell Shy about Melinda. What better way to start building her trust than to tell her about his so-called woman? Especially since he planned on cutting her loose anyway. Mike didn't have any problem being honest with Melinda about Shy. Why was it so hard to tell Shy the truth about the woman with the rolling eyes? He tried to justify not telling her. But every reason he came up with sounded too lame. Actually, he had no reason. Maybe he just wasn't ready to give Melinda up yet. *That's how the trouble starts. It can't be that hard. Bobby broke clean. Bobby doesn't mess around at all on Pam. Is there a secret to monogamy?*

"Cassandra."

"Yes, baby."

"I love it when you call me 'baby.'"

"Did you want something, or do you just like saying my name?"

"I got something else to tell you."

"What's her name?"

"Melinda."

"The honey with the eyes at the club?"

"That's her."

"I kinda had a feeling that you knew who I was talkin' about. So tell me, who is she, and what is she to you?"

"What did you say?"

Shy started to repeat herself. "I said—"

"No, I heard you. It's funny, but that's exactly what she said when I told her about you."

"Oh, you told her about me? What did you tell her?"

"I didn't have to tell her much. She already knew all she wanted to know about you. She really didn't care about you. She just wanted to know if I was fuckin' you."

"What did you tell her?"

"I told her that I had thought about it."

"What did she think about that?" Shy asked with a self-assured smile.

"She really didn't care about that either. She just wanted to know if I was going to stop fuckin' her. At the time I didn't have an answer."

"Well, what about now?" Shy asked, but she was no longer smiling.

"Now I can't think about making love to anybody but you. My relationship with Melinda is based totally on sex, nothing more. For a long time, I didn't want anything else from a woman. I want a complete person, not just an object to have sex with."

"What's the matter? You don't like having sex?" Shy joked.

"What do you think?"

CHAPTER ELEVEN

Saturday afternoon, Shy and Mike arrived in Baltimore for her family reunion. Mike went to baggage claim to get their luggage while Shy went to rent a car. Once Mike secured the bags, he went to meet Shy at the car rental agency. When he reached the counter, the attendant handed Shy the key and told her where to find the car.

"Perfect timing. I hope you don't mind, but it's red," Shy said as they walked away.

"No, I don't mind. I hope you don't mind driving, Cassandra."

"You're kidding."

"I hate to drive."

"You just don't want to drive a red car."

"No, I really hate to drive. Besides, you know the way."

"Okay. I'll drive."

With that settled, they began the drive to Shy's mother's house. Joann lived in a quiet neighborhood just outside of the city.

"The reunion always starts on Friday night with a fish fry. Which, by the way, I have never made it to. On Saturday we have lunch, which we've missed. It's kind of free style after lunch. Just about everybody hangs outside until dinner or goes shopping. Then after dinner all the men go to the den and do whatever you guys do when there are no women around. All the ladies gather in the kitchen, talk about everything and everybody, and ask me when I'm getting married. Which, by the way, is gonna be worse because of you. You know, typical family reunion stuff. Of course you know that you'll be on display, don't you?"

"I know, but I can handle it. By the way, does everybody know what you do for a living? I don't wanna say the wrong thing."

"Well, my brothers and my mother know, but that's pretty much it as far as I know. I'm sure more of them know, but they don't have the heart to step to me. I get a lecture from my mother and Harold, my self-appointed father. Watch out for him 'cause he'll try to question you," Shy said, looking very nervous about the whole thing. Bringing Mike seemed like a good idea at first, but as she got closer and closer to the house, it just seemed to be a bad idea.

"Don't look so nervous, Cassandra. Everything will be fine. Trust me," Mike said confidently. What trouble could a little family reunion be?

"You know, I never liked the way my name sounded, but when you say it, it sends chills through me." Right then they pulled up in front of the house. "Well, this is it. Are you ready?"

"Yeah. You go ahead. Do the hugs and kisses thing. I'll get the bags."

Shy got out of the car and walked to the door. The door swung open. Screams of joy rang out as family members rushed out to welcome her. Shy went inside but returned shortly with her mother. They looked a lot alike. They were about the same height. Her mother was a little heavier, but they had the same eyes.

"Mommy, this is Mike Black. This is my mother, Joann Sims."

Mike held out his hand. "It's a pleasure to meet you, Mrs. Sims," he said.

Joann looked at Mike. Then she looked down at his hand. "We're all family here. You got to come better than that." She reached out and gave Mike a big hug and a kiss on the cheek. "And call me Joann."

Joann and Shy went back inside. Mike grabbed the bags and followed them. The room was quiet. Everybody was waiting to see the man Shy brought with her.

"Everybody, this is Mike Black," Shy said, introducing him to the crowd the easy way. "You all can introduce yourselves later. But I came here to eat." Shy grabbed Mike by the hand and dragged him into the kitchen. Everyone knew of her fondness for food, so she got away with it without too many grumbles.

Shy fixed both of them a plate, and they sat outside watching the kids play. While they ate, Shy told Mike about everyone. One by one just about everybody came up and introduced themselves to him. He was introduced to Nate, a friend of Randy, the youngest of her brothers. He didn't say anything at first. Then he just laughed and walked away.

"Well, you've met just about everybody except my brothers. So come on," Shy said as she stood up, holding out her hand.

Mike stood up and accepted her hand. He kissed her on the cheek. "Showtime."

They walked around the yard, and Shy introduced Mike to each of her brothers. Each of her brothers shook his hand and smiled politely but didn't have too much else to say to him.

The rest of the day went pretty much as Shy described it. After dinner was over, as promised, Mike was separated from Shy. Her brothers escorted him into the den for questioning. Once they were in the den, the television was turned to college football on ESPN. Shortly thereafter a debate broke out, first about dinner, then about the game they were watching and then the state of the black man in America. Mike sat quietly, listening, agreeing when it was appropriate. He would be content to get through the evening watching the game. He was surprised that no one asked him any questions as Shy had warned. Then the conversation turned to merits of married life as opposed to single life. The debate raged on.

Finally, it began. George broke the ice. "What about you, Mike? You ever been married?" he asked.

Suddenly all eyes were on Mike. "No, I've never been married," he answered quickly.

Gary provided the follow-up. "So I guess you're a bachelor for life?"

"If you're asking me if I'll ever get married," Mike said, qualifying his answer, "I never have given it any thought until lately."

"Why lately?" Randy asked.

Mike turned to Randy and looked him straight in the eyes. "I met your sister," he said confidently. "I told my business partner that I had given it some thought, and he almost wrecked his car." Everybody laughed except Harold.

"How did you and Shy meet, Mike?" Gary asked.

"I saw her for the first time at a club one night. Then she just happened to come to the club that one of my business partners operates. We actually met there a week later. But to tell you the truth, I've been in love with her since the first time I saw her. But don't tell her that."

Harold stood up and moved toward the bar. "My mother tells me that you own a supper club in the Bronx," he asked as he passed Mike.

"Among other things. It's called Cuisine."

"Among other things? What else do you own?" Gary asked.

"My partners and I own a nightclub called Impressions. That's where I met your sister. Some property, a few small stores. We also own a security company. That's how we started out. Now we do mostly private security and a little personal bodyguard stuff," Mike said, trying to sound respectable. He was getting a little annoyed. He didn't like being questioned.

"Well, it seems like you've been very successful in business, Mike," Randy said, taking a seat next to Mike.

"That's good. You know Shy likes money," George joked, joining his brother at the bar. Mike thought he was being surrounded for another attack. Then as quickly as it began, the tone changed.

"Well, you just may be the kind of guy our sister needs to straighten her out," Harold said, nodding his head and looking around as if he was seeking a consensus.

All of a sudden, Randy's friend Nate started laughing uncontrollably as he walked toward Harold. Nate, like almost everyone else, had been drinking most of the day. So no one really made much of the fact that he had laughed at just about every word Mike said.

"This guy, Harold? This guy? Straighten out your sister? Harold, this guy makes your sister look like a jaywalker," Nate said, still laughing.

"What do you mean, Nate?" Harold asked.

"You don't know who Mike Black is? And y'all say you're from the Bronx?" Nate said as everybody in the room had stopped what they were doing. Now their attention was focused on Nate and Mike.

"Why you think you know so much about me?" Mike asked, trying to remember who he was and where he knew him from. Since this was supposed to be a quiet little family reunion, he left his guns in the car. It was a decision he hoped he wouldn't come to regret.

"'Cause I know you, Black. And I've known you for years," Nate said as he started walking away from him. He turned and pointed at Black.

Just then, Shy came into the room. "Hope I'm not interrupting anything."

"This gentleman is Vicious Black."

Shy dropped her head. "Oh, shit."

Harold looked at Mike. "You're Vicious Black?"

Mike didn't answer Harold. He walked up to Nate. "So you do know me. Question is, how do you know me?"

"You really don't remember me, Black? I'm hurt. But I'll try to refresh your memory. By the way, how's Bobby and Freeze?"

"They're fine."

"Heard from Nick lately? He still in the army?"

"He's out now. Callin' himself a private investigator."

"Who was the other brother y'all used to run with? What was his name?" Nate asked.

"What's goin' on, baby?" Shy asked, but Mike ignored her.

"Jamaica," Mike answered without taking his eyes off Nate.

"Yeah, right. Jamaica," Nate said as he approached Mike. "You ain't seen Jamaica in years, have you, Black? Look at me close, Black. Think about Jamaica and look at me."

Mike looked very closely at the man standing before him. Then he smiled and began to laugh. "Nathaniel?"

"I knew you'd remember," Nate said as the two men embraced. "When Randy told me that Mike Black was going to be here, I had to come. Have I changed that much?"

"Yes, you have, Na'na. How've you been?"

"Na'na? Damn, nobody's called me that in a long time."

Shy looked at the two men. "I guess y'all know each other?"

"Since the day he was born. I remember it was me, Bobby, Nick, Wanda, Perry, and his brother Jamaica walkin' to the hospital in the rain that day."

Mike, Nate, and Shy left the den and went outside, leaving a room full of confusion, fear, and unanswered questions in their wake. Seeing Nathaniel brought a rush of memories about Jamaica along with a few unanswered questions of his own.

As they walked out the back door to the yard, Shy thought, *damn, this really is a small world.*

"Have you heard from Jamaica?" Mike asked, not able to hold the question any longer.

"This morning."

Mike looked at Nate in shock. It had been nine years since anyone had seen Jamaica. Or so he thought. "Where is he?"

"He's got a little room he rents in DC."

"How is he? Is he okay?"

"He's not good, Black. He's still on that heroin bad. Every once in a while he'll say that something went wrong."

"What went wrong?"

"I don't know. That's all he says. 'Something went wrong.' That's the main reason I came here. To find out what he's talking about. I figured it had to have something to do with you. It had to be something big if he won't go back to New York."

"Can I see him?"

"Sure. I have to take you there. He won't buzz anybody in except me. I have to go to work tonight, so I'll take you there. It's on the way. But we gotta leave now."

"Where do you work?" Mike asked.

Nate reached into his pocket and handed Mike a business card.

"Doctor? I thought you joined the army."

"I was a medic in the army. When I got out, I went to med school. I'm doing my residency."

"I'll be back, Cassandra."

"Have you lost your mind? I'm not goin' back in there, not tonight."

"What's wrong?"

"Baby, be for real. Nate told everyone that you're Vicious Black. You know there'll be questions."

"I'm sorry, Shy. I don't know what happened back then. I didn't know if Black would shoot me on sight or what. I had to protect myself. Besides, I didn't know it was a secret," Nate replied, heading for the car.

"Oh, yeah. I said, 'Hey, Ma, I'm bringing a killer to the reunion with me.' Right."

Nate got into his car and started out. Mike and Shy followed him. They made the drive to Washington, DC. Mike was very quiet as Shy drove. He didn't seem to be excited about seeing an old friend he hadn't seen in years. Shy got tired of waiting for him to say something. "I could kill Nate. Bustin' out with that. What was he thinking?"

"He didn't know."

"So you and his brother used to run together?"

"Yeah."

"What was he talkin' about, something went wrong?"

"I don't know."

"I'm startin' to know you."

"What do you mean?"

"You are a talker. 'Got a story to tell' kinda brother most of the time. But when you don't want to talk about something, I get these short answers. But I understand."

"You know me too well."

"So what's up?"

Mike looked at Shy. He turned away and looked out the window and then back at Shy. He looked away again. "What I'm about to tell you, only me, Bobby, Freeze, Nick, and Jamaica know."

"See? I knew you had a story," Shy joked.

"I was pissed with André after I found out how he suckered me about Chicago. I thought that he was weak for not handling his own business. After that, a lot of things happened to confirm it. Then, one day he took me, Bobby, Nick, and Jamaica with him to a meeting on City Island with Frankie the Favorite."

"Why'd they call him that?" Shy asked.

"I have no idea. Anyway, he had us wait outside. Whatever happened in there happened, and Frankie's boys came out shootin'. Now Bobby has a sixth sense for things like that, and he sees them coming. He shot the first two, and me, Nick, and Jamaica picked the rest of them off one by one as they came out the door. We go inside, and there's André, on his knees, gun to his head, begging for his life. So I shot Frankie."

"You were supposed to die for that. How'd you get so lucky?"

"A couple of days after that, Angelo comes to my office. Says, 'Come ride with me, Mikey.'"

"Oh, shit."

"I wasn't worried. Me and Angee go too far back. And besides, if he were gonna whack me, he wouldn't have come alone. So while we're ridin', he starts talkin' about the old days. As we pull up in front of Carmine's, Angee says, 'I always liked you, Mike. That's why I saved your life.' We go in to see Carmine. Angee says, 'Tell Carmine what happened that day.' I tell my story. Then Carmine asks me why I shot Frankie. I said, 'With all due respect, do you remember when you were a soldier? If you were in my place, what would you have done?' He thanks me for coming, and Angee shows me out."

"I don't get it," Shy said, looking puzzled as she drove on.

"When we get outside, Angee tells me that André told a different story. He told Carmine that when I got inside, he had taken the gun from Frankie. And that Frankie was on his knees and unarmed when I shot him."

"Why'd he do that?"

"To save his own ass. But the way I saw it, he was trying to kill me."

"Interesting story, but what does it have to do with something going wrong?"

"I was a different kind of brother back then. I was wild. Let my nine do the thinkin' in those days. I've asked myself over and over, why?"

"Why what?"

"Maybe it was just because he was weak. Maybe it was the power. I can't really say why."

"Why what?"

"Why I killed him."

"You killed André?" Shy asked in surprise.

"And everybody else I thought might come after us."

"I never knew that."

"That was the way I planned it. Nobody knows for sure that I killed him. I didn't need anybody to know I was behind it. I already had a rep. Nobody ever suspected us. Not the cops. Nobody. Not even Carmine and them."

"How? I'm dyin' to hear this one. How did you arrange it so that you weren't the main suspect?"

"I waited. For more than a year after the thing with Frankie. I waited. Watched him. I planned it. I knew that there were enough people who hated André to go around. Cops wouldn't care, and as long as business didn't suffer, no one else would either."

"Everybody got to get paid," Shy added.

"We had to kill Ricky. Him and André started out together. He would try to take over. Benny and Dupree were loyal to André, and that was it. Those would be the only three people who would try to find the assassins. I knew that if André was dead, Cazzie would try to move on us. So he had to die too. Killin' him would be harder, but not impossible. My plan was based on the fact that for every action there is a reaction. If certain things happened, I could get people right where I needed them to be."

"Go on," Shy said, listening like a student to a professor giving a lecture.

"Benny and Dupree were the key to it all. They would make the rounds every night to collect the money from all the houses. Some Friday nights there would be more than a quarter of a million dollars. They would start at one o'clock. By three thirty, they would be coming out of the last house. That was where we hit them. Freeze and Nick hid behind their car and waited. Just when they got to the car, Freeze and Nick stood up and blasted them. They never even got off a shot. After they were dead, Nick covered while Freeze got the money."

"Clean and easy."

"Now whenever there are any problems at all, the first person to call is Ricky. Someone in the house called him to tell him about the robbery. Ricky used to operate an after-hours spot. He would sit in his office all night. He wouldn't come out of that office for shit. But as soon as he got the call about the robbery, he was supposed to call André and they would meet at André's office. So when Ricky came out of the office and started to make his way through the crowd, Bobby was waiting for him. Bobby walked up behind him, covered his mouth, stuck a knife in his back, and turned it. Then Bobby walked away. People told me that Ricky must have fallen into a chair and nobody noticed he was dead until the spot closed at eight the next morning."

"That's fucked up," Shy said. "What about that other guy, Cazzie? How does he fit into the action-reaction theory?"

"He was the wild card in all of this. He was always tryin' to bite off parts of André's territory. I knew that he would try to roll on us, and I was in no mood for a war. Problem was there was no way to control his movements the way I did with everybody else. I wanted to send Bobby after him, but Jamaica had been to his apartment and had a better idea of how to hit him. So I left the whole thing to Jamaica."

"What went wrong?"

"I don't know. Police found Caz dead in the hallway the next morning. As far as I knew, everything was cool."

"What about your boy André?"

"When he got to his office, I was waitin' for him."

"How did you know that everything went the way you planned?"

"I knew everything went smooth 'cause Freeze, Bobby, and even Jamaica beeped me when they were done."

"You had a beeper?"

"That was the only time I ever carried one. If anything went wrong, the signal was different. Three sevens if it was all good, and three nines if anything went wrong. I don't know what could have gone wrong. Everything was perfect."

"Guess not," Shy said, and he cut his eyes sharply at her.

"So André rushes into his office, and there I am, sitting on his couch . . ." Mike recounted the story for Shy.

"Black, what are you doin' here?" André said, rushing into the office.

"Waiting for you."

"Waiting for me? I'm glad you're here. We got robbed tonight."

"*I know.*"

André looked puzzled. "*Damn, word travels fast. How did you hear . . . never mind. Ricky will be here in a minute, and we'll figure out what happened.*"

"*Ricky ain't comin'.*"

"*What?*"

"*Ricky is dead. And so are you,*" *Mike said, drawing his gun and pointing it at André.* "*You've been dead for more than a year.*"

"*Stop fuckin' around, Black.*" *André looked at Mike, shocked that he would turn on him.* "*You're serious.*"

Mike stood up, took André's gun, and pushed him against the wall. "*Open the safe.*"

"*What's with you?*"

He slammed him into the wall. "*Open the fuckin' safe.*"

André opened the wall safe.

Mike threw him a bag. "*Put the money in there.*"

While André filled the bag with the money from the wall safe, Mike turned over André's desk. He kicked the carpet out of the way, revealing another safe.

"*You gonna tell me what this is about?*"

"*This ain't no fuckin' movie! Open the fuckin' safe and put the money in the bag.*"

André got down on his knees, opened the safe, filled the bag, and handed the bag to Mike. André started to get up. "*What now, Black? You gonna kill me?*"

Mike kicked André in the chest, and he fell back to the floor. He aimed his weapon at his head. "*Stay down. Get on your knees.*"

André got on his knees.

"*You remember the last time I saw you on your knees like that?*"

André paused and thought for a moment. "*You talkin' about that thing with Frankie?*"

Mike smiled. "No, it couldn't have been. You told Carmine you took the gun from Frankie. Come on. Take the gun from me the way you did Frankie," Mike said, placing the barrel of his gun on André's forehead.

André held up his hands. "Wait a minute, Black. Carmine was gonna kill me. What else could I say? I had to tell him—"

"Your weak ass had to throw me to the wolves. Is that what you were gonna say?" Mike took out his other gun. "I'm gonna give you a chance to stay alive. You take this gun from me and I won't kill you."

"Please, Black, you know I can't take no gun from you or anybody else. Please don't kill me. You can keep the money." André pleaded for his life, but Mike just smiled. He pointed both guns at him. "I'll leave the country."

"I don't think so," Mike said as he emptied the clip in André's head. He picked up the bag with the money and left through the window.

Shy continued to follow Nate as he passed the DC limits and headed downtown. Shy looked at Mike and shook her head. "Damn, you really were Vicious in those days. How much money was in the safe?"

"Your brother George said you liked money."

"Ha, ha, ha. I oughta kick his ass. How much?"

"There was a little more than three million dollars in there."

"Three mil in cash. What did you do with all that money?"

"I kept a mil, gave Bobby a mil, and I told Freeze and Nick to split whatever they took off Dupree and Benny."

"What about Jamaica? What happened to his money?"

"You ask a lotta questions. It's a good thing I love you." It was too late to call the words back. He looked at Shy. He didn't mean to say "I love you." It just came out. He tried to clean it up. "I meant to say—"

"You meant to say what?" Shy said with a girlish grin on her face. "Go ahead. Talk your smooth-talkin' ass out of that one."

Nate pulled over in front of a run-down building and got out of his car. He waited in front of the door for Shy and Mike. She parked the car behind Nate and walked toward him. Mike walked ahead of her.

Shy grabbed Mike's hand and pulled him back to her. She whispered, "Don't feel like the Lone Ranger." Shy kissed him. "'Cause I love you too."

This was really turning out to be a great day. After first finding Jamaica after all these years, and now to hear Shy say "I love you," nothing could possibly be wrong, not today.

Nate led them into the building and pushed the button for Jamaica's room. A voice came over the speaker. "Who is it?"

Nate identified himself. "It's me, Clyde. Buzz me in."

A chill ran through Mike's body as he heard that raspy voice after all these years. Finally, the Jamaica mystery would be over.

They followed Nate down the hall and up to the third floor of the rooming house. Nate opened the door to the small ten-by-ten room. The room was furnished with a single bed, one chair, and a television. The walls were peeling and needed painting. There was Jamaica sitting with his back to the door, watching TV.

"Brought some people to see you!" Nate yelled.

Jamaica answered without looking back. "I don't wanna see nobody. Send them away."

"You'll see me."

Jamaica started laughing. "Mike!" Jamaica got up and turned around, smiling. He had a gun in his hand. Shy started to reach for her gun, but Mike grabbed her hand.

"You gonna shoot me, Clyde?" Mike said, holding out his arms as he walked toward him. Jamaica and Mike hugged one another.

"No, Mike. I'm just careful. How did you find me?"

"Thank your brother. He found me."

"Who is she?" Jamaica said, pointing his gun at Shy.

"She's okay. Her name is Cassandra, but you can call her Shy," Mike said as he turned to Shy. "Cassandra, this is one of my oldest friends."

Shy stepped slowly toward Jamaica.

"You don't have to worry, sunshine. Mike says you're okay, you're okay with me." Jamaica wiped off his chair for her. "Please, have a seat. She's very pretty, Mike."

Nate stepped up to his brother and handed him something. "Cly, I gotta go to work."

"Is your home number on this card, Na'na?" Mike asked.

"No, there is a pager number on it. Just page me before you go back home."

"Don't worry, I will. And thanks for bringing me here."

Nate said goodbye to Shy and left to get ready for work.

"If I weren't so glad to see you, I'd kick your ass. What happened to you?"

Jamaica didn't answer. He looked at Shy.

"She's cool, Jamaica. I told her the whole story."

"Something went wrong, Mike."

"What happened?" Mike asked.

Jamaica sat down on the bed and recalled his story. "Mike, it was all goin' just like you said it would. I was parked around the corner from Cazzie's building. I got the pages from Nick and Bobby, so I got out, walked up the alley, and hopped the fence. I saw the light on in the room. I climbed up the fire escape, and I went in a window on the floor above. Then I went down. I waited in the hall for Nick to ring the pay phone in the hall with my .44 Mag cocked. About five minutes later, the phone rang. Caz came out to answer the phone, and I had him. I called him, he turned around, and I hit him with all six shots in the chest. I reloaded and shot him once in the head. Then I went in his apartment to get the money just like we planned."

"So what went so wrong that you left the city and no one has seen or heard from you for nine years?"

"After I paged you, I stepped inside and went straight for the safe. Mike, I was just about to open the safe when I heard a noise. I turned around quick. It was Matt, Cazzie's son. You know the rest."

"What do you mean, I know the rest?"

"When I turned around, he started to run. I shot him. I shot him, Mike. I killed Matt." Jamaica dropped his head in his hands.

Mike looked at Shy. "Is that it? Is that what went wrong?"

Jamaica nodded his head. "I didn't mean to kill him, Mike. It was reflex, that's all."

"What happened then? Why didn't you come to the meeting spot after that?"

"I killed a kid, Mike. I knew the cops would be all over me. I didn't want to bring that down on you and Nick and Bobby. So I took the money and ran. All over the country. Spent a few years in Jamaica. Finally I ended up here and got arrested for loitering. Now I'm broke."

Mike sat down on the bed next to Jamaica. "Yeah, but you ain't broke. You should've come to me, Jamaica. If you had, you would have known. You didn't kill Matt. Hey, man, you missed. You didn't even hit him. Goofy little bastard tripped over his own feet and knocked himself unconscious."

"You're kidding. Don't lie to me, Mike. We go too far back."

"I saw the bastard up on the concourse last week trying to sell some stuff he stole."

Jamaica smiled and then started laughing. "You mean I been running all these years for nothing?"

"Things are different now. It all worked out just like I said it would. Me and Bobby run things now," Mike said with a sense of pride in his voice. "Bobby is married, got four kids."

"Get the fuck outta here. Bobby, married? Who'd he marry?"

"A friend of Regina. Her name is Pam. She's a good girl."

"How is Regina?" Jamaica asked.

Shy folded her arms and rolled her eyes.

"I haven't seen or talked to her in six years," Mike said, winking at Shy.

"Things have changed," Jamaica said with just a hint of sarcasm.

"Did you know Perry is a doctor with a successful practice in Mount Vernon? And Wanda, she's a lawyer, used to work for the DA. Now she's got her own thing too. And you are a partner in both of them and a whole lotta other things. You're also the owner of Funkin' for Jamaica Incorporated. So, brother, you ain't broke."

"What?" Jamaica said in surprise.

"I cleaned out André's safe just like we planned. There was three million dollars. I kept your mil. Then Wanda set up a company for you and put the money in the bank."

"You did all that for me, Mike? Why?"

"Why did you run?"

"To protect you."

"That's right. You did it because we're family. We couldn't come up like we did and forget you. Now that you're not a child killer, let's talk about this heroin." Once again, Jamaica was silent. "You got any here?" Mike asked.

"Yes," Jamaica said, refusing to make eye contact.

Mike stood up and took off his coat. "Are you ready to kick it, or do you want to be a junkie for the rest of your life and shoot up all your money?"

"I don't know, Mike. It's been a long time. I don't know if I can."

"You can do it. It ain't gonna be easy. I'll help you. All of us will help you get through it, but only if you want to."

"Okay," Jamaica said.

Mike walked over to Shy. "I'm going to stay here with Jamaica. You go on home. Come back tomorrow to check on me."

Shy looked at Mike and shook her head. "You can't get rid of me that easy. If it's all right with Jamaica, I'd like to stay."

"You just don't want to go home."

"You catch on quick, big boy."

CHAPTER TWELVE

At about seven the following morning, Jamaica finally dropped off to sleep. Shy had fallen asleep hours earlier. She went to the store to pick up a few things, then sat up most of the night listening to Mike and Jamaica tell stories about the good old days. Shy was shocked by and yet at the same time not surprised at some of the things they had done. With both Shy and Jamaica sleeping, Mike left the room and went outside. He walked down the street to a pay phone. He wanted to call Bobby and tell him that he was with Jamaica and that everything was fine. However, it made more sense to call Wanda first.

"Hello," she answered.

"Good morning, you sexy-talkin' devil you."

"Oh, hi, Mike. What time is it?" Wanda asked, drifting back off to sleep.

"It's around seven o'clock," Mike said. "Wake up, Wanda. I got something important to tell you."

"What do you want, Mike?"

"Wanda, I'm shocked to think that you think I always want something when I call. If I hang up now, you'd be mad at me."

"Mike, it's early. Where are you? You're not in jail, are you?"

"No. I'm in DC."

"What you doin' there? Oh, yeah, the new girlfriend's little family reunion."

"How'd you know that?"

"Mike, come on. You know Bobby can't keep anything from me."

"I know."

"As soon as he saw me he had to tell me all about her. It's about time some woman stuck her claws into you. Pam says she got them in deep. So when do I get to meet Wonder Woman?" Wanda asked sarcastically.

"Wonder Woman, huh?"

"Honey, I've seen them come, and I've seen them go. I've watched you dog women to the point that I was ashamed to say I knew you. And I stood by and watched you tear yourself apart piece by piece after that bitch Regina ripped your heart out. I stood by helpless, because you wouldn't let me in, Mike. So if this honey got you, she must be from another planet. I wish it were . . . never mind. I'm happy for you. So where is she?"

"You wish it were what?"

"Never mind, Mike," she said firmly. "What did you want to tell me?"

Normally he would have pressed her for an answer, but not today. He could pursue that with her later. "I found Jamaica," he said matter-of-factly.

Wanda sat straight up in the bed. "Where is he? How is he? What happened to him? Is he with you?"

"Slow down, Wanda. He's here in DC. He's in pretty bad shape. He's still shootin' that heroin. So I want you to check on some rehab joints."

"Done."

"What are you doin' the next couple of days?" Mike asked.

"Nothing I can't get out of. You want me to come down there?"

"Yes. He says he's on probation for a weapons charge and loitering. And I want to take him home."

"Okay. I can be on a plane this morning. Give me a number where I can reach you."

"I'm at a pay phone. He lives in a rooming house. He doesn't have a phone."

"What happened to him? How'd you find him?"

"Na'na found me."

"Na'na! Na'na is there too? How'd he find you?"

"He's a doctor, doin' his internship at the same hospital Wonder Woman's brother works at. He heard I was coming to the little family reunion, so he came to see me. He looks good. I didn't even recognize him."

"Where's he been all these years? Did he say why he left?"

"It's a long story, Wanda. But you gotta promise me something."

"What's that?"

"Promise when I tell you that you won't get mad at me."

"You know I never stay mad at you long anyway."

"Good. I gotta get back to Jamaica. I'll call you back in a couple of hours to see when your flight arrives. Do me a favor and call Bobby and Perry. And when Bobby says he's coming with you, remind him that there is still a warrant for his arrest in DC."

Wanda laughed. "I guess I can see what I can do about that while I'm down there."

"Talk to you soon." He and Wanda both hung up the phone, and Mike returned to Jamaica's room. He found Shy standing in the doorway.

"Hi," Shy said, wiping the sleep out of her eyes.

"You know, you're cute when you're sleepy."

"Thanks. Where'd you go?"

"To call Wanda," Mike replied, kissing her on the cheek.

"Who is this Wanda y'all been talkin' about? Should I be jealous?"

"No, Wanda grew up with us. She's our lawyer," Mike replied. He went in the room and sat down. Jamaica was still sleeping.

"I gotta go home, get our stuff, face the music," Shy said, gathering up her belongings.

"You go ahead. We'll be all right. Give me your mother's number, and I'll call you after we relocate."

"Relocate? Where are you going?"

"To a hotel or something, but we're gettin' up outta here," Mike said, rubbing his eyes and yawning.

"You haven't been to sleep, have you?"

"No."

"Why don't you get some sleep first?"

"I'll be all right. Besides, I gotta call Wanda back in a couple of hours to see what time her plane arrives."

"She's coming down here?"

"Yes. To handle those legal matters for Jamaica so he can go home."

"Here. This is my pager number. But what about you? What are you going to do after that?"

"What did you have in mind?"

"I called E last night while I was out. He says things are goin' good, but I need to do some business soon. I met this guy a couple of months ago in Miami who does business. I need to go down there and get with him. I would like you to come with me. How long do you think you'll be tied up here?"

"Hopefully Wanda can get it done by Monday, Tuesday max. After that I'm yours." Mike started to call her Wonder Woman, but he didn't feel like explaining why. "You go on home. Apologize to everyone for me."

"Anything you need me to do before I go?" Shy asked as she sat in his lap.

"Since you put it that way . . . but I don't think he'll be able to sleep, so I'll settle for a kiss."

After Shy left, Mike nodded off for a couple of hours. When he woke up, Jamaica was still sleeping. He went back to the phone to call Wanda. She said that she told Bobby and Perry the news. They were both surprised and had many questions that she couldn't answer. As Mike expected, Bobby wanted to come with her, and it took a great deal of convincing before Bobby agreed not to come. Perry had to be in surgery that afternoon, so as much as he wanted to, he couldn't make the trip.

"So my flight arrives at Dulles at one fifteen this afternoon," Wanda said.

"Cool. We'll be there."

"Oh, you're bringing Wonder Woman with you, huh?" Wanda asked sarcastically.

"No, Wanda. She left a couple of hours ago to be with her family. I'm bringing Jamaica with me. I thought maybe you'd like to see him," Mike said sarcastically.

"Is he okay?"

"I guess. He's still sleeping. I'll wake him up when I go back up there."

"I'm really excited about this. After all these years, the debate can finally end. But you know, don't you? You know why he left," Wanda said. The lawyer in her was seeking information.

"I'll explain everything when you get here. But he did it for us."

Mike went back to the room and woke up Jamaica. He told him that Wanda would be there in a couple of hours to deal with his legal problems. He asked about Bobby and Perry. Mike explained Bobby's situation and that Perry had to operate today. Otherwise, they would be there too.

That made him happy to know that his old friends were still his friends. Over the years he thought about his friends many times. It was their friendship that got him through the hard times. Many times he thought about trying to contact them, but he was afraid he would bring the law down on them. "Mike, what about Nick? What happened to Nick?"

"About a month after you disappeared, Nick and Bobby got into it over Camille."

"Ho, bitch. I knew she would be trouble right from the start," Jamaica said.

"Everybody did, except Bobby. After that, Nick joined the army. Don't ask me why. But he got out a couple of months ago. He doesn't come around much because of that thing with Bobby, but we'll go see him when we get back to the city."

Mike told him to pack up his stuff because they were going to a hotel. Jamaica picked up his gun and put it in his pocket. He opened the door to the room, picked up the TV, and took it to the guy in the room next door. "I got nothing I wanta keep," Jamaica said, walking out the door.

They left the building, and Mike tried to hail a cab. Jamaica told him that he was wasting his time trying to get someone to stop. Mike smiled and started walking toward the corner. Jamaica followed him. Mike stopped at the corner and waited for the light to turn red. He reached into his pocket and pulled out a $100 bill. When the light turned red, Mike said, "Wait here," and made his way to a cab, which was stopped at the light. Mike showed the driver the $100 bill in his hand. When the cab driver shook his head, refusing to unlock the door, Mike showed him the gun in his other hand. The driver smiled, unlocked the door, and Mike got in. After the driver stopped to pick up Jamaica, Mike told him to take them to a hotel by Dulles.

Mike looked at Jamaica. "How you doin'?"

"I'm hungry. I could stand a shower, but other than that, I feel pretty good," Jamaica replied.

As they got close to the airport, Mike told the driver to stop at a Residence Inn. Once they checked into their room, Jamaica got in the shower, and Mike called Bobby's house and left the number with Pam for Bobby to call. He asked Pam to call and give Perry the number. Next, he paged Nate and Shy. Nate called right back. Mike told him where they were and that once Wanda cleared up his brother's legal problems, they were taking him home.

"That's good. I know deep down that he always wanted to go back to New York. Did he tell you what went wrong?"

"Yeah. It's a long story, Na. I'll let your brother tell you when he's ready. But he's okay. He's taking a shower."

"I gotta get back to work now, but I'll come out there when I get off my shift. How is Wanda doing anyway?" Nate asked. Mike could hear the smile in his voice. "It'll be good to see her."

"You still got a crush on Wanda?"

"No, man. That was a long time ago. I was just a kid."

"I'll see you tonight."

Once Jamaica got out of the shower, he and Mike went to get something to eat and brought it back to the room. After they finished eating, Mike said that it was time for them to leave to pick up Wanda.

"Black, I'm kinda tired. I'll stay here and get some rest. It will give me a chance to think. I'll be all right."

"You sure?"

"Yeah. Really, I'll be all right," Jamaica replied.

Mike really didn't want to leave Jamaica alone, but he didn't want to insist. He felt it was more important to show him that he still trusted him. Mike told him that he wouldn't be gone long and asked if there was anything he wanted.

"A new wardrobe would be nice," Jamaica said with a smile, looking at his attire. Mike said that they would go shopping after Wanda got settled.

"Thanks for lookin' out for me all these years. It means a lot to me."

"No problem," Mike replied. "What you did, you did out of friendship."

"Yeah, Mike, but you didn't know that."

"I knew. Deep inside I knew. I knew you wouldn't just go like that without a reason. I only did what you would have done for me," Mike said. He called the front desk to get a cab. When the cab arrived downstairs, Mike left for the airport.

Wanda's plane arrived on time. She got off the plane wearing a dark blue fitted jacket with pencil-leg slacks and a French-cuff shirt under her trench coat. She spotted Mike and walked toward him. "So where is he? I was all pumped up for the big 'long time no see' hugs and kisses thing."

"Hello, Wanda, it's good to see you too," Mike said as they started walking toward the shuttle.

"I'm sorry. Hello, Mike, and it's always good to see you. You look tired."

"I nodded out for about an hour."

"You should get some rest. Now where is he?"

"He said he was tired. So I left him in the room."

"You left him alone? Why? Do you think that was a good idea?"

"He didn't want to come. What was I supposed to do? Tie him up and drag him to the cab? Besides, we might as well find out now if he can be trusted. His name is on everything we own. If we can't trust him, we got a problem. Better we find out now."

"I guess you're right. So tell me, why am I going to be mad at you?"

"I'll give you the short version. I already told this story once this weekend."

"Who did you tell this weekend?"

"Shy."

"Shy!" Wanda stopped dead in her tracks. "You can tell your little drug dealer girlfriend, but you can't tell me?" Wanda said angrily, hands on her hips, head rockin' from side to side.

"Wanda, if I didn't know better, I'd think you were jealous."

"I'm not jealous," Wanda said as Mike smiled at her. "Been there, done that. Don't you remember the week we went together?"

"Sure I do. Like it was yesterday. You never forget your first time," Mike said as he thought back.

"How old were we then?" Wanda asked.

"Thirteen."

"Thirteen. How much weed did we smoke that night?" Wanda asked.

"Five or six joints. Drinkin' that Strawberry Cow. We were so fucked up. Then you started talkin' about being a virgin," Mike said as they got on the shuttle.

"Then you admitted that you were too. And that all your boys were bragging that they had done it."

"Yeah. And you said all your girlfriends had done it too. And that we might be the only virgins in the city. When you said we should just do it with each other and get it over with, I thought you were kidding until you stood up, turned off the lights, and started taking off your clothes."

Wanda laughed. "I was so shy 'cause I was so skinny."

"But look how you turned out." Wanda had grown from a tall, skinny young girl into a very attractive woman. "Then we tried to play the role," Mike said, smiling as they reminisced.

"By the end of the week, we couldn't stand each other."

"We'd been friends too long, Wanda."

"Right. That's my point. We've been friends too long. So don't think that I'm jealous of . . . what is Wonder Woman's name anyway?"

"Her name is Cassandra Sims. But everyone calls her Shy."

"Shy, huh? Anyway, please don't think I'm jealous of her. But I do love you like you were my brother. I just don't want to have to stand around while she dogs you like Regina did. If she does, I'll have to get in her ass."

"Been there, done that."

"Verrry funny. I just hope you chose wisely this time," Wanda said.

"I hope so too." They got off the shuttle and walked in silence for a moment or two as Mike thought about the days after he broke up with Regina. "I never did really say thank you for being there for me, you know, for Regina. And even if I don't tell you, I love you too. And I always will." Mike leaned over and kissed Wanda on the cheek.

"So tell me your story before I start crying," Wanda said as they walked.

While they stood by the carousel and waited for her luggage, Mike told Wanda the story of how he planned then carried out the execution of André and his associates. He explained what happened with Jamaica and why he ran.

"Why didn't you tell me?" Wanda asked, feeling left out of the loop.

"Do the words 'conspiracy to commit murder' mean anything to you, counselor? Come on, Wanda, I wanted to keep you out of that."

"But, Mike, I asked you point-blank if you killed him, and you said no."

"No, I didn't."

"Yes, you did."

"No, I didn't. You asked me if I killed him, and I didn't say anything. I just looked at you. You said, 'Good.' Then you said, 'Okay, this is what we'll do if they come after you.'" Mike gave Wanda the most innocent smile he could muster.

Wanda rolled her eyes and looked away as if it didn't matter. But it did. She felt that she should have been in on a major decision like that from the start. "That was a long time ago, Mike. No point in arguing about it now."

After claiming her luggage, they caught a cab and proceeded to the hotel. On the way, Mike told her about Jamaica's legal problems, and they discussed a course of action. When they arrived at the hotel, Wanda commented on how nervous she was.

"What about?"

"I don't know. I mean, it's not like I'm meeting him for the first time."

"I know what you mean. I got goose bumps when I first saw him."

"I don't believe that. Vicious Black got goose bumps?" Wanda laughed.

"Very funny. You just get your fine ass in the elevator."

They got out of the elevator and walked down the hall to the room. Mike unlocked the door, and Wanda walked in. Jamaica was on the couch sleeping.

"I don't want to wake him up."

"Clyde!" Mike yelled. Jamaica jumped up off the couch with his gun drawn. "He's awake now."

"Wanda!" Jamaica shouted, dropping the gun on the couch.

"It's good to see you. How are you, Jamaica?" Wanda asked as she hugged him.

"Oh, Wicked Wanda, it's good to see you too."

"How do you feel, Jay? Did you get any rest?" Mike asked.

"I'm okay, Mike. And no, I didn't get any sleep. Bobby called right after you left. I just fell asleep when you got here," Jamaica replied.

"I hope you didn't tell him that story over the phone," Wanda said.

"No, Wanda. I haven't forgotten everything," Jamaica said, looking disappointed that she even asked him that question. "Come here, let me get a good look at you, Wanda. You look good. Both of you do. I wish I could say the same for myself. I look like shit next to y'all. Feel like shit, too. I'm just now starting to realize how far gone I was on that shit. Oh, yeah, Mike. While you were gone, Shy called you. She said to tell you that she's sorry she didn't call you back sooner, but she was asleep. She wants you to page her when you get back."

"Mike, why didn't you take him to get some new clothes?"

Mike just looked at her. "Wanda, you know I hate shopping. Besides, I knew that you would want to go shopping for Jamaica. It's your thing."

"So why don't you get some sleep while we go shop? Take a shower, too. You smell like you haven't bathed in days," Wanda said with a smile.

"That's because I haven't. So y'all go ahead. See you in a few hours. Don't get carried away either, Wanda. Just get him something to wear. You can shop for him when you get back to the city."

Wanda and Jamaica left to buy him some new clothes. Mike went into the room and lay down on the bed. He called Freeze to see how everything was going. Freeze told him that everything was cool. Mike told him about Jamaica. Naturally, Freeze knew all about it. Mike told him to think of something for Jamaica to do. "I want him to feel like he never left." Freeze told Mike that Sylvia said Kenny finally called from Detroit. She said he would be back on Thursday, maybe Friday. Mike gave Freeze Shy's pager number. "As soon as you see him, you have him page me," Mike said.

"You got it."

"You seen Melinda?"

"Yeah, I saw her last night at the club. She was lookin' for you. She told me that she knows you're somewhere with that bitch. But it's cool 'cause she knows Shy ain't gonna fuck you like she does. That's a good girl, Black. Most hoes woulda been trippin' all out in the street chasin' ya down."

"She'd be one chasin' ass if she found me down here. Anyway, you know where to find me if you need me, but I know you won't." Once Mike was finished talking to Freeze, he paged Shy. He got up from the bed, went into the bathroom, and turned on the shower. Mike began to get undressed when the phone rang. He answered the phone, and as expected, it was Shy. He told her that Wanda had taken Jamaica shopping and that he was going to take a shower and get some rest before they got back.

"I was going to come over there and bring you your bag so you'll have clean clothes to put on. I promise to let you sleep," Shy said.

"Come on. Ring the room when you get here."

"I'll see you soon."

Mike took his shower and dried himself off. He sat down on the bed and laid his head down to rest. It seemed like as soon as his head hit the pillow, the phone rang. He reached out to answer the phone. "Hello," he mumbled.

"Hi, baby. I'm in the lobby. I'm on my way up," Shy said.

"Huh?"

"Open the door. I'll be up in a minute."

"How'd you get here so quick?" Mike asked, coming out of his nod.

"Baby, it's been four hours. You really are tired."

"You in the lobby?"

"Yes. Get up and unlock the door!"

Mike rolled out of bed, unlocked the door, and got right back in bed.

Shy came in, looking around for Mike. "Black, where are you?" He didn't answer. Shy looked in the room and found him in bed snoring. She kept her promise and let him sleep. She took his clothes out of the bag and hung them up. She sat down on the bed next to him. She thought about getting in bed with him, but she didn't know when Jamaica and Wanda would return from shopping.

Shy was sure of one thing—she did not wish to go back to her mom's house. The questions about her association with Vicious Black were too intense, and she didn't feel like she had to justify herself to anybody. She decided to wait there until Mike woke up. Besides, she wanted to meet Wanda since she'd heard so much about her the night before. Shy left the room, sat down on the couch, turned on the TV, and did some channel surfing. Shy called the front desk and reserved a room for herself.

After watching TV for an hour or so, Shy heard a key at the door. The door opened, and in walked Wanda, arms full of shopping bags. Shy stood up. "Hello," she said, catching Wanda by surprise. "You must be Wanda," Shy said, walking toward her.

Wanda put the bags down. She looked at Shy for a second. "And you must be Shy. I'm glad to meet you," Wanda said, extending her hand. "Where's Mike?" she asked, feeling unprepared and uncomfortable about Shy's presence.

"He's sleeping. He stayed up all night with Jamaica talking about the old days. Where is Jamaica anyway?"

"Talking to the girl at the front desk. I guess he'll be up in a while."

"What did you get at the store?"

"We got Jamaica some new clothes, and I bought an outfit for Mike. He hates to shop, so whenever I go shopping, I get something for him. I hope he likes it."

"Is it black?"

"Of course it is. I used to buy him, you know, some different colors. Anything other than black, but he just wouldn't wear it. So I stopped wasting my money," Wanda said. "So do you wear black all the time too?" Wanda asked pretentiously, noticing that Shy was dressed in black.

"No. But since I met him, black just jumps out the closet into my hands," Shy replied with a smile, choosing to overlook the tone of Wanda's question.

Wanda looked at Shy. She took a deep breath and said, "Look, it really isn't my place to be saying this, and if Mike knew he'd probably kill me, but I'm gonna say it anyway."

"What's on your mind, Wanda?"

"Well, I really don't know how to say this, so I'll just spit it out and get it over with. I love Mike. He's been more of a brother to me than my own brother. I know he really likes you. And . . . well . . . just don't hurt him."

"Look, Wanda, let me straighten you out," Shy said before she was interrupted by Jamaica's entrance into the room. Shy glanced at Jamaica. She didn't care. "You know you got a lotta heart steppin' to me like that. But I can respect that."

"Thanks," Wanda uttered with a bit of a bite.

"I didn't think you'd be soft hangin' with this crew. Black is very lucky to have a friend like you. Someone who really cares about him. I know he's been hurt, well, so have I. I'm more worried about him hurting me. You know better than I do that Black ain't no saint. So I hope you had this conversation with him."

Wanda stood silently, unable to think of a snappy comeback.

"Well, I see you two ladies have met. Where's Mike?" Jamaica asked.

"He's asleep," they both said in unison.

"Not anymore," Mike said, standing in the doorway.

"Ooops," Wanda said.

"How long you been standing there?" Shy asked.

"Long enough. Wanda, can I talk to you for a minute?" Mike said.

"I guess you don't want to see what I bought for you," Wanda said as she followed Mike into the room.

"Close the door behind you."

Once inside the room, he told her that he wasn't mad at her. How could he be when she was just trying to protect him? Mike asked her why she had to break that on Shy. "The least you could have done was wait until you got to know her. If you still felt it necessary, then by all means, bust her on down."

Wanda admitted that maybe she was just a little jealous. She apologized for the way it came out. But she refused to back off from what she said. "You can say what you want, Mike, but I meant every word I said. I will fuck her up."

As they were about to come out of the room, Mike said, "I ain't mad at you, boo. Love you too much to be mad at you for havin' my back."

When they came out of the room, Jamaica was lying on the couch, smiling. Shy was gone. Mike asked where she was. Jamaica told him that she didn't say where she was going. She just got up and left. Mike sat down in a chair by the window and asked Jamaica if she said anything.

"Yeah, she said, 'Fuck this shit!' Then she slammed the door."

Wanda smiled a devilish smile. "Sorry, Mike."

"Why you trip on sunshine like that?" Jamaica asked.

"Sunshine?" Wanda said in astonishment.

"She was cool, and her smile, like sunshine," Jamaica said.

"Sorry I ran her off. She'll be back."

Mike didn't say anything. He just shook his head. He smiled at Wanda and started laughing. Jamaica started laughing, and then Wanda joined in.

CHAPTER THIRTEEN

Shy wasn't mad at Mike. She wasn't even mad at Wanda for coming off on her the way she did. Actually, she was envious. The way they looked out for Jamaica all those years. The way Wanda jumped on her. They were more like family, not just people who grew up together. Looking out for and being supportive of one another. That was what she envied, that support. She didn't have that in her organization. Even though she and her crew had known each other since high school, most of the time Tony and E were at each other's throats. Now she questioned the support of her family. Going home to face the music, as she put it, wasn't pretty. Shy was feeling good on her way home after leaving Black and Jamaica at the room. She felt good about Black. He wasn't a vicious animal. That was all rep as far as she could see.

She arrived home after eight in the morning to find her mother along with her brothers, Harold and George, waiting. Her mother began by asking why she brought that killer to her house. Shy couldn't honestly deny that he was a killer, especially after hearing Black and Jamaica talk about some of the things they'd done. Black didn't tell her there was a war in the aftermath of André's murder. It was a bloody war, complete with drive-by shootings, cars and businesses being blown up, and people executed in public. Harold and George both had war stories of Vicious Black.

George told her that he had heard Black had walked into a quiet restaurant and approached a table where two men were enjoying their meal. He joined them and talked briefly, got up, and turned over the table. Then he shot them both in the head with his drink still in hand. He finished his drink and left.

Harold said that he heard that one night Black and Freeze were involved in a running gunfight through the streets. They shot one man on the run, and the other had run out of bullets. Black ran him down and pistol-whipped him while a crowd formed. A woman ran up on them and tried to shoot Black in the back. She missed, hitting him in the right arm. Shy remembered feeling a scar on his arm when they made love. Before she could get off another shot, Freeze shot her. Black had yelled, "That bitch shot me! Hey, muthafucka! Your bitch shot me!" Then Black had made the beaten man get on his knees, and he shot him once in the head.

The unified line was, how could she get involved with a killer like that? "Baby, you may be a criminal, but that man's a killer. You can do better than that," Joann said. It was as though they were judge and jury, having found her guilty of being involved with the wrong man. And the verdict: "Get rid of him!" Harold shouted.

"All that happened a long time ago. He's not like that anymore," was Shy's only defense. It occurred to Shy that she never met the man they were talking about. She had only heard about him. The man she knew was considerate and caring. Romantic and attentive, he was fascinating and funny. This was the man she had fallen in love with.

"People like that don't change," Joann said. "Maybe I'm not the one to be giving advice about choosing a man. You know what I been through with your father."

Shy looked at her furiously. "Why we gotta drag Chicago into this?" she asked. "If it weren't for Chicago doing what he did, we wouldn't have any of this. No house, no master's degrees, no PhDs, nothing! So let's not forget where we all came from or where we'd be without him."

"What if you're with him when somebody tries to kill him?" Joann protested.

Shy smiled. *That would give me a chance to save his life.* She didn't think this was the time to tell the family that Black saved her life when someone tried to kill her.

"He ain't nothing but a lying killer. Talking about being in love with you from the first time he saw you," Harold spit out in disgust.

"Did he say that?" Shy melted.

Her reaction only angered Harold. "He's a killer! Can't you see that?"

"You know, I would think my own family would have just a little more faith in my judgment. I don't need anyone to tell me what I should or shouldn't be doin'. I know who he is and what he's done. And you're wrong, Mommy. People do change." Shy started to walk away, and then she stopped and turned around. "I'm tired, so I'm going to bed. Or do you want to make that decision for me too?" She stormed off to her room, slamming the door behind her.

After she woke up and returned Black's call, she began to pack her things. While she packed, Joann sat on the bed and talked all around the subject of Black. When Shy finished packing, she said goodbye to her mother.

Joann stood up and hugged Shy. "I love you, baby, and I just want to see you happy."

"Mommy, I just met the guy a week ago. It's not like we're getting married in the morning. You know I'm not going to rush in. He's been hurt too. I know you don't believe that, but it's true. So we're taking it slow. I'm sorry I brought him to the reunion. But if it weren't for Nate, nobody would have ever known who he was. He really is very nice, Mommy."

"He did seem nice. Besides, anybody with eyes like that can't be all bad," Joann said with a smile.

"Ain't he fine?" Shy said with a high five.

After another round of hugs, Joann said with tears in her eyes, "I hope it works for you."

As she left, Shy said, "I love you too, Mommy."

Shy left her mother's house on her way to the hotel. Although her mother made her feel better about the situation, she still felt like they should have been supportive of her. That was why she envied the way that Black's crew was so close.

After her confrontation with Wanda, Shy drove around for a while. She stopped at a bar and had a couple of drinks. Later in the evening, she went to her brother Randy's apartment. He had a well-furnished one-bedroom apartment in DC.

"Hey, Randy."

"What's up, sis?" Randy stepped to one side, showing her in like a doorman at a fine hotel. "I been expectin' you."

"Mind if I crash here tonight?" Shy asked as she plopped down on the couch. "I guess you heard what happened."

"Not the blow-by-blow, but I sat through the pre-fight hype. I tried to tell them that who you get involved with is your business and they had no right to say anything to you unless you asked for their advice. But you know how Harold gets."

"He went off on me. Both he and George had stories about people Black killed. One of them may be true. Harold said some lady shot him in the arm, and he does have a scar there."

"Did you know that neither George nor Harold were even in the city when all that was goin' down?"

"Really?" Shy said with a mix of disbelief and anger. "The way they came off was like they had it firsthand."

"Wasn't like that. They were gone. I heard those same stories. But I was there, still goin' to City College."

"Was it as bad as they say?"

"Yeah, it was Wild, Wild West for a while. I'm tellin' you, your boy ain't no joke. But if you really wanna know about it, why don't you ask him?"

"Until now it wasn't an issue. I guess it's really not an issue now. That was a long time ago. I heard some things about him, but mostly it's rep. It's that name, Vicious Black. Makes you expect some wild man, you know? Real mean. But he's not like that at all. You met him. What did you think? I mean, like if somebody told you that Vicious Black was at the reunion, would you have picked him?"

Randy paused for a moment and thought about it. "Yes. But only 'cause of his name, Mike Black. But if I didn't know his name, hell no."

"That's what I'm sayin'. He's really not like that. At least not anymore."

"Bet they didn't mention what the war was about," Randy said.

"What?"

"After what's-his-name, ah . . ."

"André," Shy said.

"Yeah. He was large in the drug game. Anyway, after he died, Black and his crew took over. He had a meeting with the rest of the big boys. I guess to split up the territory. Black told them that he was getting out of the drug business, and anyone who worked for André could go with anybody they wanted. Which was cool, until he said that he wouldn't let anyone sell in his neighborhood. You know back then his hood was wide open. So he pissed off a lot of people 'cause they were makin' crazy money."

"That's what started it?"

"No. George told you about him killin' two guys in a restaurant, right? Well, earlier that afternoon, three of their people tried to kill him outside of his house. Black killed them. And then he went looking for the guys who sent them. He found them in that restaurant. You heard the rest of the story."

"Self-defense."

"You know, I'm surprised he likes you," Randy commented.

"Why's that?"

"I hear he hates drug dealers. And you qualify, sis. You mind if I ask you a question?"

"What's that?"

"Shy, I love you. I know how you make your money, but I know I wouldn't be where I am if it weren't for you. I appreciate what you did for me."

"You don't have to say that."

"Yes, I do, every day. Now I ain't trying to judge you, but why are you, and everyone else for that matter, all upset 'cause your boy killed a few people when you're a killer too?" Shy looked at her brother without answering. Randy explained his point. "He uses a gun. You sell cocaine. The only difference is that he faces his victims. You kill them slow and make them pay for the privilege."

Shy still had no comment. Many times she had thought about the effects of her line of work. How she was responsible for destroying peoples' lives. She had always been able to rationalize it by thinking that people make choices. She never forced anyone to do drugs. If they didn't get it from her, they would simply go elsewhere. Why shouldn't she make that money? The fact still remained, she was a killer. But she was worse. Her brand of death was slow, methodical, and deliberate.

"Not everyone who does drugs dies," she protested, but she knew it was lame when she said it.

Randy rolled his eyes at her. "That's not the point, and you know it. Some die quick, and others lose everything they own. Then it takes their self-respect. Then, if they're lucky, their body dies. But their brain is already dead."

"I know, Randy. And you're right. I'm no better than he is. At least he's got heart."

"I shouldn't have dropped that on you."

"It's cool. I'm your li'l sista. If you can't be honest with me, who can you be honest with? You're supposed to tell me what you think."

"Now that I've depressed you, I'm going to bed. I got the early shift tomorrow. How long you gonna be here?"

"Tuesday, maybe Wednesday. Why?"

"Good. I'll take you to dinner tomorrow, that is, if you have no plans. I want you to meet somebody."

"Who?"

"Her name is Renée."

"This somebody special?"

"Yes, very special. I'm gonna ask her to marry me. I want you to meet her."

"You tell anybody else?

"No."

"Then don't. You don't need to hear all that negativity Harold and them gonna talk," Shy said.

"That's why I haven't said anything to them. They're all too negative about everything."

"Well, I'm happy for you. I hope you two will be very happy together. Maybe it will be me one day," Shy said, hugging her brother.

"Thanks. I just hope she says yes." Randy paused for a moment. "One thing's for sure. Whatever Black is, he is in love with you. Says he's been in love with you since the first time he saw you."

"He really did say that?" Shy said, grinning from ear to ear.

"Practically beat his chest when he said it. Like he was proud and he wanted the world to know it," Randy said, beating his chest.

It made her feel good that, in spite of everything, he was in love with her, because she was in love with him. "What time is dinner?" Shy smiled.

"Be ready by six thirty, cool?"

"Cool. Good night, Randy."

Randy went into his room and closed the door, leaving Shy alone with her thoughts. She thought about what each member of her family said to her. She was falling victim to self-doubt. It wasn't so much about her feelings for Black—she was in love with him—but about Black himself. She remembered what her mother said about people like that not being able to change. For all she knew, Black could be behind all of her business problems. She didn't want to believe that Black could be that calculating.

"Wait a minute! This is the same man who decided to kill André and then waited a year before he did it. Yeah, he could be that calculating." He could have arranged for that guy to try to kill her so he could save her. One point rolled around in her mind. "If he really hates drug dealers, what is he doing with me? Was saving me just a way to lull me into a false sense of security? That way I wouldn't suspect him, and he could crush my business. And then he'll kill me on the street to send a message." She thought for a moment. "Stop it, girl. You trippin'."

She had sat quietly Saturday night, both in the car and in the room with Jamaica, listening to Black talk about people he had killed. He did this without showing any signs of remorse. Was he just a killing machine? Shy felt like the man she knew was considerate and attentive and he was fascinating to talk to and fun to be with. Or was all that just the mark of a powerful man doing whatever it took to get what he wanted? Until now, she accepted his assertion that he was not like that anymore.

She remembered walking with Black through his neighborhood, where the so-called war was to have taken place. Everyone knew him. Just about everyone they walked by spoke to him. Some had conversations with him. Others told him about their problems and asked him for his help in resolving their issues. They didn't fear him. They all seemed to have a great deal of respect for him. If the war was so bad, why do these people seem to love him? "He did clean up the neighborhood, made it safe, so why wouldn't they?" She didn't know what to think. Shy always considered herself a good judge of character. Could he have fooled her so completely? Was he in reality a violent and volatile personality waiting to explode? *I don't think so.*

"So what do I do now?" she asked herself. Should she continue to take it slow with Black, or call him right now and tell him that she couldn't see him again as her family suggested? "For what reason? Why should I stop seeing him? And then second-guess myself to death?" No, she would continue to take it very slow with Black. She had to admit there were some things about him that bothered her. Shy would confront him on those points at their next encounter.

CHAPTER FOURTEEN

Shy slept late the next morning. She had slept well for someone who crashed on the couch. At least it was comfortable. She got up and wandered around the apartment. Randy had already gone, but he left a key. *What time is it?* Her next thought was to call Black. It didn't take long to talk herself out of that one. She was a little put out that he had only paged her once after she left the night before. Shy decided to call the front desk to make sure that he hadn't checked out, which he hadn't. It wasn't very likely that he would have checked out since he had business that morning.

She thought about what she would do for the day. Shy decided to do what she had planned to do the day before, which was to visit with Juanita, a close friend from college who had moved to DC about two years ago, and to do a little shopping. Maybe she would buy something for Black. She really didn't like the outfit that Wanda had bought for him. Even though she liked the way Black dressed, she had to agree that he could stand to lighten up a little. However, she would break that to him slowly.

Right now she was hungry. It was after ten, so she decided to go to the Flagship for lunch. Shy called Juanita, who incidentally worked as a programmer for the DEA, and invited her to join her. They sat over lunch talking about their wild college days. And then the conversation turned.

"So what ever happened to Ricardo?" Juanita asked.

"We broke up. He was an asshole."

"Really? I thought he was nice."

"Shit, lyin' muthafucka."

"Give it up, girl. Don't leave me hangin'."

"All right, all right." So Shy proceeded to tell Juanita a bit more animated version of the story she told Black. How Ricardo told her he had been seeing someone else and that they were getting married the following week. "I said, this bitch muthafucka gonna marry some other bitch and wants me to be his toy. Girl, what I wanna say that for? Jack snatched his ass up out of his chair. And they started to beat his ass, honey. Then Jack and Tony dragged his sorry ass outside, and they beat that ass some more. I never heard from him again."

"I'm surprised he didn't press charges."

"Not a chance. If he called the cops, the case would have gone to court. I can see it now, him and Miss Thang sitting there lookin' pitiful. Then I take the stand crying. 'Yes, Your Honor, for three years I thought he was being faithful to me, but he was engaged to her the whole time.' Missy starts trippin', yelling I'm lying. No, that nigga wasn't sayin' nothing."

"If I said it once, I said it a million times: all men ain't shit. All lyin' muthafuckas."

"Yeah, you're right. Most of them are pretty bad."

"Not most of them. All men."

"I hope not. There has to be a good one out there for me."

"Yeah, but he's with some white woman, or he's doing time, or worse, he was a good man until he met that man, and now he's a good woman," Juanita said.

"You sound like you planning on switching. So which way you going, white men or women?"

"You know white men can't jump. And women, shit, ain't that much lickin' in the world. No, Shy, I got to have a nice stiff one. As sorry as black men are, they are still the only game in town for me."

"I know that's right. I met this guy last week, and he might be all right."

"Don't bank on it."

"I'm serious. This one has potential."

"Is he rich?"

"Yeah, you could say that."

"They're worse. Man with money thinks he can lie or buy his way out of anything."

Shy laughed. "That's because they can afford it."

"So what's he like?"

"He's very romantic. He cooked a candlelight dinner for me at his club. He had a band playing just for us. Then one night we took a helicopter to Atlantic City for dinner. He is very attentive, and he is fascinating to talk to. And that's what I like most, that he is so easy to talk to. Romantic, funny, and on top of that, he is so fine."

"Give him time. He'll start doggin' you soon."

"I hope not. To his credit, he has been honest with me, more honest than he really needed to be. 'Cause you know I questioned him with my nosy ass."

"What you talkin' about? I haven't met an honest man yet. That's actually a contradiction in terms." Juanita tooted up her nose. "Huh, honest man. No such thing," she shot back.

"I don't know now. Like, he didn't have to tell me all about the woman he's messing with. I didn't need to hear that, but I'm glad he told me. He's told me things about himself." She didn't think Juanita needed to know about how he killed André. "And I'm talking about some serious stuff."

"He has a motive. They all do. There is something he wants."

"He already got it." Shy smiled.

"And?" Juanita said, leaning forward in her chair.

Shy picked up her napkin, leaned back in her chair, and began to fan herself. "Girl," she said, shaking her head, "let's just say I was mad at myself for leaving him last night before I got some."

"Oh, so he's all that," Juanita said with much attitude.

"All that!" Shy said with authority.

"So what's his name?"

"Mike Black."

"Vicious Black? You're seeing Vicious Black? You come a long way from Ricardo."

"I guess you know him."

"Well, kinda. I went to one of his parties a long time ago. It was out on the island at somebody's mansion. That was the wildest party I ever went to. Plenty of food, plenty of liquor, sex, drugs, fine-ass men. The only thing missing was the drunk swinging from the chandelier," Juanita joked. "You know he used to mess with Sheila's cousin Dez. She used to talk about him all the time."

"I never met her."

"You didn't miss anything. Nasty bitch."

"Were they close?" Shy asked, hoping she'd say no.

"No. That's why I never met him. If he was at the party, she never saw him. She hung out with us the whole night. She disappeared for about an hour, but when she came back, she said she still hadn't seen him."

"When was this?" Shy asked.

"One summer I came home from college, ah, after our sophomore year. See what you missed going to summer school every year?" Juanita replied.

Shy wondered, if she had met him back then, would they have fallen in love with each other? *Probably not.* She did the math. As near as she could figure, that would have been some time after Black killed André. He was with Regina, messin' around with Dez and God only knows who else. She wouldn't have been able to stand him.

"Shy! Where are you, girl? Thinking about that man? Well, let me give you a bit of advice. Take it slow with him. Watch him. All men are dogs. And men who are all that know they're all that and like as many women as possible to know that they're all that," Juanita cautioned.

"I know that, Juanita. That's my only concern about him—women. I just hope he's serious."

"Look at the time. I gotta get back to work. When are you leaving?"

"Tomorrow, Wednesday max," Shy replied.

"Well, give me a call before you go. And let's not let so much time pass between calls."

"You could bring your ass to New York sometime," Shy said as she got up to say goodbye to Juanita.

So Shy was left alone with her thoughts. As she gazed out the window at the wharf, her mind drifted to thoughts of Black. She really wasn't all that concerned about who or how many people Black had killed. It didn't bother her. She was raised around all types of the criminal element: gangsters, hustlers, and dealers. She lay on the ground and watched him kill her attacker. *So I know he doesn't have a problem with killin'. After all, people in his line of work aren't choirboys.* She, on the other hand, considered herself a businesswoman with no interest at all in the violent side of her business. Shy had never killed anyone. She was good at pulling her gun and talking big shit. Before last Thursday, she had only needed to use it twice over the years. Shy had shot at people, not knowing if she hit anyone. But she wasn't sure if she could stand in front of someone, look them in the eyes, and pull the trigger. The closest she had come to killing someone was Ricardo. *Him, I could kill.*

No, her concern was women. After being played by Ricardo the way she had been, her biggest fear in dealing with Black was, all of a sudden, she would find he had another someone. Black had told her about Melinda. *We'll see what that's gonna be about.* He had also left the door open for her to speculate about Tara. It wouldn't be as easy for him to play her, being as high profile as he was. Ricardo was able to live his double life without her knowing because they ran in different circles. She never wanted to go with Ricardo to any of his company functions. For his part, Ricardo never quite fit in when he hung out with her. But she and Black were on the same track, knew most of the same people. It was a small wonder that they hadn't met sooner. All she knew was that the last week had been wonderful. Not that they had spent that much time together, but all the attention felt great.

After lunch, she drove around, calling herself doing a little sightseeing in the Capitol District. Finally, she ended up in Virginia at the Landmark Mall. Historically, anytime she was depressed or felt bad, she would have what she called "Be Kind to Shy Day." Shy shopped for hours like it was going out of style. She got a page from Randy. Shy went to a pay phone to call him back. He asked if she would mind meeting them at Christi's at eight because he was going to ask Renée to marry him before dinner.

"No, Randy, I don't mind, but y'all should be alone, you know, to celebrate."

"Come on, sis. I want you to meet her, help us celebrate," Randy pleaded.

Reluctantly, Shy agreed to meet them there at eight. With a new theme for the evening, Shy decided that she would need something special to wear. "Any excuse."

Shy finished her shopping and returned to the apartment to prepare for dinner with Randy and Renée. While she dressed, her pager went off. Shy checked to see who it was, hoping it was Black. And it was. She smiled but continued to get ready. Shy had bought a black suit that she was going to wear, but she changed her mind. "Nah, the green one will do nicely."

Shy wanted to give Randy and Renée some time to be alone, so she arrived at the restaurant at about eight thirty. "Will you be dining alone this evening?" the maître d' asked.

"No, my name is Cassandra Sims. I'm meeting Randy Sims and his guest here." The maître d' checked his list and had Shy escorted to the table where the newly engaged couple sipped champagne and awaited her arrival.

"Here she comes now," Randy said as he stood up the greet her. "Hello, Shy. I would like you to meet the future Mrs. Sims, Renée Grant. Renée, this is my sister, Shy."

"It's a pleasure to finally meet you. Randy talks about you all the time," Renée said as Shy sat down at the table. Randy poured his sister a glass of champagne and handed it to her. He refilled Renée's glass as well as his own.

"It's good to meet you too. And congratulations to you both. I hope you will have a very long and very happy life together," Shy said, lifting her glass to toast them.

"Thank you, Shy. I know that we will," Renée said.

"And I owe it all to you Shy," Randy said.

"Stop it, Randy. You're embarrassing me," Shy said.

"Don't be embarrassed. He says that all the time. Randy told me that you put him through med school. If it weren't for that, we would have never met," Renée said, squeezing Randy's hand.

My God, he's got her brainwashed already.

"Yeah, I'd probably still be working at the same restaurant."

"No, you wouldn't," Shy said.

"I probably would have moved up to the grill by now, but I'd still be there," Randy said to Shy, his eyes focused on Renée.

"Yeah, well, you still don't have to thank me," Shy said modestly.

Dinner was ordered and subsequently served. Throughout the evening, Shy felt like the third wheel. Although they tried to make her feel comfortable, Randy and Renée would laugh about private jokes between them and would have to explain it to Shy. Watching them together made her miss Black even more.

After dinner, Renée said to Shy, "Randy said that you were bringing a friend with you. I was hoping to meet him tonight too."

"He had some business to take care of today," Shy said, looking at Randy.

"What's his name?" Renée asked as Randy held his breath.

"Are you from New York?" Shy asked.

"No."

"His name is Mike Black," Shy said, and she winked at Randy.

"Have you two known each other long?"

"A little more than a week. It just seems longer."

"She's in love with him," Randy added.

"Let her speak for herself, Randy."

"That's right. How do you know that I'm in love with him?" Shy asked.

"We've been having these reunions since our mother moved here eight years ago. Shy has only brought two people with her. Last year she showed up with one of her flunkies, but that was just for moral support. And this year she brought Mike."

"That doesn't prove anything," Renée said.

"Well, it may be a little early, but yeah, I am kinda fond of him."

"He loves her. He got up in front of a room full of men, beat his chest, and told us how he's been in love with her since the first time he saw her," Randy said.

"That is so romantic. A man who's not afraid to show his feelings." Renée lifted her glass. "Well, here's hoping that it all works out for you."

"Thank you, I think it will. Even though I haven't had much success with men, I'm hoping this one works out."

"Had some losers, huh?"

"You just don't know." She looked at Randy. "Or maybe you do. Randy never could keep anything to himself."

"Okay, so I told her about Ricardo."

"See?" Shy said.

"Yeah, he told me. There are hundreds of studies on why men cheat, and hundreds of different conclusions have been drawn from them. It's been my experience both personally and professionally that men will only do what we let them do. Get to know him, see what kind of person he is. Become his friend. See what he's looking for in a woman. If a man doesn't see what he's looking for, he will go looking for what he needs, and he'll find it," Renée said.

"What type of medicine do you practice?" Shy asked.

"Behavioral psychology," Renée replied.

"Good, that's what we need. We are such a dysfunctional family," Shy joked.

Renée laughed, then she continued, "I'll give you an example. Randy used to mess with this girl he met while he was in med school. After we got together, he stopped seeing her, or at least that's what I thought."

"I did," Randy proclaimed.

Renée held up her hand. "Spare me, Randy. Anyway, for a while I was really busy, and I just didn't have a lot of time to spend with Randy. He would call me, and I would play him off. This went on for weeks. I remember this one night Randy called me. He wanted me to meet him for dinner. I was working on a profile, so I told him that I couldn't go. Now I never told Randy this, but later that night after I got finished, I wanted a drink. I went to this restaurant, and what do I see? Randy all up in this woman's face."

Randy looked at her in shock.

"I couldn't get too mad at him, even though I did. Randy had been calling and calling me, and I was too busy for him. So I left some room for her to exist. Then I tightened up, and now I got the rock," she said, proudly displaying her ring.

"I see your point," Shy said. "Randy wanted some attention. So when he couldn't get it, he went looking for what he couldn't get from you."

"Right."

"Wait a minute," Randy said, and he and Renée proceeded to quietly debate the pros and cons of her statement, not to mention Renée's revelation that he had cheated on her.

Shy thought about what Renée had said. It made sense. From the way he described her, Ricardo's girlfriend Susan wasn't exactly Miss Excitement. Many times he commented on how Shy and her lifestyle fascinated him. So he was looking to her for excitement. What about Black? The reality of the situation was that Black was Melinda's man and he was cheating on her. *So what is it he sees in me that he doesn't see in her?*

After a bit more small talk, Shy said her goodbyes to the happy couple. "I'm going to leave you two to celebrate. Once again, congratulations."

"Are you sure you have to go?" Renée asked.

"Yeah, I gotta go see a man about a dog," Shy said. She told Randy where she would leave the key. She thanked them both again for inviting her and left the restaurant.

Shy arrived at Randy's apartment and began to pack her things. Once she finished packing, she took a deep breath and lay down on the couch to call Black.

He answered, "Hello."

"Hi, baby."

"Hello, stranger."

"What you doin'?" Shy asked.

"Missing you."

"I miss you too. How was your day? Did you take care of your business?"

"Yes. Tomorrow morning, Jamaica will have a probation hearing and be released into Wanda's custody. Wednesday he'll be assigned a new probation officer in New York."

"Any problems?"

"Not really. A few phone calls were made. But no problems."

"Good. You gonna be up for a while?"

"Yeah, this couch ain't the most comfortable," Mike said.

"I'm on the couch too. I'll call you back in an hour," Shy said, and then she hung up the phone. She got in her car and drove to the hotel. Shy had never checked out of the room she had reserved when she left on Sunday. She went into the room and called Mike.

"Hello."

"I'm in room 319. If you're not busy, come by."

"Five minutes," Mike said. He got off the couch and put on a shirt. He left a note that read:

I'm in 319. Call and wake me up.

As promised, five minutes later, Mike was knocking at 319. Shy opened the door to let him in the dimly lit room. "Hi, baby. I missed you," she said as she kissed him.

"I missed you too," Mike said as he sat down on the couch. Shy sat in the chair directly across from him. "And I'm sorry about Wanda goin' off on you."

"It's okay, baby. I wasn't really mad at her. I just thought it was ironic."

"What do you mean?"

"I just thought it was ironic that my family thinks I should stay away from you 'cause . . . 'cause of your rep, really. My moms is worried that I'll be around when somebody tries to kill you."

"Tell Moms not to worry. I have no enemies."

"They're all dead, aren't they?"

"Yes."

"You're kind of a legend in the Bronx, aren't you? I mean, my whole family and even one of my girlfriends have Vicious Black stories."

"Probably all true."

"You think so?"

"Try me," he said.

"How did you get that scar on your right arm?" Shy asked.

"Lady tried to shoot me in the back, but she missed."

"What happened to her?"

"Freeze shot her."

"True story. You remember a woman named Dez?"

"Dez? Vaguely. Why?"

"It's nothing. She's one of my girlfriend's cousins, and you were supposed to be messin' with her back in the day. I didn't think you'd remember her."

"What's your point, Cassandra?"

"I've been doing a lot of thinking. About you, about us, and about me."

"What about you?"

"See, that's what I'm talkin' about. Most people woulda wanted to know what I was thinking about them. But not you. You wanna know about me."

"If you like, you could tell me about myself first."

"No, no, that's all right. It's just that my family is all shook up about you 'cause you're Vicious Black. That doesn't concern me," Shy said with a smile. "I ain't afraid of you."

"What's bothering you, Cassandra?" Mike asked, looking very concerned about where she was going with this. It had all the look and feel of "I never want to see you again."

"Wanda's worried that I'll hurt you. I'm worried about you hurting me."

"I know. I heard you when you said it."

"So?"

"So I'll never hurt you. Cassandra. I love you. Like I've never loved anything or anybody."

"Yeah, yeah. I love you too. But I need more than that. After what Ricardo took me through, I can't stand for a man to be messin' around on me. So you tell me, right now, what's it gonna be like, Black? Are we just going to play around with each other, have mad sex? Which wouldn't be . . . never mind," Shy said with a smile. "You just tell me."

"You want to know about me and Melinda, right?"

"For starters."

"She's done. End of story. And she knows it. If she doesn't know it, I'll make sure she does as soon as I get back to the city. I told you what the deal was with that. We're fuck buddies, period. That's not the case with us. I'm in love with everything about you. I respect you. I love talking to you. I love your sense of humor. The way you walk. The way you talk. Your smile, your eyes. Like right now, in this light, your eyes shoot through me." Mike got up off the couch and walked over to the chair where Shy was sitting. He knelt down next to her and took her hand. "Cassandra, you gotta believe me when I say I want to be with you. Not just for now or for just a little while. Forever." Mike smiled. "And that's a mighty long time."

"Okay, Prince," Shy laughed. "You know, down there on your knees like that, I thought you were about to ask me to marry you."

"Not this week. Next week maybe."

Shy looked at Mike. She smiled and shook her head. "I hope you're serious about what you say."

"Dead serious, baby. I never want this to end."

Shy leaned over toward Mike and kissed him.

"Now that I unveiled my entire campaign to you, you tell me now, what's up with you? I don't wanna have to be the last one to know."

"I think I've made myself clear. I wanna be with you too, but I don't trust you."

"That makes us even. I don't trust you. I don't trust a lot of people. I know I'll have to earn your trust just like you'll have to earn mine. But you'll see. Nobody will ever love you like I will."

"I like a brother with confidence."

CHAPTER FIFTEEN

The early morning sun rose slowly over the nation's capital. The ringing of the telephone interrupted the quiet calm of morning. Shy reached for the phone. "Hello."

"Good morning, sunshine."

"Good morning, Jamaica."

"I hate to bother you, but is Mike with you?" he asked.

Shy asked Jamaica to hold on. Shy put the phone down and began to massage and kiss Mike all over his back until he woke up and rolled into her arms. "Good morning, baby," she said, kissing him softly on his lips. As Mike started to return the greeting, Shy rolled over quickly and handed him the phone. "It's for you."

"Yeah," he said, agitated by the interruption.

"Get up," Jamaica said simply.

"Be there in fifteen minutes," Mike replied. Then he looked at Shy. "Make that half an hour." Then he hung up the phone.

"I feel special."

"Why?"

"'Cause it only took you five minutes to get to me."

"You're sick."

"And?" Shy said as she rolled closer to him.

As promised, a half hour later, Mike reluctantly got out of bed and got dressed while Shy looked on. "I should be back at one, two max. You make reservations yet?"

"No, but I will."

"What are you gonna do while I'm gone?"

"You mean other than miss you? Sleep," she answered, rolling into the fetal position.

"Miss me, huh? You wanna come with me?"

"No. There's something about being around that many law enforcement types." She frowned and shook her head. "I can't be so bothered. I'll be here when you get back."

"Well, keep it warm for me." Mike started to walk out of the room, but he stopped, turned around, and walked back to the bed. He kissed Shy gently on her lips.

"I knew you wouldn't forget," she said.

"I'll be back," Mike said, trying to sound like the Terminator. He returned to his room to get ready for the hearing.

As expected, Jamaica's hearing went exactly as Mike said it would. The board released Jamaica into Wanda's custody. There was no reason that they wouldn't. Mike had been a heavy contributor to a few local congressional candidates over the years. It was a simple matter to call Glynnis Presley, his contact in New York, who called the appropriate congressperson, who made the calls necessary for the hearing to go off without any problems. With that behind him, Mike rode to the airport with Wanda and Jamaica and saw them safely on the plane before returning to the hotel to pick up Shy and head for Miami.

He arrived at the hotel and went to Shy's room. "Cassandra, are you in here?" he yelled, but there was no response. He went into the bedroom. There was Shy, lying in the bed with the covers pulled up to her neck and a big smile on her face.

"Hi."

"Hi yourself," Mike replied as he sat on the edge of the bed.

"Did you eat yet?" she asked.

"No."

"Good." Shy removed the covers to reveal her naked body. She spread her legs slowly, and then she said, "'Cause the best restaurant in town just opened."

"What's the name of your restaurant?"

"Fit for a King."

Mike laughed as he started to unbutton his shirt. "I'm starting to like you, Cassandra."

"You loved me last night. Did I do something to displease you, Your Majesty? If I have, just tell me and I'll double my efforts to please you."

Mike took off his pants and knelt down at the foot of the bed. He leaned forward on the bed and began to kiss her feet, then her ankles, as he crawled up on his stomach. He kissed her thighs, first one then the other, then he looked Shy in the eyes and smiled. He dropped his head and rested it on her stomach. Mike pushed up, placing the weight of his body on his arms. She arched her back slightly and began to rotate her hips in perfect unison with him. He stared into Shy's eyes. "You have the most beautiful eyes I have ever seen, Cassandra. I could look in your eyes for hours."

"You gonna stay in this position for hours?"

"I could."

"I believe you," she said as her body began to quiver.

"Not yet." He rose and entered her, slowly resuming the same slow, rotating motion. Mike paused for a second, smiled at Shy, then started to move slow, then faster, and then slow again. Her body began to quiver again. He stopped. "Not yet." Then he rolled her over until she was on top.

"You know, I'm starting to think you like me up here," Shy said as he placed his hands on her hips.

"What was your first clue?" Mike said as he moved her hips in the same slow motion.

"Ah, 'cause you keep putting me up here maybe?"

He raised her and then pulled her down to his chest slowly. He placed his hands gently on her face and kissed her. Shy stretched out her legs and moved her body in unison with him, trying to anticipate his movement. "Okay, so I like you up there," Mike said as they continued to make love.

"Why?"

"I like the way you move. I like watching you move." As hard as he tried not to think about it, Mike found himself making the comparison between Melinda's and Shy's sexual abilities. There were some differences in style, but there was something else. He and Melinda would fuck like animals for hours at a time.

This was slow and deliberate.

"How does it feel making love to a person and not an object?"

Without taking the time to marvel at the idea that Shy just seemed to read his mind, or at least was thinking what he was thinking, Mike thought, *that must be it.* He was having sex for the first time in years with somebody he was in love with. Mike cared about Melinda, but he never loved her. He wasn't sure exactly how Melinda felt about him. He assumed that she was only in it for sex and money, never taking the time to find out how she felt. It simply wasn't that important.

"I'm lovin' every moment with you, Cassandra. And it ain't just sex. It's you. I'm in love with you, not your sex," Mike said, sliding his hand down her spine.

"Oooh, that sends chills through me." Shy thought how good this all felt to her. For her it wasn't just the sex, although it was great. Shy, too, was deeply in love with Mike. "I could make love to you forever. I never want to make love to anybody but you." The intensity of their lovemaking was interrupted by the annoying intrusion of Shy's pager. They didn't seem to care and continued to make love until both of their bodies shook violently in orgasm.

Shy and Mike both collapsed and drifted off to sleep. Before too long, Shy came out of her nod and reached for her pager. She looked at the number. "Tony. What's wrong now?" Shy dialed Tony's number.

Tony answered, "Hello."

"I sure hope this is important."

"Shy, we got hit again," Tony said frantically.

"Damn, who was it this time?"

"Me. At my crib."

"How much did they take?"

"About a hundred grand and ten kilos," Tony answered.

"Is everybody all right?"

"Yeah, we're cool."

"What happened?"

"Me and Rita were sitting here talking when they kicked in the door."

"How many was it?" Shy asked as Mike started to come out of his nod.

"Four. They came in, tied us up, and ransacked the place. Once they found the money and the product, they left. We've been tied up here all night. E just got here. He cut us loose."

"Where's Jack?"

"Jack's on his way. When you coming back?"

"I don't know. I'm leaving today for Miami to try to put something together. Taking this loss isn't gonna help matters. Look, I don't care how you do it, but you get up as much cash as you can and wait for my call. I may need you to meet me down there." Shy was about to hang up but then she asked, "Tony! How much product we got left?"

"That was all the reserve we had. We're done 'til we get some product."

"All right, do the best you can, and I'll talk to you later." Shy hung up the phone and buried her head in her hands.

Mike sat up in bed next to Shy and placed his hand on her shoulder. "More problems?"

Shy laid her head on his lap. "Got hit again! Most of the money, all the product."

"What are you gonna do?"

"Go to Miami and hope for the best. This is getting too hard. I'm committed to entirely too much money. I can't keep losin' money and product like this. I'll be out of business."

"I think that's the point. Someone wants you out of business. Question is whether it's personal or business."

"What do you mean personal?"

"Like when I killed André, that was business, but it was purely for a personal reason, you know what I'm saying?"

"I see your point. I didn't think I had any enemies until these last few weeks."

"Well, you got one. A very smart one. One so smart and careful that Freeze can't get anything on them. Even Angelo doesn't know anything about them. Not much gets past those two."

"Angelo, damn." Shy sat up. A cold chill came over her. "If I live through this, he's gonna kill me, as much money as I owe him."

"How much do you owe him?"

"Quarter of a mil."

"Angee won't kill you."

"How do you know he won't?"

"'Cause I'll tell him not to," Mike said confidently.

"Seems like I'm only safe when I'm with you."

"I'll never let anything happen to you, Cassandra. I love you."

"I know that, Black, but it just seems like everything is crashing down around me."

Mike wrapped his arms around her like a blanket. She moved closer, resting her head on his chest. He kissed her on top of her head, then lifted it up gently and kissed her lips. "It's gonna be all right, trust me," he said.

Shy felt safe. Once again she was the little girl in her father's arms, and nothing could harm her there. "Baby, there's something I want to tell you. I was gonna tell you Friday, but I got a little sidetracked. And besides, I didn't wanna worry you with my problems. I know how you men hate a woman with problems," she said quietly.

"That's what I'm here for. What do you want to tell me?"

"Thursday night we did business. It went all right, but when we came out, we got pinned down. I didn't know what was goin' on. We must have gotten in the middle of somebody's war, 'cause no one was shooting at us. We were just stuck there. I'm tellin' you, it was scary out there. All of a sudden, they just started shooting in another direction and we got away." She looked at Mike, anticipating his reaction to her announcement that someone had once again been shooting at her. Or at least in her direction. She wanted to hear him say one more time that everything would be all right.

Mike looked away from her for a moment. "I have a confession to make, Cassandra," Mike said, breaking the spell she had just cast.

"Not another girlfriend."

"Not this time."

"I'm listening."

"I know all about what happened Thursday."

"I'm not surprised. You get around."

"Well, there's a reason I know," Mike said reluctantly.

"Spit it out, Black. What you trying to tell me?"

"Since the day you got robbed and that girl died, you've had a bodyguard," he said with a sense of relief, like a weight being lifted from his shoulders. Telling the truth was so liberating.

"What?" Shy pushed him away, vaulting from the bed. "You been spying on me!" she said angrily.

"It's not like that. It's not like that at all. I never wanted to know where you were or what you were doin'. I just wanted to keep you alive."

"Yeah, right."

"Serious."

"Who's been following me?" Shy asked, not hiding her disbelief.

"Jap. He's been on you all the time unless you were with me. Except for that day. I was planning on picking you up that afternoon, but when you didn't call, I had to send Freeze to find you. He found out where you were goin' and was waiting there for you with Jap. I was on the phone with him when the shooting started. Freeze and Jap drew their fire long enough for you to get away."

Shy looked at him in disgust. She plopped down on the bed and bounced up again. "Damn it, Black, I don't know whether I should thank you or slap the shit out of you."

"Both."

"Don't be funny."

"I'm sorry, Cassandra. I know it was wrong, but I just couldn't stand by and let something happen to you."

"I can take care of myself." Shy thought about what she had just said and smiled. "I know I haven't been doing such a good job so far, but I can. And don't get me wrong, I appreciate you looking out for me. I mean, that's twice you saved my life. But you could have told me."

"If I had told you, would you have agreed?"

"No."

"See?"

"That's not the point. The point is—"

Mike cut her off. "The point is you're alive."

"But that don't make it right." She turned around and started for the shower, but she stopped. She turned around again and pointed at Mike as she walked toward him. "I know what your problem is. You're used to running over people. Doing whatever you wanna do. Well, let me straighten you out, Vicious Black. That shit don't work here." Shy walked into the bathroom and came right back out. "You know, it's shit like this that makes it hard for me to trust you."

"I was wrong. I'm sorry," he said, thinking he really had finally met his match.

"No, you're not."

Mike smiled at Shy and got under the covers. Shy stood there for a moment, expecting some type of response. When one didn't seem to be forthcoming, she turned once again for the bathroom. "Yeah, you're right," he said, and Shy turned around.

Mike propped the pillows up against the headboard. He crossed his legs and folded his hands behind his head. "No, I'm not sorry I did it. I am sorry I didn't tell you. I'm really sorry you're mad about it. But no, I will not apologize for you being alive."

Shy took a deep breath and put her hands on her hips, her anger seemingly defused. "You know you had no right to do that, baby."

Mike leaned forward. "I know. But believe me, I wasn't tryin' to spy on you. I love you, and I only want you to be safe."

Shy walked back to the bed and looked at him for a second before sitting down on the edge of the bed. "You're making it really hard for me to be mad at you. And I am. I'm mad as hell."

"And you're so cute when you're mad. Eyes get all Chinese and shit," Mike said jokingly. "Come on, smile. That shit was funny."

Shy smiled and tapped him on the arm. "You have to respect my privacy."

"I do. I know it doesn't seem like it, but I do. I wasn't spyin' on you."

"I wasn't doing anything worth talking about anyway. Until you came along, my whole life was my business. You know, it was so easy when I started. No problems. Just lots of fun and lots of money."

"You're gettin' large. Somebody wants what you have."

"I'm almost ready to say they can have it. I'm not built for this gangster stuff. I'm a businesswoman. At least for now."

"Well, let's think about that for a minute."

"What?" she asked.

"It's not somebody tryin' to ruin your business."

"What makes you say that?"

"'Cause you're still doin' business. You're not makin' any money, but you're still doin' business. No, this isn't business. It's personal."

"I say again, what makes you say that?"

"What, you had five, six people robbed? Bandits hit quick, but they took the time to tie people up. If I was tryin' put you out of business or even take over, I woulda killed everybody. Not just some girl on a humbug. I'm talkin' everybody. This way there's no witnesses, nobody comes after you. No, Miss Sims, it's you."

"Thanks, I really needed to hear that. Why me?"

"You think about that. You think about everyone who would want to hurt you. Who wouldn't mind killin' you, who doesn't care about your little dope business. Someone who wants you dead."

"I don't mind telling you that I'm scared," Shy said, laying her head on his shoulder.

"They probably won't try to kill you again, at least not while you're so well protected."

"No. No, I don't want anybody following me."

"I was talkin' about myself," he said, beating his chest. "I guess I can't let you out of my sight until this is over."

"I don't think so."

"Okay, you can go to the bathroom by yourself," Mike said with a straight face.

"You sound like a fool," Shy said as she got out of bed and started once again for the bathroom. "Well, this time I'm really going to take a shower. You wanna come . . . with me?" Shy turned around quick and went into the bathroom, followed closely by Mike, like an animal who had the scent of his prey.

CHAPTER SIXTEEN

During the ride to the airport as well as the flight to Miami, Shy was very quiet. She sat on the plane, staring aimlessly out the window. Her mind was consumed with thoughts of murder. Who were her enemies? Black had given her entire situation a brand-new flavor. It had been easier for her to think that all this was business. However, what he said made perfect sense. It had to be her. Shy had gone to great pains to ensure that her operation wouldn't interfere with anybody else's business, being spread out and so diverse. It was that diversity that had put her into a position for her operation to grow. Now it was the thing that was dragging her down.

She was too spread out.

Everybody who got hit was holding large quantities of product. Some of her associates were hurt pretty bad. It would have been easier to kill them. No, whoever it was wanted her out of the way and her operation intact. Her first thought was Ricardo. She didn't think he would have the heart to take over her business, much less kill her. But he was the only person she could think of with a reason. After all, that was quite a beating Jack and Tony issued. He wouldn't do any of the work himself, but Shy had no problem believing that he would pay someone to do his dirty work. Ricardo had met many people during his association with Shy. He could have developed a relationship with someone and paid them to kill her and take over.

Upon arrival at Miami International Airport, they caught a cab and headed for her meeting. The cab driver asked, "Where to?"

"Miami Beach. The Beekman Hotel on Collins Avenue," Shy replied.

"The Beekman?" Mike asked with a frown on his face.

Shy leaned closer to him and whispered, "The deal is that I am supposed to check into that hotel and ask for messages. It will have instructions."

Mike laughed and shook his head. "Sounds like something from an old spy movie."

"Don't it?" she replied.

The cab arrived at the hotel, and Shy checked in. "Are there any messages for me?" While the desk clerk went to check for messages, Shy turned to Mike. "This is the part when the shady little man walks up with his henchmen and escorts you away at gunpoint."

The clerk returned and handed Shy a note, which read:

The pool at 10 tonight. You will be contacted.

Shy handed it to Mike, who laughed. "A cheap spy movie."

"Well, since we have some time, let's go eat," Shy said.

"At Fit for a King?" Mike replied eagerly.

"No, baby, I'm hungry. I haven't eaten a thing all day. After we eat, then we can play. But I got a taste for seafood."

They returned to the hotel shortly before ten and went directly to the pool. They took seats at poolside and waited. Shy sat facing the ocean.

"This is really beautiful. I love the beach," Shy said.

"I do too. But this doesn't compare to the beaches in the islands. Maybe once things quiet down we can—"

Mike was interrupted when a gentleman approached the table from behind him. "Miss Sims?" the gentleman said.

"Yes?"

"Mr. Villanueva will join you shortly," said the shady little man Shy was expecting. Shortly thereafter, they were joined by Hector Villanueva, whom Shy had met months earlier and who had offered her a deal on product.

"Shy, it's good to see you again," Hector said, kissing her hand.

"Hello, Hector."

"May I join you?" he said, reaching for a chair.

"Please have a seat."

"Thank you," Hector said as he took a seat at the table, taking a glance at Mike.

"My associate, Mike—"

Hector cut her off. "Black! What are you doin' here? You don't do this type of business!" Hector said as soon as he recognized him.

"Hello, Hector, it's good to see you again too. And to answer your question, I'm just keeping the lady company."

"I guess you two know each other?" Shy asked.

"Yeah, me and Hector go back a long way." Mike smiled. "By the way, how is Nina?"

"Why do you disrespect me in front of the lady, Black?" Hector said furiously. "Why do you want to know, Black? So you can fuck her again?"

Shy's jaw dropped.

"Hector, I didn't fuck your wife."

"Why do you continue to deny it, Black? You fucked her!"

"Hector, please lower your voice. Did you ask her about it?"

"Yes, and of course she lied too."

"Hector, I'm gonna say this one more time. I did not fuck Nina."

"You fucked her, Black, more than once," Hector argued.

"Hector, what can I say to convince you?"

"Don't say anything to me, Black. You and I both know you fucked Nina."

"Cool. I won't say anything."

"Is there anybody you don't know, Black?" Shy asked.

Mike didn't answer. He just smiled at Hector without taking his eyes off him.

"You should be careful of the company you keep, Shy."

Shy leaned forward and pointed in Hector's face. "Look, if you don't want to talk to him, that's fine. But I definitely don't want you talking to me about him. Are we clear?"

"My apologies." Hector looked angrily at Mike, but then proceeded to the business at hand. "What can I do for you, Shy?"

"When I met you, we discussed a business arrangement," she said, turning on her considerable charm. "I wanted to know if the offer was still good."

Hector paused for a minute. "You know I used to live and do business in New York. I still have many friends and many business associates there. Some have told me about the problems you are having. In fact, they tell me that just last night you took another loss. Is this true?"

"Yes. But I am moving to correct that situation," Shy said quickly.

"Shy, it hurts me deeply to tell you this, but I must retract my offer."

"Why?"

"You're not a good risk at this time. Please understand, once you have settled these matters, I would have no problem extending the offer," Hector said.

"Just like that?" Disappointment manifested in her voice and her eyes.

"Well, of course you can always do it all on the front end."

"I can't do that."

"Yes, I know, due to your problems. Of course, if Black were to guarantee your investment, that would eliminate all of my objections."

"Hector, you know better than most that, as a matter of principle, I will not do that," Mike said, "and you insult me by mentioning it."

"My apologies, Black," Hector said bitterly. "Once again, Shy, I'm sorry we cannot work together."

Mike saw the disappointed look on Shy's face. "Well, Hector, I do have a better idea." Shy and Hector both looked at Black.

"I'm listening," Hector said.

"It's simple. You extend to her the same deal that you offered her."

"No, Black!" Hector shouted. "Only if you stand with her."

"Hector, listen to me. All I am asking is that you stand behind your word. I know that you are an honorable man."

"Understand me, Black. I can't do that," Hector said as Shy looked on, feeling left out of her own business.

"Hector, look at me," Mike said, looking Hector in the eyes. "I would consider it a personal favor if you would stand behind your word and do this for her."

Hector sat back in his chair and pondered Mike's proposal. Shy sat quietly, looking back and forth at both of them. Finally, Hector said, "Shy, it would be my pleasure to do business with you." He got up from the table and handed Shy a card. "Call this number in New York when you are ready to do business. It is always a pleasure to see you, Shy. And you, Black. I hope this concludes our business together," Hector said as he and his associate walked away.

As they walked away, Shy looked at Mike curiously. "You mind if I ask you a question?"

"Sure. I knew you'd have questions," Mike said, continuing to watch Hector until he was out of sight.

"Well, thank you. I only have a few questions. First of all, what just happened?"

"Hector owed me a favor."

"What was that?"

"I introduced him to Angee."

"That's it?"

"Yeah. Hector used to buy from André back in the day. André hated Puerto Ricans, so he was killin' him on price. So one night I was at the club, and Hector was there when Angee came in."

"I can't see Angelo hanging out," Shy said.

"Why? Nobody would bother with Angee. One, 'cause everyone knew Angee wouldn't care about killin' them, and two, 'cause everybody knew I had his back. And besides, Angee likes black women. Anyway, Angee talks to me for a while, and then he sees a woman he likes and walked off. Hector runs up in my face, tellin' me how André was beatin' him down on price and all that. So I asked him, 'Yo, Hector, why are you tellin' me all this?'"

"You know Angelo, right?"

"So what are you tryin' to say, Hector?"

"Can you introduce me to Angelo? Please?"

"Hector, let me make sure I understand you. You buy from André, who pays me. And now you want me to introduce you to Angelo so you can stop buyin' from André, who pays me. Is that what you're asking me? Let me make sure I understand you. You want me to take money out of my pocket to help you. Is that what you're sayin', Hector?"

"Yes, Black," Hector said.

"You owe me a favor, Hector."

"Okay," Shy said.

"So I take Hector over to Angee and I say, 'Yo, Angee, this is Hector Villanueva. He's an honorable man and deserves to be taken seriously.' So Angee dismisses the honey he's talkin' to. He says to me, 'Is he a good guy, Mikey?' I said, 'I wouldn't introduce him if he weren't.' That's why he owed me."

"That's what all that honorable man stuff was about. You were reminding him that he owed you," Shy said.

"You catch on quick, college girl," Mike said.

"Now did you fuck his wife?" Shy asked, praying he'd say no.

"Yes."

"Damn it, Black."

"I didn't know she was Hector's wife, or that she was even married for that matter."

"Sure," Shy said, as she got up from the table and started walking toward the beach.

Mike got up and followed her. "Slow down, Cassandra. Come on, wait up."

"What?" She stopped and faced Mike. "You must have fucked her after you did him that favor?"

"Years."

"When?"

"Five years ago," Mike said.

"How long were you with her?"

"Off and on for about a year."

"So you're telling me that you were having sex with this woman for a year and didn't know she was married?"

"Yes. She never wore a ring, and I never asked her any questions. I never called her. I never even knew her number. She never knew mine. I'd see her around, we'd hook up, then I wouldn't see her for a while," Mike said.

"So when did you find out she was married?" Shy asked as she began to calm down. She started walking along the beach.

Mike walked alongside her and offered his explanation. "I saw her one night on the street, and she walks up on me. We talked awhile, and then she says, 'Oh, shit, here comes my husband.' So I'm like, 'You're married? To who?' and she points at Hector. I never saw her again after that day."

"Never?" Shy said in disbelief.

"No. Not too long after that, Hector shipped her down here."

"That's probably why you never saw her again."

"No, that's not it. I don't mess with married women."

"I guess that's something I just have to get used to. Women from your past. I don't know. I just don't know if I can."

"I know I said this before, but I'm not like that anymore."

"So you told me."

"But you don't believe me, do you?" he said, challenging her.

"It's not that I don't believe you. It's just that I've heard that so many times from so many men. I want to believe you. I really do. I'm just gonna need some time. That's all."

"I got all the time you need. Which brings up another point."

"And what might that be?"

"When do you want to go back to the city?"

"Why, you in a hurry?"

"No, I wanna go to the beach."

"Baby, I hate to be the one to break this to you, but we are on the beach," Shy said.

Mike stopped in his tracks and looked around. He shook his head and said, "No, let me show you a beach."

He took Shy by the hand and practically dragged her to their room. Mike picked up the yellow pages and began to thumb through until he found the number of the charter service he was looking for.

"Baby, it's too late to charter a plane. Everything's probably closed at this hour."

Mike continued undaunted by her comment.

"Pete's Charter Service. Pete speakin'."

"Pete, my name is Mike Black. I'd like to charter a plane tonight to Grand Bahama Island."

"The Bahamas," Shy said.

"It's too late tonight. We can get you there first thing in the morning," Pete said.

"Really? My friend in New York who referred me to you said that time wouldn't be a problem," Mike replied.

"Oh, yeah, who's that?" Pete questioned.

"Carmine Fortine."

"Why didn't you say so?" Pete said with a new attitude.

"I don't like droppin' his name unless I have to."

"Any cargo?"

"No cargo, just two passengers."

"How long before you get here?" Pete asked.

"Half hour," Mike replied.

"I'll have it gassed up and ready," Pete said as Mike hung up the phone.

"Grand Bahama Island. I never been to the Bahamas. You're going to spoil me, Mike Black," Shy said, falling into his arms.

"That was my intention, babe."

CHAPTER SEVENTEEN

Jack emerged from Tony's apartment, heading for his car. E came out behind him. They spent the day together trying to regroup from their latest setback. They had given up on figuring out who was robbing them, focusing instead on a way out of the situation.

"There he is again, Jack," E said, looking down the street.

"Who, Freeze?" Jack replied while walking back toward E.

"Every time I look around, there he is."

"I know. He's been on me too. What pisses me off is that he don't even try to hide," Jack observed. "Like he don't care if we do know he's following us."

"We oughta just roll around behind him and kill him."

"You must have a death wish. You kill Freeze and Black will kill us all. Shy too. But I'm startin' to think that maybe you're right about them being involved," Jack said. "He's damn sure up to something."

"I been trying to tell y'all. It's been Black all along."

"Maybe not all along." Jack started for his car. "But since he's been at Shy, Freeze has been at us. But as long as he stays out of my way, I don't care what he does."

At that moment, Bobby drove down the street. He noticed Freeze double-parked and thought nothing of it. He continued down the street until he saw Jack and E. Bobby made a U-turn and pulled up across the street from Freeze. He got out of his Cadillac and got in the

Rodeo with Freeze. "What are you doing?" he asked Freeze.

"What's up, Bobby?" Freeze replied. "What does it look like I'm doin'? I'm protecting our interest."

"Looks like you're involving us in that woman's business. That's how it looks to me. Probably how it looks to them." Bobby shook his head. "You don't see how what you're doin' makes it look like we're involved in this madness."

"We are involved, can't you see that?" Freeze replied angrily. "As soon as Black started fuckin' around with Shy, her problems became our problems."

"Mike know what you're doing?"

"He knows I got his back." Freeze paused a moment, eyes still focused on Jack and E. "I don't wanna argue with you. But these boys are sloppy and careless. You know they got robbed again last night?"

"How do you know that?"

Freeze simply looked at Bobby and smiled.

"Anyone get killed this time?"

"Not this time. But tell me something. If somebody were trying to kill Black, would you let him go out of town to do business by himself?"

"No."

"Now do you get my drift? The way they handle her security puts Black at risk. She got her shit rollin' tight, you know what I'm sayin'? But these bitch-ass gangsters can't handle it."

Bobby thought for a minute. Freeze was definitely sizing them up. What was he up to? It was obvious that both Freeze and Mike admired Shy's operation. But after all they had gone through to get out of the drug business, he didn't think Mike would drag them back in, especially without discussing it with him first. "Black ain't thinkin' about getting back in the game?"

"Hell no!" Freeze protested. "At least I don't think he is. And if he is, I need to know what they got. Makes it easier to take over."

"What you gonna do with them when you take over?" Bobby joked as E and Jack drove away.

"Them low-stress gangsters? Shit. I'll bleed them quick," Freeze replied.

Bobby started to get out. "You're a dangerous man, Freeze."

CHAPTER EIGHTEEN

After a quick cab ride, Mike and Shy found themselves at Pete's Charter Service.

"Anybody here?" Shy yelled.

Pete came out of the back room. He was a short, heavy-set guy, dressed in a beat-down flight suit and looking like he needed to make friends with a razor. Badly. "What can I do for you folks?" Pete asked.

"I'm Mike Black. I talked to you a while ago about a charter."

Pete looked at Mike, and his expression spoke volumes. "Okay, we'll be ready to leave in a little while. Just make yourselves comfortable. I'll be right back." Pete returned to his office. He flipped through his Rolodex, picked up the phone, and dialed a number.

Mike leaned over and said to Shy, "He wasn't expecting us to be black."

"So what's he doing now?" Shy whispered.

"He callin' to check us out," Mike replied.

The phone rang and was answered. "Yeah."

"This Jimmy?" Pete asked.

"Yeah, who's this?" Jimmy asked.

"This is Pete down in Miami. Is Mr. Collette around?"

"Hold on, Pete."

After a while, Angelo came to the phone. "Pete! How's it hangin'?"

"Everything's great, Mr. Collette. Listen, I got a couple of moolies here," Pete said. "The guy says Carmine referred him."

"No shit, Petey. What's his name?" Angelo asked.

"Says his name is Mike Black."

"Pete, I want you to listen to me very carefully," Angelo said. "You apologize to Mr. Black for keepin' him waiting. Then you take him wherever he wants to go."

"Yes, sir," Pete said sheepishly.

"Let me talk to Mike. Oh, and one more thing, Pete. You don't charge him shit! You got that?" barked Angelo.

"Yes, Mr. Collette."

"Good. Now let me talk to Mike," Angelo said.

Pete went back to the lobby where Mike and Shy were waiting. He motioned to Mike to come into the office. Shy asked, "What's happening now?"

"Angelo wants to talk to me. Come on," Mike replied.

"Mr. Collette would like to speak to you, Mr. Black," Pete said, handing the phone to Mike.

"Angee! What's up?"

"Nothin', Mikey. Listen, you let me know if that scumbag doesn't treat you right, okay?"

"Done."

"Where you goin'?"

"Bahamas," Mike replied.

"Mind if I ask a personal question, Mikey?" Angelo said.

"Fire away."

"Shy with you?"

"She's right here. You wanna talk to her?"

"No. Just tell her I was hopin' to see her soon, or should I be talkin' to you about that?" Angelo said.

"Nope. But I'll give her the message," Mike replied.

"Have a good trip."

"Thanks, Angee. We'll talk when I get back." Mike hung up the phone, turning his attention back to Pete.

"Sorry to keep you waiting, Mr. Black. If you follow me, I'll show you to the plane. We'll take off whenever you're ready," Pete said with a newfound sense of respect. Pete led the way, and Mike and Shy followed him.

"What did Angelo say?" Shy asked.

"That he was hopin' to see you," Mike replied.

"Great. He's gonna kill me," Shy said.

"You let me worry about Angee."

"What am I gonna do?"

Mike stopped and grabbed Shy by the shoulders. "You're gonna get your fine ass on that plane, and then you're gonna have some fun for the next couple of days. Think you can handle that?"

"I can handle that," Shy said, shaking her head.

"Good. The island of love awaits us," Mike said as he and Shy boarded the plane.

CHAPTER NINETEEN

Looking out the airplane window, they could see the lights of Freeport on Grand Bahama Island. The plane flew low over the water, close enough to a catamaran to see the people partying on the deck. When Pete landed at the airport, it was just after midnight.

Shy looked around as they got off the plane and took a deep breath. "Do you smell it?" she asked.

"Smell what?"

"Fresh air," Shy replied, her wraparound skirt blowing in the wind.

"You want me to come back for you?" Pete asked.

"No," Shy said, walking away. "You don't ever have to come back for us."

Mike walked over to Pete and handed him five $100 bills. "Be back for us about ten o'clock Saturday morning."

"Mr. Collette said I shouldn't charge yous no money," Pete said, trying to give Mike back the money. "I can't take that."

"I know. This is your tip, Pete."

Pete smiled and took the money. He agreed to return Saturday morning. After passing quickly through customs, they caught a cab to the Lucayan Beach Hotel. Once they arrived at the hotel, Mike started to go inside to check in. Apparently, Shy had other ideas. She started walking away from the lobby doors.

"Where are you going, Cassandra?"

"Hey, you promised me a beach, didn't you? Why waste time?"

Shy walked alongside the hotel. She stopped at the edge of the sand and took off her shoes. Mike followed suit and rolled up his pants. They walked toward the edge of the water. "Isn't that a beautiful moon?" Shy said, sticking her foot in the water. "And this water is so warm." She turned around and kissed Mike on the cheek. "This is wonderful."

"Is this the first time you've been to the islands, girl?" Mike asked with an accent as they walked through the sand.

"Well, sorta. I've been to Aruba with Ricardo," Shy replied, rolling her eyes. "But it rained just about the whole time we were there."

"That sounds fun."

"Woulda been better if I were rained in with you," she said, rubbing his inner thigh. "This time, I wanna do something. I wanna do a lot of this, too," she said, easing her hand higher on his thigh. "I didn't have any fun."

Mike leaned slowly toward her lips. "We can't have that," he said softly as their lips met. "Come on!" Grabbing her hand, he ran down the beach, practically dragging Shy behind him. Mike ran into the water. "I want to show you everything, not the tourist stuff. I mean, the island."

"You must come down here a lot," Shy said, struggling to keep up.

"Yeah, I've been to a lot of the islands, but this is my favorite. So I'll be your very personal guide. You tell me what you want to do. Your every desire is my passion to satisfy."

"Hmm, really." Shy stopped in her tracks. Mike stopped, turned, and walked back to her.

"You know what I really wanna do, don't you?" Shy whispered to him in a very sensuous voice, drawing him closer. "I wanna go dancing!"

"I know just the spot. Come on," Mike said, grabbing her by the hand again and running. They ran toward the Rivera Towers and went into the outdoor bar at the Coral Beach Hotel. As Mike headed straight for the bar, Shy stopped and scanned the crowd.

"I hope this isn't what you ran me down the beach for, is it?" Shy said, looking around the bar with a frown. "This looks like a tourist spot to me."

"This place? Hell no!" Mike looked around. "We just came here to get a drink and catch a cab." He turned to the bartender. "Gombay Smash please. And one for the lady."

"What kind of smash?" Shy asked.

"Trust me."

After being served their drinks at the bar, they got in a cab. "Freeport Inn," Mike said to the driver.

Before too long, they were on the dance floor at the Freeport Inn, dancing to reggae and soca music, only leaving the floor to get more drinks. After a while they stopped dancing to the beat of the music. They danced cheek to cheek, swaying back and forth, talking, laughing, kissing. They remained on the dance floor well into the early hours of the morning.

The crowd started to thin out, and they drifted out with them. They took a cab and got out by the canal. "Let's go for a walk on the beach," Shy suggested. "I'm about Gombay Smashed, and the walk will do me good."

Along the edge of the water by some private homes, they walked and talked. Shy stopped to play in the water. She started splashing at Mike, and got his shirt very wet. Mike began to get undressed. "What are you doin'?" she asked.

"Takin' off these wet clothes so they'll dry," Mike replied, dropping his shirt in the sand.

"Yeah, right, any excuse to be naked."

"Right," he said and began splashing her and then ran through the sand. Shy gave chase. Mike faked left and then went right. Shy tried to grab him but slipped and fell on her side. Mike stopped. "Are you all right, Cassandra?"

"Yeah, I'm all right, but this skirt is shot."

Mike smiled, then began laughing hysterically.

Shy started laughing too. "It ain't funny."

"You shoulda taken it off."

Shy got up and stripped down to her bra and panties. "Okay, see how you do me? But it's cool. I'll get you." Shy ran straight at him. Mike smiled and stood, waiting, then took off just as she was about to grab him. Mike dodged back and forth for a while, and then she said, "Got ya!"

"I let you catch me," Mike said, allowing Shy to push him to the ground. Mike rolled over on his back and pulled Shy on top of him.

"To the victor go the spoils," she said, kissing him passionately. "Ouch, your belt buckle is sticking me."

"Lucky buckle. Wish I were sticking you," Mike said, unfastening the buckle. "Is that better?"

Shy lay back down on his chest and kissed him. "Much."

"Rise up a second."

"No, people live in those houses. Someone will see us," Shy said, but she did it anyway.

"They oughta be asleep anyway," Mike replied, sliding his pants down a little. He slid her panties to one side. Shy placed her hands on his chest and slid down on him slowly.

On their way back to the hotel, the sky began breaking in anticipation of the sun. When they arrived, Shy allowed Mike to check in before they gave away the room. "Good morning, sir. Welcome to the Lucayan Beach Hotel."

"You have a reservation for me, Mike Black."

"Yes, I do, and welcome back, Mr. Black. We have your usual room ready."

"Your usual room?" Shy commented mockingly as she walked away. "Probably the presidential suite."

Mike went through the formalities of checking in. Shy wandered through the hotel lobby, finally ending up back on the beach.

"Thought I'd find you here," Mike said, walking up behind her, putting his arms around her waist.

Shy spun around and kissed him. "This was a great idea. Thank you for bringing me here."

"I wasn't just talkin' when I said it is my passion to satisfy you."

"I haven't seen the sun rise since . . . I don't know when," Shy said, turning back toward the sun.

"I never watched it until last week."

"You've never seen the sun rise?" she asked.

"I've seen it plenty of times, but the first time I watched it was last week."

"Get outta here, really?"

"Really. I was thinking about you. I couldn't sleep. I hadn't slept all night. So I went outside and sat on the porch. I watched the sun come up and wished I were with you. And now here we are. And I can't tell which is more beautiful: you or the sunrise."

"I'm friendlier."

"Softer too," Mike said, sliding one hand across her stomach, the other across her breasts.

"I know. So choose wisely." It wasn't that hard a choice. They walked hand in hand into the hotel and took the elevator to their room.

"This is your usual room?" Shy asked, seemingly disappointed that it wasn't the presidential suite.

"It's not the room, Cassandra," Mike said, walking out on the balcony. "It's the view." From the balcony, there was a breathtaking view of the Atlantic Ocean.

"It is a beautiful view," Shy said. After a few moments she went back inside and lay down on the bed. Mike came in and lay down next to her. Before too long, they found themselves naked and making love.

Caught up in all the magic that was their lovemaking, they forgot to put the DO NOT DISTURB sign on the doorknob. A knock came to the door as it opened.

"Housekeeping," the attendant said as she came in the room. By reflex, Mike rolled over, grabbed his gun from the nightstand, and pointed it at the attendant.

"Oh, my God," she said, staring down the barrel of Mike's gun.

Mike put the gun down and motioned for her to be quiet and wait in the hall for a minute. She closed the door and waited patiently outside. Mike got out of bed and put his pants on. Then he gathered up the towels and Shy's clothes. He opened the door, apologized for scaring her, and got some fresh towels. Mike handed her a $50 bill.

"If it's not too much trouble, can you take these to the laundry and have them dry-cleaned and pressed, please?"

The attendant agreed. He finished getting dressed, kissed Shy on the forehead, and left the room.

Mike caught a cab to the International Bazaar to shop. He wanted to buy a sundress and swimwear for Shy and a black shorts set for himself. He entered the shop, being greeted by a tall, older, somewhat chesty woman.

"Can I help you find somet'ing?" she asked with a heavy accent.

"I hope so. I wanna get a sundress for a lady," Mike replied, wandering and looking around the shop.

"Do you know what size she wear?" the woman asked.

"No."

"Well, how you expect to find somet'ing for she you don't know she size?"

"That's where you come in. What's your name?"

"Lulu."

"Not Bong Bong?" Mike asked.

"In me younger days, but Lulu gone away. And don't you ask me who is Bong Bong now that Lulu gone away, 'cause me don't know," she replied.

"I promise I won't ask, Lulu." Mike smiled. "My name is Black."

"It's good to met you, Black. Now what she look like?"

"She's about five eight, maybe five nine."

"'Bout my height?" Lulu asked, thumbing through a rack of dresses.

"Not quite, but close. I like that one. What size is it?"

"This a size three," Lulu said, checking the label. "She have to be skinny and flat chested to wear this, ya know."

"That is definitely not her," Mike replied.

"So she busty like me then?" Lulu said, leaning toward him.

"No, now she ain't got it like all that, but she holds her own," Mike said, laughing as they continued to look. "She's about a hundred forty pounds. You know, she's like this." He placed his hands in front of his chest to show her size. "And like that in the hips."

"Size seven should do she nicely." Lulu pulled a dress from the rack and handed it to Mike. It was a white dress with thin straps and a yellow bird on the front and back. "This should fit she fine, like this and like that," Lulu said, motioning with her hands.

"Excellent. I'll take that, and now I need some swimwear for both of us, preferably something in black," he said, trying to stay in character.

Lulu picked out a black and green bikini for Shy and a pair of matching trunks for him. Lulu bagged it, and Mike was outta there. As he walked to the cab, he realized that in his haste to end the shopping experience, he forgot to get something for himself to wear. Mike turned around and cruised the bazaar for a moment when he saw an outdoor vendor with a black shorts set. It was his size, but he was apprehensive about buying it because it had a yellow bird on the shirt, similar to the one he had bought for Shy. He decided to go with it. "She'll think it's cute."

Black returned to the room to find Shy coming out of the bathroom with a towel wrapped around her. "Hello, Cassandra."

"Hi. Where you been?"

"Did you miss me?"

"Yes."

"You been up long?" Mike asked.

"No. I woke up thinking that I was gonna get some."

"Sorry. I had something I had to do."

"So I got up and took a shower. Since you wouldn't let me bring any clothes, I rinsed out the essentials. Which brings up another point. Where are my clothes?" Shy asked as Mike sat down next to her on the bed.

"I sent your clothes to the laundry. Then I went to the International Bazaar and bought something for you to wear."

He was about to show her the dress when Shy said, "Time-out. You went shopping? But you hate to shop. Never mind. Let's see what you bought." She was prepared to see something black and was pleasantly surprised. "Black, I love it. It's beautiful. What else did you buy?"

"I got us some swimwear and some shorts for me," Mike said, showing her the swimwear.

"Thank you, baby. This means more to me than anything else you've done. You hate shopping, but you got up and went shopping for me. That is so . . ." Shy was unable to complete her sentence when she saw the shorts set he bought for himself. "No, you didn't buy us matching outfits."

"Yours is white and mine's black," Mike said.

"You know what I'm talking about. They both have yellow birds on them. That is so romantic," Shy said as Mike got up and began to undress.

"I started not to get it, but I knew you'd say that."

"Think you know me already, don't you?"

"No, but I'm learning more every day. I'm going to take a shower so we can get out of here."

"No, you're not. *We're* going to take a shower," she said, following Mike to the bathroom. The shower was small, but that was all right with them. It gave them one more excuse to be close to each other. They took turns bathing one another and then toweled each other down. Mike got dressed while Shy pondered what to do with her hair.

"This has all the feel of a ponytail day." Shy put on her bra and reached for her panties.

"You don't need those," Mike said, taking them away from her.

"Why not?" she asked.

"They'll just be in the way," he said with a smile.

"There goes that slick West Indian smile again," Shy said, putting on her dress. "Zip me up and we'll be ready to go."

"What do you want to do first, Cassandra?" he asked as he zipped up her dress.

"What do you think? I want to eat," she said, turning around. "So how do I look?"

"Outstanding as usual. Now let's get outta here. We have just enough time to have lunch at the Princess."

Another cab ride passed quickly, and they found themselves at the Bahama Princess Hotel. By the time they arrived, most of the crowd had departed, so they requested a table by the window. They were seated, and before long a waiter arrived. Naturally, Mike ordered champagne to go with their meal. "Dom Pérignon of course," Shy said in anticipation of his order.

"No, this seems more like a Bollinger type of day. What do you think?" he asked, turning to the waiter.

"Excellent choice, sir," he remarked.

Sampling items from the large variety of foods, Shy came across something she couldn't identify but tried anyway. "This is good. What is it?"

"That, my love, is steamed conch."

"What is conch?" she inquired.

"Shellfish. This is conch chowder, and that is conch salad."

"You must like this stuff," she said between mouthfuls.

"As a matter of fact, I love it. It's a legendary Bahamian aphrodisiac."

"I don't think either one of us need any help there."

In the period following lunch, Mike asked what she wanted to do next. Shy answered sheepishly, "I wanna play tourist for a while and go shopping."

Mike looked at her. "Okay," he said. "On two conditions: one, that we go to one other tourist spot, and two, that I don't have to go with you."

Shy frowned and folded her arms. "Why can't you go with me? I promise I'll go easy on you."

Mike folded his arms and frowned. "Baby, please, I've already done the shopping thing once today. And besides it will give me a chance to make some arrangements." Shy agreed after Mike promised to go shopping with her before they left the island. They arranged to meet in an hour, both of them knowing it would be closer to an hour and a half.

He left Shy at the bazaar and went to see a friend of his named Percival to make transportation arrangements. Percival was a handsome man in his early fifties who had a way with women. He ran a charter boat service and rented cars on the island. Mike asked Percival to borrow a car for a couple of days. Also, Mike wanted him to meet them later that afternoon on the beach in Williamstown to take them out in his boat. Percival told Mike that it would be no problem to take them out on the boat. However, he didn't have a rental available.

"What about the Benzo?" Mike asked.

After Percival talked a little shit, he handed Mike the keys to his Mercedes-Benz 450SL convertible.

"Thanks. I promise not to dog it," Mike said as he raced the engine and sped away to pick up Shy.

Mike arrived at the prearranged spot. However, Shy was not there. He got out and leaned on the car. Not too much time passed before Shy arrived with an armful of bags. Shy got in the car and showed Mike what she had bought for them as they drove. "So what tourist trap are you taking me to?"

"Trust me. I'm sure a rare beauty like you can appreciate rare beauty."

Mike took her to the Garden of the Groves. They parked and entered through the gate. Mike took her by the hand, quickly pointing out the museum on his right as they went down the path on his left. A few short steps later, they were standing on a platform watching the flamingos. Shy looked around her. "I love flamingos. They are so beautiful. I love watching them move. It's like they're tiptoeing through the water." She laughed.

"They're so delicate and graceful, like you, Cassandra."

"Flattery will get you everywhere, Mr. Black. Mike Black." She smiled.

"Don't tell me. Bond fan, too?"

Shy smiled her response as he led her back down the path. "What's that building?" she asked as they approached a chapel.

He stopped at the door, smiled his response, and led her inside.

Shy scanned the room quickly. "You trying to give me a hint?"

"I told you, not this week."

"I know, I know. Next week maybe," she said, turning quickly and leaving the chapel. They walked through the array of flora and color. She stopped to admire their beauty and bask in their scent. Mike stopped to admire Shy.

"You ever think about getting married, Cassandra?" he asked as they walked.

"Once. And I promised myself I'd never even consider it again."

"Ricardo?"

"Good guess. What about you?" she asked, anticipating another sad story about Regina.

"Never," he lied quickly, smiling to himself as he thought about Bobby almost wrecking the car the last time he divulged that piece of information. He was confident that telling Shy wouldn't produce a similar effect. But why risk it?

Shy paused on the bridge to look at their reflection in the water.

"Your smile," he said. "You look extremely happy, Cassandra."

"That's because I am," she said quietly as they continued down the path. "I've never done anything like this before. Just up and go like this. When I was a little girl, I used to say I was gonna make a lot of money so I could travel, see the world, and shop of course. Well, I got the shopping part down to a science. I've been to Aruba with an asshole. I've been to Jersey, naturally, L.A., Miami, and New Orleans, but I've never done anything like this."

"Why not?"

"I got a business to run."

"So do I. That never stopped me."

"I'm not spontaneous like you are. I'm a planner."

"So am I. That never stops me."

"So I guess I have no excuse."

"What good is having money if you don't enjoy it?" Mike laughed out loud when he said it.

"What so funny?"

"I asked myself that same question a couple of weeks ago. Then I met you."

After leaving the garden, they proceeded to the beach. Shy enjoyed the scenery as Mike drove. Although she was having a good time, her mind was still on business. Who would want to do this to her and why? She knew that she would have to deal with it when they returned to the city. Deep down inside, Shy wanted Mike to handle this entire matter for her. She looked over at him. *He always appears so in control of everything.* Shy admired his strength.

Not wanting to allow it to get in the way of her enjoying herself with Mike, she forced her problems to the back of her mind. For the first time in a long while, she was happy. Still, she was curious about why he hated drug dealers. She was about to ask him when they arrived at the beach. They changed into their swimsuits in the car, resisting the temptation to make love. They got out of the car and walked toward the water. There were a few people on the beach. Some kids ran around, playing in the sand. Mike spread out a blanket, and they sat down under a tree.

Mike stood and picked Shy up, cradling her in his arms. Shy screamed, but she was loving every minute of it. He ran into the water, then stopped and threw her in. Shy seemed to enjoy getting dunked, so he went for it again. Mike swam under the water and came up under her, picking her up, kissed her, and then threw her in. For an hour or so, they played in the water like children. Mike told Shy to look up so she could watch someone parasailing. Shy said that she would like to try that before they left. Mike saw a speedboat approaching. As promised, Percival had come to take them out on the ocean.

"Come on, we're going," he said to Shy. While they gathered their things, Percival stopped the boat in the shallow water. "Percival, this is Cassandra."

"Hi, Percival."

"You didn't tell me she was a goddess, Black," Percival said, kissing her hand.

"You're right. Why do you think that is?" Mike said, helping Shy into the boat.

"I'm disappointed, Black," Percival said while he loaded their things into the boat. "You'd think that you didn't trust me around your woman."

"Right."

"Where are we going?" Shy asked as they sped away.

"Nowhere fast," Percival replied.

They cruised around the ocean for a couple of hours. Percival brought along a gallon jug of Bahama Mamas. Shy said that it tasted like Kool-Aid. Mike tried to warn her that it would sneak up on her, so to be careful. "Bahama Mamas will get you fucked up," Mike said, but she didn't seem to care. The afternoon passed quickly and was filled with laughter, good conversation, and plenty of Bahama Mamas. They got quietly drunk.

When Percival returned them to the beach, most of the people were gone. Shy told Mike that she was in the mood. "For more conch, that is."

"I know just the place," Mike replied. Returning to the car, they changed clothes again and proceeded to Williamstown. Shortly thereafter, they arrived at Traveler's Rest, home of the Annual Conch Cracking

Contest. "On Easter Monday, they have a conch cracking contest here," Mike explained.

"We need to mark that day on our calendar for sure," Shy said as they went in.

After stuffing themselves with conch chowder, conch salad, conch fritters, crab and rice, and sheep's tongue, they drove around Williamstown. They parked the car and walked around, ending up back on the beach in time to watch the sunset. The view was absolutely breathtaking.

"Baby, this is so beautiful. I wish we could stay forever," Shy said, watching the sun disappear from the sky.

"I've got nowhere to be and nothing to do. But some of us can't say that," Mike replied, knowing that he wanted to be anywhere Shy was. Spending the rest of his life with Shy on the island of love was a dream. Mike never was much on dreams. However, he never expected to be in the Bahamas on the beach with a woman he loved, thinking about the future. *Things change.* Until recently, he thought love was something for suckers, trick boys, and weak men.

"Look at that," Shy said, walking away.

"Look at what?"

"That house. It's adorable. And it's for sale," Shy said, walking around the house and looking through the windows. She walked around back. "I wish we could see inside, baby. Baby? Where are you?"

The back door opened. Shy screamed.

"It's only me, Cassandra. Come on in."

They walked throughout the house. Shy played interior decorator, describing in detail what she would do with each room. "And this would be our room."

"Since we claimed the house, we have to christen it."

"Whatever do you mean, Mr. Black?"

"Bend over and grab your ankles, and I'll show you, Ms. Sims."

After making one last pass through the house, they walked back to the car and returned to the hotel in Lucaya. After a shower and a change of clothes, they were on the go again. Shy wore a turquoise hand-dyed bias-cut dress in silk gauze with scarves to match. She laid out a silk shorts set for him to put on. It was midnight blue. He put it on without a word.

Mike put the top down on the Benz. In honor of that afternoon's attire, they drank Yellow Birds all night. Before the night was through, they had been to every bar in every hotel and danced at every nightclub they could find. They even crashed a private beach party. Quickly they became the talk of the party. People were amazed at how even and rich their tans were. When the lady whose party they had crashed approached them, Shy told Mike to let her handle it.

"I met John earlier on the beach, but I don't see him. Anyway, he said it would be all right if we came. I hope we're not imposing," Shy said, walking away with the lady. Mike watched as Shy laughed and talked with the lady for the next ten minutes as if she had known her all her life. When she returned, she said, "If there is one thing I learned from Chicago, it's how to talk to people."

"You can turn that on anytime you feel like it, can't you?" Mike asked, ordering two more Yellow Birds from the waiter as he passed.

"I sure can. You control the conversation by making people feel like they're in control of the situation."

They stayed long enough to finish their drinks and dance one more time. At least the band was good. The evening ended with them sitting quietly on the beach wrapped in each other's arms.

***

They lay in bed late the following morning.

"So what do you want to do today, Cassandra?" Mike asked.

"Spend the day with you."

"I'm really starting to like you, Cassandra."

"Starting? Like? You know you love me. Why you tryin' to front?"

"I don't want to give you a big head. But I see it's too late," Mike said.

"So what are you tryin' to say?"

"That I love you."

"I love you too, but yesterday is going to be hard to top."

"Try me."

"Okay. Something romantic," Shy said, rolling into his arms.

"One romantic evening, coming up. Let's go to New Providence."

"Where?"

"Nassau."

"What's in Nassau?"

"Trust me."

Without delay, Mike made arrangements to fly to Nassau. A plane was chartered, and by three o'clock that afternoon, they were on the streets of Nassau. Mike hadn't spent as much time in Nassau as he had in Freeport. "So all I know here are the tourist spots."

"Then why are we here?" Shy asked, hands placed firmly on her hips.

"Trust me."

He didn't know anyone in Nassau to lend him a Benz, so they had to settle for a rental car. After checking into a beachfront condo at the Grand Hotel, they proceeded to drive around the countryside. Shy rested her head on Mike's shoulder, and they just talked. They visited the waterfall at the 66 steps and drove around Lyford Cay. They started back to the city just as the sun began to set.

He parked the car and went around to open the door for Shy. Holding his hand as they walked, Shy said, "This really has been a nice afternoon. Just you and me. Kinda quiet, you know what I mean? I couldn't think of a more romantic way to spend the day."

He put his arm around her. He never thought that something as simple as a quiet ride together would be so romantic, still knowing that he had saved the best for last. "I ain't through. But what I am is hungry."

"This is gonna sound corny, but you took the words right out of my mouth," Shy said as they wandered into the first restaurant they saw and had dinner.

Leaving the restaurant after dark, they walked for a while when suddenly Mike said, "Wait here." He ran off down the street and around the corner.

Shy wondered where he was going. She started to follow him or at least peek around the corner. She fought the impulse. She walked around the area, looking in a few store windows to pass the time. She turned around and looked up. There was Mike standing next to a horse-drawn carriage.

"Your carriage awaits you, Ms. Sims," Mike said, extending his hand to help her into the carriage.

"Oh, baby, this is so romantic," Shy said, kissing him on the cheek.

"I'm glad you're happy," he said, squeezing her hand a little tighter. "I love to see you smile. Just like a kid with a new toy."

"I am. Only my new toy is tall, dark, and very sexy."

The coachman rode them around Nassau into the morning hours, telling stories and pointing out some points of interest. He gave them a brief history lesson, even though at points their kissing prevented them from paying attention. He told them, "In 1492, Christopher Columbus made his first landing in the New World in the Bahamas on an island that was then inhabited by the Arawak Indians. He claimed it for Spain, naming it San Salvador. He also explained that the island was a stronghold for buccaneers and pirates, most notably the infamous Blackbeard."

"No relation," Mike said.

As the evening wore on, the coachman stopped talking and left the lovebirds to their own resources. He dropped them off at their car. Mike jumped down, and then he turned to help Shy.

"Baby, this has been the most romantic day I've ever spent. There is no place I'd rather be than right here with you," Shy said.

"I feel the same way too."

"I wish it never had to end."

"Why does it have to?" Mike asked.

"'Cause, like you said, one of us has someplace to be," she replied, walking away and looking very sad. She couldn't stay and she knew it.

"What do you wanna do now?" Mike asked.

Suddenly the smile returned to her face as she turned and walked toward him. "I wanna make love," she said, putting her arms around him. "I wanna make love until the sun comes up." Mike drew her close and kissed her passionately. "I wanna fall asleep in your arms, wake up, and make love again. Do you think you can handle that?"

"I know I can," Mike replied.

"You're pretty sure of yourself, aren't you?"

"Self-confidence never was one of my weaknesses," Mike said, walking to the car.

Things went pretty much as they had discussed for the rest of the early morning hours and well into the afternoon. Afterward, they debated whether to call room service or go out. They settled on the hotel restaurant. The closer it came to Saturday morning, the more Shy thought about her situation. The last three days were wonderful. Mike was wonderful. Still, there was one thing that bothered her. "Mind if I ask you a question?" Shy asked.

"Shoot."

"What did you mean when you told Hector that as a matter of principle you wouldn't guarantee my deal?" she asked.

"You know I don't do that type of business, Cassandra. And as a matter of principle, I don't like having my name associated with it."

"Yeah, yeah, I know all that, but why?" Before he could answer, Shy said, "Everyone's been telling me that you hate dealers, but here you are with me."

"What somebody does for a living is none of my business as long as it doesn't conflict with my business. One has very little to do with the other. I'm in love with you for who you are. I just don't want no part of your occupation."

"The question still stands. Why?" she asked again. "You're not going to answer me, are you?"

Mike stared into her eyes and began eating. Then he said, almost as an afterthought, "When we were coming up, there was another member of the crew."

"Was?" Shy asked.

"Her name was Vickie."

"What happened to her?"

"I killed her."

"What?" Shy said in shock.

"I killed her."

Shy stared at him for a while, expecting an explanation of that one. All types of things ran through her mind. Perhaps she was wrong about him. Maybe he was as vicious as his reputation after all.

"Comin' up, all of us knew where we were goin' and were moving toward it. Perry and Wanda were in college. But not Vickie. She just wanted to have fun. Hangin' with me, Bobby, Nick, and Jamaica was all she wanted to do."

"Who is this Nick y'all keep talkin' about?"

"Nick came up with us."

"What happened to him?"

"He joined the army, got into some black bag stuff. You'll meet him. Anyway, we took care of her. All of us did. She had a key to the crib, the whole nine, and that was cool. We had it like that, and she was down with us."

"How did you kill her, Black?" Shy asked seriously.

"I've never done cocaine in my life, but back in the day I would always keep some around 'cause hoes—I mean, women—would freak for it."

"You have a real problem with calling women hoes," Shy remarked.

"Until I met you."

"Go on."

"We were hangin' out one night. I saw André, and he gave me some pure. I didn't get home until like nine the next morning. I was getting ready to put a cut on it, but I was blasted and didn't feel like it. So I threw the bag on the coffee table and crashed on the couch. I had been asleep a couple of hours, I guess, when Vickie came in. We kicked it for a minute, and then I passed out again. I woke up again and decided to get in the bed. But the door to my room was locked. I knocked on the door, but she didn't answer. After a while, I kicked the door in. I found her lying on the floor, naked, with the pipe still in her hand."

"Was she dead?" Shy asked.

"Yes."

"What did you do?"

"I called 911. Ambulance came, and so did the cops. They wanted to charge me, but André took care of that."

"I'm sorry," Shy said, feeling bad that she had pushed it.

"Don't sweat it. How would you know that I killed her?"

"You didn't kill her, baby. But being the type of guy you are, you tortured yourself about it."

"I did. André had to send me away for a couple of months 'cause I just started killin' everybody he'd send me at. That's when I really earned the name." Mike stood up and reached for Shy's hand. They walked out together. "Vickie and Jamaica were real close. He took it badly too. He got off into that heroin strong after that. And you see how that turned out."

"I didn't know. I shoulda let it go."

"Don't look like that, baby. You look so sad. Now we have to do something to recapture the mood. I know." Mike began walking faster and grabbed Shy by the hand.

"You think you got me figured out?" Shy said as they approached the beach.

"Not yet. But I'm learning more and more every day," Mike said. He was right. The beach brought the smile back to her face. Then it started to rain.

"'Walkin' in the Rain with the One I Love,'" Shy said.

"Love Unlimited."

"Ever since I heard that song, I always wanted to do this," Shy said as raindrops ran down her cheeks. "Did you arrange this too?"

"I can't take credit for this one. Changing the weather is more than I can handle," Mike said as they walked for a while longer. "There's something else I like doing in the rain."

"Me too. I'll race you back to the condo."

By the time they got there, they were both drenched. "One more excuse to be naked," Shy joked.

They both began to remove their wet clothes. Shy took her .22 out of her back pocket and laid it down on the nightstand. Mike asked, "I've been meaning to ask you, do you know how to use that thing?"

"Yes, baby, I know how to use it."

"You ever kill anybody with it?"

"No."

"Think you could?"

"I don't know. I've been thinking about that for a while. More recently, for obvious reasons. But hopefully I'll never have to find out. I'm no gangster, baby. Maybe that's why I'm having all these problems. Maybe you can give me some pointers?" Shy asked.

"Maybe tomorrow. I'm still on vacation."

Later that evening, they chartered a boat and sailed back to Freeport. The dream ended when Shy saw Pete on Saturday morning.

CHAPTER TWENTY

Upon arrival in New York on Saturday evening, Mike and Shy took a cab to Cuisine. They sat quietly in the back seat of the cab, holding hands, neither one wanting to be back in New York. Freeport was beautiful. Shy wished they could have stayed forever. However, she felt she had no choice. She had to return and face her responsibilities. Staying in the Bahamas seemed too much like running away. Had she chosen that course, she would not be able to face herself. Now the reality of her situation came back into focus. First, there was the small matter of the quarter of a million dollars she owed Angelo. Although she felt that Black planned on covering her debt, it wasn't his responsibility. Shy became determined to find her attackers and destroy them before they destroyed her.

Mike had called Sylvia from the airport and told her to have Freeze and Kenny, who had finally returned from Detroit, meet him there. Shy called Jack and told him to do the same. The last time Kenny called, he told Sylvia that he had a few strong leads. Mike was anxious to hear what he had. Hopefully, there would be something, anything, that would lead him to whoever was trying to do harm to Shy.

"Hello, Sylvia."

"Welcome back, Black. Everyone's waiting for you."

"Good. Sylvia, this is Shy," Mike said as he passed her desk.

"It's nice to finally meet you," Sylvia said.

"Same here," Shy said as she rushed past her.

"You had a call from someone named Tony. He said he would meet you here."

"When he gets here, please send him in."

They entered the office to find Kenny and Jack seated in the two chairs in front of Mike's desk. Freeze was sitting behind the desk with his feet up. "What's up, Black?" Freeze said as he got up from the desk, taking a seat on the couch.

"Did you enjoy the vacation, Kenny?" Mike said as he went behind his desk. After saying hello to Jack, Shy sat down on the couch next to Freeze.

"I was working, Black," Kenny said, pleading his case.

"Okay then, working vacation." Mike sat down at his desk. "Long as you been gone, you should know who it is, where they are, and what they're havin' for dinner tonight."

"Leon wasn't easy to track down."

"Nothing about this is," Shy said matter-of-factly. "What'd you find out?"

"What I got is the address of an art studio in Manhattan. This is where the first meet was supposed to be. The way I got it is that whoever paid for the hit met Leon there a little more than a month ago."

"That's about when we first got hit. What else?" Shy got up from the couch and stood before Kenny, demanding more information.

"After that, Leon goes back to Detroit. The hit was set up then. But it didn't get paid for until a week or so later in Detroit."

"You know where that was?"

"No."

"You get a description?" Shy asked.

"Not a good one. Black man wearin' a hat and sunglasses, about five eight, maybe five ten."

"That's it?" Mike asked.

"There's a place in Brooklyn, a chop shop. Guy there named James Kerns is supposed to have arranged the meet with Leon."

"Shy, that's the place you sent Tony that night. That guy Tim just played him off. But now we got a name," Jack said.

Shy turned and said to Mike, "E said he had a tip that someone there knew something about it. When Tony went there, he thought it was a setup, like they were expecting me to be there."

"Freeze, you ever hear of James Kerns?"

Freeze shook his head.

"Check it out. See if you can get something on him. Then—" Mike said.

Shy turned quickly. She looked at Mike, and then she leaned across the desk. "Baby, let me handle my business."

Mike leaned back in the chair with his hands up in surrender. Shy turned to Freeze. "Freeze, I would appreciate it if you checked him out, but you don't go out there without Tony."

Freeze looked at Mike, who nodded in approval.

"Jack, let's go check out that studio." He got up and started for the door.

"Freeze, Kenny, would you two excuse me? I wanna talk to Black."

Mike motioned for them to leave. Shy followed them to the door and closed it behind them. "I'm sorry for cutting you off, but this isn't your problem," Shy said as she walked over to him and sat in his lap. "I appreciate your help, but I gotta do this."

"I don't want you to get hurt," he said.

Shy kissed him. "I can't hide behind you. So don't have anybody following us. I'll be all right with Jack. And besides," Shy said with a smile as she got up and started for the door, "don't you got something to do?"

"I get your point. But you call me here as soon as you leave there."

"I promise."

"Send Freeze in for me please."

"I will," Shy said, closing the door behind her.

She and Jack made their way across the restaurant floor and out to the street. As they walked to Jack's car, Tony pulled up in his BMW and walked toward them. Shy told Tony the information Kenny had gotten in Detroit. "I want you to go back out there with Freeze. Where's E?" Shy asked.

"He's makin' the rounds. We should be ready to do business in a couple of days," Tony replied.

"Cool. You beep him. Let him know what's going on. After you check this Kerns guy out, you call me on Jack's cell phone," Shy ordered before getting in the car with Jack. Tony went inside to get Freeze.

When Jack started to pull away, a woman got out of a car that had parked a short way down the street. As she walked closer, Shy could see that it was Melinda.

"Slow down, Jack. I wanna make sure this bitch sees me." They drove past slowly, but Melinda wasn't looking. "Honk the horn," Shy said to Jack.

Melinda looked at the car, and Shy mouthed the words, "He's mine," then motioned to Jack to drive on. Melinda looked away and went inside.

While Shy was marking her territory outside, Freeze returned to Mike's office to see what he wanted. "You wanted to see me, Black?"

"Yeah, I do want you to check out that spot in Brooklyn, but I want you to check out this Ricardo guy first."

"Who is that?"

"Some guy she used to go with. Tony will know how to find him."

"Done." Freeze paused as he was about to leave the office. "Yo, Black, we gettin' back in the dope game?"

"You lost your mind? Hell no!" The question made him angry, but he knew it had to be answered. "Sit down, Freeze. Look, I know that we been committing a lot of time and resources to this, but we are by no means gettin' back in the game." He gestured with his hands to emphasize his point.

"Just wanted to know if I should start recruitin'. Yo, watch out when you see Bobby. He's gonna come at you hard about this, so be ready."

"Yeah, right. I'm sure he won't be the only one." He knew Wanda would have some more to say on the subject. "Get outta here. But yo, Freeze, good lookin' out."

"Yo, ain't that what you pay me the phat cash for?" Freeze said, closing the door to the office.

After leaving Mike's office, Freeze approached Tony at the bar. "You ready?"

"Yeah, let's go."

"Yo, man, Black wants us to check out some guy named Ricardo. You know how to find him?"

"Ricardo? Yeah, I know where he lives. After he dissed her, Shy had to see who he dropped her for. So me and her followed him 'til we saw her. She was kinda fly. Anyway, they got a house in White Plains." Tony thought for a minute about the type of guy Ricardo was. "Now that I think about it, I wouldn't put this past him. He's too weak to do it himself, but he got money."

"Let's do this," Freeze said, starting for the door.

"Hold up. Let me call Shy, tell her where we're goin'," Tony said.

"No. She don't need to know all that. Let's just go do this."

"You're right. She'll just start beefin' with a nigga."

CHAPTER TWENTY-ONE

"Hello, Black," Melinda said as she entered the office.

"Hello, Melinda," Mike said with the phone in his hand.

"It's good to see you." She sat down on the couch and crossed her legs.

"I was just about to call you," he said as he put the receiver back in the cradle.

"To tell me it's over?" she said, nodding her head and rocking her leg in perfect rhythm.

"Yes," Mike said without emotion.

"I knew it wouldn't take long," Melinda said in much the same manner.

"I'm gonna order dinner. Want me to order something for you?"

"If I'm gonna get kicked to the curb, it might as well be over steak and lobster."

Mike called the kitchen and ordered their meals, then escorted Melinda to his table. Diane brought Mike a drink and asked Melinda if she wanted a cocktail with her meal. "Double black Russian," Melinda replied. "So I saw your little drug dealer girlfriend on the way in. Is she the one?"

"Yes."

"I thought so. I always knew this would happen. I just didn't think it would be this soon."

"This isn't easy for me, Melinda."

"I know. And I'm not gonna make it any easier for you. It was easy for you to fuck her. So what's the big deal? What's so special about her?"

"I love her."

"You love her. Ain't that a bitch. You love her. Well, I love you."

"What?"

"I know I never said it before, but I do."

"I never knew." Genuinely caught off guard, he continued, "I never knew how you felt. I always thought you were in it for the money."

"It wasn't your money, baby. Sex maybe, but not money."

Mike laughed. "We were good together."

"She any good?"

"She's not on your level, but nobody is," Mike lied as Diane returned to the table with Melinda's drink. She placed it in front of her. Melinda thanked her and took a sip.

"You treated me better than any man I've ever known. And I'm not just talkin' about sex. You always treated me with respect. Never called me anything but my name. Never raised a hand to me. You didn't even lie to me. That's what made me love you. You made me feel like I was somebody. Somebody special."

"You are special, and I do care about you, but—"

Before Mike could finish, Melinda said, "But you don't love me. You never did. I knew you messed around, but you always came back. I thought that you would learn to love me. That you would sorta grow into it, you know. And you would love me, just like I love you."

"Why didn't you ever say any of this before?"

"I thought it would run you off."

"Maybe."

"I always thought I'd have more time. I just never counted on you falling in love," Melinda said tearfully. "I gotta go, Black." Melinda got up quietly from the table. "It ain't over between us, Black."

Diane brought their meal. Mike watched Melinda walk quickly out of the restaurant. He looked at Diane, who had started to serve. Mike held up his hand to stop her. "I don't think the lady will be joining me. Take mine to the office."

"You okay, Black?"

"No."

Mike finished his drink, got up from the table, and returned to his office. He sat on the couch, put his feet up on the chair, and closed his eyes. Mike picked up the remote, turned on the CD player, and pressed the random button. As the music began to play, there was a knock at the door. "Who is it?"

"Diane. I got your dinner."

"Come on in." Diane came in, carrying a tray. "Just put it anywhere," Mike said, and Diane placed the tray on the desk.

"You want me to fix you a drink?" she asked, picking up the bottle of Remy from the credenza.

"Thanks," Mike said without opening his eyes.

"You broke that girl's heart, didn't you?"

"Yeah."

"Feelin' kinda shitty about it, too?" Diane asked in a very dry tone.

"Yeah."

"Good."

Mike opened his eyes.

"You should feel shitty when you break someone's heart. I wouldn't have any respect for you if you didn't." Diane handed him his drink and started for the door. "I stopped in the kitchen and got you some extra shrimp scampi."

"Thanks, Diane. For everything."

Diane closed the door leaving Mike alone with the scampi, the cognac, and Coltrane playing a slow melodic tune. "This is depressing the shit out of me." He got up and turned it off, picking up the case to see what was playing. "'Like Someone in Love.' Figures."

He took the cover off the tray, picked up a shrimp, and took a bite. Diane had hit right at the heart of it. Mike felt shitty. He really felt bad about breaking Melinda's heart. He had actually convinced himself that she was only with him for the money. Mike felt insensitive. Since he had broken up with Regina, just about every woman he had met was all about the money. No reason to think Melinda was any different. That was how she came off. Maybe at first that was how it was. Perhaps as time went on her feelings changed. Now he felt as if he had used her.

Although he felt badly about hurting Melinda, Mike knew he was in love with Shy. He wondered where she was and if she was safe.

CHAPTER TWENTY-TWO

As Jack drove downtown, Shy stared aimlessly out the window. Every now and then, she would look behind her to see if Jap or somebody was following them. Although she had told Mike that she had to handle this, there was a part of her that wished he could make it all go away. Shy slowly came to the realization that this was way over her head. So far Black had saved her life twice, and he intervened when Hector told her no money, no product. It was Black who sent Kenny to Detroit, providing them with the first real leads they had. This was Black's domain, and he excelled at it.

They arrived at the studio and went inside. The studio was open to the public, and patrons of the arts wandered around, admiring the assembled collection. Shy and Jack split up and walked around the studio, looking at the art and checking out the people. When Jack stopped to admire a painting, Shy wandered over to him.

They stood quietly for a moment. Finally, Jack said, "This might sound like a stupid question, but I'm gonna go with it anyway. Just what are we looking for?"

Shy started to answer, but then she thought about it. "Just follow my lead," she said, not wanting to let on that she really wasn't sure. They stood in front of a large portrait of palm trees with the sun setting on the horizon. As Shy stood there, she was taken back to the Bahamas. Her daydream was interrupted by the presence of a lady standing next to her.

"It is a fine work, isn't it?" The woman turned and faced Shy with a smile and an extended hand. "Hi, my name is Wendy. I'm the curator here."

Shy smiled a fake smile and shook her hand. "Hi, my name is Sandy. It's a pleasure to meet you, Wendy, and my yes, it is absolutely breathtaking."

Jack rolled his eyes and excused himself. "That girl's somethin' else," he said as he wandered away. As Jack continued to look around, he noticed two men who didn't look like patrons of the arts coming out of a door in the back of the studio. He positioned himself in an area of the studio where he could watch Shy and the door without drawing attention to himself. Jack looked on as Shy continued to walk and talk art with Wendy.

A white woman entered the studio and headed straight for the door. Five minutes later, she came out and left. Jack watched as the pattern continued in much the same manner for the next fifteen minutes. He walked over to Shy, who was still listening to Wendy run her mouth.

"It took him over two years. And believe it or not, the artist painted this entire canvas in the nude," Wendy said of a rendering of two birds flying through some clouds.

"Sandy," Jack interrupted. "Wendy, would you excuse us for a moment? There's a phenomenal portrait that I must share with her," he said, practically dragging Shy away.

"I think I know which one you're talking about. It has the same effect on me," Wendy said as they walked away quickly.

"Thanks. That was by far the most boring woman I've ever met," she said, trying to shake herself out of it. "What's up?"

"I think they rollin' here," Jack said quietly.

"What? Where?" Shy said in disbelief.

Jack pointed at the door. "I been standing here watching people come in, go straight in there, and come out a few minutes later."

"That don't mean they're rollin'."

"Shy, I know a stop and cop when I see one. Just watch," Jack said, and he walked away, leaving Shy to see for herself. She watched as two black men came in the studio and went straight for the door. One of them went in while the other stood outside like a posted sentry. He stood and watched Shy watching him. The other emerged, and the two left quickly, the sentry pointing at Shy as they left. Jack rejoined Shy. "See what I mean? Them boys probably think you're a cop and this place is under surveillance."

"You're right. I wonder if they're rollin' with our product," Shy said angrily.

"Probably," Jack replied.

"Let's get outta here," Shy said.

She and Jack left the studio, got in Jack's car, and drove away. "You want me to put someone down here?"

"No," Shy said, still fuming at the thought that they were selling her product. "I don't want to tip our hand. I think we finally got an ace. See if you can find out who's supplying them."

Shy picked up the phone and called Black at Cuisine. The night receptionist told her that Black had left a half hour ago and didn't say where he was going. She tried calling him at Impressions.

"Impressions, how may I direct your call?" the receptionist said.

"Mike Black, please," Shy said.

"Mr. Black isn't in. Can somebody else help you?"

"Is Mr. Ray in?" Shy asked.

"Who should I say is calling?"

"Shy."

"Hold, please."

The receptionist placed her on hold. Shy wondered if Black was somewhere with Melinda. If he was with her, was he telling her that it was over between them, or had they continued their sexual relationship?

"Hello, Shy. How was your trip?" Bobby asked.

"I had the time of my life. I hated to leave," Shy replied.

"You know Mike's not here. So what can I do for you?" Bobby asked.

"Please tell him it's very important that I talk to him."

"Are you all right? Where are you?"

"I'm fine, Bobby. I'm in Manhattan, but I'm on my way home," Shy replied.

"Who's with you? Do you want me to send someone?"

"Not you too. Jack's with me, and no, I don't want you to send somebody. Have you talked to Black since we got back?" Shy asked.

"No," Bobby answered.

Shy started to ask if Melinda was there but thought that was a little pushy. "Well, like I said, I'm on my way home. Just give him that message for me."

"You got it. Hey, what are you doing for dinner tomorrow?"

"I don't have any plans. Why?"

"If you're not doin' anything, why don't you come to my house for dinner? My wife, Pam, is dying to meet you."

Shy smiled. She wanted to meet Pam anyway. "I would love to meet your wife. But let me talk to Black first."

"What, you can't come without him?"

"It's not that."

"Then we'll see you tomorrow," Bobby said.

"Okay, what time?" Shy asked.

"Seven, okay?"

"See you at seven. Tell Pam I'm looking forward to meeting her." Shy hung up the phone. She looked at Jack.

"Goin' to meet the family?" he asked.

"Ha, ha, ha. Very funny. Just shut up and take me home. I wonder why Tony hasn't called."

CHAPTER TWENTY-THREE

Tony drove along the winding road of the Hutchinson River Parkway on the way to Ricardo's White Plains home. Freeze sat listening as Tony tried to impress him. He talked about his being robbed and what he was gonna do when he found the bandits. It wasn't working.

Finally, Freeze grew weary and asked, "So what's the deal with this Ricardo guy anyway?"

"He used to go with Shy," Tony said as he drove. "They came to a parting of the ways about a year ago."

"I know that. Black wouldn't send me out here for nothing. What happened?"

"He got married."

"And?"

"He waited until the week before to tell her."

Freeze started laughing. "Oh, shit."

"He broke that shit on her one night at the club outta nowhere." Tony began laughing too. "Shy didn't even know he had another woman."

"Must be more to it than that."

"Hold up, it gets better. After he tells her that, kid says that she can still see him on the down-low after he's married."

"I know Shy musta freaked," Freeze said.

"Yeah, Shy was about to shoot him when we got to her. When she told us that shit, Jack snatched him out his chair, and we beat him down. Dragged him outside, beat him down some more."

"Yeah, I remember hearin' about that. Where was E while all this beatin' down was goin' on?" Freeze asked.

"He grabbed the gun from her. Then he stayed inside with Shy. She was trippin' pretty hard for a while behind that, cryin' and shit. E helped her get through a lot of that. He got a real type a thing for Shy, even though he'll never admit it."

"Oh, really?" Freeze said, making a mental note of that comment. "I think that gives Ricardo a reason to want to get back at her."

"Yeah, we fucked him up pretty bad," Tony replied. "All right, so we know he got some heart. Takes heart to say some illin' shit like that to a woman. Especially one who's armed. What else you got?"

"He was like this smooth-talkin' businessman. Had a little job on Wall Street. He was paid though, always had mad cash on him. But the more I think about it, he used to always try to involve himself in our business. Almost cost us big time one night."

"Wannabe gangster," Freeze said, shaking his head.

"That was him, real wannabe," Tony said.

Like you, Freeze said to himself. Freeze didn't have a lot of respect for Tony, or any of Shy's boys for that matter. Although they knew one another from junior high school, they weren't cool. Well, there was the time that girl came in the boys' bathroom with them, but other than that, they rarely spoke. Freeze always thought Tony was too soft.

They arrived at the house just after eight o'clock. Tony rang the bell as Freeze looked around the outside of the house. Ricardo's wife, Susan, answered the door.

"Hello. Is Ricardo home?" Tony said.

"Wait just a minute. I'll get him," Susan said, leaving the door cracked while she went for her husband. Freeze joined Tony at the door.

Shortly thereafter, Ricardo came to the door. He stuck his head out. "Tony, what are you doing here?" he asked.

"We wanna talk to you."

"Well, let's talk out here." Ricardo started out the door. "I don't want—"

Before Ricardo could finish what he was saying, Freeze pushed Ricardo in the house. "Nobody asked you what you don't want. Get inside."

"Honey, is everything all right?" Susan said, hearing the commotion. Freeze took out his gun and pointed it at Ricardo's head.

"Everything's fine, honey," Ricardo said, fearing for his life.

"Smart man. Now get in there," Freeze said, pushing him into the living room. "Sit down."

"What's this all about, Tony? I don't have much money here."

Freeze pulled a wad of money out of his pocket and slapped Ricardo in the face with it. "If I wanted your money, I'd be countin' it now, and you'd be dead," Freeze said calmly.

"Who are you?" Ricardo said.

Freeze sat down on the couch next to Ricardo. "We gonna cover this one time, okay?" He removed the silencer from his pocket. "Next time you say somethin' and nobody asked you nothin', we gonna have a problem, understand?" Freeze put the silencer on the gun.

Ricardo nodded his head.

"You know James Kerns, runs a chop shop in Brooklyn?" Tony said.

"No," Ricardo said, without taking his eyes off Freeze.

"What about Leon Thomas? You know him, don't you?" Tony asked.

"No, I never heard of him either. What's this about?" Ricardo asked, and with that Freeze chopped him in the head with the barrel of his gun.

"Look, Babalu, you ain't payin' attention. You don't ask shit here." Ricardo nodded his head again. Tony continued to ask Ricardo questions for a while, always receiving the same answer.

"I told you, I don't know anything about it!"

Appearing bored by it all, Freeze got up. He began to look around. "Nice artwork. You buy through a broker?"

"No, my wife bought all of it," Ricardo answered.

"You remember that night in Jersey when you almost blew that deal for us? You always wanted to play the role. Hey, you still carry around all that cash, Ricardo?" Tony asked.

"I knew that's what this was about," Ricardo said. Freeze began to move toward him. "No!" Ricardo said quickly. "I do all my transactions via credit card. I was just frontin' with that money. I would skim some of the interest off my clients' accounts at night and put it back in the morning."

Freeze said to Tony, "Go get Lucy. Get her purse, too."

Ricardo started to speak.

"Don't say it, Babalu." Freeze leaned over the couch and tapped Ricardo on the shoulder. "Hey, Ricky Ricardo, if you really love Lucy, you'll make sure she behaves herself. It's on you," Freeze said, pointing his gun at Ricardo.

Tony went upstairs, returning shortly with Susan and her purse. Seeing her husband sitting on the couch with a gun pointed at him, Susan ran and sat beside him. "Are you all right, honey?"

"I'm all right. Just be quiet and do what they say," he said to her.

"Lucy . . . I'm sorry, what's your name?" Freeze asked.

When Susan didn't answer him right away, Ricardo yelled, "Answer him!"

"Susan!" she cried out.

"Chill out, Susan. I'm not gonna hurt you," Freeze said calmly. He put away his gun. "I'm just gonna ask you two or three questions. Then I want you to get something for me. After that, we up outta here, okay?"

"Okay. Can I ask you what this is all about?" Susan asked.

"Come here, Susan. I'll be happy to tell you," Freeze said, taking her purse from Tony. Freeze waved her on as he walked into the dining room.

Ricardo looked at Susan. She looked at him. He looked terrified. Susan got up and followed Freeze into the dining room.

Freeze pulled out a chair for her at the table. "Please, sit down." Susan sat down at the table. She looked at Ricardo and smiled, seeming to enjoy seeing him so unsettled at what Freeze would tell her. Freeze spoke softly, "A former associate of your husband is having some problems. I need you to help me prove that he doesn't have anything to do with it."

"I understand," Susan said.

Ricardo yelled out, "He's lying!"

Freeze smiled. "Now see, you might wanna ask him about that and think about who's been lyin' to who."

"You can tell me," Susan said.

"No. That's between you and your husband. And I don't go there. Now, who buys your art? It really is a nice collection."

Susan looked at Freeze in disbelief that he asked about their art collection. She thought for a second. "I bought it all myself. I go to different galleries. I go to shows, some local, but most of it I bought in Europe. Why?"

"You and your husband ever been to a studio on Twenty-third Street in Manhattan?" Freeze asked, ignoring her question.

"I haven't. I can't say if Ricardo has. But I doubt it."

"Has he gone out of town in the last month or so?"

"No," replied a still-confused Susan.

"I want you to get your credit cards out and then go get the last statement for them, okay?" instructed Freeze.

"You want to see if there are any airline or hotel charges on them, don't you? Well, I can tell you now that there aren't," Susan said loud enough for Ricardo to hear her. She watched Ricardo squirm as she placed each of her many cards carefully on the table before Freeze. "I go over the statements very carefully, looking for unexplained charges like that. I've found them before. If this associate was a woman, would you tell me?" she whispered. Then she looked at Ricardo. "A couple of years ago there were some charges for plane tickets to Aruba."

When Tony heard "tickets to Aruba," he looked at Ricardo and started laughing, remembering Ricardo had taken Shy to Aruba one summer.

Susan got up from the table and led Freeze back through the living room, past Ricardo and into their office. "That's what this is about, isn't it, Ricardo? That little bitch you took to Aruba!"

Once in the office, Susan showed Freeze a statement for each of her credit cards. Freeze looked each one over carefully. Periodically Susan would ask Freeze questions about the story Ricardo told her of his trip to Aruba. Freeze ignored her until he had satisfied himself with the statements. "He told me that he had been laundering money for her. Please, can't you tell me anything?" Susan pleaded.

Freeze took Susan's hand. "Look, Susan, I don't know anything about the lady and your husband or what business they had. I'm just doin' a favor for a friend. You seem like a nice person, too nice to have to get involved in somethin' like this. Havin' to be bothered by people like me."

"I don't think you're such a bad person," Susan said, looking into his eyes.

"Susan, you just don't know how bad a person I am." Susan smiled like she was willing to find out. "But you check your man. I'm sorry if I frightened you." Freeze got up and walked back through the living room on his way out the door. "Let's go."

Tony walked to the door behind him. Ricardo got up and followed them outside. He ran up to the car as they were about to get in.

"Tony!" he said, looking back at Susan standing in the door. "How is Shy? Is she in trouble?"

"What if she is?"

"Hey, you have to believe me. I would never do anything to hurt her. I loved her. I still do." Freeze waved his hand in Ricardo's face and got in the car. "Tony, you tell her that I'd never hurt her, not again."

Tony slammed the door in his face and drove away, leaving Ricardo standing in the street. He looked up, and there was Susan staring him in the face.

"Come on in, honey. We need to talk."

Tony and Freeze drove away and started back for the city. After a long silence, Tony asked Freeze, "Do you believe him?"

"To a point. But I'll go see Susan tomorrow to be sure. She'll get more out of him tonight than I ever will."

"I don't think he knew anything," Tony said.

"I'll tell you what I do think. I think it's somebody real close to y'all. Someone who knew you had the product that night."

"What makes you say that?" Tony asked.

"'Cause y'all been rotatin' it every night."

"How'd you know that? Shy doesn't even know that."

"Because I been checkin' up on y'all. I hear shit. All kinds of shit."

"Why you so interested?"

"I protect Black's interest. What he needs, I get done. He's interested in Shy. Her problems are somethin' I need to know about 'cause it affects Black. I'll tell you somethin' else. Y'all doin' that girl a disservice the way y'all handle her security."

"What are you talkin' about?"

"Stupid, if I can find that shit out, anybody else who really wanted to know who had the product that night could find out too."

Tony said little else during the drive back. He did ask Freeze if he wanted to go straight to Brooklyn to check out the chop shop. Freeze said no but told him to head for Brooklyn anyway. There were a few people Freeze wanted to talk to first. "I hate fallin' up in places unprepared."

Freeze had given Tony a lot to think about. He was right. Tony hadn't been prepared for any of this. He, too, began to realize that they were in over their heads. It had all been business before all this began. Tony now knew he did not possess the skills to get information by force if necessary.

Watching Freeze work fascinated him. He would have allowed Ricardo to talk outside, so he would have never gotten in the house to see the art collection. Tony never would have thought to question Susan. The way Freeze was all over the whole credit card thing. The way he separated Susan from Ricardo and turned her. Then he used her to get what he wanted. E was on the right track with the lead on the chop shop, but he handled it wrong. Tony walked in there with nothing and came out the same way. This time he'd be ready. Freeze would see to that. He felt useless to Freeze, but he was enjoying the education he was receiving. Now his thoughts turned to Shy and Jack. He wondered if Jack was having as much fun as he was.

Later that evening, Freeze and Tony arrived in Brooklyn. Freeze told Tony to roll by Prospect Park and cruise. After cruising around the outside of the park for twenty minutes, Freeze said, "Pull over." Tony pulled over as requested and parked the car. "Wait here." Freeze got out of the car and approached two attractive ladies. Each greeted him with a hug and a kiss on the cheek, and then Freeze walked away with one of them. Tony watched as Freeze talked with her for a while then returned to the car.

"Let's rock and roll," Freeze said, and Tony drove away.

"Where to now?" Tony asked.

"To the chop shop," Freeze replied. Tony drove as Freeze explained that James Kerns was definitely a contractor and that he most likely arranged the hit on Shy. "He's connected to one of the Brooklyn crews. He's a fat white boy, in his forties, wears black-frame Coke-bottle glasses. Drives a white sedan DeVille. He's got access to a few low-grade hitters. But somethin' ain't right."

"What's that?" Tony asked.

"Most times the hitter never meets the client. But according to Kenny, they met twice."

"Maybe Kerns knew the client well enough to put him in touch with Leon direct. Either way, Kerns knows who the client is," Tony said.

"You armed?" Freeze asked.

"Hell yeah."

"Why did you think it was a setup when you went there before?" Freeze asked.

"While I was talkin' to Tim, the phone rang. I could only hear parts of what he said, but I heard him say, 'No, she's not with him.' Then he tried to rush me out. I saw I wasn't getting anywhere, so I left."

"Let's assume it was a setup. They might open up on us as soon as they see you, so be ready," Freeze said while he checked his weapons.

When they got to their destination, Tony said, "This is it," as he started to pull into the small lot.

Freeze said, "No, park around the side."

After Tony parked the car on the side of the building, he and Freeze walked around to the back of the garage to have a look. Tony climbed up on the dumpster and looked in the window. "How many?" Freeze asked.

"Four."

"You see our boy?"

"No."

"Hardware?" Freeze asked.

"None that I can see. Wait a minute. I got him. There are some offices upstairs. He just came out of one of the offices. There's somebody in the office, but I can't see his face."

"Let's see if there's another way in. I don't wanna try the front door," Freeze said as he and Tony walked around the building, looking for another way in. They walked around the entire building only to find that the only ways in were the front door and the garage door in the back.

"Guess we got no choice," Tony said. He and Freeze went in the front door. Freeze took the lead. Tim, the same guy who played Tony off, greeted them. Tony hung back and kept his head down so he wouldn't be recognized right away.

Tim said, "Can I help yous guys?"

"My name is Freeze. A friend in Yonkers tells me I can find James Kerns here." Both of his hands were in his coat pockets with his fingers on the triggers.

"Who told you that?" Tim asked.

"He doesn't like his name mentioned," Freeze said.

"Gimme a name."

"Angelo," Freeze answered.

His answer raised an eyebrow. Tim looked at Freeze for a moment, then said, "Wait here." Tim went in the back to the garage.

Freeze thought that maybe saying his name was a mistake. If whoever was behind it all knew their operation, they would also know that Shy was involved with Black. It was too late to worry about that now. Freeze nodded at Tony, then took out both guns and crossed his arms to conceal his weapons. Tony removed his gun from its holster, crossing his hands behind his back.

Tim appeared at the door long enough to say, "Come on back," then disappeared from view.

Freeze looked at Tony, then proceeded into the garage behind Tim. They entered the garage carefully, walking down the center aisle with cars on both sides. There was no longer anybody to be seen in the garage. Freeze stopped and looked around. The garage door slowly began to open. Freeze looked at Tony. "Get the car and pick me up in the back!"

"But—" Tony said.

"Go!"

Tony ran out of the garage as Kerns's DeVille started up and drove quickly out of the garage. Freeze started to run through the garage. He followed the car out the door as shots were fired at him from both sides. Freeze ran through the garage, firing back in both directions. Tony pulled up in the Beemer.

"How well can you drive this muthafucka?"

Tony laughed, "Put your seat belt on," then took off after the Caddy. Tony turned the corner and sped away, handling the car as if it were an extension of his body.

"Glad you ain't drivin' Miss Daisy," Freeze said.

"Do you see them?"

Freeze looked ahead. "Over there, on your right. About five cars ahead," Freeze answered as Tony weaved in and out through the traffic.

The Caddy turned sharp onto Atlantic Avenue with Tony in pursuit. As they crossed Flatbush Avenue, the light turned yellow. Tony floored it. The light turned red, but he made it across, swerving to avoid the oncoming cars.

"Stay on him, man. Don't lose him," Freeze said as they approached the Brooklyn-Queens Expressway.

"I got them. So what's the plan?" Tony asked. "You gonna jump on top of the car like Action Jackson?"

"Nigga, please. You just catch them," Freeze said.

Just then, the Caddy cut across lanes and went onto the on-ramp, causing the cars to crash in front of Tony.

"Shit!" Tony said, driving up on the median to avoid the wrecked cars. He slammed on his brakes, turned sharply, and continued up the on ramp.

Freeze shouted, "You lose them and I'll shoot you myself."

"Lighten up. I ain't new to this. I'm true to this. I used to boost cars. I won't lose them," Tony said as he drove. "Wait a minute, I got an idea."

"Make it good."

"How well do you shoot?" Tony asked, closing the distance.

"'Bout as good as you drive. Why?"

"Think you can hit a taillight?"

"Hell yeah."

"You shoot out a taillight, and then I'll drop back a little. Make them think they lost us. Then we can follow them, see where they go," Tony said.

Freeze pushed the button to open his window. "Get closer." Freeze took careful aim, preparing to fire. "Keep it steady."

As Freeze was about to shoot the taillight, Tony hit a pothole in the pavement, causing Freeze to miss the taillight, hitting the left rear tire instead. The Caddy spun out of control and slammed into the guardrail. Tony pulled over ahead of the wrecked Caddy. With guns drawn, he and Freeze approached the Caddy slowly. There were two men in the car, and both of them appeared to be alive. However, neither one was Kerns.

"He ain't in there," Freeze said.

"Shit, let's get back to the garage," Tony said.

They got back in the Beemer and returned to the garage. Once they arrived, they noticed that a crowd was forming outside the garage. "This is not good. Something's goin' on up there, Freeze," Tony said as they approached slowly.

"I can see that," Freeze replied with contempt, seeing the police lights, an ambulance, and the coroner's wagon.

"Pull over here. We'll walk up there. Find out what happened." Tony pulled over, and he and Freeze got out and approached the crowd. As they got closer, they could see the coroner rolling out a body bag.

Freeze walked over to a young lady in the crowd. "Excuse me, do you know what happened?" he asked.

"Yeah, guy who owns the garage got shot."

"You know what his name was?" Freeze asked.

"No, but he was a fat white man with a dope Caddy," she said.

"Cops know who killed him?" Tony asked.

"Nope, but I heard that three guys rolled up in masks and blew everybody away."

"Thanks." Freeze turned to Tony. "Let's get out of here." They walked quietly back to the car and drove away.

"I think our boy beat us to him," Tony said, but Freeze didn't answer. Tony picked up his phone and called Jack.

"This is Jack."

"Jack, where's Shy?"

"I took her home," Jack replied.

"What! Is Black with her?" Tony asked.

"I don't think so. What's up? What happened with Kerns?" Jack asked.

"You left her alone?" Tony yelled.

"She said she'd be all right. You know how she gets when she makes up her mind. What's wrong? What happened with Kerns?" Jack repeated.

"He's dead," Tony said.

"Y'all killed him?"

"No. When . . ." As he was about to continue, Freeze turned quickly and stared at Tony. "No time to explain. You just get back to Shy, now! I'll explain when I see you. Just go!" Tony shouted, then hung up and called Shy.

"Now you see what I mean? Y'all doin' that girl a disservice. You just drop me at Impressions first," Freeze said.

Shy answered the phone. "What?"

"Shy, it's Tony."

"What took you so long to call? I was about to—"

Tony cut her off. "Is Black there?"

"No."

"I told Jack to get back over there and stay with you."

"You told who to do what?" said a now-angry Shy.

"Kerns is dead. I'm on my way over there. I'll explain then." Tony hung up.

Shy sat there for a second, holding the phone. "What now?" she asked. Then she got up and walked to the window. Then she went and got her gun out of her purse. She dragged the love seat in front of the door before returning to the window and taking a seat.

CHAPTER TWENTY-FOUR

Shortly after one in the morning, a cab pulled up in front of Impressions. Mike got out of the back seat, paid the driver, and went inside. After leaving Cuisine, he walked around the neighborhood for hours. He thought about Shy, naturally, as he was very much in love with her. Mostly he thought about Melinda, trying to reconcile how he felt about telling her it was over. He thought that he would be able to tell her and walk away—no regrets, no sorrows. This was not to be the case.

So he walked no place in particular, just around. Finally, he got in a cab and ended up at the club. Mike wandered around the club for a while, half looking for Melinda but not finding her. After all, she was there every night. He felt he should have said something more than he did.

Tara walked up to him and asked, "Have you seen Melinda?"

"Why?" Mike looked at Tara as if she had lost her mind. For obvious reasons, she and Melinda never got along.

"I was just wondering if she was gonna work tonight," Tara said.

"Work? Work where?" Mike said curiously.

"Here, silly. You do know she still works here."

"She does? Doin' what?"

"Don't you remember? You told me to hire her in hospitality over a year ago."

"I always wondered why she was here every night." Mike walked away, laughing. He went upstairs to Bobby's office. He busted through the door in his normal fashion and headed straight for the bar. "What up, Bob?" Mike said as he poured a drink for himself and Bobby.

"Good trip?"

"Yeah, it was cool."

"Grand Bahama is cool this time of year," Bobby commented.

"Where's Jamaica?" Mike asked.

"Wanda's got him in a rehab program out on the island," Bobby replied.

"How long?"

"Until he's ready to leave."

"When's visiting hours?"

"Between three and five and seven to nine during the week. All day on the weekends," Bobby replied.

"He'll be all right," Mike said.

"Mind if I ask you a question?" Bobby asked, leaning back in his chair.

"No, we're not gettin' back in the dope game," Mike fired back without waiting to be asked.

"Mind if I ask you a question?"

"What, Bobby?"

"I know we ain't gettin' back in the game. Ain't no reason for me to think that we were. What I wanna know is, since we ain't gettin' back in the game, what were you doin' in Miami with Hector? By the way, is he still pissed about Nina?"

"Yeah, I'd say he's still a little pissed," Mike said with a smile.

"So since he's still pissed at you, you decided to guarantee her investment?"

"What?" That one caught him off guard. "I didn't guarantee shit."

"You didn't?"

"Hell no. Hector wanted me to, but you know I'd never do no shit like that. I told him that I would consider it a personal favor if he would do business with her."

"Favor for what?" Bobby asked.

"For introducing him to Angee."

"Well, maybe we should have a talk with Hector's boy."

"Who? Orlando."

"No, Carlos. He's been goin' around tellin' anybody who'd listen that we're guaranteeing her."

"So?"

"Mike, when you decided to get out, honestly, I wasn't sure about it. But I went along with it 'cause I knew it was the right thing to do. Even if it wasn't good for business. We fought a war to get out. Now I don't wanna go back."

"You think I do?"

"No, but let's think for a minute about how this looks. You and Shy, in Miami, hangin' around with Hector. You got Freeze checkin' on their security like we gettin' ready to take over. And before you say you didn't tell him to do it, he is. Freeze anticipates what you want. That's his job," Bobby said.

"You're right."

"Where's Freeze now?" Bobby asked.

"Checkin' out something for me," Mike replied.

"You mean checkin' out something for Shy. You see what I'm sayin', Mike. People think we're back in the game, they start coming after us. And I'm just not in the mood."

"We'll go see Orlando tomorrow. Put a stop to this shit."

"We! Tell me what you mean, we?"

"Yeah, we got to do this. It won't have the same impact on him if we sent Freeze. Or would you rather I go alone?"

"Shit, wild horses, three pigs, two mules, and the bull couldn't keep me from going with you."

"I noticed that list doesn't include Pam." He derailed Bobby from his point.

"Why you gotta go there?" Bobby asked as Freeze entered the office. Bobby would have to sit on his point for now. "What's up, Freeze? Tell me a story."

"Yeah, and I got one for you." Freeze began to recount the story for Mike and Bobby. "I think it's somebody close to them, but that punk Ricardo ain't the one."

"What you get on Kerns?"

"He was definitely the contractor. Oh, and he's dead. Did I forget to mention that?" Freeze told them how when the shooting started, he had gone after Kerns's Caddy, but Kerns wasn't in it when it crashed.

"You're gettin' careless, Freeze," Bobby joked.

"Fuck you, Bobby," Freeze fired back. "I wasn't gonna stay and shoot it out with them. Since I was leaving anyway, I followed the car."

"Go on, man. I was just fuckin' with you."

"When we got back, cops were bringing him out in a body bag."

"Who killed him?" Mike asked.

"I don't know. Little honey in the crowd said it was three guys in masks. I'll confirm that tomorrow."

"No. Back up off it," Mike said, walking toward the window and looking out at the club. "Bobby's right. We've involved ourselves and our organization too deeply in this. And like the lady said, it's not our business."

"Good," Freeze said with a sense of relief.

"Oh, yeah, Mike, I forgot to tell you. Shy called you a couple of hours ago. She wants you to call her at home."

"Thanks, Bobby," Mike said, walking toward the phone.

"Oh, yeah, Black, Shy's alone. Did I forget to mention that?" Freeze asked.

"She told me Jack was with her," Bobby said as Mike dialed her number.

"Yeah, well, she sent Jack home. But Tony sent him back, and he's on his way there now," Freeze said. Mike just looked at Freeze and Bobby. He smiled and shook his head.

Shy answered the phone. "Hello."

"You all right?"

"Yeah. A little confused, but I'm fine. What's goin' on?" Shy asked.

"Is Jack there?"

"Yes, baby, he's here," Shy said. "What happened out there?"

"Tony's on his way there now. He'll explain everything," Mike said, not wanting to alarm her. "When he gets there, have them drop you off here."

"Good. I've gotten used to waking up with you next to me," Shy said.

"I have too. I'll see you soon," Mike said as he hung up the phone. He turned to face Freeze and Bobby, who looked at each other and busted out laughing.

Bobby began to tease him. "'I love you, Shy. If I don't see you soon, I'll die.'"

CHAPTER TWENTY-FIVE

Tony finally got to Shy's apartment. He looked around briefly for Jack's car. Not seeing it, he ran into the building and into the elevator. He banged furiously on the door until Jack opened it.

"What you in such a panic about, Tony?" Jack asked as Tony came into the apartment.

"Where's Shy?"

"I'm right here, Tony. What's happened?" Shy yelled from the bedroom as she packed a few things.

Tony went into the bedroom. "Where you goin' now?"

"I'm gonna stay with Black for a while."

"Good, you'll be safer with him."

"So what happened?" Shy asked.

"Kerns is dead. They were a step ahead of us all the way. While me and Freeze chased Kerns's car, somebody wasted Kerns and all his boys. There was a man in Kerns's office, but I couldn't see his face. I think that was our boy. I think he knew we were gettin' close to Kerns, so he killed him. I thought they would come after you next. That's why I sent Jack here to protect you," Tony said.

"Any idea who it was in the office with Kerns?" Shy asked Tony as she left the bedroom, taking a seat in her favorite spot by the window.

Tony followed her to the window. "No, but I think it's somebody real close to us."

"That thought has crossed my mind once or twice," Shy said, staring out the window.

"Did you tell anybody we were going there?" Tony asked.

"No," Shy said, walking back into the bedroom and preparing to leave.

"What about E?" Tony said.

"I beeped him, but he never called back," Shy said, coming out of the bedroom with a gun in each hand. Tony stopped talking, and Jack simply stared at her in disbelief. "What?" Shy held up the guns. "Oh, these. I just thought I needed a little extra firepower, that's all," she said as Tony helped her on with her coat.

"You been hangin' around Black too long," Jack said, taking her bags. Tony opened the door. Shy put her guns in the pockets and closed the door behind her.

On the way to Impressions, Shy told Tony about what happened at the art gallery. She thought that if it were somebody that close to them, they wouldn't have seen what was goin' on in the gallery. "No, I think it's somebody with a grudge. Somebody who used to work for us. You know, the disgruntled postal worker type. Somebody I did wrong or something like that. I was thinking about checkin' out Ricardo."

"Me and Freeze went out there tonight," Tony said.

"And just whose bright idea was that?" Shy asked, but Tony didn't answer. "Never mind, it had to be Black's idea."

"Yeah, it was Black," Tony said.

"Why didn't you tell me?" Shy asked.

"If I told you I was going to White Plains to sweat Ricardo, you would've gone ballistic on me."

"Okay, okay. Anyway, what did you find out?" Shy asked.

"I didn't find out shit. It was all Freeze. Yo, Jack, it blew me away watching Freeze work. We just been playin' the role. That muthafucka is dangerous."

"Beat him down bad, huh?" Jack asked.

"No, he only hit him once for not doin' what he was told," Tony replied.

"So what was so dangerous about that?" Jack asked.

"It was the way he did it more than what he did."

"What did Ricardo have to say?" Shy asked.

"He said to tell you that he loved you and would never hurt you."

"Whatever. With all the money he had, I thought he might have paid somebody to do it after the beating y'all dealt," Shy said.

"Not," Tony said. "He was just frontin' that cash. He would skim money off his clients' accounts. Old girl controls the money."

"He was embezzling," Shy said.

"Not. Kid would just put the money back in the morning."

"Fake. He was a fake from start to finish, Shy," Jack said.

Shy knew that all too well and did not wish to be reminded of it. Still, she was glad that Ricardo didn't appear to be involved.

Impressions was crowded, as usual, when they arrived. Shy made her way through the club looking for Black. She stopped at the bar to get a glass of wine. After receiving her drink, she took out some money. "How much?" she asked.

"The gentleman at the end of the bar said to tell you that your money's no good here."

Shy looked to see who paid. She smiled when she saw it was Black. They walked toward one another, each not taking their eyes off the other.

"Hello, beautiful," Mike said.

"Hello yourself."

"You ready to go?"

"Yeah, I'm ready. Ready to make love to you," Shy said with a kiss.

"Oh, really? Well, we got to get you out of here."

"I gotta find Jack to get my bags. Baby, do you mind if I stay with you for a few days?"

"I was just gonna suggest that," Mike replied.

"See? It's true. Great minds do think alike," Shy said.

They found Jack and he drove them to Mike's house. He carried in her bags and took them straight to the bedroom. Shy unpacked her clothes and put them away. Once she had finished, Shy wandered around through the house, looking for Mike. It was a modest house, not what she'd expect from someone with the kind of money he had. There were three large bedrooms, two of which were not furnished. Downstairs was nicely furnished, in black of course. Since Mike hated to shop, Shy wondered if he had picked it out himself or whether Wanda or maybe Regina bought it all for him. She opened a door, which led to the basement.

Shy called to him, "Black, you down there?" Not getting an answer, Shy sat down in a chair by the window.

"That's my favorite spot," Mike said, seeming to appear from nowhere.

"Where were you?"

"In the basement."

"Why didn't you answer me?"

"I had something in my mouth," Mike replied.

"What?" Shy inquired.

"This," Mike said, handing her a jewelry case.

Shy opened the case, which contained a diamond-studded necklace. "Thank you, Black. It's beautiful."

"You're welcome. It's nothing really. I've had it for, damn, eighteen years, I guess. Me and Angee robbed a jewelry store. First job we ever did together. I thought it was pretty, so I didn't let him take it to the fence. I figured I'd give it to somebody special. But back then there was nobody special to give it to," Mike said while he put the necklace around her neck. "I found it when I moved here."

"This really is a nice house."

"Yeah, Regina liked it too." Mike turned and walked away. "I bought the house for her before we broke up. Whenever we'd drive down this street, she'd always say how much she liked it. So when it went on the market I bought it. I was going to surprise her with it after the wedding."

"Time-out. What wedding?"

Mike smiled and sat down next to Shy. "Bobby and Pam's wedding."

"Oh," said a relieved Shy.

"Well, I guess you know how that worked out. So it stayed empty until I decided to move. Since it was already paid for, I moved in. And besides, it really is a nice house."

"You know, sometimes I don't know how to take you."

"What do you mean, Cassandra?" He put his arm around her.

Shy put her head on his shoulder. "I mean, you gave me this beautiful necklace, which is so romantic. Then you bust my bubble and tell me it's stolen. Then you tell me that you waited eighteen years for somebody special to give it to. And I melt. Then you tell me you bought this housed to surprise what's-her-face. Which is romantic. But I could've gone all year without hearing it."

"Sorry, but I feel strangely compelled to tell you everything."

"That's all right. I would rather that than have you lyin' to me all the time. So what's-her-face never knew you bought it for her?" Shy asked.

"Nope. I guess by now Pam told her that I live here, and she figured out it was the same house."

"She and Pam still friends?"

"They aren't tight like they used to be. But they still talk."

"How come they aren't still tight?"

"Pam thought Regina messed up her wedding day."

Shy got up and started up the stairs. "That makes tomorrow night all the more interesting."

"Tomorrow night? What's happening tomorrow night?"

"You don't know? Well, I guess you're not invited," Shy said, continuing up the stairs. Mike followed her upstairs to the bedroom. Shy lay down on the bed.

"Invited where?" Mike asked.

"Bobby invited me to dinner tomorrow at his house. Pam is dying to meet me. I told him I would love to meet his wife but to let me talk to you first. He said, 'What, you can't come without him?' So I guess you're not invited."

"That's cool. If you want to go have dinner with Bobby and the interrogator by yourself, be my guest," Mike said, laughing as he lay down next to her.

"What did you call her?"

"Pam's the interrogator. And if you think you have questions, wait."

"She's the inquisitive type, huh?"

"No, Pam's just plain nosy. Pam will sit there and ask question after question. So what makes tomorrow so interesting?"

"I know Pam will have to make a full report about me. And I want what's-her-face to know she can cancel the comeback."

"You're kinda territorial, aren't you?"

"Very. And selfish, too, when it comes to a man. I don't like to share. Which reminds me, you handle your business?"

"Yes."

"And?"

"And that's that," Mike said.

Shy smiled at him and moved a little closer. "It wasn't as easy as you thought, was it?"

"No."

"Wasn't just sex and money either. She was in love with you, wasn't she?"

"Yes."

"I don't know whether to call you insensitive or be thankful that you were so blind."

"Yeah, right," Mike said, looking away.

"She probably cried, too. That was to make you weak for her."

"Think so?"

"Yeah, but let me stop. You probably feel bad enough already."

"I don't know. It just seems like I should have said something."

"To make her feel better about it? Think about how you sound. You told her you were leaving her for another woman. A hell of a woman, yes, but still. Nothing you said would make her feel any better about that."

"I guess you're right," Mike said. Shy kissed him on the cheek. "What was that for?"

"To make you feel better," Shy replied.

"I'm feelin' really bad."

Shy kissed him on the lips this time. "How was that?"

"Better. Thanks."

"Baby, can we just stay here tomorrow until it's time to go to dinner? We been on the run since we left here last Friday. Even in the Bahamas, I had a great time, but we were always doing something. I just want to do absolutely nothing."

"Sure we can. We won't leave this bed."

"Except to eat," Shy said.

CHAPTER TWENTY-SIX

Early the next morning, the calm was interrupted once again by Shy's pager. Shy looked at the pager. Not recognizing the number, she rolled over and went back to sleep. Seventeen minutes later, it went off again.

"That's why I hate those things. People don't care what time they page you," Mike mumbled.

Once again, Shy grabbed the pager. Once again, it was the same number. Shy picked up the phone and dialed the number.

"Yeah." It was E paging her.

"This is Shy."

"What's up, Shy? Where you at?" E said.

"Oh, what's up, E? I'm at Black's house. What's wrong?"

"I need to see you sometime today. We can do this thing with Hector and them anytime you're ready," E said.

"You seen Jack or Tony?" Shy asked.

"Nope, I been rollin' all night tryin' to get this thing together for you."

"That's why you're the man, E. I know I can always count on you. Listen, what time is it anyway?" Shy asked.

"Quarter to nine."

"Hold on." Shy turned to Mike. "Baby, wake up. You mind if E comes here?"

"Why would I mind?" Mike mumbled. Shy told E where Mike lived and told him to be there at one o'clock. Shy hung up the phone, turned her pager off, kissed Mike on his back, and drifted back off to sleep.

Shy woke up a little after twelve in the afternoon. She reached in the bed next to her for Mike, but he was gone. Shy got out of bed and wandered through the house. Mike was nowhere to be found again. Shy returned to the bedroom and removed her gun from under the pillow. She went into the bathroom, put the gun down on the sink, and turned on the shower. Then she heard a noise behind her. She reached for her gun, turned quickly, and aimed.

"Safety's on," Mike said with a smile.

"Don't do that," she said, lowering her gun.

"Rule number one: when you pick it up, make sure one's in the chamber. Oh, yeah. And make sure the safety's off, too. Remember, one shot in the head."

"Yes, sir," she said and got in the shower.

E knocked on the door at Mike's house at about one thirty. Mike was in the basement working out when E arrived. Remembering what Mike said, Shy checked her weapon, removed the safety, went to the door, and let him in.

"Come on in, E."

"So this is it, Vicious Black's house. I expected more."

"So did I, but come in anyway."

Shy led E into the living room. He sat down in the chair by the window.

"So we work for this nigga now?"

"No!" Shy answered with a frown. "What makes you say that?"

"The way Freeze been rollin' around, peepin' out the operation. And with him guaranteeing our purchase, I just thought we worked for him."

"Hold up. Black didn't guarantee anything. Okay, so he used his influence so I could make the deal with Hector. But that don't mean we work for him."

"That's not what I hear."

"What you talkin' about, E?" Shy fired.

"Can he hear us?"

"Let's go outside." Shy grabbed her coat and put her gun in the pocket. E led Shy away from the house to his car. "Now what you talkin' about, E?"

"I been hearing for a long time that Black was behind the robberies all along. He hates drug dealers and wanted to put us out of business 'cause we operate too close to this area. He got a real thing about people doin' business here."

"Nobody rolls around here. Everyone knows that. But we're not even close."

"Well, Shy, that's not entirely true."

"What you mean, E?" Shy asked.

"I have a little spot two blocks from the dead zone," E said.

"Why didn't you tell me that before?"

"You never wanted to know where I was doin' business before. It was outside the fuckin' dead zone. I didn't think they'd give a shit. But that's not what I been hearin' lately."

"What now?"

"Now since he's all in love with you, he figures he can just take over our organization, since it's so spread out, and expand his gambling operation. With his influence with the cops and his muscle, no one could fight him off for long. He probably arranged for Hector to turn you down so he could guarantee it."

"He didn't guarantee it!" Shy shouted.

"That's not what I hear!" E said all up in her face.

"Don't you think I thought of all that? But why would he do that? It's not like he needs the money," she said angrily.

"Man like that never has enough money. It's the power he needs."

"I just don't think it's like that!" Shy said all up in his face.

"Look, Shy," E said, backin' up off her, "I don't wanna argue with you. Besides, if it's true, we'll all make mad dough anyway. I just wanna know what's up, that's all I'm sayin'. Open your eyes. See this thing with Black for what it is. This ain't no fairy tale. Y'all ain't gonna live happily ever after. This is business!"

E got in his car. "Page me as soon as you know what's up with Orlando." E slammed the door and drove away before Shy could tell him what went on the night before.

Shy thought about all that E had said. She still refused to believe that Black was involved in any way. How could he be involved when she loved him so much? However, she could no longer ignore the possibility. Other than his word that he wasn't involved, there was no reason that he couldn't be. It would be easy for Vicious Black to have arranged it all. There was no telling how long he'd had somebody following her so he would know enough about her operation to pull off the robberies. He could have set it up to be able to use his influence with Hector. Shy walked back in the house, thinking about how things had worked out so that she would need him. If he were planning to take over, it would only be logical to have Freeze checking them out.

Shy went upstairs to the bedroom and closed the door. She took off her coat and removed the gun from her pocket. She paced back and forth, gun in hand. E's words kept rolling around in her mind. The more she thought, the angrier she got. If his intention was only to take over her organization, how could she ever trust him? She thought about going straight downstairs and confronting Mike. "No," she said, sitting down on the bed. "Just play it cool and see where this all leads." Shy got up and started down the steps, heading straight for the basement. "Fuck all that 'play it cool' shit," she said, not giving any thought to the gun in her left hand. "Black! Black!" she shouted.

Mike came running up from the basement and ran right into Shy's arms. "Cassandra, is everything all right?"

"You and I need to have a conversation," Shy said, separating herself from his arms. Seeing the gun in her hand, Mike stepped back.

"What's the gun for, Cassandra?" Mike said to her in a tone she had never heard. "You wanna shoot me?"

Shy looked at the gun. "Is it you?"

"What? What are you talkin' about?"

"You know exactly what I'm talkin' about, Black. Don't play me like I'm stupid. Are you planning to take over?" Shy said, the gun still at her side.

Mike began to walk toward her slowly. "If you think I am, go ahead and shoot."

"Answer me!"

"No! You think all this is about taking over your little bullshittin'-ass dope business? You wanna tell me why I'm doin' this?"

Shy didn't answer.

"You talk to me. This is too important. You tell me what that bitch-made nigga said to make you walk up on me with a gun."

Shy looked at the gun again and smiled. "I'm not gonna shoot you. People just been sayin' you've been behind this all along. But now since you're in love with me you figured you can just take over my operation since it's so diverse. Once you took over, you'd expand your gambling interests. The talk is that with your influence with the cops and your muscle," she said, smiling, watching the sweat drip off him, "no one could fight you off for long. That's why you arranged for Hector to turn me down so you could guarantee it."

"I know. Bobby heard the same thing."

"So what's up, Black? More money? More power?"

"Money! I don't fuckin' believe this. Money! Baby, please. I got enough cash in this house to do your deal with Hector and pay off Angee."

"Why don't you?"

"Why don't I what? Pay off Angee?"

"Yeah."

"I told him no."

"He asked you?"

"Yeah."

"When?" Shy asked.

"Before we left for the islands."

"What did he say?"

"I told you. Angee said he was hopin' to see you," Mike said.

"And?"

"He wanted to know if he should be talkin' to me about that now. I told him no."

"You did?" Shy said in surprise.

"But I shouldn't have, should I? The thing to do is pay Angee. And while I'm at it, why don't I just do your deal with Hector? That would put me in control, wouldn't it? That's it. Come here," Mike said, grabbing Shy by the hand. He led her into the den. He opened the closet and pulled out a metal briefcase. "Open it," he said, handing her the case.

"What's in it?"

"Open it," Mike said as he sat down.

Shy opened the case, and as she expected, it was filled with money. "How much money is in here?"

"Three hundred grand. The quarter mil you owe Angee, plus fifty for making him wait for his money. Take it," Mike said quietly. "Now you don't have to deal with Hector. So much for my guarantee. Save me and Bobby the trouble of going to see Orlando tonight."

"I can't take this," Shy said, starting to feel bad about asking him.

"You already did," Mike said, leaving Shy in the den. He went into the living room, sat down by the window, and looked out.

Shy closed the case and followed him into the living room. She put the case down on the floor next to the couch and sat down. "I don't wanna believe it, baby."

"But there's something that tells you, 'Yeah, it could be Black.'"

"Yes. So I had to ask. I had to look in your eyes and hear you say one more time that it isn't you."

"I'm not the one. You're just going to have to trust me." He stood to proclaim his innocence.

"I know. Just be patient with me," Shy said.

Mike sat down next to her and reached for her hand. "All I wanna do is love you, Cassandra. If you don't believe anything else I told you, believe that."

"The only thing I am sure about is that I love you."

They kissed and made up.

CHAPTER TWENTY-SEVEN

Pam got the girls ready to take to her sister Monica's house for the evening. Bobby watched the football game in the living room with Bobby Jr. He sat close to his father, hoping he would say that he didn't have to go with his sisters. He didn't really like going to his aunt Monica's house. It was a little too girlie for him. Since Aunt Monica had two daughters of her own, there was never much for him to do.

"Bobby, let's go," Pam yelled from the front door.

"Your mother's callin' you," Bobby said to his son.

"I don't wanna go, Daddy," he replied. "I wanna stay here with you and Uncle Mike." They had invited Mike to come with Shy to dinner after all.

"You need to go so you can look out for your sisters. You know you're the man of the family when I'm not around."

"I know that, but I still don't wanna go, Daddy."

"I'll make a deal with you, chief. You go with your sisters, and me, you, and Uncle Mike will go to the game next week."

"Bobby Ray Jr., I'm not gonna tell you again. Let's go," Pam yelled again.

Bobby picked his son up in his arms and carried him to the door. Seeing them coming, Pam gathered the girls together and went to the car. Pam gave Bobby last-minute cooking instructions before leaving for her sister's. "I'll be back in an hour. Please don't let the duck burn," Pam pleaded.

"Don't worry, baby. I'm all over this."

"That's what bothers me," Pam said, slamming the car door and driving away.

Bobby went back inside and back to the game. When Pam returned an hour later, she found her husband asleep in the chair, as she expected. That was why she'd set the oven to warm before leaving the house.

"Bobby. Bobby, wake up. You remember the last thing, the only thing, I asked you to do before I left?

"I remember the roast duck."

"It's toast."

"Can you do anything with it?" Bobby said, coming out of his nod.

"Nothing but call a caterer," Pam said with a smile. "I guess we can eat out."

Bobby looked at Pam and noticed her smile. "You're a little too calm for someone whose day's work just got trashed. Nothing's wrong with that duck, is there?"

"You're no fun," Pam said.

"I'm lots of fun. You just ain't slick," Bobby said, following Pam to the kitchen.

"You know me too well, Bobby. What time did you tell them to come?"

"Seven. Let's see. It's six thirty now, so he should be here any—" The doorbell rang. "Right on cue. Mike's always early."

"Don't open the door yet, I look like Hazel," Pam said, running by Bobby and up the stairs. Once Pam had made it safely in the bedroom, Bobby opened the door.

"Pam had to run upstairs?" Mike asked as they entered.

"Something about lookin' like Hazel. How are you, Shy?" Bobby asked, kissing her hand.

"Just fine, Bobby. Thank you for inviting me," Shy replied graciously.

"You gonna kiss my hand, too?" Mike said jokingly.

"Come on in and have a seat. Pam will be down after a while." Bobby led Shy on his arm into the living room.

"You want something to drink, Cassandra?" Mike asked, making himself at home.

"Surprise me. Something fruity."

Bobby excused himself and went upstairs, leaving Mike and Shy alone. While Mike fixed her drink, Shy wandered around the room, looking at the many pictures spread throughout the room. "Are these their kids?"

"That's the crew," Mike said, without looking up. "From left to right that's Bobby Jr., Barbara, Bonita, and Brenda."

"I think I'd go crazy with four little kids like that. How old are they?"

Mike walked over and handed Shy her drink. "Bobby's five, Barbara's four, and the twins are almost two."

"What's this?" Shy asked, holding her drink up in front of the light.

"Something fruity," Mike answered. He returned to the bar and poured himself a drink.

"What's in it?"

"Taste it and I'll tell you."

Shy took a sip. "That's pretty good. It's got a little kick to it. What's in it?"

"Spiced rum, Absolut, peach schnapps, orange and pineapple juices, and a teaspoon of grenadine for color." He sat down on the couch.

Shy continued to look around. She stopped in front of Bobby and Pam's wedding picture. Shy stood a while, smiled at Mike, and sat down next to him. "How come there are no pictures of you? Or Bobby for that matter? Other than the wedding picture, that is."

"There's only one picture of me and Bobby."

"I don't see it," Shy said, scanning the room.

"Cabinet, under the lamp," Mike replied.

Shy opened the cabinet, reached in, and took out an album. "The wedding pictures," she said as she handed the album to Mike, and he turned to the only picture of him and Bobby.

He handed the album to Shy. She flipped a few pages, stopping on the picture of the bridal party. "Is that Regina?"

"Yes," Mike said, without looking at the picture.

"She's very pretty, Black," she said, looking at another picture of Regina.

"Yes, she is."

"And very foolish," Shy said, closing the album.

"You think so? Huh, a couple of hours ago you were thinking about shootin' me."

"You see I didn't shoot. Seriously, I am sorry about that. You're probably not gonna believe this, but I wasn't even thinkin' about shootin' you. The gun just happened to be in my hand," Shy said, laughing. "I really wasn't all that mad."

"I know, baby," Mike said as he kissed her. "The gun just made it seem that way."

"Excuse me," Bobby said. "Y'all wanna use the guest room? I know how that feeling gets."

"That's why we have four kids," Pam said, walking past Bobby toward Shy. "Hi, I'm Pam."

Shy stood up to greet her. "My name is Cassandra, but please call me Shy. It's nice to meet you."

"It's good to finally meet you too. What did Wanda call you?"

"Pam," Mike said.

"What did she call me?"

"You're startin' shit now, Pam," Bobby said.

"I don't remember what she said. It wasn't anything bad. I thought it was kinda cute. Well, since you're early, dinner will be a while. Shy, you make yourself at home. Mike always does."

"Thank you. Do you need any help?"

"Not right now, but I'll let you know if I need you," Pam said, going into the kitchen.

A short while later Pam announced that dinner was ready. Bobby filled each glass with champagne, Dom Pérignon 1982. Along with the roast duck, Pam had prepared pasta and sautéed vegetables with a cream sauce. Dinner conversation was polite and casual at first.

Shy was expecting Pam to ask her many questions. She asked where Shy bought her outfit and whether she could cook. "I can cook anything that requires boiling water. Other than that, I'm lost in the kitchen."

"A woman of the new millennium," Bobby said.

"That's me," Shy replied. "I can't cook, and I have somebody who comes in to clean my apartment."

"Are you an only child?" Bobby asked.

"No, I come from a big family. I'm the youngest of five."

"That's too many kids. I can't say a thing with the crew I got," Pam said.

"Your children are beautiful," Shy said.

"Thank you. Do you have any, Shy?" Pam asked.

"No."

"Do you want any?" Bobby asked.

"I never gave it much thought. I like kids, but I'm not in any hurry to have any. No disrespect to you, Pam."

"None taken. But I'll give you some advice. Until you're ready for your life as you know it to end, don't have any. I barely remember who I was five years ago."

"Tell me something, Shy. How did you get started in the game?" Bobby asked. "I'm sure you're quite intelligent. I can tell you got some education. You carry yourself well and all that shit. How did you become a player?"

"When I graduated from college with a dual degree in management and marketing, I knew I was set. My brother Randy was waiting tables at a little restaurant in

Brooklyn, tryin' to get into medical school. So I told him when I got a job I would help him pay for med school. But I couldn't find a job. After a while, both of us were waitin' tables. I decided then."

"That's interesting. I put someone through med school too," Bobby said.

"Oh, really, who was that?" Shy asked.

"His name is Perry," Bobby said.

"Someone y'all grew up with, right?"

"Yeah, Mike probably mentioned him."

"No. Mr. Black don't give up information freely. If you don't ask, he ain't sayin'."

"Unlike some people," Mike remarked.

"Oh, so you sayin' I talk too much?" Bobby asked. But Mike didn't answer him. So he turned his attention back to Shy. "You think you've got your business problems worked out?"

"I hope so, Bobby. It's causing friction where I don't need it," Shy said, looking at Mike. He winked at her. "I'd rather leave all that gangster stuff to you and Black."

"Cassandra thinks we wanna take over her business, Bob."

"No, Shy, we got no desire to get back in the game. Ain't that right, Mike? Besides, all that you got goin' on is too messy. That ain't old Vicious Black here's style. He would do it a lot smoother than that."

"Oh, really? So just how would you handle it, Vicious Black?" Shy asked.

Mike stopped eating and looked in her eyes. "I'd cut off your supply. None of that robbin' and shootin' women in the back. I'd want you to have cash, but nowhere to spend it. I'd lock you out of the product completely. I'd have the cops sweatin' you every day. Lockin' you and your people up on sight, so everyone would be afraid to come near you. By the time I was done with you, even the

Dominicans wouldn't do business with you. Then, when you were weak and demoralized, you'd have to come to me," he said, staring in her eyes the entire time.

The look in his eyes, the tone of his voice, and the way he spit out "weak and demoralized" sent chills through her body. Shy shook off the chill. She couldn't help feeling that she had just met Vicious Black. "That's deep, baby. You'd do me like that?" Shy asked.

"Of course not, Cassandra. I love you," Mike replied.

"That is so sweet," Pam said.

"You ever think about the future? I mean, what are you gonna do when the game dries up?" Bobby asked.

"Sometimes I think about it, but not much. I try to save tomorrow for tomorrow."

"You got some money put away for your retirement?" Bobby asked as if he were a lawyer and Shy were on trial.

"Not anymore. All my reserves have gone to digging out of this hole."

"Bobby, let her eat in peace," Pam said.

"Does that answer your question, Bob?" Mike said.

Sensing an opportunity to change the subject, Shy said, "Pam, everything tastes so good. Did you make this cream sauce yourself?"

"Yes, I did. Thank you, Shy. You just earned an invitation back."

Bobby didn't ask any more questions through the remainder of the meal. After dinner was over, Pam began to clear the table. Shy insisted on helping with the dishes. Pam carried the remaining food into the kitchen while Shy got the plates and the silverware.

"Got time for a quick one, Mike?" Bobby asked.

"Always got time to beat you," Mike replied, and they disappeared into the den.

"Where are they going?" Shy asked.

"To play chess. It's what they live for," Pam replied. "Do you play chess?"

"My father taught me when I was a kid, but I haven't played in years," Shy replied.

Pam put away the leftovers while Shy prepared to do the dishes. "Sit down, honey. I'll do that," Pam said, taking the dishes from her.

Shy sat down at the kitchen table. "I wanted to thank you again for inviting me."

"Thank you for coming. I've never seen Mike smile that much. And the way he looks at you, the way you look at each other . . ."

"Hope we didn't make you sick."

"No, of course not. I see what you like. Mike is good people. He's the big brother I never had. I'm just happy for you two."

"I am too. And thank you for making me feel so comfortable."

"Not the interrogator you were expecting, huh? Mike probably told you I was just goin' to sit there and ask you a whole group of questions, didn't he?" Pam asked.

"He sure did."

"But you see who asked the questions?"

"Yeah, and thanks for getting Bobby off me."

"They are a very closed bunch and very protective of one another."

"I wonder why I'm not surprised. I got the same kind of reception from Wanda. Only she went straight for my throat."

"That's it! Wonder Woman!"

"Excuse me?"

"That's what Wanda calls you, Wonder Woman. She said you must be from another planet," Pam said, laughing.

Shy laughed too. But now she had questions. "Why does she think that?"

"Honey, please. What's it been, less than a month? You came in and set up camp quick. Mortal women been tryin' to lock Mike Black down for years."

Shy didn't comment. She just smiled a very satisfied smile.

"Jamaica told me how Wanda flipped on you," Pam continued. "Heard you got her up off you, too."

"Quick," Shy said with a snap of her finger.

"You go, girl. I went through my thing with Wanda, too. She tried to pledge me, but she doesn't mean any harm. She's pretty cool once you get to know her."

"What about Black? Did he try to pledge you too?" Shy asked.

"Mike, no. He's a sweetheart. I knew Mike for three years before I met Bobby. He used to get Wanda up off me," Pam replied.

Now that the kitchen was clean and the food was put away, Pam led Shy to the den, where the chess game was in progress. "Who do you think is winning?" Shy asked as they walked.

"If they're still playing the first game, Mike is. Bobby plays cutthroat. He comes after you with everything he's got. When he wins, he wins quick. Mike plots, he lays traps, he gets you looking one way, and then he attacks from another. He anticipates countermoves."

"Action and reaction," Shy said.

"Exactly. That's the way he thinks. So he plays beyond the next move. He plans, and then he executes those plans. He gets you to move the way he wants you to move, and then he's got you. I think that's what makes him vicious. You heard him, and you saw the look in his eyes while he described how he would come after you if he were going to take over your business," Pam said.

"I know. It sent chills through me." Shy considered the possibility one more time, that in spite of what he said, Black was the mastermind behind it all.

"That's what I'm talkin' about," Pam agreed. "Back when they got out of the dope game, they were always outmanned and outgunned. But Mike crushed them. It was frightening, and at the same time, it was very exciting just to be around them. It's not what he does, Shy. It's the way that he does it."

"Check," Mike said as the ladies joined them.

"I didn't see that," Bobby said.

"What'd I say?" Pam said.

"You called it," Shy said. Pam's description of Vicious Black made Shy anxious. *Trust has to start somewhere,* she thought and pushed the feeling away.

"What'd you call, baby?" Bobby said, pondering his next move.

"I was tellin' Shy how Mike plays."

Bobby made a move. Mike looked carefully at the board. He moved his knight to unveil his queen. "Checkmate."

"Yes," Shy said, giving the victor a kiss.

"Cassandra, me and Bobby need to go take care of that matter we discussed earlier."

"What, Orlando?" Shy asked.

"Right. It shouldn't take more than an hour. Do you mind staying here with Pam?"

"You're going to leave me, baby?" Shy said, trying her best to sound weak and demoralized.

Mike smiled at her attempt. "Don't worry. Pam's raw with a nine."

"That's right. You can ride with me to pick up the kids," Pam said.

"No. If you're going to leave the house, call the club and get Jap or Kenny to drive you there," Bobby said.

"That's all right. I don't want anything to happen while the kids are around." Shy walked toward Mike. She put her arms around him. "Why can't I go with you?"

"I don't wanna dis Orlando in front of you. If you're there, he'll have to do something about it," Mike replied.

"What are you gonna say to him?" Shy asked.

"I don't know. Something will come to me," Mike said, kissing Shy goodbye.

"Something always does," Bobby remarked as he and Mike walked out of the house.

Mike came back in. "No matter what Monica says, those are not my kids." He kissed Shy again and left.

Pam called the club. Jap told her he would be right over. She hung up the phone and smiled at Shy. "I bet you want me to explain that."

"The thought had crossed my mind."

"Well, Monica is my sister. Like I said, we've known Mike for eleven years. Regina always thought they had a little thing goin' on when they first met."

"Did they?"

"Both of them say no. Anyway, about a month after I met Bobby, Monica got married to Norman. A month after they got married, she got pregnant and had Angela. Three months after they had Yvette, Norman got fired from his job. They caught him hittin' the pipe in the bathroom. Things got bad after that. He started stealing her money to get high, beatin' her and the kids. She didn't want to tell me or my mother 'cause she knew my moms would freak. So she called Mike. Monica wouldn't take money from Mike 'cause she thought Norman would steal it. So Mike would take food over there for her and the kids, or he would take them out and make sure they ate every day. That's why she says they're his kids."

"'Cause he fed them?'" Shy asked.

"You never heard that old sayin'? If you feed them long enough, they'll start lookin' like you."

Shy laughed. "No, that's a new one on me."

"Well, they don't look like Mike. Norman was high yellow."

"What happened to Norman? Did he get some help for himself?"

"No. Some people say Mike and Bobby killed him. Others say he's suckin' dick on Third Avenue," Pam said.

"That's too bad. How'd she get away from him?" Shy asked.

"After we got married and were on our honeymoon, Norman tried to kill her because she wouldn't give him the money Mike sent for her. He took the money, then beat her. Then he locked Monica in a closet for four hours while he got high. That's how she lost her job."

"Thought you said she wouldn't take money."

"Did Mike tell you anything about what happened between him and Regina at my wedding?"

"Yeah, he told me how she flipped on him."

"That's puttin' it mildly."

"Did that put a strain on your friendship?" Shy asked, trying to shake out more information about Regina. Not that Shy was worried about her. She just wanted to know.

"It did. To this day she never has said why she went off on Mike that day. I always thought that she was just jealous. We were always competing with each other growing up. Me marrying Bobby after us only being together two years must have been too much for her to take, I don't know. She and Mike had been together five years and the words 'marry me' never came out of Mike's mouth."

"Oh, really?" Shy said, her smile growing.

"He never seemed interested in marrying her. Anyway, we stayed gone for about two months on our honeymoon, and I didn't talk to her for at least a month after I got back. We've been talking more often in the last couple of years. But she almost messed up one of the biggest days of my life. No, Shy, it took me a long time to get over that one.

"Anyway, Mike was pretty down after that, so he sent Freeze to take Monica shopping. She can't stand Freeze, and she didn't wanna go anywhere with him, so she took the money. Norman saw Freeze give her the money, and after Freeze left, he went crazy. So she called Mike."

"Vicious Black to the rescue."

"He got her and the girls outta there. He took care of them until she got herself together. Got her a job and found her a place to stay. He's not vicious. Like I said, he's just a sweetheart."

"I know. That's why I love him," Shy said as Pam went to open the door for Jap.

On the way to Monica's house, Shy thought about Pam's story. For her it was a bittersweet story. Bitter because once again it forced her to deal with the tragic side effects of her business. Sweet because it was one of the few nice things she had heard anybody say about Vicious Black.

CHAPTER TWENTY-EIGHT

Bobby drove slowly along the concourse, looking for Orlando. They had already checked out a couple of his hangouts without success. Bobby had been unusually quiet since they left the last spot. Mike was in a good mood, so he didn't care. Finally, Bobby could no longer contain himself.

"Mike, let me run something by you. We're out here, ridin' around looking for Orlando. For what? To tell him that we ain't guaranteeing no drug deal. Hopin' that will kill all the talk. But it's out there now. Not much we can do about that."

"Right. So far I'm with you."

"Hearing all that talk, your girl is worried that we're tryin' to take over her little business. Which we're not. But everybody thinks that we are. So no matter what we do with Orlando tonight, people are still gonna believe what they wanna believe anyway."

"What are you sayin'? You don't wanna talk to Orlando?"

"No, that's not what I'm sayin'," Bobby said.

"Well, what's your point?" Mike asked, knowing Bobby had a tendency to be long-winded.

"Suppose that was the point all along."

"Okay. You lost me."

"Mike, I like Shy. She seems like cool people. And I know you're all in love with her and shit. But did you ever think that maybe she's usin' you?"

"Huh?"

"Not just usin' you. Usin' us, usin' our reputation," Bobby said.

"I'm still in the tunnel, Bobby."

"Your involvement with her does make her a stronger player. And maybe that's all she wanted. See the light now?"

"Right. Now I see. You think she arranged for somebody to try to kill her so I could save her."

"No, but since you brought it up, just you seein' the attempt would have the same effect. But I'm willin' to concede all that was real. Somebody is at her."

"Willing to concede? You been hangin' around Wanda, haven't you?" Mike asked with a smile.

"Fuck all that!" Bobby smiled, knowing it was true. He and Wanda had talked about it on the way to and from checking Jamaica into rehab. "All I'm sayin' is she coulda pushed up on you because of everything that she got goin' on. Mike, you're a powerful and influential man."

"So I've been told," Mike said, staring at Bobby. "Okay, let's say that was her plan from the jump. How'd she know I'd go for it?"

"Nigga, please. I guess you ain't looked at her lately. Shy is one fine-ass muthafucka, and I'm sure she knows. Who wouldn't go for it? If she had pushed up on me, I'd be out there just like you," Bobby said, pointing in his face.

"I'm surrounded by paranoia here. She thinks I'm tryin' to dog her. You think she's doggin' me." How could she be all he wanted and not be real? It wouldn't be the first time a woman became what a man wanted so she could use him. He refused to entertain the thought.

Bobby wouldn't let up. "You can make all of her problems go away. And you are. If you haven't done it already, you're gonna give her the quarter mil to pay Angelo. You arranged for her to get cheaper product from Hector. And don't even think about sayin' you didn't. And even though you told him to back off, Freeze will find who's robbin' her. And he'll kill them. Or you'll kill them. Or we'll kill them. Either way, it's all good. Her problems are gone," Bobby fired back quickly.

Bobby parked the car outside a bar just off Grand Concourse. Mike sat quietly, checking out the front of the bar. "Let's go." He got out of the car and started walking toward the bar. He stopped suddenly and turned back to face Bobby. "Is that what you believe?"

"It's possible. That's all I'm sayin'."

Mike sat down on the hood of the car. Bobby came and sat down next to him. "So what if she is doggin' me? I've never met anyone like her. It's like she's inside my mind, knowing what I want, feeling what I feel. When we're together, it's like nothing else even exists. And I'm lovin' every minute of it."

"That's a real pretty picture you're painting, but like the man said, 'It ain't 5th grade, and these ain't nursery rhymes.'"

"Who said that?" Mike asked.

"LL Cool J. Look, what's gonna happen is gonna happen. All I want you to do is see what's in front of you 'cause we got your back. And when she kicks your dumb ass to the curb, we'll still be here," Bobby said sarcastically.

"Thanks. That's very comforting. You know, just when you think things are going good, here comes some old drag to fuck it up. Let's go."

"'Cause that's what friends," Bobby sang, following him into the club, "real friends are for."

Once inside the club, they looked around for Orlando. It was a small club with mostly Hispanic patrons and live salsa music blasting in the background. Mike approached the bar and asked the bartender, "Is Orlando here?" The bartender said he didn't know anybody named Orlando and started to walk away. "Well, give me two double shots of Rémy Martin VSOP, straight up."

The bartender walked away to fix their drinks. He called over another man and whispered something to him. He looked at Mike and Bobby and immediately came from behind the bar. He went through a door marked KEEP OUT. The bartender returned with their drinks.

"Thanks for announcing us, asshole," Bobby said. They walked away from the bar, taking a seat at a table by the door. The band broke into an upbeat version of Santana's "*Oye Como Va*," and shortly thereafter, a beautiful woman wearing a black dress joined them at the table.

"Mind if I join you?" she said, looking at Bobby.

"Have a seat," Bobby said.

She sat down next to him and put her hand on his thigh. "I've never seen you here before."

"No, you haven't," Bobby said, grinning.

"We're looking for Orlando. You seen him?" Mike asked, trying to stay on task.

She smiled at Bobby. "Who are you?"

"Mike Black and Bobby Ray," Mike replied, demanding her attention.

"Wait here." She frowned and left the table.

"They shoulda played 'Black Magic Woman.' It woulda really set off her entrance," Bobby joked, but Mike was not amused.

She returned to the table. "Come with me." They followed her through the door and down a short hallway. She knocked on the door. The door opened, and she showed them in, closing the door behind her as she left. There was Orlando, seated behind a desk along with Carlos and another man.

Orlando got up and came out from behind his desk. "Black, Bobby, long time no see. How've you been?"

"See, Bobby, I tried to tell you he does know me," Mike said, staring at Carlos but walking straight for Orlando. He grabbed him by the back of his neck and put his gun to Orlando's forehead.

Bobby pulled out two guns and pointed them at Orlando's boys. "Don't do it. Nobody's gonna die here tonight."

"You know me, Orlando! You know I ain't no fuckin' drug dealer!"

"I know that, Black."

"Then you tell me why I hear you been talkin' about me guaranteein' some fuckin' drug deal!"

"Hector told me—" Orlando started, but Mike cut him off.

"Oh, fuckin' Hector told you! Where's the fuckin' phone so I can call fuckin' Hector!"

"Black, all right, I am responsible. It is wrong for anybody to say that about you. I just thought—"

Mike quickly cut him off again. "Fuckin' Hector doesn't fuckin' pay you to fuckin' think! So if I hear that shit again, from anybody, I'm gonna fuckin' kill you first! Then I'm gonna fuck your wife before I kill her! Then I'll burn your fuckin' house to the fuckin' ground!" Mike shouted.

Then he let Orlando go, lowered his gun, and said calmly, "'Cause I ain't no fuckin' drug dealer. I kill people. That's what I do."

"Okay, Black. I didn't mean you any disrespect. It won't happen again, will it, Carlos?" Orlando said.

"No, Orlando, never again," Carlos said.

"I'm glad we understand each other," Mike said as he left the office.

"Good to see you again, Orlando," Bobby said, backing out the door.

Mike and Bobby left the office, making their way quickly through the club. They did, however, stop to admire the lady in the black dress.

As they drove away, Bobby said, "You just had a fuckin' fit in there. What was all that fuckin' this and fuckin' that all about?"

"Hey, hey, it's what came to me," Mike said with a smile.

"And that thing about fuckin' his wife. Where did that come from?"

"That was for Hector."

"Thought so. Listen, man, about what I said earlier," Bobby said.

"Don't sweat it. I never even saw that as a possibility, but I need to. I have to look at it objectively. Like you said, what I do affects all of us. I'm sure Wanda pointed that out too. I know she had a hand in this," Mike said.

"Pam and Perry, too."

"Damn, this has all the feel of a hostile takeover."

"Come on, man, it ain't like that at all. It started out with me and Wanda talkin' on the way to drop off Jamaica. When we got back to the house, Pam was on the phone talking to Glenda. We got Perry on speakerphone, and here it is."

"I got it in check, Bobby. Y'all don't have to worry."

"We don't wanna see you get dogged again. And we damn sure don't wanna go to jail. Like I said, I like her, Jamaica loves her. She and Pam seemed to get along okay. And you know how Wanda is."

"She'll come around."

"Watch her, that's all I'm sayin'. A little paranoia is healthy in any new relationship," Bobby said.

"I do love her, Bobby. Last week was great. I can't remember ever being this happy. I miss her now, and we've only been gone for a couple of hours."

"You got it bad."

"Whatever. All I know is I'm in a hurry to get back to her. So I'd appreciate it if you drove faster. Maybe she is usin' me, but it feels good. And I hope she never stops."

"You mean she can just keep on usin' you until she uses you up."

"I said I was in love, not stupid."

CHAPTER TWENTY-NINE

Monday afternoon turned out to be a very nice fall day in New York. It was mild enough for Mike to feel like driving the Corvette and letting the top down. So he decided to ride out to the island to visit Jamaica. Shy wanted to go with him. After she got dressed, Shy called Orlando and made arrangements to meet and transact their business later that evening.

They arrived at the clinic after three. Jamaica was glad to see them since he wasn't expecting anybody that day. Perry and his family had come out early Sunday morning. But after that, it was pretty depressing watching other people visiting with their families. Mike and Shy told him all about dinner with the Rays. Shy told Jamaica how nice Pam was to her and how she had to get Bobby up off her when he tried to question her. Jamaica told her that Bobby wasn't the one, and that she still had to watch Wanda. "You only slowed her down. She'll be back at you again."

"Pam used to think Wanda was such a bitch," Mike said.

Shy started to say, "That's because she is," but she kept that to herself. "What's her trip anyway?" she asked instead.

"Wanda just needs a man, that's all," Mike replied.

"Why do men think that's the solution to all of a woman's problems?" Shy asked.

Mike and Jamaica looked at one another. "'Cause they do," they both said.

"Her problem is that she eats most men up. Most men just aren't strong enough to handle her," Mike said.

"She still a control freak?" Jamaica asked.

"It's gotten worse. Don't get me wrong, Wanda's my girl. She's made us a whole group of money. But she just has that way about her. She got to run things. But she gets it done. So I ain't sayin' nothin'," Mike said.

"Well, if she comes after me again, she better be ready 'cause I got something for her."

"Have you thought about what you want to do now?" Mike said to Jamaica.

"I don't know. I been thinking about it, but I really don't know."

"You could come work for me," Shy said jokingly.

"No, sunshine, I don't think so. Your business is a little too hectic."

They remained until visiting hours were over. Jamaica said that there was nothing to do on the weekends. So Mike said that he would be there Friday at three to check him out for the weekend. When they were ready to leave, Shy promised she would come back next time Mike came out. Mike said he would be back tomorrow. "But don't hold me to it."

As they drove slowly back to the city, Shy commented, "This is so relaxing. This is just what I needed. Put all that drama aside, even if it's just for a little while."

"If I didn't know better, I'd think you were tired of dealin' with all this."

"I am."

"You mean you're not havin' the time of your life?"

Shy smiled. "I am, but that's only because of you."

"They say relationships that begin under extreme circumstances never last."

"Maybe for other people, but not us."

"That's what we talkin' about."

"This love thang we got goin' on, Black, I feel so good when I'm with you. It's like escapism."

"I know what you mean. But somebody told me last night that this 'ain't 5th grade, and these ain't nursery rhymes.'"

"Who you tellin'? But that's the problem with escapism. When you come off the high, reality is still there waiting to slap you in the face."

"Maybe we should see about making the fairly tale a reality."

"I know you got money, but I don't think you can buy a new reality. This is real life, and that's what we got to deal with," Shy said sadly.

"O ye of little faith. I'm not talkin' about changing the world, I just wanna change our reality. The rest of the world can come along."

"Black, can I ask you something?"

"What's that, Cassandra?"

"I'm getting tired of callin' you Black."

"Call me whatever you want."

"It's like when your friends are talkin' about you, they're talkin' about a different person. They're talkin' about some nice guy named Mike. Maybe I'm just jealous, but I wanna call you Mike too."

"You could call me muthafucka if you wanted to. It would still sound good coming from you."

"You say the sweetest things."

"All true, Cassandra, all true."

"Mike. Now it feels funny saying it. Anyway, I have a small confession to make."

"What's that?"

"I didn't just happen to come to Impressions that night."

A cold chill ran through Mike.

"The first night I saw you, it hit me too. You looked so good. I came there hoping I'd see you."

Mike didn't say anything for a moment or two, and then he just looked at her. Had she said that last week or anytime before yesterday, he would have been overjoyed. But not now. Now he felt like he had awakened to find his nightmare was real. Now Bobby's words echoed in his mind.

"What's wrong?" she asked, sensing his mood had changed.

"Nothing."

"I know you, Mike Black. Tell me and I promise I'll make it better."

Once again, Mike went silent. Should he confront her with what Bobby said about her? What would he say? "Yo, Shy, are you using me?" and then be afraid to hear her answer? No point in asking. If it were true, she'd only deny it anyway. "It doesn't matter."

"Yes, it does. If something's bothering you, I wanna know."

"Just be for real. I couldn't stand it if all you turned out to be was a perpetrator."

"Perpetrator! Perpetrating what? Where did that come from?"

"Like I said, it doesn't matter, perpetrator or not."

"What did he say?" Shy asked.

"Who?"

"Don't play stupid. Bobby! What did he say to make you call me a perpetrator? Baby, it don't get no more real than this. Please, talk to me." Shy smiled. "Doesn't this feel like déjà vu? I mean, isn't this how we spent yesterday afternoon?"

"Only difference is you had a gun in your hand." They both laughed.

"I told you, baby, the gun just happened to be in my hand."

"Say it again," Mike said.

"What? The gun just happened to be in my hand."

"No, call me baby again."

"Baby," she said again, looking seductively into his eyes. "What could possibly be wrong?"

"No, I am not letting you off the hook that easy. You're going to tell me what Bobby said. Oh, and in case you didn't know, I am in love with you. I'm a little dick whipped, too, but we'll pass that for now. Now you tell me, what did he say?"

"That you may just be here to make your problems go away."

The smile on Shy's face turned to anger, and just as quickly the anger gave way to hurt. "Is that what you believe? Do you really think I would do you like that?"

"No, I really don't. I wasn't even going to mention it."

"No, you were just gonna go around thinking I'm a perpetrator. I wouldn't play with your feelings like that, much less mine. How could you believe that, Black?"

"I don't, and even if you could, please don't stop. It's been great bein' with you. Now I can't imagine living without you."

"I can't either. I've never felt like this about anybody. That's why I can't understand how you could even think that," Shy said.

"Déjà vu."

"Okay, okay, hypothetically, let's just say I was like that and that I stepped to you just to get your help."

"And protection," Mike added.

"And protection. How'd I know you'd go for it?"

Mike started laughing.

"What?" Shy asked, wondering what could be so funny.

"I asked Bobby that very same question."

"Well, that makes me feel a little better. At least you had some confidence in me. What did Bobby say to that?"

"He asked me if I had looked at you lately."

Shy looked at herself, smiled, and started laughing too. "What's that supposed to mean?" she said, fishing for the compliment.

"Cassandra, you are the most beautiful woman, the most beautiful person, I've ever met. And I've met some fly ones. But they can't compete with you. You've come to show me that loving you is what's been missing in my life," Mike said, reaching for her hand.

"Please believe me. Better yet, I'll just have to prove it to you. Prove it to everybody. Baby, I'm for real."

"You don't have anything to prove, at least not to me."

"I know I got nothing to prove, but you stick around. Because I'm here to stay."

"I got no problem with that."

When they got back to the city, it was almost ten. Mike drove straight to Impressions. He told Shy that he needed to catch Bobby before he went home. That was all right with her. She might have a thing or two to say to him. Shy asked what Bobby was doing there when the club was closed. He explained that every other Monday they had a staff meeting.

Once they arrived at the club, Mike went to Bobby's office. Shy used the phone at the front door to call E. She told him where she was and to pick her up there. After hanging up, she went to join Mike in the office.

Mike wanted to talk to Bobby about Jamaica. He wanted to have some options to discuss with Jamaica when he went to see him the following day. It wasn't easy since they hadn't seen Jamaica in nine years. They didn't really know him or what he was interested in doing. They kicked around a few things, but they both agreed that it should be his choice.

Shy entered the office. "Bobby," she said calmly. "I have something to say to you."

"What's that?" Bobby asked.

"You're wrong."

"Wrong about what?"

"I said what I had to say, and now I'm done with it."

"Done with what?" Bobby asked, becoming a little agitated.

"How's Pam and the kids? Oh, Bobby, your kids are so adorable. And your son, he's quite the little man, isn't he? And a gentleman. He opened the car door for me, tried to help me on with my coat. They are all so polite. You and Pam have done an excellent job with them. You must be very proud."

"Oh, all right, that's cool. I see how it's gonna be, and yes, I am proud of them."

"Good, I'm glad you see how it's gonna be. Oh, yeah, one more thing I'd like to say, too."

"What's that?"

"I didn't thank you for having us to dinner last night."

"You're welcome. Mike, what am I wrong about?" Bobby asked.

"Cassandra."

"Yes, baby?"

"Bobby's talking to you."

"Hey, Bobby. Did you wanna ask me something?"

"Never mind. The two of you belong together. Neither one of you can answer a straight question." Everybody laughed.

"What time are you meeting Orlando and them?" Mike asked.

"Midnight at a warehouse in the South Bronx."

"You be careful," Bobby said. Shy looked surprised by his comment. "I want you to know that I don't have anything against you. I like you. I'm just protecting our interest, that's all."

"I like you too, Bobby. And I can understand that. But you are wrong about me. End of story. We don't need to discuss this any further," Shy said, extending her hand in friendship.

Bobby shook her hand.

"I hope we can get past this," Shy said as the phone rang, and Bobby answered it. He told Shy that E was downstairs waiting for her.

"I guess I'll see you later, baby. Where are you going to be in a couple of hours?" Shy asked.

"I don't know. I have something I need to do," Mike replied.

"Here you go, Mike." Bobby threw him a cellular phone. "Join the new millennium," he said, writing down the number and handing it to Shy.

"I guess you can call me," Mike said.

"Don't worry about it. We got a lot to do afterward, so it will be late. Why don't I just see you in the morning?" Shy said.

"Call me anyway when you're done. Doesn't matter what time."

"Okay. Now you promise me that you're not gonna send Jap or Freeze to follow me."

"I promise. I will not send Jap or Freeze to follow you," Mike said, raising his right hand. Shy kissed him goodbye and left to handle her business. As soon as the door closed, Mike said, "Bobby, follow her."

"I knew you were gonna say that." Bobby got up and armed himself. "Why can't you follow her?"

"I have someplace to go," Mike replied.

"Now you got me runnin' behind her. Call Pam and let her know what I'm doing. She won't go off on you. I'll call you if I need you. Where you goin'?"

"Home."

CHAPTER THIRTY

There is a certain feeling that comes over you when you drive down the street that you grew up on, the familiarity of being home. Mike parked the Corvette in front of his mother's house and went inside. Not very much had changed over the years. A few new knickknacks, a new picture of Malcolm X, but other than that, nothing had changed. He sat down on the couch.

"Who's that? Who's in here?" Emily shouted from her bedroom.

"It's just me, Ma. Did I wake you up?"

"Michael? What are you doing here?" she asked.

"I'm fine, Ma. How are you?" Mike asked.

"I'm sorry, Michael. I'm fine, and no, you didn't wake me up. I was just reading."

"What ya reading?"

"Just the paper. But you still haven't answered my question. What are you doing here at this hour?" Emily asked.

"I hadn't seen you for a couple of weeks, so I came to see you."

"What's wrong, Michael?"

"What makes you think something's wrong?"

"Well, it's after eleven. Most people don't just drop by at this hour just to say, 'Hi, Mommy, how are you?' Now what's on your mind?"

"I wanted to ask you a question," Mike said, returning to the couch.

"I'm all ears."

"If I were to leave New York, leave the country, would you come with me?"

"Where are you talking about going?"

"Back to the islands, the Bahamas. Saint Vincent maybe," Mike said.

"Saint Vincent? What brought this on? You're not in trouble, are you?"

"No, Ma, nothing like that. I've just been thinking about it a lot lately."

"Saint Vincent. I haven't been there in, my God, thirty years."

"I never told you this, but I went there about twelve years ago."

"You went looking for your father." Emily reached for his hand and squeezed it tight. "Why didn't you tell me?"

"Didn't want to upset you. Anytime I'd mention it, you'd get mad at me."

"Did you see him?"

"Yes."

"How'd you find him?"

"It's amazing what you can do with money. I found someone who knew him, and I paid them to introduce me to him. Socially, of course."

"Well?"

"I introduced myself as Mike Black. Told him that my mother was born there and that her name is Emily Black. He didn't remember you."

"Michael, back then I was a different person. I was eighteen and I was so fast."

"You? Fast? I have a hard time believing that," Mike said.

"It's true. Having you changed my life." Emily smiled. "I met him one night at a dance. I was so drunk. That's why I stopped drinking. I never saw him again after that night, never even tried."

"Why didn't you tell me this before?"

"Pride. You were too young when you used to ask. Besides, it wasn't your business. When you got older, you stopped asking. I didn't think it mattered to you anymore. I didn't know that man. Only thing I do remember about him is that he was kind of arrogant."

"Yeah, I noticed that. But he's a cop, so that figured," Mike said.

"You look a lot like him."

"I noticed that, too. It was funny, the way he kept looking at me, sayin' how familiar I looked to him. He showed me a picture of his wife and kids. I have two brothers and a sister."

"Why didn't you tell him that he was your father?"

"Because he's not. I mean, biologically he is, but Mr. Smith was more of a father to me than he was."

"I never knew you thought of old Smithy that way. I do remember how upset you were when he died. But you still haven't answered my question."

"You haven't answered mine."

"Of course I'd go, Michael, but what would you do?"

"Open a reggae supper club on the beach."

"For years I prayed for this day. I never thought I'd hear you say that you wanted to quit being a criminal. You caused me so much grief and so much pain."

"I'm sorry."

"And embarrassment. I couldn't walk down the street or even go to church without somebody pointing a finger and whispering. It wasn't easy being Vicious Black's mother. I used to wonder where I had gone wrong with you. Then you took the neighborhood to war," Emily said, shaking her head in disgust. "Day after day, having to hear who and how many people my son killed today. I was ashamed of my own son."

"I did what I thought was best."

"But then things changed. No more drugs, no more drive-bys. Building a community center for the kids. People needing help started asking me to talk to you. And you would always do what you could to help them. Even the finger pointers started speaking again, which I could have done without. I can't stand them anyway. Too gossipy for my taste," Emily said with a smile.

"Who, Mrs. Hawkins and them?"

"Yes, she was the main one always asking for favors. 'Could you ask Michael to do this and tell Michael to do that.'"

"She got on my nerves too," Mike said.

"I just thank God for answering my prayers. Now you tell me, what brought all this on?" Emily asked.

"I met somebody," he replied quickly, like a kid who couldn't wait to tell a secret.

Emily saw the excitement in his eyes. "Look at you. She must be somebody important."

"Yeah, she's pretty important. Her name is Cassandra Sims," he said, "and I'm in love with her."

"In love with her!" Emily said, caught completely by surprise. "How does she feel about this move?"

"I haven't told her yet."

"I feel honored that you would tell me first. Do you think she'll be willing to go with you?"

"I think so. But she has a lot going on right now."

"I knew that's what it would take. Someone to come along and show you a better way. What does she do for a living?" Emily asked, totally unprepared for the answer. "I hope she's a step up from those tramps and that shake dancer you run around with."

Mike dropped his head. "Actually she distributes cocaine."

"You sure can pick them," Emily said, shaking her head. "So when do I get to meet her?"

"Maybe I'll bring her by tomorrow."

"Well, Michael, I think I've had enough excitement for one day. You're in love and retiring, and I'm going to bed."

"I'm a little tired myself. Do you mind if I sleep in my old room?"

"This is your home, Michael. You don't have to ask me that. If you're still here in the morning, we'll have breakfast together."

"That would be nice. I can't remember the last time you cooked for me. Thank you."

"Good night, Michael." And with that, Emily went to bed.

Mike went to his old room. He sat on the bed he hadn't slept in since he was 15. Mike looked around the room. The walls were still covered with movie and basketball posters. "The '69–'70 New York Knicks. Greatest team in NBA history." He got up and opened the closet door and pulled out three suitcases that were hidden in a false compartment. Mike placed them on the bed and opened them up. Each case was filled with money. There was $10 million in those cases. Mike closed the cases and put them on the floor. He got undressed, turned off the light, and went to sleep.

CHAPTER THIRTY-ONE

Meanwhile, Shy arrived at the warehouse to transact her business with Orlando. Bobby was able to follow them there with no problem. He parked his car across the street so he could watch the warehouse, but not close enough to be seen. On the way there, Shy had to listen to E argue with Tony and tell her again how it was Black behind their problems. Her mind was focused on making this deal and getting back on track. They entered the warehouse, led by Shy. Jack carried the money while E and Tony brought up the rear. One of Orlando's men met them at the door and escorted them to the warehouse floor.

The warehouse was empty for the most part, except for two cars and a table in the middle of the warehouse floor. Shy looked around, checking for another exit. There was one marked exit next to the loading dock in the rear of the building. To the right of the dock there were steps leading upstairs. Orlando stood waiting, flanked on either side by five of his men. All were standing around a table with four metal briefcases on it.

Orlando greeted them. "Shy, you are looking more beautiful than I remembered."

"Thank you, Orlando. How have you been?" Shy asked.

"Very well, thank you. I am better tonight than I was last night, isn't that right, Carlos?" Orlando said, looking around. "Oh, yes, I forgot, he is no longer with us, in case somebody asks. Shall we get down to business?"

"By all means," Shy said.

Tony stepped to the front with his testing kit. Orlando handed Tony a kilo from one of the four cases. "Not that one," Shy said, walking to the table. "May I?" she said, pointing to the metal cases.

"By all means, Shy. Be my guest." Orlando stepped back as Shy came around to the other side of the table.

She opened another case and handed Tony another kilo. "This one."

Tony proceeded to work. All stood quietly, waiting for the contents of the tester to change color. E stepped up, stuck his finger in, and tasted the product. He nodded at Shy in approval.

"It's got the color we want," Tony said.

"Jack."

Jack stepped up, placing the case on the table and opening it before Orlando.

E leaned toward Shy. "I'll get the car."

"Okay," Shy said, and E walked off.

"I'm sure there's no need to count it."

"But I insist. Please, count it," Shy said.

"Shy, may I speak with you for a moment?" Orlando said, motioning for her to join him as he stepped away from the table. Shy walked toward him. "Black came to see me last night about a problem. Please tell him I have dealt with that problem, and ask him to accept my apology."

"I'll be sure to tell him if I see him." Shy shook Orlando's hand. "Pleasure doing business with you."

"Let's hope it will be a profitable relationship for both of us," Orlando said.

Bobby sat impatiently in his car checking his watch, thinking that they should be out shortly. He thought he saw someone moving on the side of the building. Bobby turned back to the front door as E came out of the building. Bobby watched as E stopped on the steps and lit a cigarette. E started walking toward his car as two men in police vests ran past him. Then E calmly got in the car and drove away. Two more cars arrived. Bobby thought it was strange that the cars were unmarked. Another six men in police vests got out of the cars and entered the building. The cars were then driven away from the building. Police cars arrived, no lights or no sirens, taking up positions outside the building.

Back inside the warehouse, the police moved into position. "Police! Nobody move!"

Orlando and Shy looked at each other, both thinking that the cops came for the other. Tony looked at Shy and took out his gun.

"Tony, no!" Shy shouted.

Tony opened fire on the police. They returned fire, hitting Tony with three shots in the chest. Shy pulled out one of her guns and began shooting as she ran to the table.

"Shit!"

She took cover under the table and reloaded. Jack took cover with Orlando's men and was drawing fire from the police. Orlando grabbed the case with the money and ran to the steps.

"This way, Shy!"

Shy took a deep breath, stood up, and began shooting as she followed Orlando to the steps. Orlando ran up the steps to a window that led to a fire escape to the alley on the side of the building. He opened the window and was shot immediately. Shy hid behind a large box against the wall as a cop entered the building through the window. He aimed his weapon, looking left in her direction and then to the right. As he turned back, Shy came out of hiding and fired twice. The first shot grazed his temple, and the second shot hit him in the chest. The cop fell to the ground and dropped his gun, but he was moving, still alive. He was wearing a bulletproof vest. Shy was glad that she didn't have to kill him. Quickly, she moved toward the window, kicking the cop's gun out of his reach as she passed. She looked at Orlando. He was dead. Shy picked up the case with the money and placed it on the fire escape.

"Freeze!" yelled a cop at the top of the steps.

Shy turned and pointed her gun at the cop. He fired, hitting Shy in the upper right chest, in the shoulder area. She returned fire as she fell, one shot to his head.

Shy struggled to get to her feet. She checked her wound. It hurt like hell, and she was bleeding profusely. But she was all right.

"Damn!" she said, looking at the cop slumped over the top of the steps. Shy decided not to take the time to ponder the ramifications of killing a cop. She went out the window and looked around for more cops. Not seeing any, she picked up the case and proceeded down the fire escape. She lowered the ladder, dropping the case as she climbed down. The alley was a dead end. Shy had only one choice. She picked up the case and started running toward the street. She hit the corner and ran to the right. Two cops fell in behind her and opened fire.

Bobby saw Shy come running out of the alley. He started the car and went after her. "I'm impressed."

Her arm felt more like she was carrying rocks than money, but she kept running. Bobby pulled up alongside them, got out quickly, and began running after them. Shy stopped, turned around quick, and shot one of the cops in the leg. Bobby shot him again as he ran past and then shot the other cop in the back of the head.

Shy didn't see Bobby and kept running.

"Where is she going?" Bobby ran back to his car and caught up with her at the next corner. He turned in front of her. "Hello, Shy. Need a ride?" He got out of the car and helped Shy into the back seat. Bobby got back in the car and drove away. "Are you all right?"

"No! I'm shot!" Shy screamed in pain. Bobby looked back at Shy, seeing that she was bleeding.

"How bad are you hit?"

"It's bad, Bobby," Shy replied.

"Hang on, Shy. I'll get you to a doctor." Bobby picked up his cell phone and called Mike.

"Hello."

"Mike, it's Bobby."

"What's up, Bobby? How'd it go?"

"Not good. Cops raided the place."

"Where's Shy?" Mike asked as he got out of bed and began to get dressed.

"She's with me, but she's been shot. I'm on my way to Perry now. Call him and tell him to be ready," Bobby said.

"Where's she hit?" Mike asked.

"In the chest, by her right shoulder. She's bleeding pretty bad."

"Okay, I'll meet you there." Mike headed out the door. "Bobby . . . thanks."

"Yeah, yeah, I'll send you the bill for cleaning my back seat."

Mike got in the car, dialing Perry's number as he drove. "Hello."

"Glenda, it's Mike. Let me speak to Perry."

Glenda handed the phone to her husband. Perry asked who it was. "It's Mike," she said.

"What's wrong, Mike?" Perry asked.

"Sorry to bother you, man, but I need you and Glenda to meet me at your office as soon as you can. Bobby's on his way there now. He's bringing you a patient, gunshot wound in the chest by her shoulder."

"Her? Her who?" Perry asked.

"Never mind that now. I'll explain when I get there." Mike hung up the phone and called Freeze.

Being entertained by Paulleen, he answered the phone with fury, "This better be important."

"Where are you?" Mike asked.

"I was about to get fucked. What's up?"

"Meet me at Perry's office now," Mike said.

"On my way," Freeze answered.

Mike arrived at the office. Perry and Glenda were inside waiting for him, prepping for surgery. Mike stood outside, looking for Bobby's car. "Where is he?" He called Bobby.

"Yeah," Bobby answered.

"Where are you?" Mike asked.

"I'm a couple of blocks down the street."

"How's Shy?"

"Looks like she passed out, but I think she still hangin'."

"I'll get a stretcher and meet you outside." Mike ran inside and returned with the stretcher as Bobby arrived. Mike opened the car door and checked for a pulse. Shy was still alive. "Cassandra," Mike said as he and Bobby took her out of the car and put her on the stretcher.

Shy opened her eyes. "Black."

"You're gonna be all right, baby. Just hold on." He wheeled her into the operating room.

After taking Shy into the operating room, Mike and Bobby went outside to wait. "What happened, Bobby?" Mike asked.

"They had been in there about fifteen minutes when cops started showing up outta thin air."

"How'd she get away?"

"I don't know. A while after the cops went in, I see her come runnin' out of the alley carrying . . . I almost forgot. She came out with a briefcase." Bobby walked back to the car and opened the back door and removed the briefcase.

"Mike, come here."

Mike went to the car.

"Look at this."

Mike looked inside the car and was horrified by how much blood Shy had lost. He looked at Bobby, picked up the briefcase, and walked away. "Send me the bill." Mike put the case in the Corvette and slammed the car door.

"Hey, Mike, I'm sorry. I shouldn't have gone there," Bobby said.

"It's cool." Mike sat down on the curb. "Anybody else get out?"

"E got out before Shy. After she came out, I went after her."

"E? How did he get out?"

"He came out before the cops went in," Bobby said as Freeze pulled up.

"What's up?"

"Cops raided Shy's buy," Bobby said.

"Is she all right?" Freeze asked.

"She took one in the chest," Bobby replied.

"What the fuck do you mean he came out before the cops went in?"

"I didn't stutter. He came out, lit up a square, and walked. What was funny about that was the cops ran right past him."

Freeze and Mike both looked at Bobby. "You're tellin' me that the cops were about to raid the building, but E walks out and the cops don't bother with him?" Freeze questioned.

"What does that tell us, boys and girls?"

"He set her up," Freeze said.

"Freeze, I want you to make inquiries, find out what happened. I wanna know who the cops were after: Shy or Orlando. Find out who's dead, who's in jail, the whole nine. But stay away from Orlando's people. They're probably pissed at us anyway. And, Freeze, you find him," Mike ordered.

"What do you want me to do when I find him?" Freeze asked.

"Nothing. And don't mention anything about a setup to anyone, especially to Shy. If he is the one, I want him to think he got away with it."

"I'm out," Freeze said.

As Freeze drove away, Mike and Bobby went back inside. They sat quietly in the waiting room for what seemed like hours. Actually, it was only forty-five minutes or so before Perry came out. Mike jumped to his feet.

"How is she?"

"I removed the bullet, but she's lost a lot of blood. She'll be weak for a couple of days, and she should take in as much fluid as possible, but she's going to be fine," Perry replied.

"Thanks, Perry."

"No problem. I'll send you my bill," Perry joked.

"Damn, this is gettin' expensive."

"You'll need to change her dressing every four hours or so. I'll give you something for pain and an antibiotic for her. The question is, who is she?"

"You mean you don't know? Well, you better ask somebody. That's Wonder Woman," Bobby said.

"Can't be Wonder Woman, Bobby. Wonder Woman got those wristbands. Bullets can't hurt her. So who is she, Mike?" Perry asked.

"Her name is Cassandra. But you can call her Shy."

"So this is the infamous Shy. I figured that's who she was. Wanda told us about her. You know nobody around here can keep anything. Well, don't worry. She'll be fine in a couple of days. I hope she's not a bitch like Regina," Perry said, as Glenda came out of the operating room. "How's our patient?" he asked.

"She's doing just fine. Hi, Mike. Hi, Bobby. And no, she's not a bitch. Pam says she's nice."

"Y'all got a regular hotline goin'. Can't get nothin' by you," Mike said.

"And if she hangs around a while, she'll be in on it too," Glenda said.

"Yeah, well, that remains to be seen," Mike said.

"Do you want her to stay with us while she recovers?" Perry asked.

"Can we move her?" Mike asked.

"Yes, but don't give her too many bumps. It may reopen the wound. You're not taking her in the Vette, are you?"

"I was gonna let Drivin' Miss Daisy here take her."

"'Cause I can call a friend of mine who runs a private ambulance service."

"Where are you gonna take her, Mike?" Bobby asked.

"I'll take her to my mom's house. She can change her dressing."

"How is Miss Black gonna feel about you bringing a drug dealer into her house?" asked an exhausted Glenda. "She hates dealers more than you do."

"Don't worry, she's expecting us." But this wasn't what he had in mind when he said it.

Perry sat down and rested his head on his wife's shoulder. "By the way, Mike, how'd your 'I got no use for no drug dealer' ass get hooked up with a drug dealer anyway?"

"I guess since Glenda was in there you didn't look at her," Bobby said.

"I asked myself that too." He stared at her through the glass. "But I love her."

The ambulance got to Perry's office at about two thirty and took Shy to Mike's mother's house. He had Freeze send a couple of men to watch the house.

Not wanting to wake Emily, Mike carried her in and took her to his room. For the next two hours, he sat holding her hand and staring at her. He wanted to be the first thing she saw when she opened her eyes. Once, he felt her squeeze his hand. The events of the evening strengthened his resolve to get Shy away from all this. He couldn't stand to lose her.

Finally, he got up and went into the living room and lay down on the couch. He drifted off to sleep shortly thereafter.

CHAPTER THIRTY-TWO

Emily woke up early the following morning to find Mike asleep on the couch. She didn't wake him. She went into the kitchen to cook breakfast. When it was almost ready, Emily went back into the living room. "Michael, wake up," she said several times before finally having to shake him.

"Good morning, Ma," Mike said with a deep yawn and stretch.

"What are you doing sleeping on the couch? You know it's not good for your back. Anyway, breakfast is almost ready. Just come on when you're ready," Emily said on her way back to the kitchen. Mike gathered his thoughts and went into the kitchen.

"Ma," he said, sitting down at the table, "got something to tell you."

"What's that, Michael?" Emily said, bringing him his food.

"Actually," he said, scratching his day's growth of beard, "I need you to do something for me."

"Ask me what you wanna ask me," Emily said, sitting down to eat.

"Remember I said that I'd bring Cassandra by today to meet you?"

"So what time are you going to bring her by?"

"Well, she's in my room. She's been shot."

"Oh God."

"Perry took the bullet out last night, but she is gonna need to have her dressing changed every four hours."

"When was the last time it was changed?" Emily asked.

"Glenda dressed it about two, I guess."

"It hasn't been changed since then?" Emily said excitedly, getting up from the table.

"No," Mike said, following her to his room.

"My goodness, Michael, why didn't you wake me up? Sometimes I wonder where your mind is. That dressing should have been changed hours ago." Emily opened the door and went in.

"Ma, this is Cassandra."

Emily sat down on the bed, and Mike handed her the bag Perry had sent for her. She cleaned and redressed the wound.

"She's very pretty, Michael."

"I hope you like her. She really is wonderful," Mike said, looking at her with pride.

"Now I understand. You have to get her away from New York," Emily said as she went back to the kitchen.

"I know that, Ma."

"You got to get her away from that life."

"I know that, Ma."

"She could have been killed."

"I know that, Ma."

"That's a very dirty and dangerous business to be in, especially for a woman."

"I know that, Ma," Mike said, feeling more like a kid each time he said it.

"How did it happen?" asked Emily.

"I don't know. But I have a good idea," Mike said.

"I hope you're not involved. What am I saying? I hope you're not involved too deeply in this, are you, Michael?"

"No, Ma. She is very quick to remind me that this is her business." Mike finished eating and got up from the table.

"I have to go out for a while. I shouldn't be gone long, but I have a couple of people outside watching the house. If you want, I can get one to stay in here with you."

"Is it really necessary to have one of them in my house?"

"No, but I thought it would make you feel more comfortable," Mike said.

"No, having a hoodlum in my house wouldn't make me feel more comfortable."

"I've got a cellular phone that Bobby gave me. You can call me if anything happens."

After Mike left, Emily dusted off her old medical bag and went in to check on Shy. Shy still had not regained consciousness, so she checked her vital signs and left the room.

Mike called Bobby. He wanted Bobby to ride with him and told him that he would be there in about an hour to pick him up.

"You're something else, driving your own car, talkin' on the cell phone. And they say that miracles never cease," Bobby joked.

Then he called Freeze for an update.

Freeze answered, "Yo."

"Where is he, Freeze?" Mike asked.

"Nothing yet. I got everyone out lookin' for him," Freeze said.

"What about the rest of her crew?"

"Tony's dead. Jack's in jail," Freeze replied.

"Orlando?"

"He's dead too. Two more of his people are dead. The rest are in jail. It was definitely a setup, Black. Cops got a tip that there was a big deal goin' down. No word on who the target was."

"Well, stay on finding E."

"Where are you gonna be?" Freeze asked.

"I'm on my way home. Bobby gave me one of his cell phones, so call me if you get something. Freeze, find him. Don't kill him."

"Understood."

Mike went in his house. After a quick shower and shave, he was back on the street. He got into the Seville, taking with him the briefcase that he had given to Shy. On the way to pick up Bobby, he called Wanda at her office. Wanda's secretary put him right through.

"Good morning, Mike. How is she?" Wanda asked.

"She hasn't come out of it yet," Mike said.

"Glenda said she would probably be out for a while. She lost a lot of blood. Where is she?"

"At my mother's."

"Will she be safe there?" Wanda asked.

"Freeze has some people outside the house. I've got a run to make, but I'll be back there in a couple of hours," Mike said.

"We need to talk."

"Why don't you meet me at my mom's around one?"

"That's cool. I'll see you there. Mike, I'm sorry."

"Thanks, Wanda," Mike said, arriving at Bobby's house.

Bobby came out and got in the car. "Where we goin'?" Bobby asked as Mike drove away.

"Yonkers. And don't you say a thing," Mike said.

"I wasn't gonna say anything," Bobby said, laughing.

"I'm getting out, Bobby."

"What?"

"I'm leaving the country with Shy," Mike said.

"Don't you think you're overreacting?"

"No. I got to get her away from here. I should have done this before. I could have handled all her business for her," Mike said.

"She told you that it is her business. What were you supposed to do?"

"We shoulda just stayed in the Bahamas. If we had, none of this woulda happened."

"Mike, come on, you can't blame yourself for this. It's a rough business she chose to be in."

"It is my fault, Bobby, as if I had pulled the trigger myself. I shoulda been there for her."

"Okay, I understand your wanting to get her out of here. She shot at least one cop, so they'll be all over her. But please, man, give this some thought."

"I have, even before this happened. Think about it, Bob. We don't need to live like this anymore. We got plenty of money. Until recently, we really haven't been involved in the business anyway."

"I guess you're right, Mike. Pam's been at me to get all the way out since we started getting back involved. But what would we do? Where would we go?"

"I'm goin' back home."

"To the islands?"

"Yeap. Open up a little spot on the beach. All I'm asking you to do is think about it. Shy may still die, and I can't stand to lose any more friends."

Mike parked outside of Angelo's spot. Uncharacteristically, there was no one outside. Bobby got out and went in, but he was stopped at the door.

"Can I help yous two?"

"I'm lookin' for fat-ass Jimmy," Bobby said.

"Is that fuckin' Bobby? Is that fuckin' Bobby I hear? How the fuck are you? How's the family?" Jimmy asked.

"They're fine, Jimmy. I'm tryin' to keep up with you. I heard that your wife had another baby."

"That's six. We're working every day on number seven," replied Jimmy.

Angelo came out of his office. "Is that fuckin' Bobby? I don't fuckin' believe it! Pam let you out?" Mike came in, carrying the briefcase. "I knew this guy shouldn't be far behind. How's it goin', Mikey? Come on back, gentlemen." Angelo led them back to the office. "What's in the case, Mikey?"

"The quarter mil our friend owed you, plus fifty grand for making you wait," Mike replied, handing Angelo the case.

"Look, Mikey, I heard about what happened. I'm sorry. Is she all right?"

"She'll be fine in a couple of days."

"Anything I can do, anything at all, just tell me," Angelo said.

"I need to get her out of the country, Angee."

"Tell me what you need."

"I need an airplane, Angee. You know black people don't have airplanes."

"Tell him the rest, Mike," Bobby said.

"Rest of what?"

"I'm goin' with her."

"Are you surprised, Bobby? I'd follow her too. No disrespect to you, Mike. You thinking about getting out, huh? You need money or anything?"

"No, Angee, just the plane. I'll be fine once she's safe."

"You ever need anything, and I mean anything at all, you make sure you call, Mikey. I'm serious. You call me and let me know where you are."

"Bobby will know where I am. You take care of yourself, Angee. I'll be back to see you after things quiet down," Mike said, attempting to shake Angelo's hand.

"Sorry, Mikey, but that's not gonna cut it." Angelo got up from behind his desk, arms extended. Angelo hugged Mike and kissed him on each cheek.

"Isn't this just the most touching scene you ever wanted to see? You can call this gangster love," Bobby said.

"I'm gonna miss you, Mikey," Angelo said as he watched Mike and Bobby leave his office.

CHAPTER THIRTY-THREE

"Tony, no!" Shy shouted.

Seeing the police open fire on Tony and watching as he fell to the ground, Shy took a deep breath.

She tossed and turned. "Tony's dead." She was having a nightmare: hearing Orlando's voice say, "This way, Shy!" then seeing him die.

"Freeze!"

The cop fired.

Shy sat straight up in the bed. She awoke to a big movie poster of Pam Grier as Coffy. Shy looked around the room, wondering where she was. There was a framed poster of Prince and The Revolution from *Purple Rain* right next to James Brown's *Sex Machine* album cover. She tried to get up, but she was too weak.

Emily heard stirring coming from Mike's room and went in. "Hello. How do you feel?" Emily asked.

"It feels like my shoulder is about to fall off. I'm a little groggy, but other than that I feel fine," Shy said as she lay back down in the bed.

"Let me change this dressing for you," Emily said.

"Thank you." Shy lay still and quiet while Emily changed her dressing. Once she was finished, Shy said, "I hope you don't mind me asking you this, but who are you and where am I?"

"I am sorry. I don't know where my manners are. I'm Michael's mother, and you're in his old room at my house."

"Michael?"

"You know, Vicious Black. I guess I'm the only one who still calls him Michael."

"It's a real pleasure to meet you. I didn't know he had a mother," Shy said, not thinking about how that sounded.

"What did you think, he was created in a laboratory or something?" Emily said with a smile.

"No, it's just that he never mentioned you or his father. We walked by here, I guess it was here, a couple of weeks ago. But he never talks about you."

"I'm not surprised. Michael and I didn't speak for ten years. I just couldn't deal with what he had become."

"What brought you two back together?"

"Wanda came to see me one day. She said Michael was going through a bad time. And he wanted to see me. How could I refuse? My son needed me."

"How long ago was that?" Shy asked.

"About six years ago," Emily replied.

Shy did her math and knew that the bad time was Regina. "I know it couldn't have been easy for you. I hear Black was a bad boy back in the day. But he's not like that anymore."

"I know he's not, but back in the day, as you say, I thought that I had failed him."

"I think you did a fine job. He is the sweetest person I ever met."

"That's because you're in love," Emily said.

Shy let out a little laugh. "Yeah, maybe I am." But it hurt.

"Here take this. It's for the pain. I know he thinks a lot of you too."

Shy and Emily sat there for more than an hour. They talked about a little of everything, but mostly about Mike. Emily told Shy how she felt about what Mike did for a living. She spoke of how those feelings led to their ten-year separation. How the pain of not speaking to him finally outweighed the hurt that she felt about what he had done.

"I still don't approve of what Michael does, but he has done some good things, too. So what's your story? Why is my son so in love with you?"

Shy smiled and told the short version of her life story. She was quite candid about what she felt were the mistakes she had made. "I should've gotten out years ago, as soon as Randy graduated. My first excuse was that he wouldn't be able to afford to pay for me to go to grad school on residence pay. But I was only fooling myself. If I was serious about going back to school, I woulda been putting money away. If I had, Miss Black—"

"Please call me Emily."

"If I had, Emily, I wouldn't be lying here now. But I would have never met Michael." Shy paused briefly. "Michael. I think I like the sound of that. Anyway, it's definitely better than calling him Black."

"Why didn't you want to go back to school?" asked Emily.

"The money. I was making more money than I ever thought possible. And the power. I was surprised at how much I got off on the power. To me it was all just business. This is what I went to school for—management and marketing. I was managing people and marketing a product. I was the CEO of a company worth $4.2 million dollars a year."

"That all sounds good, but that's a far cry from where you are now. What went so wrong?"

Surprisingly Shy told her the whole story and how it led her to be in need of Emily's nursing skills. Emily was easy to talk to, so she told her about the attempts on her life. "This is the third time in as many weeks that Michael has either saved my life or been responsible for saving my life."

"Is that why you love him?"

"I've asked myself that question over and over again. Each time I come up with the same answer: no. He's just a sweetheart. He's considerate, and he's so much fun to be with. I love talkin' to him. He's easy to talk to, just like you."

"Thank you, Cassandra. I've enjoyed talking to you."

"I should be thanking you. For allowing me in your home, for taking care of me, and honestly, I've enjoyed talking to you too."

"Michael was right. You're not the average drug dealer."

"Excuse me—former drug dealer. I just don't want to do that anymore. I don't know what I'm gonna do yet, but I know it won't have anything to do with drugs."

"That's good. I'm glad to hear you say that," Emily said, knowing what Mike was thinking. Her willingness to quit distributing cocaine would make it easier. "You get some rest now. Are you hungry?"

"Always."

"Good. I'll wake you when lunch is ready," Emily said as she left the room.

Emily returned to the kitchen to prepare lunch. Cooking was her passion. Therefore, she was excited about having someone to cook for. Emily had enjoyed talking with Shy. She was everything that Mike said she would be. Emily had hoped that someday he would become serious about another woman, but she had always assumed that it would be Wanda. During the years that she and Mike didn't speak, a day wouldn't go by without hearing from Wanda. Emily and Wanda shared a mother-daughter relationship. In spite of that, she was just happy for him, happy that he was in love with someone nice. Happy that he was finally ready to put the gangster life behind him. Happy for herself because he wanted her to be a part of his future. Now Emily had visions of grandchildren running in the island sand. She knew it was a little premature, but it felt marvelous.

While Emily cooked lunch for Shy, Mike returned from Angelo's. He came in quietly so he wouldn't disturb Shy. He came into the kitchen and spoke to Emily. She told him that Shy had awakened, but she was resting. Mike excused himself and went to see Shy. As he opened the door, Shy opened her eyes.

"Hello, beautiful," Mike said, leaning down to kiss her gently.

"Hi, baby," Shy replied, accepting his kiss with a smile.

"How do you feel?"

"Like I've been shot."

Mike laughed a little. "Hmm, I wonder why that is." He knelt down next to the bed.

"Why didn't you ever say anything about your mother?"

"I don't know. Just never came up."

"She's wonderful. She's very serious, and at the same time, she's very warm and friendly and so easy to talk to. A lot like you," she said, leaning forward to kiss him on the cheek. "Baby, I'm sorry for being so much trouble to you."

"It's okay. I'm just glad you're gonna be all right," Mike said, smiling at her. "Cassandra, I got something I wanna talk to you about."

"I got something I wanna talk to you about too, Michael."

"Michael? You have been talking to my mother. She's the only one who ever calls me Michael. What do you want to tell me?" Mike asked.

"No, you go first."

"No, you go first," he insisted.

"Okay, okay. I just wanted to say thank you for everything you've done for me. You saved my life again."

"Actually, Bobby saved your life."

"Which reminds me, didn't you promise not to have anybody following me?"

"No, I promised not to have Freeze or Jap follow you."

"Hmm. Anyway, I'm glad you did," Shy said, taking his hand.

"So am I."

"Anyway, you don't have to worry about me anymore."

"What do you mean?" Mike said, horrified at what she would say.

"Stop looking like that. All I wanna say is that I don't wanna do that anymore. Sitting in the back seat of Bobby's car, I thought I was going to die. It's just not worth the risk. My life is more important than business. For a while that's all there was. But I have you in my life, and now everything is different. I don't wanna lose you. I wanna be with you always. I love you so much. I never want to do anything that puts that in jeopardy."

"You just made me the happiest man alive. I love you too, Cassandra. I want to spend the rest of my life lovin' you. And I promise never to put that in jeopardy either."

"Do you mean it? Do you really want to spend your life with me?"

"Yes, and I want us to leave here. Start a new life together. Will you come with me?"

"That sounds good to me. Where will we go? No, let me guess. The Bahamas!" she shouted.

"You think you're smart, don't you, college girl?"

"No, I just know my baby. And we can buy that adorable little house by the beach. Oh, Michael, yes, yes, of course I'll go with you," she said, leaning forward quickly and hugging him, without thinking about her wound. "I forgot about that," she said, laughing, on the verge of tears.

Emily came in carrying a tray with lunch for Shy. Seeing Mike on his knees like that, she thought he was proposing to Shy. "Oh, I'm sorry. Am I interrupting something?" She asked.

"As a matter of fact, you are. You're interrupting the two happiest people in the world," Mike said, getting up to take the tray from her. "But we have plenty of happiness to share with you."

"My goodness, Michael. I've never seen you smile like that," Emily said.

"Ain't he cute when he smiles?"

"What did you do to my son, Cassandra?"

"Just lovin' him, that's all."

"That's so nice. You both look so happy," Emily said, leaving the room. "Do you want me to bring you something to eat, Michael?"

"I'll be out soon. There are still some things that I need to talk to Cassandra about," Mike answered.

"Yeah, there are still some loose ends to tie up," Shy said as Mike closed the door behind Emily.

"What happened? Tell me every detail, and don't leave anything out."

"It was a done deal. E had just gone to get the car. I was talking to Orlando, and then there were cops everywhere." Shy recounted in detail the events of the previous evening while she ate. "This is so good. I see where you got your cooking skills from. Anyway, after that is when Bobby came out of nowhere and picked me up."

"That's it?"

"That's all of it. It was a setup, wasn't it?"

"Yeah, cops were tipped. Any idea who?"

"No. But that's nothing new. I've been wandering through this with my glasses blurred from the jump," Shy said. Mike got up and walked to the window. "Tony's dead, isn't he?"

"Yes."

"Damn. It was so fucked up watching him die. What about Jack and E? Are they dead too?"

"No. Jack is in jail. E got away," Mike answered, still looking out the window.

"I gotta get Jack out of jail. I'm glad E got away though."

Mike turned and walked toward her. "Yeah, Bobby said that E came out, lit up a cigarette, and walked right by the cops when they went in."

"What did you say?"

"He walked right by the cops when they went in," repeated Mike.

"No, he lit a cigarette? E don't smoke. He set me up!" Shy said angrily. "It's been him all along. And I trusted him. Where is he?" Shy started to get out of bed, but Mike laid her down gently.

"Calm down, Vicious Shy. Freeze is looking for him as we speak."

"You knew it all along. Didn't you?"

"Not all along. We figured it out last night, even without the cigarette."

"Why didn't you tell me? Why all the drama?"

"I thought it was important for you to see it for yourself."

"You're right. I wouldn't have believed it if you had told me."

There was a knock at the door while Mike and Shy continued talking. Emily opened the door. Wanda had come to talk to Mike about the situation. She sat on the couch awhile, talking with Emily. "But enough of that, I can tell by that look that you came to see Michael. I'll get him for you," Emily said, getting up and heading toward the room. She knocked on the door and stuck her head in. "Michael, Wanda is here to see you."

"I'll be right back. Don't go anywhere," Mike said, kissing Shy.

"Yeah, right, where am I goin'?" she replied as Mike closed the door behind him. At first, she was a little annoyed that she was not a part of the discussion about her situation. But at the same time, she was relieved that, for her, it was over.

"How you doin', Wanda?"

"Hello, Mike. How is she?"

"She's fine," Mike said, sitting down next to Wanda.

"Can she be moved?"

"Moved her here. I don't see why not. Give me the bad news."

"You know she killed one cop and wounded another?"

"Yeah, she was just tellin' me."

"Cops are all over this. They have her name and a good description of her. It won't be long before they link her to you. It's not safe for her to be here."

"Legally?"

"Right now, it's just harboring a fugitive, but with all the talk about your involvement, it could easily turn into accessory to murder," Wanda said.

"Okay, as soon as it's dark we'll move her. What else?" Mike asked, getting up from the couch.

"One of her people is in jail. He was arraigned this morning for murder, conspiracy to distribute, attempted murder, and accessory to murder. For the time being, he's not talking, not even to his court-appointed lawyer. But that may change if they don't get her. Somebody's gotta fry. Other than the one Wonder Woman capped, four more cops were killed in the shoot-out," Wanda explained.

"Get him out of there."

"No, Mike, if we do that, it will point right to us," Wanda said.

"Don't argue with me. Just get him out of there. Get some Jew lawyer in Brooklyn to get him out."

"Mike, listen to me, he's charged with murdering New York City police officers. No judge is going to release him on bail."

"I guess you're right. Do what you can for him. What about her boy? What kind of deal did he make with the cops?" Mike asked.

"They thought they'd catch her in the act, no need for him to testify. So basically, he just pointed the finger, but killing cops will change that quick. They're probably looking for him to lead them to her. Bobby said he told Shy it was you behind it, so you can just imagine what he'll tell the police."

"Shit."

"I knew this would happen," Wanda said.

"Go ahead and say it, 'I told you so.'"

"Well, I did, but do you listen? No."

"Okay, Wanda. What about the two cops Bobby dropped?"

"Nobody knows anything about Bobby even being in the area, much less killing two cops. I don't know how he does it."

"Okay, best case."

"If what's-his-name . . . Jack doesn't give you up just to make a deal, without her and the snitch, there's nothing to link any of this to us," Wanda said.

"Okay," Mike said before turning to head back to Shy.

"What do you want me to do, Mike?" said Wanda.

"Nothing. Do what you can for Jack. Make sure he knows that it was E who set them up. At this point, the less we're involved, the better."

CHAPTER THIRTY-FOUR

After the sun went down, Mike prepared to move Shy to a safer location. Freeze, along with Jap and Kenny, arrived to provide extra security. Emily wrapped Shy in a blanket and said her goodbyes. "Take good care of yourself, and I'll see you soon," Emily said, giving her a kiss on the cheek.

They formed a circle around Shy, led by Mike, flanked on each side by Jap and Kenny, and Freeze brought up the rear. As they were about to put Shy in the car, Larry came running up. "Yo, Black, yo, Black. Wait up, man, wait up!" he yelled as he ran up.

Mike kissed Shy on the cheek and put her in the car. "Wait here," he said to her, turning to Freeze and motioning for Freeze to follow him. "What's up, Larry?"

"I got some information for you. You know that guy you're looking for?" Larry began whispering in Mike's ear.

"No shit." Mike smiled, then walked back toward the car. "You go ahead. I have something to check out," he said to Shy.

"What is it? I'm going with you," Shy said quietly and started getting out of the car.

"Excuse me, but aren't you retired?" Mike asked.

"Okay, okay."

"Look, it's probably nothing, but it's worth checking out."

"Liar. If you thought it was nothing, you wouldn't be going. You'd send somebody to check it out and report. But it's cool. I'll be a good girl and sit this one out."

"You know me a little too well, beautiful. I'll see you soon."

"Be careful, baby. There's no point in both of us getting shot over this," she said, kissing Mike gently. Mike closed the car door, and Jap drove off.

Mike watched them drive away before joining Freeze and Larry in the Rodeo. Now Larry provided the best lead to E. Mike asked Larry to elaborate in his story. "So where did you get the info?"

"After Freeze told me that he was lookin' for him, I remembered somebody sayin' that he was fuckin' Tony's girl Rita on the down-low. So I rolled by her crib and chilled for a while. A couple of hours ago, she went out. She came back about an hour later with a suitcase. It was full, 'cause she had to drag it in."

"Could be, Black," Freeze said.

"May be something, may be nothing. None of y'all checked her out?"

"No, I was gonna roll by there tomorrow, see if she needed anything," Freeze replied.

"It's still the best lead we got," Mike said.

"So what you wanna do? Go in there and blast that ass?" Freeze asked.

"No, we don't know if he's in there, and if he's not, we'll just be tippin' our hand. For all we know, the cops could be all over the place waiting for Shy to show up."

"So what you wanna do?"

"You were going to stop by to offer your help, right? Let's do it now. I have a plan."

Meanwhile, Jap continued to drive Shy to a more secure location. Shy asked Jap to pull over so she could use the pay phone.

"I don't think that's a good idea, Shy," Jap replied.

"Is anybody following us?" Shy asked.

"No, I don't think so."

"Well, ride around the block a few times and then stop at that pay phone, please."

Jap did as Shy asked, returning to the pay phone. Kenny got out and looked around. There was no one in sight. Shy and Jap got out and they walked toward the phone.

"You got any spare change?" She dialed the phone. She wanted to call Rita and tell her how sorry she was about Tony.

"Hello," Rita answered.

"Hello, Rita. This is Shy."

"Shy," Rita said loudly. E was lying next to her in bed.

"I can't stay on long, but I wanted to say that I'm sorry about what happened to Tony. He was a good man," Shy said.

"Thank you, Shy. I know it wasn't your fault. Cops been here looking for you. They said Tony shot at them first," Rita replied.

"I tried to stop him. But it was too late," Shy said.

"I know you did what you could, but don't worry about me. I'll be all right. You just take care of yourself."

"When is the funeral?" Shy asked.

"The day after tomorrow," Rita replied.

"You know I won't be there. By the way, have you seen E?"

"E?" she said loudly. E motioned for the phone. "He's right here." E took the phone from Rita.

Hearing that E was there with Rita, Shy became excited and angry all at once.

"Shy, you all right?"

"Yeah, E, I'm fine. Are you all right?"

"Yeah, I'm all right. Where are you?" E asked.

"I'm with my peeps in Baltimore. It's better if you don't know where."

"I understand. I'm gonna lie low here until things quiet down, and then I'm gonna try to get down there to you. We can start over," E said.

"I gotta go, but I'll see you soon." Shy angrily slammed down the phone. "That muthafucka. I'll kill him," she said, dialing the phone to warn her mother. "Collect from Cassandra."

"Hi, baby, how are you?"

"I'm okay, Mommy, but listen, the police will be coming. You haven't seen or heard from me in months. I'll explain later. I love you." She hung up the phone quickly. Shy started for the car, saying, "Let's go, Jap. I know where E is."

Kenny looked at Jap and walked away, laughing.

"Shy, please. Do you want Black to kill me? Look, he's with Freeze. We can call and let them know where he is. But I gotta get you off the streets now. So please get in the car, and let's go."

"Okay, let's go," she said grudgingly. "I don't know if I'm ready to retire yet."

E hung up the phone with Shy and began to dial the phone. Rita asked him, "Who are you calling?"

"Forty-seventh precinct."

"Detective Kirkland please," E said.

After a short wait, Detective Kirkland came to the phone. "Kirkland."

"Yeah, Kirk, you can find our friend in Baltimore with her family."

"You got an address?" Kirkland said.

"No, but you're a detective. You'll find her." E replied. He hung up the phone, smiling. "This is working out better than I planned it."

E had been in love with Shy for years, but she never saw anything in him other than dollar signs. He made money for Shy. *Money. That's all she ever cared about.*

It was torture to see Shy with that punk bitch Ricardo all those years. After Ricardo broke her heart, Shy turned to him, and for a while, he had hope. *But she used me. Sucked all the life out of me. And when she had taken all I had, she put me back on the shelf.*

He looked at Rita for maybe the first time. At that moment, it became apparent to him that his interest in Rita was driven solely by his hatred for Tony. "Your boy is dead, Jack's in jail, Shy's on the run, and that leaves Black to take the weight." He never really meant for Shy to get hurt. Not at first anyway. He just wanted to scare her, to drive her closer to him. But then she met Black and everything changed. He wanted her dead. Even though he hoped that Shy would be killed in the shoot-out, this was just as good. E laughed out loud.

Just then, there was a knock at the door.

"Shhh," Rita said, grabbing a robe as E hid, and she went to answer the door. "Who is it?" she yelled.

"It's Freeze, Rita."

"Just a minute. I gotta put something on," Rita said, as E prepared himself to go up against Freeze. When he was set, he motioned for her to open the door.

Freeze stood back away from the door. Mike stood behind him, facedown, not making eye contact with Rita.

"Hello, Rita. I just came to say how sorry I am about what happened to Tony," Freeze said.

"Thank you, Freeze. I'm a little shook up about it. I don't know what I'm gonna do. Tony meant so much to me," she lied.

"If there's anything I can do, anything," Freeze said, looking Rita up and down, "you make sure you call me. You need any money for the funeral?"

"No, I got it covered. It will be the day after tomorrow."

Freeze started to walk away. "By the way, you seen E?"

"No, I haven't. You want me to tell him that you're looking for him?"

Mike looked Rita in the eye. "He knows I'm looking for him." He walked down the hall.

Mike and Freeze returned to the car. Larry handed Mike the phone. "Shy wants you to call her, Black."

He dialed the phone. Kenny answered and handed the phone to Shy. "Hello, Cassandra."

"Baby, I know where E is. He's at Tony's girlfriend Rita's apartment."

"That's probably because he's fuckin' her," Mike said.

"Whaaat, really? That's why they were always at each other. He's gotta die. You know where she lives?"

"I know. We're there right now as a matter of fact," Mike said calmly.

"Did you kill him?"

"No. I have a plan."

"Why not! You should've blasted that ass and been done with it!" Shy said.

"Cassandra, please. I have a plan. Just chill, and I'll see you soon."

"Okay, I'll chill out. But you get here soon 'cause I miss you."

"I'm on my way."

CHAPTER THIRTY-FIVE

It rained most of the morning on the day of Tony's funeral. There was just a little drizzle when the funeral procession made it to the cemetery. E sat next to Rita, holding her hand, appearing to comfort her in her time of loss. She cried and sobbed a few times to keep up appearances. Mike and Freeze stood across from them, smiling. E refused to look in that direction. Detectives Kirkland and Richards were there, staring at Mike. From time to time, Mike would smile and wink at Kirk.

The minister spoke, "Into the ground we commit this body, ashes to ashes, dust to dust."

As the funeral party began to disburse, Rita and E made their way to the limousine. Mike and Freeze followed them to the limousine, still smiling. As they were about to get into the limo, Detective Kirkland approached Mike. E stopped to watch.

"Vicious Black," Kirkland said.

"Kirk, what's up?" Mike said.

"What does it feel like to be at a funeral that you weren't responsible for?"

"Kirk, now you know I've never been responsible for any funerals. Look at my record. I'm still batting a thousand."

"Anyway, Black, I need to ask you some questions," Kirkland said.

"Do you have a warrant, Detective?" Mike asked sarcastically.

"No, but I can get one."

"I don't think so, Kirk. If you could get one, you'd have one. You're too good a cop not to have covered all the bases. Anyway, what do you wanna ask me about?"

"Drug deal went bad the other night. Five police officers were killed in the line of duty. You know anything about that?" Kirkland asked.

"Drugs?" Mike said, appearing to be surprised and insulted by the word. "Kirk, you know I don't know anything about drugs. But I'll be happy to answer any and all questions you have. Do you want me to come in?"

"Yeah, why don't you ride to the station with us?"

"Cool," Mike said, thinking that this was working out better than he had planned it.

"You wanna have your lawyer meet you down there?" Kirkland asked as he started for the car.

"Why, you planning on charging me with something?"

"No, just some questions."

"I think you just wanna see Wanda again, Detective. Let's go." Mike whispered something to Freeze before going along with the detectives.

E watched happily as Mike got into the car with Kirkland. He got into the limo with Rita, confident that it was over and he was on top. Seeing Kirk take Black into custody was the icing on the cake.

The limo turned onto Rita's block, coming to a stop in front of her building. The driver got out and opened the door for them. E got out and looked around. It was fairly quiet on the block. There were a few people walking down the street. An old bag lady was digging through the garbage, and of course, the regulars were in their usual spot on the corner. Rita thanked the driver and started for the door as the driver pulled off.

E stood in the middle of the street, looking around. He pounded his chest. "Who's the man!" he shouted. "Who's the muthafuckin' man!"

"Stop pattin' yourself on the back and get out of the street," Rita said as E walked toward her.

"Got any spare change?" the bag lady asked as she approached them.

"Why don't you get a fuckin' job instead of being out here beggin' all day?" E said with disdain.

"Oh, give her some money. It ain't like you ain't got it like that," Rita said.

E stepped toward the bag lady, reaching into his pocket and pulling out his money. He peeled off a $10 bill. "Here," he said, shoving the bill in her face. "Go buy you a rock, bitch." E looked up. "Shy."

"You ain't the man," Shy said, raising her gun. She fired two shots to his head.

Rita screamed as E fell to the ground, and Shy turned the gun on her.

"This is for Tony, cheatin' bitch." Shy fired again, hitting Rita with two shots to her head.

Shy looked down at E as people began to slowly move toward her. Kenny pulled up in a panel truck. Jap opened the sliding door. "No time to admire your work. Let's go!"

Shy dropped the gun on E's chest and walked slowly to the truck. Jap got out and picked up the gun. Shy sat on the floor of the truck with her head down. She was glad that she could put it all behind her and start a new life.

Kenny drove to a private airfield in Westchester, where Angelo had arranged for a small plane to take them to the Bahamas. There was nothing for her to do now except wait for Mike to arrive.

CHAPTER THIRTY-SIX

Kirkland and Richards grilled Mike for more than two hours. Kirkland questioned his relationship with Shy, while Richards tried to link him to Orlando. They had heard the rumors that Mike was ready to get back in the dope game. "I heard those rumors too. That's why I went to see Orlando. To kill that noise," Mike said with a smile.

The afternoon dragged on as they went over the same points over and over again. They repeated their assertion that Mike had the connections and the muscle to take over not only Shy's business but anyone else who opposed him. "I heard that too." Mike sat through the entire thing calmly, answering each question. He knew they were just fishing, hoping he would bite, but that wasn't part of the plan.

The story Mike told was pretty close to the truth. He told them that he and Shy went out a few times. "End of story. I guess if I'd gone out with a woman who owned a chain of restaurants, I'd be planning a hostile takeover," he said contemptuously. "Come on, fellas, let's live in reality. You don't have shit."

Mike had been questioned more times than he cared to count. Each session ended in the same manner, with the words, "Okay, Black, you're free to go." On top of that, if all had gone as he planned, Shy was waiting for him at the airport and E was dead, so there would be no one to testify against him. It was only a matter of time before Detective Kirkland would have enough and release him.

A knock came at the door. A uniformed officer came in and whispered to Kirkland. He looked at Mike. "Okay, Black, you're free to go," Kirkland said, opening the door to the interrogation room for Mike.

"Tired of my company already?" Mike asked as he walked toward the door. Kirkland walked out alongside Mike.

"We just got a report that Eddie Miles and Rita Collins were just murdered on the street in front of her apartment building by a bag lady. Probably the Sims woman. So until we catch her, and we will catch her, there's nothing to link any of this to you. But I'll get you sooner or later, Black. I'll get you."

"Walk me out, Kirk. I got something I wanna say to you."

As they left the building, Mike said, "I wanna tell you that I always had a lot of respect for you, even though you're a cop."

"Thanks. For a crook, you're not so bad yourself," Kirk replied.

Once they were outside the station, Mike said, "I'm gettin' out, Kirk, so you'll have to find yourself a new project."

"You're going to leave the country with her, aren't you?" Kirk asked.

"If I told you that, I'd have to kill you," Mike said.

"Well, then don't tell me," Kirk joked. "Well, good luck, Black. It's been real," he said, shaking Mike's hand. "You want me to get a car to take you somewhere?"

"No. Freeze will be here soon, but thanks. And good luck with your case."

"Don't sweat it. The guys she shot weren't cops anyway. Just some low-life scumbags dressed like cops tryin' to rip her off. We caught one of them. They were supposed to confiscate the drugs and the money, then slip away in the confusion when the real cops got there."

"When were you planning on tellin' me that shit?" Mike asked.

"You said you barely knew the woman. Why should you care?" Kirkland said, going back into the station.

Mike leaned against the fence and laughed to himself. He marveled at how his plan had worked out even better than he had planned. Killing a drug dealer and a couple of guys he sent to rob her was a long way from killing cops. Freeze arrived shortly after that, and he drove Mike to the airfield.

Shy gazed out the airplane window. *What's taking him so long?* she thought, tapping her foot and looking at her watch. Impatience was definitely something else she and Mike had in common. The wait did give her time to reflect on her actions, more time than she wanted, actually. Shy trusted E, and he betrayed her. She killed him for it. She faced him, saw the terror in his eyes, and shot him, almost without thinking. She felt vile and corrupt, but at the same time, she felt justified. *Fuck that. He deserved to die.*

She had sat in judgment of Mike having killed people. Now she realized how death was a by-product of their occupation. She would be happy to put it all behind her. The only thing that would make her happier was . . .

"Here they come now," Kenny said.

Kenny and Jap said goodbye to Shy and got off the plane. Shy watched through the window as Mike said goodbye to his boys. It was kind of touching to watch as Freeze hugged him. Mike got on board and told the pilot to take off.

He sat down next to Shy. "You ready?" he asked, kissing her lips.

"Baby, I've been ready for this all my life," Shy said.

"Oh, really?"

"Yeah, it's like a fairy tale. You know, the handsome prince rescues the damsel in distress. They fall in love and fly away together."

"Do they live happily ever after?" Mike asked.

"I don't know," Shy said, kissing him on the cheek. "Story's not over yet."

EPILOGUE

One Year Later

After island-hopping for three months, Mike and Shy settled on Grand Bahama Island. They bought that adorable little house by the beach that Shy liked so much. Armed with a fake passport, Shy filled most her days shopping in Miami for just the right piece. Mike began to oversee construction of a reggae supper club on the beach. He wanted to name it Cassandra's Paradise. She thought it should be called Vicious Black's. Each thought that the other's idea was too pretentious, so they settled on Black's Paradise.

Naturally, they had it built within walking distance of the house.

Mike had been to New York five or six times over the last year. He would never stay long, not being able to stay away from Shy for more than three days at a time. Once they settled into the house, Mike moved Emily out of New York. Shy insisted that M, as she had become fond of calling her, stay with them. Since her arrival, Percival had become quite enamored with her and she with him.

Once the house was decorated, Mike noticed that Shy was getting restless and just a little bored. She was a businesswoman without a business to run. With no desire for her to die a slow death, Mike invited her to be his partner in the operation of the club. She gladly accepted and she excelled.

"Yo, Bobby!" Freeze yelled from across the bar at Paradise. "Throw me another brew. This one's hot." This was the first time Freeze had been to the island. He now had complete control of the New York operation.

Bobby reached into the cooler and pulled out a Kalik, a Bahamian-made beer. He and Pam had made several trips to the island, staying longer each time.

"If you would drink it instead of runnin' your mouth, it wouldn't get hot." Pam was dying to make the move, but being the die-hard New Yorker he was, Bobby's will remained strong.

"I know you ain't go there, talkin' about somebody runnin' their mouth," Mike said. It was just like old times, with Freeze and Bobby going back and forth about every issue. He missed them.

"Some people got nerves of steel," Jamaica said as he walked outside to get some air. After successful completion of the rehab program, Jamaica came to visit and became the houseguest who wouldn't leave. Finally, he decided to stay and bought a house.

"When are we going to get started?" Perry asked, pouring himself another drink. Perry, Glenda, and their kids had been down to visit a few times. "If I keep drinkin' these Bahama Mamas, I won't be able to stand up."

"As soon as Cassandra gets back from picking up Wanda," Mike answered.

"I still don't see why she had to go," Bobby commented impatiently. "I could've picked up Wanda."

"She felt like they needed to talk."

"I hear that M is responsible for this little party," Perry said. "Who gave Miss Black the nickname M, anyway?"

"Cassandra tagged her with it after we watched *Die Another Day,* and it just stuck, but yeah, she flexed on us big time. I was here one afternoon, when Cassandra comes in and says she thinks M moved out. I'm like,

'What do you mean she moved out?' Cassandra says, 'I mean, I looked in her room, and all her stuff is gone.'"

"Where did she go?" Freeze asked.

"The Princess. Quiet as it's kept, she's become quite the gambler. You can find her there most afternoons playing the slots."

"What, she wanted to be closer to the slots?" Bobby said jokingly.

"Anyway, I roll up there. Go to her room. She's just sitting there like everything's just lovely. So I ask her, 'Ma, what's wrong?' She said, 'Michael, I just can't live in that house any longer.' So I'm like, 'What, do we make too much noise? Is that it?' She gives me that look and says, 'No, Michael, I just can't live in that house with you two living in sin.' 'Okay, Ma, I'll be back for you. I gotta go have a talk with Cassandra.'"

"Now that's what I call flex," Perry said.

"Hold up, it gets better. So I look around the room, and none of her stuff is in there. So I say, 'Ma, where's all your stuff?' She smiles and says she had Percival move it into one of the other rooms in the house."

Just then, Jamaica came back inside. "Black, come see this."

Everybody got up and followed Jamaica out the door, and they were shocked at what they saw. Shy was back from picking up Wanda, and there they were, getting out of the Corvette, laughing and talking like they were the best of friends.

"Baby, what are y'all doin' here?" Shy asked Mike as everybody greeted Wanda. "I get to the house ready to get married and I gotta go find the groom. What's up with that?"

"I should be askin' you that. What's up with you and Wanda?"

"We got our thing straight. I'll tell you all about that later. But, baby, I'm not wanted for murder anymore."

"What do you mean?"

"I mean, without them having the murder weapon or any witnesses to place me at the scene, Wanda got the murder and conspiracy to commit murder warrants dropped."

"She did?"

"I sure did. It wasn't easy, but I got it done. There's still a warrant for conspiracy to distribute. I haven't made any headway with that. But give me time. I'm just sorry I couldn't do anything for Jack. He got five years," Wanda said, joining them at the car as everybody else left to go back to the house. "Now you two need to go on and get ready."

"Get ready for what?" they both said.

"Get dressed to get married," Wanda said. They both had on shorts and shirts.

"Wanda," Shy said, "this is about as dressed as we ever get." She handed Wanda the keys. "But you go on and freshen up. All of us aren't gettin' in that Vette. We'll walk."

Mike took Shy's hand and started walking, leaving Wanda standing there, mouth open.

"That's a good idea, Cassandra. That's why I love you."